IN THE LAND OF THE LIVING

IN THE LAND
OF THE LIVING

A Novel

Austin Ratner

A REAGAN ARTHUR BOOK

Little, Brown and Company

NEW YORK BOSTON LONDON

Copyright © 2013 by Marathon Lit LLC

Reagan Arthur Books/Little, Brown and Company
Hachette Book Group
237 Park Avenue, New York, NY 10017
reaganarthurbooks.com

First Edition: March 2013

Reagan Arthur Books is an imprint of Little, Brown and Company, a division of Hachette Book Group, Inc. The Reagan Arthur Books name and logo are trademarks of Hachette Book Group, Inc.

The Hachette Speakers Bureau provides a wide range of authors for speaking events. To find out more, go to hachettespeakersbureau.com or call (866) 376-6591.

From the David Merrick–Bernard Delfont Production *THE ROAR OF THE GREASEPAINT— The Smell of the Crowd,* "A WONDERFUL DAY LIKE TODAY." Words and Music by Leslie Bricusse and Anthony Newley. Copyright © 1964 (renewed) Concord Music Ltd., London, England; TRO—Musical Comedy Productions, Inc., New York, controls all rights for the U.S.A. and Canada. Used by permission.

Library of Congress Cataloging-in-Publication Data
Ratner, Austin.
  In the land of the living : a novel / Austin Ratner.—1st ed.
    p. cm.
  ISBN 978-0-316-20609-9
  1. Loss (Psychology)—Fiction. 2. Families—Fiction. 3. Grief—Fiction. I. Title.
  PS3618.A875I5 2013
  813'.6—dc23   2012028730

10 9 8 7 6 5 4 3 2 1

RRD-C

Printed in the United States of America

To James Ratner

Corpore de patrio parvum phoenica renasci;
cum dedit huic aetas vires, onerique ferendo est,
ponderibus nidi ramos levat arboris altae
fertque pius cunasque suas patriumque sepulcrum
perque leves auras Hyperionis urbe potitus
ante fores sacras Hyperionis aede reponit.

And from his father's body, so they say, a little phoenix
springs up which is destined to attain the same length of
years. When age has given him strength, and he is able to
carry burdens, he relieves the tall palm's branches of the
heavy nest, piously bears his own cradle and his father's
tomb through the thin air, until, having reached the city of
the Sun, he lays the nest down before the sacred doors of
the Sun's temple.

Ovid, *Metamorphoses*
Frank Justus Miller, trans.

Contents

Part I—Nine Worthy and the Best That Ever Were

1—Of the Mad King on a Bicycle All Green   5

2—Of Isidore's Quest for a Damosel   32

3—Of the King of Genes   39

4—How Isidore, Arrayed Like a Poor Knight,
Came to the Demesne of Laura's Father   48

5—How Isidore Went to Sea without a Proper
Surcoat   59

6—How Isidore Auberon Was Chastened   70

7—How the Ghost of Dr. Austrian Appelled
James and Isidore of Grievous Sins   73

8—How Isidore Spake to his Aunt at the Feast
of Saint Rufus   79

9—How the Lords of Chaos Came to Isidore
and Made War Against Him   84

Part II—The Little Boys Lost

1—Grand Canyon   107

2—Red Right 88 / The Wampa   121

3—Labiaphobia   133

Contents

4—The Island of Neverything Ad Ban Cappen   154

5—The Abattoir   161

6—Yalensis   177

Part III—Highway 1 and Highway 2

1—Lizard Tail   225

2—The Portland Rose Garden   237

3—The Cairns of the Kootenai   266

4—The Hog Butcher   282

5—Dead Man's Curve   287

6—Wedding at the Metropolitan Ballroom   298

Acknowledgments   *309*

PART I

Nine Worthy and the Best That Ever Were

That there lived a man named Isidore Auberon, there can be no dispute. There is the reflex hammer with the reddish rubber tomahawk head bearing his initials. There is the red shirt, thick and coarse like Indian jute, with black buttons, in which he appears in many photographs. And in many other places there are many other things, and many people will give accounts of him.

"It is notoriously known through the universal world," William Caxton said, "that there be nine worthy and the best that ever were." Three pagans—Hector, Alexander the Great, Julius Caesar; and three Jews—Joshua, David, Judas Maccabaeus; and three Christians—King Arthur, Charlemagne, and Godfrey of Boulogne. Many stories portray them, and we know that they lived in this world. It must be so with Isidore Auberon.

I.

OF THE MAD KING ON A BICYCLE ALL
GREEN; OF THAT BOY FAIRLY SHAPED AND
YCLEPT ISIDORE, WHO FORSOOTH HAD BUT
LITTLE SAVE SHIRT AND BREECHES; HOW
ISIDORE WAXED BIG AND STRONG AND SMOTE
THE KING OF THE HARD HAND WITH
SHIVEROUS WORDS AND BLOWS; AND EKE
HOW HE DEPARTED FROM THERE

THEIR FATHER PEDDLED certain lies the same way he pedaled his
bicycle to and from his many jobs all over Cleveland Heights,
with his monstrous canvas bag balanced on his back and his giant
toolbox strapped to the bike with a three-pronged canvas belt.
He pedaled his bicycle slowly and resolutely, so that he never got
up any momentum, as if momentum would have been cheating,
pressing and pressing on the pedals, advancing up the sidewalk
righteously, slate by slate, lie by lie, without caring when he
got there, without knowing he was lying. His first name was
a lie: Ezer. It sounded like one of the seven dwarves, but Ezer
didn't whistle, except through his asshole. His last name was a
lie, though perhaps it wasn't his own lie: Auberon, some Ellis
Island gag on Abramowicz or whatever it had been, which was
itself a Polish joke on whatever it had been before that, maybe

nothing. Another of Ezer's false propositions was "corned beef soup," being the grease water in which a hunk of corned beef had been boiled, served in three bowls as unmatched and misbegotten as the brothers who sat before them: Burt, the oldest, Isidore (his father called him Isser), and Dennis, the youngest. And Ezer didn't like football—that was still another lie. "Such a rough game, they kill each other," he said. But when he entered the house at 6 P.M. and sat at the table like a sphinx with sawdust sticking to his face and on his shirt, he himself was rough. When Burt reached for the jam, Ezer said without warning, "Enough jam! Jam is for breakfast!" and seized Burt's wrist and lowered his whitish face like a hobgoblin's, and he didn't let go until the boy's hand was pale as wax. Then the man got up and went off to lie in his bed with sweaty sawdust on his face. Burt held the cool jar in a hand now electric and red, and his mother let him dip his painful sleeping finger in the cold jam.

Of course, their father wasn't a hobgoblin. No, he was human, with coarse unruly hair that he'd given to his sons, and a terrible gut that made the house reek, and a fleck of corned beef on his eyeglasses when he ate his lunch, and only one suit, and watery eyes cracked with tortuous red lines, lines twisted like the twisted history of life in the hovels of Jedwabne from which he'd come. And his eyelids were sad and slanted like the sad and slanted life of the shtetl and when he took his eyeglasses off, the sad hooded froggy eyes were disarming in their softness, as were the smithereen tiny purple veins across his contused rosaceous nose.

Isidore's mother, Sophia, came over from Europe in 1937. Her brother owned a grocery store in Cleveland and had a little money. The brother sent his wife to Poland to get Sophia, but it was hard to get out by then, and the sister-in-law came back without her. So her brother sent money, and somehow she escaped the jaws of the beast in time. Sophia never learned to speak

English, and the tale of her passage to Cleveland was lost to the chasms of language, of marriage, of the Atlantic Ocean, and most of all to death. Her other brother in Poland didn't come, or anyway, he never arrived, and there might have been a photograph of him somewhere, but there was never a sound.

Now Sophia was in New York in a hospital bed, alone except for a woman from the International Ladies' Garment Workers' Union who mailed her letters for her. Her brother and sister-in-law had sent her there for treatments to her stomach, Ezer said, because they had something in New York that Ezer called "the radiation." The war, the ship full of rotting tubercles, the rains of Cleveland, and the garment factory on East Sixty-sixth Street couldn't kill her, but after all that, it turned out she'd not been particularly strong, just lucky. Delivered at last and undamaged to the unassailable well-being of America and its International Ladies' Garment Workers' Union, she got cancer of the stomach. Her letters were addressed to Burt because, Isidore told himself, she hated Ezer like they did, and Burt was the only one of them who could read Yiddish. "Remember that I love you, Burt," she wrote. "Take care of your brothers." She was a soft, nice sort of mommy. He wished she'd put his name on the envelope.

Isidore waited outside the house where his father was fixing somebody's faucet—one that as usual he'd already fixed before—and wondered if he was to see his mother again.

His baby brother, Dennis, had asked for a picture. Isidore drew a tank on the cold Invermere Avenue sidewalk with great big chalky clouds of smoke arising from the superheated wreckage of a battle. It was a busier sidewalk than the one outside their own house on Hildana Road.

"Is that a tank?" Dennis said.

"Yep."

"And what's that?" Dennis said, pointing.

"That's wreckage."

"That's a good cabbage," Dennis said.

"It's not a cabbage."

"That's a good tank," Dennis said. "I can't draw that tank."

"You're four," Isidore said. "I'm older."

"I could maybe draw a cabbage, though. Why is there a cabbage under the tank?"

"It's not a cabbage," Isidore said. "It's wreckage."

"Oh," Dennis said, thinking. "I can't draw a tank. You can draw it because you're older."

"You'll be older too," Isidore said.

"Why did the lady say we could use the chalk?" Dennis said. "It's not ours."

"I guess she wanted to share it."

A rubber-tipped cane stabbed down into the chalk drawing. "Watch it!" said the woman who belonged to the cane. She pounded her cane once more at a crack in the sidewalk and limped on. She was lugging a heavy shopping bag.

"Why did she yell?" Dennis said.

"Shhh," Isidore said, and pointed to the woman. He watched her plodding ahead on the sidewalk with her heavy bag.

"Why did she yell?" Dennis said, more quietly.

"I don't know," Isidore said. "She was mad."

"Was she mad because she has a cane?"

"Quiet, Dennis! Maybe. I don't know."

"Or because she was old? If I get old, I'll be mad. Because your face cracks off and your eyeballs fall out and your brain falls out your eyeholes and they put you inside a pyramid. And your hair falls off too and then you're bald. And you have nothing to drink." Dennis looked down sadly.

"She wasn't old, really," Isidore said. "She looked young."

"Then was she mad because you drew on the sidewalk? I'm not mad. That's a *good* tank. I *like* it. Because you're a good drawer."

"Thanks, Dennis. Come on, let's go inside."

"I don't want to go in there. Who lives there? That lady who gave us the chalk?"

"Just come on. Let's go," Isidore said. "Aren't you cold?"

"Are we gonna go see Mommy now?" Dennis said. "I'm not going in till we go see Mommy. I'll just go to New York myself. I'll just walk. Which way is it?"

It was cold and getting colder. They hadn't worn any jackets because no one had told them to. Isidore took a butter cookie out of his pocket and told Dennis if he came into the house he could have it.

All the way home, walking behind their father, who stopped pushing at his bike occasionally to turn around and tell them to hurry up, Isidore kept thinking about the woman with the cane. He'd forget her and then she'd intrude into his thoughts yet again, much as she had into his chalk drawing. He wished he'd thought to get out of her way. But the moment had come and gone. The woman was somewhere else and he wouldn't ever see her again.

They came to Hildana with its familiar hydrant with the rusted chains and its flat and square front lawns littered with yellow leaves. Then they came to their house, which seemed to be half the size of the houses on either side of it—the green one on the left with the listing portico over the drive and columns and a low brick wall along the front of the porch and a third floor, and the house on the right with two porches, one on the first floor and one above and a high triangular roof above that over a third floor. The house where they lived, in between, had a porch too, but its steps had no railing, and there was no brick wall. Their house had no third floor, either—or rather, it had no second floor, as its second floor looked more like a third floor, with a dormer window like the other houses had on their third floors and a roof that slanted up from the gutter on top of the porch.

Their father said he had to go to the store, and the three boys went inside and sat down on the floor of the dark living room without the lights on. Isidore took the army surplus blanket from the arm of the sofa (it was so scratchy, Dennis wouldn't touch that one), and Dennis took the plaid wool one that he considered to be "his." Burt never used the blankets, even if it was cold. Sometimes he slept on top of his covers. They heard their father's bicycle chain clanking in the back of the house.

Burt tried to build a house of cards. Isidore drew a picture of the woman with the cane on the back of an envelope with a pencil and Dennis watched him.

"Her face is a skull?" Dennis said.

"Yep."

"I thought you said she wasn't old."

"She wasn't. It's just a picture. And old people don't have skulls for faces, Dennis! They still have *skin!*"

"Oh," Dennis said. "Izzy, I want some milk."

"You want milk?" Isidore said, and sighed. "Okay."

Isidore put his pencil down and stood up, and Burt's cards fell.

"Ah, I can't build a second level," Burt said, "I don't know how Moseley does it, I'm no good at this," and he started collecting the cards into a pile.

"Who's Moseley?" Dennis said.

"What?" Burt said. "He's just a kid at school."

Isidore went up the steps into the kitchen and he didn't expect to see what he did: his father under the sink. He thought his father had gone out, but there he was, right on the kitchen floor, grunting and kicking with his face up under the sink as though trying to wrestle himself inside the jungle of pipes back there. You never knew when he'd decide to try to fix something, and neither did the people he worked for, it seemed, since they were often surprised to see him when he showed up, and angry that he hadn't showed up sooner.

"Tateh," Isidore said, "are we gonna go to New York to see Mommy?"

His father didn't answer.

"Do you know what her favorite book is? I was just wondering. I never asked her." The only things his father liked to talk about were books and labor unions, but he only read Yiddish books. He still didn't answer.

"Tateh," Isidore said, "why would a young woman have a cane?"

Instead of an answer, a towel came flying out from under the sink and landed near Isidore's shoe. It had brown grease on it.

"Watch it!" Isidore said suddenly, though he hadn't meant to. It was too much to feel guilt just then, and he blurted something else: "Ezer."

Ezer peered out at him from under the sink. The low sun coruscated orange on every piece of glass, and outshone the dim light of the fixture on the ceiling. His father's face looked naked and small without his glasses on. Ezer rolled himself over quickly, so quickly that he bumped his head under the sink, but he persevered and fought back against the bottles and the pipes; he clobbered the pipes with his elbows and upset the bleach bottles and at last emancipated himself from the kitchen cabinet. Ezer heaved himself off the floor with a merciless inconsideration toward the hinges of the cabinet doors and toward his own stiff joints. He kicked at the greasy towel. Meanwhile, the cabinet doors, as if to deny the sincerity of Ezer's struggle with the pipes and bottles, stood agreeably open behind him and displayed sticky paper with mocking roses up and down them.

"Of a dirty towel, you are afraid?" his father said with foreign-sounding, Yiddish consonants that inflected his speech with bad portents.

"No," Isidore said, and kicked at the towel himself.

"Am I to worry about you, too?" his father said.

"Huh? I'm just getting some milk for Dennis."

"For Dennis, I worry, because he is small. For Burt, I worry, because he is . . . Burt. For you, I cannot worry."

"Burt's right in there," Isidore whispered. "He could hear you." Isidore was by now fully awake to the long history of unequal warfare between his father and his older brother, who had according to Ezer failed—failed to recite Yiddish verses, failed to clean the dishes properly, who was always dropping things and making a mess, who had failed, who had failed, who had failed. The history seemed for both combatants to be rich with memorable incident and lay fresh in his father's memory like a disappointment he was not yet ready to accept. He yelled at Burt often and by now Burt always yelled back. He shoved Burt and Burt slapped blindly at their father's arms. Now that their mother was sick, there was no one besides Isidore to referee.

"From a baby, Burt made worries for your mother!" his father said loudly. "She worries so, it makes her sick! She worries so, she thinks of nothing but Burt! She does not think even of me, her husband! And now her stomach—the radiation destroys it! Fills it with burns because your uncle Mo took her to New York for treatments that I tell him are no good! And a debt, he says I owe him for the treatments! He blames *me* for the cancer, he says! He told her it should be a divorce between us, he says! She agrees. She wants it, he says! A divorce! Well, then I divorce *her!*" He swished his hands together as though ridding them of dirt. "Mo, he should drop dead! And your aunt Mara, too!" He swiped at the air.

A slow-melting fire had arisen in the kitchen window behind Ezer and the weird, doomed light made Isidore feel that something terrible was about to happen and that he'd been appointed to this moment for some time without knowing it—perhaps since before he was born, even.

"Her worries over *Burt* made a cancer in her stomach! I should know! As if Mo knows a single thing about my house! And I am one man!" Ezer yelled. "How much worry am I to bear all alone? Worry from boys who never know one day of work, even! Who never even know a worry! I fix the sink—for *you* to fill your greedy mouth without we have leaks and smells and holes and bugs! A child, I worked! Do you? You see this house? These walls? *My* walls?" He slapped his hand against the wall. "Insulated! Strong! Warm! My house in Jedwabne, it burned! To the ground! Gone! We lived in a cellar! That is no *bubbe meise,* that is truth what I saw with my own skull! And when we get a new house, Russian soldiers take it and again we sleep in the cellar! Unbelievable, I think. Again, here am I in a cellar with bugs! And for my brothers and sisters are the nice places. Warm! Dry! For me, the youngest almost, except for the baby what is bited by a rat and *dies* in that cellar, I sleep on dirt with rats and bugs, everywhere bugs, afraid that I too should die! One of those soldiers, he almost *kills* my father! What do you know from worry? Do you see Russian soldiers on Hildana Road? Do you see guns? Do you see fire? Do you see cold and dirt and rats?"

Ezer reserved most tirades for Burt. This marked something very different, it seemed, a mutation in the atoms of the air and the ground, and Isidore felt himself compelled to memorize the light of the sun before it disappeared, as if it might not ever return.

"What name do you call me?" his father said.

"I called you Tateh."

"After."

"After what?" Isidore said.

"After the dirty towel that you wish it doesn't touch your foot! Sir Isser!"

"I called you Tateh!" Isidore said loudly.

"You said Ezer!"

"Okay, Tateh," Isidore said quickly, "I'm sorry!"

Ezer looked into the living room, where Burt was standing on the steps with Dennis behind him. "This doesn't concern you!" Ezer said. "For once!" Again, he chopped at the air.

"You're wrong, not him!" Burt yelled, leaning forward into the yell and stepping halfway up into the kitchen.

"Zol zein shah!" Ezer yelled.

Burt scrambled up the steps, ran into Ezer, and slapped at his arms. Ezer swung Burt around in a sort of awkward dance step and Burt fell against the stove and got back up. Then, employing a technique he'd presumably learned at the Kishinev School of Cossack Child-Rearing, Ezer picked up a pot and knocked Burt in the head with it.

"Don't you trip! Don't you stumble, you actor!" Ezer yelled. "Don't you cry! A boxer, I'm not! I didn't hit you hard. I didn't *touch* you."

The sun was gone now. The yard had rapidly capitulated to a darkness that sealed the boys and their father up tight in the small kitchen as inside a coffin ship: the windows became dim, distorting mirrors, and displayed not the outdoors, but a bad replica of the kitchen instead. The yard and the glass seemed to collaborate to encircle them with warped images of themselves.

"Don't look at *me* with hate!" his father yelled.

"I'm not!" Isidore said.

"Do not judge me, Isser! You know nothing! You're a child!"

"He didn't mean to, Tateh!" Dennis cried out from the bottom of the steps into the kitchen. "I asked him to get me some milk."

"I have a terrible headache," Ezer said, suddenly quiet, and he clutched his head. "I am going to bed."

He mumbled some Yiddish curses, things about dark dreams for devils such as his sons, and he said the word *chaloshes* and said it again. As he went up the stairs, he mumbled on, about weakness, *shvachkeit,* and what happens to weakness in this world, which he said like "oiled" with a "V" on the front. The word made Isidore think of a valley with its "V," the *voiled,* valley of darkness and toil.

They did not see their mother. She was already dead.

It would have been a good time to get help from the boys' aunt and uncle, Sophia's brother and sister-in-law, Mo and Mara, but Ezer wouldn't speak to them anymore, because Mo said Ezer owed them money. It would have been a good time to get help from Ezer's brother, Hermann, who was a furrier in New York and made a decent living, but Ezer had cut Hermann off years ago, and pointedly hadn't even spoken to him when Sophia went to New York for her treatments. Ezer had a sister who might have helped too, but Ezer hated her husband. And while he *was* on speaking terms with his other sister, who ran an antique shop, she and her husband had no kids and they said they wouldn't know what to do with one, let alone three. For a time the Jewish family service sent housekeepers to look after the boys.

Then one day Ezer told them Burt would be sent to Bellefaire, an orphanage on Fairmount Boulevard. Isidore and Dennis, he said, would go to a foster home in University Heights. The brothers stood together before their father and one and all held on to each others' shirts.

At times like these, their father surprised them. He didn't care what they wanted, but he also didn't fight. Instead he called the foster home, as if it merely hadn't occurred to him that there might be room for Burt.

So an old woman came in a green car with a bent antenna and all three boys climbed in. Ezer kissed Dennis hard on the head, but he didn't kiss Isidore or Burt.

As the car rolled slowly backward toward the street, the old woman repeatedly slammed on the brakes, which slammed the boys' heads into the unforgiving vinyl behind them.

Their father called out to them from the top of the brick steps that had no railing: "You must come back to visit to me!" And he waved slowly from under the dark porch, with eyes sadder than ever, as if the boys were abandoning him, when in fact he had sent them away.

The foster parents were old, and they lived not so far away from Hildana, in University Heights in a house that smelled like dogs, but it felt like another country. The old lady had her own kids, one who still lived there and seemed quite old himself, and two dogs, and she didn't hear well, but that first day she did give them some cranberry bread and it seemed to be edible. There was evidence that the old man's ears were fine, but he seemed disinclined to use them. He liked to play with the dogs in the backyard and had a bunch of weird magazines next to his bed that had pictures of women in their underwear. They said MAN on them in big letters. The boys went to the foster home in University Heights in the winter, and Isidore changed schools.

They shared a room and a dresser and even socks and underwear, and Isidore opened the drawers for Dennis and showed Burt that you had to lift as you pulled or they wouldn't open at all. It seemed important that the top drawer should be for those sacred articles worn against the privates, and that was where he'd put their underwear, even though that drawer was slightly too high to reach into comfortably and hurt the elbow and the armpit to reach into the back of it, where he kept his mother's lilac blouse. After their first dinner he came back to the bedroom and scraped his elbow while pulling out the blouse. He went into the closet with it and brushed a sticky spiderweb off it, and there he unrolled the blouse and tried to smell her on it, but all he could smell was the unfamiliar chest of drawers and the musty closet. In the hot stuffy air underneath his winter coat, with his elbow burning, he cried till his nose ran and his brothers heard and came to him and, for their sakes, he made himself stop.

Ezer did visit them after all, and especially in the winter they dreaded news of his arrival. In the winter, when other carpenters picked up side jobs, Ezer collected unemployment. He would bring the boys back to Hildana Road and sit around in their old house reading *Morgen Freiheit,* the Yiddish communist newspaper, and bitch at the air in Yiddish. Isidore figured that he sent them to Yiddish school three days a week at *Der Arbeter Ring* instead of Hebrew school just so he'd have someone around who could understand his bitching. In the summers, when he was working, he came to see them less and sometimes he took them to the picnics that the Jewish communists threw on Sundays, and those were best—not because the picnics were any fun (they weren't, though there were generally hot dogs), but because Ezer could complain to sympathetic ears about the plight of the workingman, or talk about the Yiddish theater, and the boys usually got through the picnics without any shouting matches between Ezer and Burt.

At the end of three years at the foster home, Ezer got married to a woman whom the boys called the Bitch. Her son was a drug dealer, and one time he threatened Burt with a gun. Ezer bought a new house, on Meadowbrook Boulevard. A few months later and, as far as they could tell, having nothing whatsoever to do with the loaded gun in Burt's face, Ezer and the Bitch were divorced. But the Meadowbrook house was big enough and the boys were old enough to move into it with or without a Bitch.

By the time Ezer took the boys back, Isidore didn't think of himself as a boy anymore. He could ride a bike and do his own laundry. He could make scrambled eggs. He had seen weird pictures of women in their underwear, and could throw a baseball and a football, could tell time both by hour and minute (you had to consider them separately, then add them back together), he could multiply, and he could read anything, even the *Cleveland Press* or *Morgen Freiheit*.

There were enough bedrooms for the boys to sleep separately—which was desirable considering the odor and quantity of Burt's farts. But Burt didn't even have to say anything. When it got late enough to go to sleep, Isidore and Burt dragged his mattress into the room with the other beds and they stayed all together in one room as it had been at the foster home. Their father didn't know or care where they slept, and the other bedrooms remained empty, without any shades on the windows.

To eyes less jaded than Isidore's, the new photographs on the wall of the dining room might have hinted at new developments in Ezer's soul, but Isidore perceived immediately that his father was unchanged. For one thing, while new to the dining room wall, the photos were otherwise old. One showed Ezer and his brother, Hermann, but Ezer had evidently cut the picture in half and thrown his brother away so that it was just Ezer by himself now, reaching off the edge of the world toward a space that had formerly been Hermann, but was now just the brown underboard of the picture frame. There was another of Ezer and Sophia, which had a magic force about it, as though it had caused something new to exist that didn't before, but again, his parents' youth, while new to Isidore's eyes, in fact belonged to the past. His mother was not smiling and her skin looked the color of porcelain and hard—another lie. Ezer looked smart and radical in it, like a 1930s socialist playwright or somebody like that. Aunt Mara said he'd wanted to be a Yiddish-school teacher and in fact had tried to get certified once and, before he met Sophia, Mara said, he'd even acted a bit in the Yiddish theater in New York.

There was a picture of Ezer's father, Nachem, on the wall also, with a visage remnant from another era and cold-blooded, just exactly like the haunting, cold, reptilian visage of a crocodile with eyes that move but do not seem to see. The crocodile on the wall had made and sold barrels. It had been that cooper and father of eleven whose bed the Russian officer had slept in, that man whom the Russian officer had driven into the basement with his wife and eleven children and threatened to shoot in the head when the cooper stuck it through the cellar door to ask for water while the soldiers were at cards.

Perhaps it was that crocodilian old cooper whose iron grip on past and future had stunted Ezer's means of expression in English. True, Ezer had no ambition anymore and never tried to learn English really well, but it also seemed that for him there was hardly any need for those tenses apart from the present; for past was merely the stain of injury on the film of the present; and future the corresponding photogravure of permanent resentment. He couldn't change himself any more than he could change the expression of that old cooper on the wall.

Their neighbor, Mrs. Polanska, said she was sorry for Ezer. "He just needs a lady friend to help keep the house," she said, but suggestions as to who were not forthcoming.

Like the Bitch, perhaps? She had not seemed like much of a housekeeper. Mrs. Polanska and her shtetl ways! She couldn't help Isidore, or his brothers, either. He had to take care of his little brother, Dennis, and of his older brother, who told Isidore he was the closest thing he had to a mother. They didn't even have a cousin or an uncle worth half a pancake. Their foster mother would write, she said, and Isidore believed her. Yet he had known from the day the green car with the bad antenna rolled up their drive: he had his own mind and his own body and his sense of humor and a belief in something better, if only mind and body and humor hungered after it hard enough—and that was it.

Before he had finished grade school, Isidore had learned not to try to change his father, but to circumnavigate him instead. False apology, the oldest of their strategies, remained available to them, but as they got older, they acquired new and more powerful means of resistance, like the boot full of coins they called their *unger bluzen* fund. He and Dennis regularly trolled the gutters for old Coke bottles and traded them in at the grocery store for a nickel or a couple of pennies. They put the coins in a boot in the bedroom closet and when a fight erupted between Ezer and Burt, and Ezer went to bed with a headache in the middle of the afternoon and refused to go grocery shopping, they could buy cereal and milk with their *unger bluzen* coins even if their father lay in bed all day. No one had to utter a single false apology.

That strategy was standard operating procedure until high school, when Isidore quickly grew and became bigger than his father, much bigger, in fact. (When he was six feet tall, Mrs. Polanska started calling him a "long noodle.") If it came to it, he could defend his brother with his body. For example, one night when Burt was making dinner, he dropped a hot dog on the floor and Ezer started to ride him for being a klutz and they yelled, nose to nose. Ezer got so mad he went and grabbed a crowbar out of the basement and chased Burt up the stairs with it. But before it ended up lodged in Burt's cranium, Isidore wrested the weapon from his father's hands. He threw it out the back door into the snow, where it landed with a pleasingly dull thud.

The old era came to a close with evident permanence the night before they went to wash the garbage trucks. By the back steps, Burt slammed the garbage can down and kicked it twice and ripped his shirt open, stripping off the buttons and tearing the shirt, which he probably did (knowing Burt) just to give himself a reason to open up their father's *verboten* sewing kit.

Burt rode out on the trucks on Saturdays in spring and summer, when garbage smelled worst. He'd wed himself to the job, like Sisyphus to his stone, for three years. Isidore had worked the garbage route between Cedar Road and Lake View Cemetery the summer before, and he'd signed up to do it this year too, since he needed a job and told Burt he would, but he'd be goddamned if he ever did it again.

"Don't torture yourself on account of him," Isidore said.

"The old fart would let me work in a coal mine before he gave me a nickel." Burt let loose a wild laugh.

"There are a hundred other things you could do," Isidore said.

"There are a hundred things *you* could do, Izzy."

"And you."

Burt seemed not to hear and cursed his father up and down. He picked up the rusted crowbar they'd found on the little hill in back of the house. The snow had melted and there it was one day, the weapon, and they remembered the bad fight—something to do with a hot dog—and they wondered if Ezer would feel bad when he saw it. When Ezer came home Isidore asked him why he had the crowbar in the first place, and for what job, and Ezer said he didn't remember ever seeing it and that it probably belonged to the Polanskas. Isidore put it outside with the trash, but the garbage men had not taken it away, and there it was again, like an albatross that can't be gotten rid of. So Burt picked it up and whacked the trash cans in the guts with it until they were badly dented. A couple of terrified squirrels raced up the tree behind the house and a startled dove flapped away off the roof. Somewhere during the tantrum, the buttons popped off Burt's shirt.

"Ah shit, I shouldn't have done that," Burt said, examining the shirt. "Now I gotta sew this up."

"Don't do it, Burt," Isidore said. "He'll go crazy."

"I don't have that many shirts, Izzy. I have one good one left clean, and tomorrow night I got a date."

"I'll give you one of mine."

It was about the middle of April and it must have been a Monday that Burt tore up his shirt because they washed the garbage trucks on Tuesday mornings. Burt collected up the shirt buttons he could find in the dirt beside the garbage cans, and then he entered the house with his shirt hanging open and his big chest exposed. He went into the closet and took the sewing kit down from the shelf. It seemed he made sure to commence work on the damaged shirt in the most public manner possible, disposed on the front of the living room couch, as though he wanted Ezer to find him there.

That April at the end of Isidore's junior year was a warm one that sweated up the sticky carpet in the lightless upstairs hall, and refreshed the fusty air of the living room with small and faraway sounds of cars on wet pavement and kids at the playground, and refreshed the kitchen air with new air that smelled like it had come even farther, from mountains and meadows somewhere. The fresh air and the strange sight of Burt sewing at his shirt while he was still wearing it cast a pall of instability on the living room, and Isidore went out of it, into the kitchen, and turned on the oven.

The squabbling over the sewing kit had over years imbued it with unnatural significance—like a house where someone famous once lived, or a much-sought-after treasure chest that's discovered not to have any treasure in it. The kit was a square wicker basket with a lid, painted pink—it had of course belonged to their mother—but over the years the basket had changed complexion from pink to the color of flesh. A long time ago Isidore played with the buttons inside it. How many and how varied in size and color were those buttons, unfastened and heaped on the floor of the kit, under the clear plastic tray full of needles and thread. In a house that was frequently out of toilet paper, it was a marvel to see so much of anything accumulated in one place. Burt and Isidore had once played a game with the buttons where they flicked them across the dining room table at each other. But Ezer, who frequently used the sewing kit in the evenings to mend his socks, did not like this debit on his button ledger. He warned the boys to stay out of the sewing kit, and Isidore did stay out (and made fun of his father behind his back: "Keep away from my buttons! Keep away from my buttons!"). Since it had been their mother's, however, the boys privately agreed it was theirs now, and the warning to stay away of course caused in Burt more interest in the sewing kit rather than less.

Isidore heard his father's bicycle chain clanking and the kitchen door opened.

"Burt!" Isidore said, but it was too late.

"Where is Burt?" his father said.

Isidore didn't answer or raise his eyes from the meat loaf on his plate. His father went down into the living room. Isidore followed him with his dinner half-eaten on the plate.

Ezer did not yell, "Keep away from my buttons!"

He didn't yell anything. He approached the couch, and stood over Burt, and Burt calmly continued with the hopeless project of fixing his buttonless shirt, which he was still wearing. Still, Ezer did not yell. Burt put the end of the thread into his mouth without looking up at his father and tried again to guide it through the eye of the needle. Ezer took the lid of the sewing kit and held it firm, watching.

"And now we will see," Ezer said, "if a boy who cannot remember his verses and cannot carry a hot dog from the icebox to the stove can sew even one button."

"I'm not a boy anymore, Tateh," Burt said, and reached into the kit. "A pin, a pin," he said. All the boys had observed their father pinning buttons into place before attaching them with needle and thread. "Let's see, a pin, a pin," Burt said, and rummaged through the tray of the kit.

"The pincushion, idiot!" Ezer said, squeezing the lid of the little sewing basket so hard that his knuckles turned white. Burt looked up helplessly. *"There!"* Ezer shouted again, and he snapped the lid down onto Burt's hand. Burt leaped off the couch and screamed.

"Ah! Ah! You stabbed me, you *shtunk!"* Burt hopped off the floor and hopped again, holding out his finger, which had blood on the end of it. He made a fist of his wounded hand, and feinted toward his father, who didn't move.

"My heart breaks, *zuninkeh,"* Ezer said. "Because you cannot sew a *button!"*

And instead of yelling any more, Burt hung his head—because

24

he thought the things his father said were true; he thought he wasn't good enough to sew a button.

"Don't listen to his bullshit!" Isidore shouted, almost letting the meat loaf slide off the plate.

His father began to curse in Yiddish.

"You shut your mouth, you sick old Yid!" Isidore said. "Don't make me any madder or I don't know what I'll do to you, I really don't! I have had it up to here with your bullshit! You ride Burt and you ride him. Why don't you ride yourself, you lazy bum? What the fuck did you ever do, you fucking lousy bum?"

"What did I ever do?" his father screamed, and added more Yiddish curses. "I came here. I made you an American. You are here because of me that I fight to be here, where you have such a luxury to complain over a little stick with a pin. What is it that *you* do, that it can't be done in all the world? You *never* sleep in the cellar, without a roof, with black night and stars cold like knives whining and scraping at the cellar door! My father slept with a table leg so it wouldn't be a Russian come and take our food and rape my mother and my sisters! You never hear the wind in Jedwabne at the cellar door, a sound it should make you believe in a devil and a *dybbuk!* Except that I, without help from nobody, no brother no father no God, hold tight to reason, not such *bubbe meises,* even in the darkness of Jedwabne, and I give to you this reason! I give to you America! And that is enough! That is a future, I give to you!"

With a cry of primal hatred, Isidore shattered the plate and the meat loaf against the wall.

His father stopped yelling and looked in disbelief.

"This you will clean," Ezer said, "or you will find another house to sleep tonight."

"You clean it!" Isidore yelled. "You're lucky I didn't put that plate in your fucking ear!"

"Nah, it's my fault," Burt said. "I deserved it. Don't blame Izzy for that, Tateh. I'll get you a new dish, Tateh. I will." And he started up the uncarpeted stairs with his buttonless shirt hanging open and his shoulders in a miserable hump.

"Gimme a break!" Isidore shouted after him. "Did that ridiculous speech about the Jedwabne stars and Russian rapists make you feel sorry for him? *Nobody* deserves him!"

Burt went on creaking up the stairs.

"Don't you care about anybody, you troll?" Isidore said to his father. His ears felt full of blood, but it was just his own heart pouring blood into his skull, a heart that wished to kill. "You think Mama would like what you did? But you, you'd eat your lunch on Mama's grave, you *black hole.*"

Isidore looked forlornly at his ruined dinner and then collected his schoolbooks and left the house. He went to the pool hall where he sometimes bussed the tables and he opened his books on the green felt of a table in the back. Under its dim light, through which climbed tapes of boa-like smoke, he read about the Gold Standard Act of 1900 and the McKinley assassination. (Emma Goldman claimed innocence, the book said, not because she was sorry he got killed, but because McKinley was "too insignificant" for her to bother murdering.) He read till midnight, when he found himself leaning over the book, half-asleep, and the bartender told him to go.

In his dream, he was juggling balls of yarn in a house with big holes in the roof, and a pair of girls yelled at him from the bottom of some stairs, and he threw the balls of yarn down at them but couldn't move his arms fast enough to hurl them with any aim or force. He also dreamed of a knife fight where he didn't have a knife but only a blunt-tipped meat thermometer, and he was about to push the meat thermometer into someone's chest when the alarm clock rang. It was 4 A.M. and Burt lay sleeping on his back like a slain warrior with his mouth open and his Adam's apple poking up unbeautifully. Izzy could hear the loud engine of their ride waiting on Meadowbrook, which looked like a road in a different world at this hour, a road through mist and purple darkness with curbs hard and cold as tombstones. They drove in woozy silence along that road. It led to the unholy terminus of the sanitation department, where a smell of ash and rotting food spoiled the dark air before the heat and light of the sun could begin to chasten it. They banged the trucks to scare off the crows and fired their hoses.

When he'd returned from washing trucks, Isidore washed himself, twice from head to toe, and ironed his shirt on the dining room table and got himself dressed. A warm shirt made him think of his mother, and even if she was mostly an idea now, he still felt sniffly and foolish. He went on anyway sniffling a bit over his cereal and made himself a lunch. He made it with the only food in the house now that the meat loaf was gone, some stale bread from the Invermere bakery and an avocado that was turning black, and he put the sandwich in a bag and took it to school. At lunch they laughed at his black avocado sandwich and passed it around and said, "Oh my God, look at that!" And the sandwich went around the lunch table and Isidore waited for it to come back to him. When the sandwich came back he said, "It's pretty ugly, huh, this sandwich?" and the kid who had first taken it said, "No, it's beautiful," and Isidore raised the sandwich to his lips like he was going to eat it but instead of biting it he flung it into the kid's face.

Before the next class he went and said hi to everybody he knew in the hallway. As he passed them at their lockers he touched them on the elbow or clapped his arm around their shoulders whether they liked it or not, even if he still smelled like garbage—he didn't know and he didn't care. And the guys said hey and the girls smiled; it was mostly a nice group there at Heights High and he was the president of his class, and it made him feel better about the black avocado and the broken plate.

He walked home with a girl named Ellie who lived on Chelton Road. The week before at Bonsdorf's ice cream shop, he'd bought Ellie a root beer float, with Mr. Bonsdorf watching them benignly from behind the glass.

"He doesn't realize we're Jews," Isidore said.

He liked her because she'd said it wasn't stupid at all that he was going to apply to Harvard even though he had no money. He'd said he was hoping to go to Miami of Ohio and that it looked so beautiful in the brochure, just like what college was supposed to be, a million miles away from the Old Country of his father, and she'd said she was applying there too, and they said they'd get another ice cream together when they were down in Oxford, since they wouldn't know anybody.

Isidore purposely avoided his own street, Meadowbrook, on the way home, but by some cosmicomic misfortune, they ran across Ezer anyway, pedaling up Tullamore Road on his green bicycle with knees rising and falling slowly, rising and falling, rising and falling, rising and falling, the heavy canvas bag balanced on his back and the toolbox strapped to his bike with the three-pronged canvas strap.

Ezer squeezed the brake handles several times, and the old bike jerked, shuddered, and groaned to a stop. Ezer steadied the rickety machine and pulled his sweaty shirt from inside the waist of his pants as though he were proud of it. "You will come home now, please, and do the wash," he said. "And you will eat on a newspaper like a dog."

"You know this guy?" Isidore said.

"No," Ellie said.

"There is no plate for you," Ezer said.

"Never mind him. He's the Crazy Old Man of Meadowbrook Boulevard. Goes around sticking his fingers in kids' ears." Isidore wanted to lift up the manhole cover in the street and climb in.

Ezer jerked his head toward Ellie and said, *"Aroisgevorfene gelt."* A waste of money.

Isidore was so tired his eyes burned, and his fingers were sore from wrestling the high-pressure hoses to keep them trained on the garbage trucks; his biceps ached, and he was so hungry and faint because he'd thrown his sandwich away that the ground seemed to be slowly rising like leavening dough.

When he came back to the sunny drive of the house on Meadowbrook, his father was standing outside the house on the steaming asphalt with a hose, watering the grass with a limp stream. The sweat itched on Isidore's neck and chafed between his legs, and the air smelled of hose water and dead grass uncovered by melted snow. Isidore figured he'd see if Dennis was home yet and maybe cash his paycheck and buy them dinner somewhere. But once he was on the drive, which was bleeding silver rivers from the coreopsis bush in front of the spigot, the words *aroisgevorfene gelt,* a waste of money, pulsed in his ears and he walked up to his father without saying anything and shoved him so hard that he tumbled onto the wet lawn and his glasses came flying off and landed in the grass. His father sat up and looked down slowly at the wet blades of grass stuck to his elbow and then looked slowly up at Isidore and then slowly back at his elbow.

"Yeah, I'm terrible!" Isidore shouted. "That's right, *I'm* terrible! I'm the monster! This, from the troll who lives under the bridge!"

But at night he cried, thinking of his father without his glasses and with water stains on his pants—thinking even of the inimical stars over the cellar door in Jedwabne. He cried not because he loved his father, which he really didn't, but because it could be, he thought, that he, too, was a monster. It could be that monstrosity was a family trait passed down from that old crocodile on the wall. He cried harder than he had since the day they arrived at the foster home in University Heights in the car with the bent antenna.

"What's the matter?" Dennis said.

Burt just rolled over and said in a voice muddy with sleep, "I'll break your knuckles, you consternummpin-ffffffff."

Isidore couldn't even answer. All he could say was "I'm sorry! I'm sorry! I'm sorry I woke you up. Go back to sleep, Denny. Go back to sleep. I'll ruin your sleep."

And the next day, Isidore was late to school. He guessed he was late so he would get a demerit and have to apologize to somebody who wasn't his father.

"I'm sorry," he said to Mr. Connelly, the homeroom teacher, who didn't give him a demerit but looked him in the eye with priestly significance. He wished he hadn't said he was sorry then and he sat down at his desk. It was a crude and bloody thing to be alive! But if he had to choose blood to be alive, then he chose blood. He watched Mr. Connelly, and said in a low voice, "Up yours, shit-for-brains."

His father didn't forgive people and neither did he. After his Harvard interview, he'd begun to believe he could really get in, because he'd told how he quit his job with the butcher, who'd thumbed his scale and sold bad meat, and the interviewer had seemed to like that story quite a bit. When he got the envelope, a gigantic thing like a letter from a king, he was surprised anyway and very proud, not only because it was Harvard but because he'd been rewarded for years of corned beef soup and emptying garbage cans when it was too early to smell anything like that,

and for years of collecting Coke bottles from the gutters of Warrensville Center Road, years of looking after his brothers when
he himself was so new and small he had to push a kitchen chair
up to the counter and climb on it just to get himself or Dennis a
cup to drink out of. He had no interest in telling his father, but
there was also no hiding the big, fancy envelope with VE–RI–TAS
spelled out on three little books on a crimson crest. "Harvard,"
his father said. "A *groyser tzuleyger* now, I guess." A big shot. And
when Isidore came back to Cleveland in the summer, he didn't
call to tell his father he was back in town. He was free. He would
let his hatred wrestle his father's hatred in some realm of eternal
hatred, some rank of the inferno cold and dark forever.

2.

OF ISIDORE'S QUEST FOR A DAMOSEL FOR TO
MAKE A HOME AND HOW HE GREW NIGH
WEARY OF IT, AND ALSO OF HIS DOLOROUS
ADVISION AT NIGHT AND HOW HE ROVE
HIMSELF THROUGH THE THIGH

PHONY HARVARD HIPPIES with their daddies' money in their wallets and their prep school degrees. He saw them watching him from the table by the window. He saw them sneering and sniggering. *Yeah, I serve you lunch in the dining hall. Yeah, I do your dishes, and so what? You think you're better than me? That makes me better than you, you shitheads.* He would rip their heads off and drink their blood. He'd crack their skulls and grease the skids of his own career with their spinal fluid. He'd—

"And you ordered a roasted chicken?" the waitress said.

"Yes, please," Isidore said.

"I'll be right back with that."

"Thank you very much," he said.

James's girlfriend, Joyce, a girl from Smith, spilled a glass of water all over the table. James said they were living in the age when all the heroes had been destroyed. John F. Kennedy was dead. Joyce and James seemed to be having another fight.

"What do you know about heroes?" Joyce said. "Your hero is Burt Lancaster."

"An imaginary hero is as good as any in this day and age," James said. James was another Cleveland Jew without any money. They were dishwashers living in the basement of Dunster House. But five more years and they'd be golden, they'd be doctors.

Joyce had brought along a friend from Smith named Danielle. She'd been advertised as good-looking, and in fact she wasn't bad. She liked to talk on and on about Bull Connor and the South. At least she cared, which was better than the last girl. But she was one of these girls who puckered her lips knowingly and nodded slowly like she was bringing everybody else the news, news that was by now old.

Isidore drank up two beers and felt he would fall asleep. He let his arms and legs fall where they would and wondered if he had mono.

"You're really a great big teddy bear, aren't you?" Danielle said.

"Oh, sorry," Isidore said, and pulled his legs together under the table and crossed his arms.

"A great big teddy bear."

"Uh," he said.

When Joyce burst into tears and climbed over James and out of the booth, James clutched his head in both hands and, his black hair standing up in a sheaf, chased after her.

"That was awkward," Danielle said.

"Uh, happens a lot with those two," Isidore said.

"Hey," she said. "You're pre-med, aren't you? Would you look at my hand? I was on vacation in Florida and I fell on it. That's what I get for trying to play volleyball for the first time!"

"You know, they don't teach much about volleyball injuries in organic chemistry."

"That's okay. Do you think it's sprained?"

He took her hand. "Not really swollen. Does it hurt?"

"A little, when I move it like this."

He saw very clearly what she was up to, but he tapped the back of her wrist. "Well, it's not broken at least."

"James told me about you," she said. "He's very impressed with you."

She wore her brown hair in a bob swept across the top of her head and hairsprayed perfectly round and wore thick, dark eyeliner or eye shadow or whatever it was and dark mascara, which he liked. A pointy bra with fairly big breasts underneath and good thick thighs you could bounce a coin off.

"Darn that Florida sun," she said, scratching at the neck of her sweater. "That darn volleyball game gave me a sunburn, too."

"Well, I'll have to make a thorough examination of that!" he said, because he guessed that was what she wanted to hear.

"Ah, ah, ah!" she said, and waved her finger no, but her eyes flashed yes like meteors, bridal white.

It would be nice to see her tan lines. But he was tired, and what he wanted more than sex was something else, maybe to be seen and felt as well as he could see and feel.

"I think you'll be a good doctor," Danielle said.

Isidore didn't have a chance to answer because James came back in with his hair still standing up and his eyes a bit teary, which he made no effort to hide. He sat down next to Isidore and grabbed him around the neck with the cold rolling off him like he'd just come out of a meat locker.

"You all right, mate?" Isidore said.

"Ahoy. Bring me the hogshead," James said, pulling Isidore close to him and kissing his hair. "This here Jack Tar, Danielle, he's going all the way. Don't you worry, I'm looking after him. He's got a world-class arm and I won't let him waste it on men in tights that carry around wet feathers."

"What does that mean?" Danielle said, looking horrified.

"He thinks he's a poet," James said. "He goes around reading Romantic poetry and writing poems!"

"Don't mind him," Isidore said, "he has Osgood-Schlatter disease."

James laughed.

"What is that?" Danielle said.

"Doesn't that typically affect the knees?" James said.

"In rare cases it affects the brain. Apparently."

"I mean," James said, "he's the hard-luck kid with the world-class fastball and I can't wait to see the World Series, that's all. Now bring me the hogshead!"

Joyce came back but would not speak to James. Isidore and James waited with the girls under the light of a dim and frozen lamp-post to see what would happen, and if Joyce would soften up again, but she didn't. She stared straight ahead until the bus came barreling in on tortured brakes, a hard and hardy machine lighting up the bleached asphalt from within, grinding salt under its wheels and boiling sulfur in its engine. It sat in gusts of white vapor from its own tailpipe, the lamplight shining on its black windshield.

"I'll call you," James said.

"Don't bother," Joyce said.

Isidore walked the girls to the door of the bus and kissed Danielle courteously. "I had fun with you girls," he said. "Thanks for making the trip, Danielle, you're sweet."

"Never mind Joyce!" she said. "You call me! You make sure and call me!"

"Maybe next month," he said. "There's a dance."

When the bus had roared off, they walked onto the bridge and James said, "Are you gonna call her?"

"No. But Joyce did well. She really tried this time."

"Izzy?" James said seriously.

"Yes?"

"Do we have oranges in the room?"

"Oranges? No. There might be some peanut butter left on one of the mousetraps, though."

"I think I have plague."

"You want to buy some orange juice?" Isidore said, looking around for a store. "Jesus, what time is it? It's been dark since lunch. It's like the North Pole."

The cold Charles River flowed under the bridge like the path of a nightmare down into darkness. Above the numb and dimly lit spires of Harvard, the moon was bright as a C sharp on a trumpet against the black sky. Harvard was a city upon a hill. Its ivy and polished windows and legion of janitors showed its power and its age. And he was a part of it. Of those to whom much is given, much is required, Kennedy had said. But the assholes at the other table could still fuck themselves, fucking cocksuckers, more was required of them than they would ever give.

"How much do you honor the dream," he wrote to Dennis. "Sorry if I was incoherent when you called. I was half-asleep," he wrote. "Remember that I believe in you, okay? And remember," he wrote, "if you have an emergency, the parking lot of the grocery store is the best place for a last-minute bottle collection." And he opened up the wine-red book to the dusty lines by Wordsworth. On onionskin paper, he typed up the lines of the poem that suited him.

But yet I know, where'er I go,
That there hath pass'd away a glory from the earth. . . .

But there's a tree, of many, one,
A single field which I have look'd upon,
Both of them speak of something that is gone. . . .

The homely nurse doth all she can
To make her foster-child, her Inmate Man,
Forget the glories he hath known,
And that imperial palace whence he came.

Behold the Child . . .
A six year [old]. . . .

But for those first affections,
Those shadowy recollections,
Which, be they what they may,
Are yet the fountain-light of all our day,
Are yet a master-light of all our seeing. . . .

Though inland far we be,
Our souls have sight of that immortal sea
Which brought us hither. . . .

What though the radiance which was once so bright
Be now for ever taken from my sight,
Though nothing can bring back the hour
Of splendour in the grass, of glory in the flower;
We will grieve not, rather find—

And he could read, type no more. And he was blinded by his tears. And he thought of the lilac blouse, but didn't get it out of his underwear drawer, just as he dared not allow the word "Mama" into his mind or the crow that had flown out of the tree and landed on her casket. If he did—

And he remembered the warmth and light of some home kind of place that had once shone on him, some home kind of person whom he would never see again. He remembered a warm place on a familiar chair, a leather chair, someone had been sitting there, sitting there, and he pressed his face where she had been until the leather went cold as rocks and was never warm again. And neither her warmth nor tucking in up under his chin, nor even her name returned again. He later discovered that the chair itself had not been theirs; his father had dragged it in off the street, Burt said, and banished a beetle from the hole in its leg.

3.

OF THE KING OF GENES, WHO PERADVENTURE
WAS FRIEND TO ISIDORE'S SOUL; HOW ISIDORE
SERVED THE KING; OF THE KING'S DAUGHTER,
THAT WAS GOOD AND FAIR, WITH A BAND OF
GOLD BEFORE HER EYES THAT MADE
WONDERMENT IN MANY AN ERRANT
BACHELOR; HOW ISIDORE CAST HIS
GAUNTLET AT THE GRANARY

HE ASSUMED, FOR no particular reason, that he'd meet his future wife in Boston. Which is to say, he expected very little in the way of romance in the summer of 1966, because he was not living in Boston then. He was living in Cleveland—Cleveland, with its ring of beautiful suburbs and long burning avenues leading straight down to ruin. But, it had to be admitted, there was a man there named Dr. Neuwalder, a wonderful wizard of a man who made you believe the universe was not an accident and was after all rightly governed. And Isidore went to work in Neuwalder's lab, which was no small thing, as Dr. Neuwalder had five years before become famous across the world; he'd shown for the first time that DNA from a healthy cell could cure a genetically diseased one.

Neuwalder looked to be about eight feet tall. (That is, he was six foot three.)

He said he always asked his short wife, "Are you standing in a ditch?"

He was busy, as people at that level tended to be. His time, if he gave it to you, was valuable in and of itself, like medicine.

Isidore asked him one day if he wanted the new test tube warmers on the first bench or the second.

"Either one," he said.

Whoa. Isidore told James, "That guy is amazing." *Either one.*

"What if he's gonna help you?" James said.

"People have tried it before," Isidore said. "I'd say I'm fucked regardless."

Building Isidore up seemed to make James feel virtuous. Or maybe it just distracted him from himself. "Neuwalder makes things happen," he said.

Neuwalder did have power. That was clear, because he had the sort of gentle humility about him that only the most powerful people can afford. His power and wisdom went almost beyond that, into indifference. Once, Isidore saw him looking out the window at the clouds with an expression that was hard to describe—the sort of docility you see in some fine race horses.

As Isidore drove east on Warrensville in Dr. Neuwalder's much-abused truck, the new Beatles song "Got to Get You into My Life" played in his mind over the sick grinding of the gears. He guessed the song had come into his mind because he'd met Dr. Neuwalder's daughter and she was good-looking. But as he pulled back up the drive to Neuwalder's house, he purposely scuttled the Beatles refrain and sang out loud: "I am I, Don Quixote, the Lord of La Mancha!"

And there she was again—Laura, she'd said—sitting and writing something in the garden, sitting on a moss-grown patio of cracked red brick, amid the slow helicopter circles of the carpenter bees. A lock of dark hair with a blond streak in it hung down from her forehead as she looked over her papers with a warm, contemplative face. There was something deeply familiar about her, as though he'd seen her not one hour ago but ten years ago—a feeling of two places or moments separated by much time but linked by strong resemblance in the way that an adult's face is linked to her baby picture or vice versa.

He tossed the gardening gloves onto a sack of birdseed and called out, "Hello there!" He felt like a dog must feel when he discovers a happy scent in the air—of a beef stew bubbling on the stove—or of another dog—or of wind—or of a person's crotch! And just as he suspected, the letters aligned in pen across her notebook paper had been shaped with care. They were mature, they were steadfast, and beautiful.

"So what did your father do with his old water heaters before he had lab assistants?" Isidore said.

"Oh, we didn't have any hot water," she said. "You should have seen the place before we had lab assistants."

Mr. Bonsdorf seemed to approve of them from behind the counter, and Isidore once again felt that Bonsdorf had only given out his ice cream to Jews by an unwitting mistake—but maybe that was paranoia.

Frigid air from the ice cream bins flowed over the glass and the long banquet tables loaded with Christmas-looking parcels, tinsel, chocolate, and canisters of Poppycock. It all looked like it hadn't been touched since a Christmas many years past. But Isidore had brought the chief's daughter there because it reminded him of something happy and long ago, something that was real but that he couldn't quite hold in his mind, like the concept of pi.

"This place is frozen in time," he said.

"He knows how to make a root beer float," Laura said with a sunniness that meant she didn't completely understand.

"You'd never know anything happened outside the door— that we went to space or that JFK was shot or there were race riots and a mother shot dead in a window in Hough," he said. "I wonder if Bonsdorf would have let a colored man have a glass of water in here."

They remembered together, and that was better: porcelain water fountains with drains patinaed like a grate in an old rainy garden. The smell of cut grass, of chalkboards, of antique pipes and pencil shavings. Stiff springs in bus seats that poked your sit bones through oily green plastic, and red rubber kickballs that pealed like bells. The smell of old library books with yellow pages soft as butterfly wings.

He didn't want to see her again, because he sensed a trap, because he felt a very particular, dangerous old dream reanimating itself like the undead sailors in "The Rime of the Ancient Mariner." He used to imagine that his father wasn't his real father, that his mother wasn't dead, and that he'd be restored someday to his real family, and he felt tantalized by this dream again, by the chief of medicine and his beautiful daughter, even though he knew that dreams were dangerous. There was no escape in September, as she went to school in Boston too, at Brandeis.

So he drove his brother Dennis's rusted Eldorado to the day care center where Laura worked. He knew just how to say it, gently and firmly, so she'd know it might be good-bye forever at the end of the summer—and after all, it really might be. He wouldn't have to say more. She was too perceptive a girl not to get it.

When he opened the front doors to the white brick building at around three o'clock, she was right there in the dark front hall kneeling down before a boy of three or four whose face was splashed with tears. She had made a cartoon on a piece of notebook paper with a ballpoint pen, a little storybook of saying good-bye. The boy watched intently, as she explained it to him.

"See, this is your mommy in the coffee shop across the street, waiting for you," she said. "And this is you seeing your mommy again!"

She said to the mother, "He actually did much better today. Sometimes the feelings come out when they see their moms."

The mother looked at Laura with such relief on her face, she looked like she'd just received a verdict of "not guilty!"

"You see, this nice lady Miss Neuwalder is here to look after you!" the mother said. "She says you can do it! So you can do it!"

Isidore held the door open and the boy walked out with his mother.

"I'm never going back in there," the boy said, but still he clutched the story in his small hand like a treasure map.

"Oh, yes you are!" the mother said as the glass door swung closed again.

Laura smiled at Isidore as if she knew what he was thinking, and what the mother was thinking and what the boy was thinking. He helped haul her up from her squatting position.

"It's hard to get back on your feet in a skirt," she said.

"You're pretty valuable around here," Isidore said. "How much are they paying you?"

"Come on, this is social work," Laura said, and she tried to smooth the wrinkles in her skirt as another mother came out of the hallway, dragging a little girl behind her.

"Susan did not eat lunch," the woman said hysterically. "Look at this!" She held up an open lunch box full of glassine papers.

It seemed there might be a confrontation, but again Laura

stood there calmly in her wrinkled skirt, as though she had glassine papers waved in her face every day of her life—as though
she didn't even mind it, like a surgeon doesn't mind a gall stone.
He just removes it.

"Carol, Carol," Laura said, "it doesn't matter if she eats her
lunch." She said it so compassionately and authoritatively that the
mother seemed to be soothed by it, even while she kept staring
into the disaster of the lunch box, which indicated that day care
and everything that had necessitated it would be the death of the
child. "Susan is doing great," Laura said.

The mother listened with a squished look on her face like she
was trying to evacuate something from her colon.

"Her job is really just to get used to the place and to separate.
And she's doing that. Believe me, she won't starve. The food is
there when she decides she wants it."

The mother went away not exactly with gratitude but without the squished look on her face. In fact, she looked as if
she'd heard something that had improved her like gospel in
church—because Laura seemed to know by intuition all the
numberless, nameless idioms of worry in the souls of children
and adults and it didn't matter if the child cried and didn't eat
lunch. It didn't matter if the moms were still *upset* that the
child cried and didn't eat lunch. There was someone to call,
and someone to talk to, and that was all anybody ever wanted
anyway.

What was wrong with these Neuwalder people? Why weren't
they a mess like everybody else?

When Isidore and Laura had sat down in the decaying sky-
blue Eldorado, Isidore said, "I really like you."

"Well, thanks. You're so-so."

"And I think it's great we'll both be in Boston this fall."

"Yeah...?" Laura said with suspicion. It appeared she had already begun to figure this picture out, even before he'd finished shaping it for her, and to figure out its underlayers too. You couldn't hide too much from this girl. "Yeah, you think it's great?" she said.

He realized she'd put on more makeup than usual today. She looked pretty.

"I just don't know what it will be like," he said, carrying on to the bitter end. "I'm going to be busy, and I want to see you, but I don't know, and we'll have to wait and see."

The frown disappeared. She laughed. Her laugh was as if to say, *I thought you had a better curveball.* "Of course we'll have to wait and see. What else would we do?"

He eased the Eldorado into the street with all its exhausted, beaten parts straining and grinding uneasily against one another.

"How do you know so much about kids?" he asked.

"It's just common sense really."

She took a peek at herself in the mirror on the visor, thought about fussing with herself for a moment, and gave up and flipped the visor up again.

When they got back to his place, she asked him what he had been like as a child. He offered to show her some pictures.

"Don't you have an album?" she said, when the pictures were emptied from the envelope.

"I should get one," he said.

"Is this you?" she said. "Everybody's smiling but you look so sad."

"Yeah," he said. "My mother had just died."

"Oh no," she said, and somehow the sympathy on her face did not mollify, whether because it was too uncomprehending about this particular thing or because nothing could mollify at all.

"That's Ed. He's not smiling either, see? That's because I shoved a football into his face that day."

"He probably deserved it."

"We always had cheap, horrible clothes. He was making fun of my shirt, I think." He had cried over that fight too. He showed her his watch and confessed: "It says Seamaster, but it's a fake."

"So?" Laura said. "There are probably more fake men with real watches than the other way around."

He wanted to make a joke, but the pictures had sobered him.

"I'm sorry about earlier, in the car."

"No need. You're not the first man I've dated."

"I have no doubt many men have tried," Isidore said. "I guess, in the car before, I was just tensing up."

"You? Tense?" She laughed. "My father always says about the house staff that the ones you have to worry about are the ones without a care in the world. They're the ones who kill people. I mean, I wouldn't really know myself, but I see the point."

"What's wrong with you? Why aren't you a mess like everybody else?"

"Oh, isn't everybody a mess, when it comes down to it?"

"I'm not sure. How many Harvard guys do you know? Some of those guys are like . . . printed at U.S. Steel. You wonder if they have adrenal glands."

"That's all a front," she said. "They're like anybody else and so am I. I have nightmares." She told him how they'd operated on her eye when she was three. Her father had stood in the door and wouldn't come and she'd breathed the ether and tumbled backward, falling and falling into space. And every night before sleep, when she was a child, she would think of a ballerina turning and turning around and around and slowing down, and as the ballerina made the last turn and came to a stop you saw that her face had changed to a skull.

They drank cheap wine and wondered whether it was any good and he laid his head on her big and pretty breasts, and she kept saying, Why not? Why not? So they climbed out the window and onto the roof with Vivaldi playing on the record player (because they were so young that Vivaldi was still fresh on their ears). He saw the scars high up on her legs. She pulled her skirt down over them and told him about the puppet show in front of the fire and her black pants and how she'd ignored the heat because, well, the show must go on! Then she'd had to peel off the dressings and the dead skin for weeks after and the fire had left a pattern of pale welts on her thighs as if it had touched her with evil fingers and left behind an anarchy of faint fingerprints like a Seurat.

Her healed injuries, the wine, and the major key of the Vivaldi made him believe with a total sincerity, without sentimentality, or romanticism, or self-delusion, or desperation, that things could be healed.

"Why not?" she said.

4.

How Isidore, Arrayed Like a Poor Knight, Came to the Demesne of Laura's Father, Leo Neuwalder, Lord of the Eerie Lake, and How the King Would Fain Gird Isidore Betimes with the Sextant of Sir Oliver Hazard Perry

LAURA TOOK A heavy course load that year so she could graduate early, at the same time as Isidore would graduate, just in case there would be some need for that, and kept quiet about having done so with a shrewdness unknown to most women in regard to the male psyche. And by the time the mild air of spring came around and began to revive the dead world of Boston, Isidore knew what he would do.

On Labor Day weekend of 1967, the last weekend before medical school was to begin at Case Western Reserve in Cleveland, they went out to South Bass Island to join her parents and her sisters. As they waited on the roof of the ferry, Isidore kept saying they were late, and it was a shame to be late, and Laura kept saying it didn't matter and why was he in such a weird mood.

"You can control what you can control," she said. This was

yet another distillation of her father's Confucian wisdom, and it only made Isidore more nervous. He knew all her father's sayings from Laura's frequent quotations: my father says you must respect a patient's denial; that most things get better by themselves; that a peach is best slightly underripe; that McCarthy stripped the State Department of all the brains on the Far East and that was why they got into Vietnam; that the key to life is recognizing what you can't control, which is everything.

"Sorry," he said, "I have a bug up my ass today. I don't mean to."

Isidore's ass literally itched like there was a family of bugs up in it. He'd in fact bled from his hemorrhoids that morning.

"I think you'll like our house," she said. "It's not Martha's Vineyard, and it's kind of ramshackle, but it's a nice place to sit by the lake and have wine."

Isidore watched the clouds over Lake Erie, aloft like airships high above their own shadows.

When they arrived, Dr. Neuwalder's other two daughters and their boyfriends cheered and disentangled themselves from the picnic table in the yard. They came with red wine in paper cups, and Dr. and Mrs. Neuwalder came from their Adirondack chairs with books. There was still light in the sky.

"Let me get a good look at you," Mrs. Neuwalder said, and put her glasses on. "What's wrong with him? He looks ill."

"The famous Isidore Auberon," Dr. Neuwalder said. He was gray at the temples, tall, with tan arms that were naked of hair, and chapped lips. The boyfriends called him Doc.

Isidore could barely stop himself from uttering some hosanna about how Doc had cured sickle-cell anemia in a test tube and invented gene therapy, which was the entire future of medicine. He had never seen Dr. Neuwalder outside the lab, and it was a little like seeing one of your teachers outside class in elementary school.

"Would you like bourbon? Or some ice wine?" Doc said. "It's

nothing special, but they make it right here on the island. No, you need the bourbon, I see. Evelyn, get him some bourbon, would you?"

Evelyn Neuwalder brought him some bourbon in a Mason jar. She was a child psychoanalyst.

"I always take my bourbon in a Mason jar, served by a psychoanalyst," Isidore said. "How did you know?"

"Ha!" she said, and told him a dirty joke about a priest, a minister, and a rabbi taking the train to an ecumenical convention in Pittsburgh. The woman selling train tickets had big breasts, she said, and wore a low-cut blouse that showed a lot of cleavage and turned the clergymen into stuttering fools: the minister asked for his change in nipples and dimes; the rabbi asked for two pickets to Tittsburgh; but the priest would not be pushed on his heels and wouldn't let the woman's brazen apparel go without comment and declared, "When you get to Heaven, Saint Finger's gonna shake his peter at you!"

Isidore was grateful for the bourbon and the bosoms, and he helped grill the walleye without feeling even a trace of garbageman. The clouds drifted unfettered across the sky, and sailboats crossed below.

After dinner, while the girls were upstairs washing up, Doc brought Isidore through a doorway lit up with red light from across Lake Erie and into a sitting room with a blue-and-white painting of many ship masts at harbor and a view of the water.

"Do you like boats?" Doc said.

"I've been in a rowboat," Isidore said, looking out at the oceanic lake. "And I read *Moby-Dick,* but that's as far as it goes. I imagine people sail a lot out here."

"I don't get out here as much as I'd like anymore," Doc said. "But my brother sails in the merchant marine."

"So he's a real sailor."

"I guess you could say that," Doc said. His eyes twinkled as if to presage a laugh or the telling of a joke.

"I mean, I'm sure you're a real sailor too," Isidore said.

Doc crossed the Persian rug and put his jar of bourbon down on the shelf beside an old nautical instrument and blew the dust off the instrument and held it over the lamp.

"Was sickle-cell the first disease you tried?" Isidore said. "That was genius. The newspapers got it, but they have no idea how big it truly is."

Doc looked at him with benevolence. "Edison forgot to mention luck in his inspiration-perspiration formula. But let's have a vacation," he said. "I want to show off my sextant here. This one belonged to Oliver Hazard Perry. You remember him? Of course you do, because you were in high school less than ten years ago. It's been a little longer for me. Go ahead. Take a look." Isidore took the instrument and Doc leaned up against the window and tapped on the windowpane behind him with the knuckle of his middle finger. "Perry repelled the British right out there in the Battle of Lake Erie, 1813. It happened. Isn't that something? The sextant reminds me that it really happened. That the past really happened."

Isidore couldn't think of what to say so he said nothing. He wanted to ask Doc his question, but the question seemed to create its own weather and rocked his boat and upset his timing whenever he thought he would get the words out.

"There's a huge painting of Perry in the capitol," Doc said. "It's crazy-looking. The canvas is probably three hundred square feet and all you can see are Perry's eyes. Have you seen that?"

"No, sir," Isidore said. Goddamn the question!

"It was given to me by a teacher of mine. He got it from his teacher, who got it from William Osler, who got it from Perry's nephew or cousin or somebody who had goiter. 'We have met the enemy and they are ours.'"

"You're right," Isidore said distractedly. "It's like holding a piece of history in your hands."

Doc turned around and leaned on the windowsill and looked out at Lake Erie. "There's nothing like the sea, is there?"

"Cure for the November of the soul," Isidore said, and he put the sextant back on the shelf. He felt emboldened by the thought of Herman Melville and almost asked what he had to ask. Instead he said, "Has your brother ever taken you aboard a freighter?"

"Me?" Doc said. "Oh, I was in the Pacific Fleet in the war. That was quite enough for me. I just tootle around in a Sunfish nowadays."

"Oh, that. The war." Isidore looked at the titles of the books behind the sextant, running from the floor high up above him: *The Axis 1945, Iwo Jima, Survival in Auschwitz*.

"Would you like the sextant?" Doc asked.

"What do you mean?"

"Take it."

"No, no. I don't have anyplace to put it in my bag."

"I'll send it to you."

"That doesn't make sense. I'll forget to give it back."

"I mean take it. To keep," Doc said, and he drank a bit more bourbon and sang part of an old sea song. "'From Ushant to Scilly is thirty-five leagues. . . .' I'm drunk."

At dusk, Doc led Isidore out onto the coarse wet grass. Windows shone yellow up and down the side of the dark house. Someone was playing records and in the window on the third floor there was a slim silhouette with big breasts, which must have been Laura's. She looked like she was in front of the mirror and doing something to her hair. Isidore scratched his ankle on the thorns of a barberry bush.

Doc held up the sextant to the imperial blue of the evening sky and said with a cigarette clamped in his mouth, "Arcturus."

He handed Isidore the sextant and Isidore peered through it uselessly. "I can't see anything."

"It hasn't been cleaned since the Battle of Lake Erie."

"I thought you saw Arcturus," Isidore said.

"That's just something I say when I look through a sextant."

Isidore sat on the end of the picnic table bench, but Doc remained standing, and exhaled a stream of smoke with chin up-lifted. Isidore stood again and he almost asked his question but instead he said, "They say the navy is the way to go. You think so?"

Doc looked at him in a calm and gentle way, as though no question could surprise or trouble him. And he hesitated, as if he had mixed feelings about giving a speech, but felt compelled to do it anyway because of the danger posed by Vietnam or because Isidore was nervous and wasn't saying much or because of the special circumstance of marrying off his daughters before the electric dimness of the Great Lake and the barberry bushes fading into obscurity.

"The navy?" he said. "Well, Izzy—can I call you Izzy? Do you mind? This mess in Vietnam is a whole different war from the one I was in. You should stay out of it. You have a deferment for now, and there's military money at NIH. Hard to get, but I'll talk to you more about that, I think you could get it. I'll help you to get it. Now, World War Two was a different conflict, you see, but you should be glad to be away from any war there ever was and you should steer clear of any war there ever will be, even if it's against Nazis. The military is like anything else made out of people, which is to say, sometimes very great, and usually very badly fucked up. But it's different from anything else in that it's a bunch of fuckups with guns that can blow your head off. I knew a few great military men and not all of them were former civilians, either, some of them were career men who not only cared about their work but thought about it too—you know, men of honor who used all that power they had wisely, prudently, and on behalf of good causes. A navy can move a mountain and come to the rescue. But even in that just war against gangsters and murderers, I spent ninety-eight percent of the time doing complete chickenshit for men with salt in their brainpans and the other two percent I felt like we were running into each other like football players in blindfolds. And that's before we even got near the enemy."

Doc waited to see if Isidore would talk. He didn't.

"The navy is supposed to be safer, I guess, but it didn't seem safe at the time. You felt the threat of extinction from zeros and submarines all the time, while you played cards, in the john, in your sleep. People say you should live every day as if it's your last—and maybe that works for people who have no idea what a last day on earth is like. I say, you live every day like you're gonna live forever. Which means, by the way, stay out of wars. The *Thomas Jefferson* was an attack transport, so we were shelled. One guy I knew, who later got killed, described it as having a speeding train thrown at you from out of the sky. And I treated some of the kids who came off the beaches at Okinawa. The ones that had prerenal failure or got hit in the liver. It seems to me since then that a person's a homunculus, and the child is the greater part of the self, and everything that comes after in life is by comparison a veneer. It's easily stripped away and then the child is right out there, out of its shell, quivering and bleeding. But then those boys were actual children. And the ones who go home feel old whether they can grow a beard or not. They feel separate because the facts of life have come to roost directly in their kitchen window and they know the secret of the universe now, about death and the homunculus. I see it in the hospital, too. There's a lot of death in the world. The world is a brutal enough place without inviting any more trouble from it. So no, there is no branch of the armed services that's the way to go. The best branch for you is NIH. Laura told me about your mother, I hope you don't mind. She told me because I was in a foster home too, and my mother died when I was three. You sure you don't want to smoke?"

Doc smoked for a little while. Isidore asked Doc about his mother and Doc said he guessed she'd had enough babies and tried to get rid of the last one with a wire hanger, yours? Isidore said cancer of the stomach, and they both laughed a good laugh about their little punch line, but it hurt Isidore to laugh and Isidore guessed it hurt Doc, too.

Doc offered Isidore a cigarette again and smoked for a while longer. Then he said, "Have you ever seen an eagle in the wild? You know why an eagle is a war emblem? Because you get the sense a pigeon might get a joke, and a sparrow might make one, but an eagle would do neither. An eagle has no sense of humor. That's why he's on the national seal. When I was in California, I saw an eagle eating a fish on the limb of a tree. I'll never forget him, the way he straightened his plumage and refolded his wings when he was done pulling at the fish carcass, how he retested the wind and prepared himself for the next thing. An eagle has skill. That's all expertise is, you know? It's training and knowledge you get because you need it to survive. Nature makes an expert out of you if you want to survive. That's a war. Just like life. Just trying to survive. You know, I don't feel awe when I see an eagle. I feel sad. I feel sorry for him. There he is, him and me and you, experts in our jobs, because of the constant threat of extinction. In my view, war is just like life, only more of it per square inch." Doc examined the end of his cigarette and pulled the ash off bit by bit with his fingers as though he were debriding it. "Well, you asked a simple question a while ago and I told you the story of my life! Forgive me, it's unlike me. I drank one too many bourbons! And I have only daughters, you know. You seem like a fine young man, is all, and I wouldn't like to see you go to Vietnam. But you have a deferment."

Now Doc sat down on the picnic table, and Isidore sat down too.

"I think I'll take a cigarette after all," Isidore said.

"Usually I'm pretty good at not scaring off the boyfriends," Doc said. "Ah well, nobody's perfect."

"If it's all right with you," Isidore said, "I'd like to marry Laura."

"If it's all right with me?" Doc said. "Hey hey!" Doc threw an arm around Isidore and raised his glass. "By God, you're a gentleman and a scholar and a fine judge of whiskey!"

They drank.

"You feel better now?" Doc said.

"Did you know I was going to ask?" Isidore said.

"Laura tipped me off a little," Doc said.

"But she doesn't know."

"Well, she seems to suspect something."

Isidore raised his glass again. "Fine judge of whiskey—fine judge of women, is what!"

"You're right about that," Doc said seriously. "I love her. And I love that you love her. *L'Chaim!*"

They drank again.

"My father made me study Yiddish at the Workmen's Circle," Isidore said. "I hated it, but I admit there are words in Yiddish we just don't have. Like *tachlis*. You ever heard of that? It means 'brass tacks' or something like that. You don't get to talk *tachlis* every day, or hardly at all." The alcohol was beginning to affect him, and he felt so much looser after asking his question that he stood up straight and shook his fist theatrically at the sky and said: *"Tsi zaynen shteyner in himl nor kedey tsu dunern!"*

"What was that, now?"

"'Are there no stones in Heaven but what serve for the thunder?' By the great Yiddish playwright William Shakespeare. It's from *Othello*."

"You just stay out of wars, young man," Doc said. "How do you say that in Yiddish? My father spoke Yiddish but I don't speak a word."

"I don't know 'war.' I just know the Yiddish for getting your ass kicked."

Doc liked that joke so well that he recited a limerick:

> *There once was a fellow McSweeney*
> *Who spilled him some gin on his weenie.*
> *Just to be couth*
> *He added vermouth*
> *And slipped his girlfriend a martini.*

"You made the right choice, Isidore. You'll never meet another girl with a father like me." And he told Isidore another one:

> *A koala came down from the trees*
> *For the treasure between Mary's knees*
> *Though Mary would marry*
> *Koalas don't tarry;*
> *The marsupial eats bushes and leaves.*

And Isidore said the only limerick he knew:

An old man from Kalamazoo
Wrote limericks that stopped at line two.

"I asked about boats because my brother is the president of one of the seamen's unions and he could get you a stint in the merchant marine. You have next summer—your last summer of freedom for the rest of your life—"

"Ugh, don't say that."

"No, no, you get real busy and then it calms down again, and then you get real busy again—"

"If I can do it, I'll do it."

"You can do it," Doc said. "I ought to know."

Doc lit a new cigarette on the ember of the old one and inhaled through it until the end of the new one glowed.

"When you're at sea, you take the ashes off your cigarette like this," Doc said, peeling them off with his fingers, "so they don't fly up in the wind and get in your hair—or worse, somebody else's. Sailors don't like ash in their faces."

They sat in silence and away out in the dark somewhere, a buoy clanged and clanged again. And Doc told him some more raunchy rhymes and they sang sea songs till the youngest Neuwalder girl called them in.

5.

How Isidore Went to Sea without a Proper Surcoat and Slept Full Little in a High Rocking Bed; and of a Marvellous Savage Who Loved Bottles of Glistering Gold; and How Isidore Stood the Fiend a Stroke of His Gisarme and the Fiend Repayest Him with His Finest Weeds and a Helm Polished with Linseed Oil

Isidore had been to an ocean beach just four times, but it was a holy place to him, and he liked the days of rough seas and high wind best. On a windy day, the sand stirred up into the wind and flowed over the beach in low and sinuous currents like marauding fingers searching for signs of life. Wind blasted the waves in slow explosions that upset the phases of matter and burst the ambits of sea and sky. The screen of lifted sand divided near and far, as did sea-spray, which diffused in the distance into a shining vapor, an almost photographic filter, and made of the far end of the beach a nostalgic scene, a memory, a mystery half-known. As did sea-sun, which changed distant people, lifeguard chairs, kites, dogs, and sailboats to vulcan shadows, burned them down to essence like Giacometti sculptures come to life, dark thin figures engulfed in magic fire and living in a far-off golden realm.

On another day, a colder day, in another mood, he heard the millstone of time turning in the waves, felt the floury sand on his toes like the offals of that turning stone: there on the shore of the ocean you remembered that your mother was dead, and that you would die too. Days themselves were the offals shattered on the wheel of time. He wrote a poem about the sand and nothingness and the lime bones of the clams and birds. *Days are offals shattered on the wheel of time.*

And he felt a great hunger for that forlorn communion with nature as he set off to see a little of the world.

At the Brooklyn Port Authority, the men of the *Garfield* sat in plastic chairs like zombies. Except for one sailor who kept cursing the officers and saying, "The goddamn *officers* don't wait," the men didn't talk to each other, but merely smoked or played solitaire or sat helpless and idle like illiterates in a doctor's waiting room. If you asked them for a light, they seemed almost confused, and couldn't figure what to do or say. They seemed ill at ease. But at sea, the zombies came right to life, and never stopped talking, least of all Happy.

"You're in the upper bunk, Cork Fender," Happy said. "You'll like it up there in a typhoon."

The answer to that was easy, really: "Okay."

"It's a real nice place to love yourself. 'Cause you ain't gettin' no love down here, Cork Fender."

Isidore threw his duffel onto the top bunk. The tiny room smelled like engine oil and hummed with the distant sound of motors at work. The steel walls were cold.

"Do like I say," Happy said. "You don't do like I say, and you might have an accident. You get it? You might get mistaken for one of them niggerheads on deck and get wound up in a rope. You get it?"

"Yeah," Isidore said, "I think I do."

"I might accidentally forget to not throw you overboard. You believe that?" Happy stood up and took the measure of Isidore from head to toe. "You believe I could do that? To a six-footer like you? What are you, two hundred pounds? 'Cause I done it before, and not to no cork fender who don't know which is the bow and which is the head." Happy scratched his jaw with the stump of the half-amputated ring finger of his left hand. He had a buzz cut and wore army pants and waders and had a blurry American flag tattooed on his left shoulder in ink that had badly bled.

Isidore stuck his hand out and said his name.

"I'll shake your hand," Happy said, "sure I will," and he squeezed Isidore's hand hard. "And I won't even wash it after. Isidore? Is a door for slamming?" He laughed outrageously.

"The way you laugh reminds me of my brother," Isidore said. "So—just so I know who to blame when you throw me overboard—who are you?"

"Who am I? I ain't your brother. And I ain't a door like you, Is a Door." Happy waited, maybe for him to laugh or to jibe back at him. "Ah, I wish Cooper was here! He was a riot! Shit, I love that dumb cracker." And Happy swatted the air in front of Isidore as if he were swatting at a fly, and crouched before his footlocker, and opened it up.

The footlocker contained at least seven bottles of Red Stag Kentucky bourbon, and some smaller bottles of a lighter yellow stuff, with strips of cloth tape on each that said LINSEED OIL in blue marker. Happy pulled out one of the small bottles of yellow oil and poured it into his palm and started oiling his hat, a new sou'wester.

Happy said, "Since you don't know how to do shit else, they're gonna give you the watch. And what I'm tryin' to tell ya is: on

the watch. On the bow. If you feel spray out there. Go to the
fly bridge or the waves will swallow you whole and no man's the
wiser." Happy laughed hideously, then stopped. "What are *you*
laughing for?"

"Because you're joking," Isidore said, and he stopped laughing.
"Aren't you?"

"Oh, you ain't long for this world, Cork Fender. You got
yourself tangled this time!"

In the mess hall, Isidore learned that the other sailors did not
call his roommate Happy. He called himself Happy, but they
mostly called him Chips because he was the carpenter. And he
learned that even though he was called Chips, the carpenter
didn't work with wood. That was the joiner. The carpenter
battened the hatches with a ratchet that was kept on his person
at all times. A cork fender, Isidore figured out, was something
that hung over the side of a boat to buffer its collisions with
the pier. "It isn't so bad if I call you a cork fender," another
sailor explained, "it just means you're a useless piece of shit!"

"Good old Is a Door," Happy said. "His father's name is Is a
Floor. And I guess his mother is . . . Is a Whore. Get it?"

"Ah, Happy," Isidore said, "you know the way to my heart."

"I wish Coop was here!" Happy said. "He knows a good joke!
Me and Coop, we've had some times together! In the marines
they cut him loose in the woods of Tennessee and told him to
live off the land for a couple weeks—so he broke into chicken
coops, that crazy cracker, and ate the farmers' chickens like a
fox!"

The sailors did not exactly talk *to* each other but rather *near* each
other. But the food was good. And when Happy challenged Isidore to an arm wrestling match, and Isidore pushed Happy's hand
down toward the table, he pretended to tire and let Happy come

back up to ninety degrees and then win. Soon after that, Isidore graduated from Cork Fender to Schooner Rig.

"It means you're green and you got the wrong gear and you're fucked!"

The SS *President Garfield* was more than five hundred feet long, so when you were on the watch, alone in the dark at the bow of the ship, sailing fifty feet above the waves at twenty knots, you were not only alone in the middle of the Pacific Ocean but far from midships and the life that persisted in its heat and light like a campfire in a dark wilderness of waves. Between you and the fo'c'sle there was nobody and nothing besides the inhuman towers of the booms, which groaned like pterodactyls but had no preference between port or storm, between waves or the frigid sand at the bottom of the sea. You were to call the bridge on a little phone if you saw a light. You were to say, "Two points off starboard bow" or however many points it was, or say "port bow" if it was port. It was so black out there, sometimes the lights of your brain mingled with the dark of the ocean and you saw sea dragons with electric scales, and sometimes you heard a malevolent sound against the hull like the serpent arms of a sea monster, pulling the whole ship down, down, down into the inhuman, ugly deep. In the morning, such thoughts looked ridiculous, but the next night, they returned unabated.

The second night on the watch, the boat rode into heavier seas that came before the wind came. He didn't know what calm felt like or what high seas were, but he did feel a change, a different tension in his legs, and then he heard the waves and felt the spray on his face. He was fifty feet in the air up on the bow and the only wind was from the boat pushing through the still, dank, black air. He remembered what Happy had said and hurried up the deck, under the giant, lonely booms that screeched like pterodactyls and reared disconcertingly back, back, back, so he tumbled downhill toward midships and gripped the rail tight. The bumpy steel of the deck was shining and over the rail was a yawning blackness of no sight or sound. Before he got to the fly bridge, the ship came over the swell. It pitched down the back of the wave and smashed into the next trough with a horrible shuddering and groaning of booms, and the jolt knocked Isidore's feet out from under him and he slammed down on his tailbone and rolled against the side rail with the speeding blackness just beyond it. He scrambled to his feet, and made it up to the fly bridge as the *Garfield* crashed into another swell and he nearly lost his teeth on the forward rail. Down below, liquid tons of seawater poured into the deck lights, washed over the entire bow, and rained out the scuppers as the booms again reared back and the ship pushed up the face of another swell.

It seemed at that moment he'd made a terrible mistake, and his hunger was still a hunger, but not for the alien desert waves. He saw in his mind the lamp at home on the bedside table, and the oven mitts on a hook by the kitchen window, and the exact place beside the sink where Laura kept her hairbrush, and her bathrobe, warm and dry in the early morning hours.

"I can't say I'm sorry you didn't drown," Happy said.

The upper bunk seemed to roll through an arc of 180 degrees and to try to dump Isidore out of his bed each time, or to punish his aching tailbone, and every other minute the foghorn, which was next door, would blow Isidore's ears out.

"Sleep tight, sweetie," Happy said. And then he added, "You ain't been in my locker, have you?"

Isidore answered in the negative.

"I told you what I did to the kid I caught stealing from me? The little kid in Vietnam, cleaning the ship? I caught him in my locker. So I said, 'You want to go in my locker?' And you should know by now I'm a stone-cold killer, Schooner Rig. I held his wrist with one hand and with the other I took my whiskey bottles out of the locker and put them under my mattress. And I stuffed the little gook inside my locker and locked him up inside. It was tough to get him in there. I had to fold him up. And you think I let him out?"

Isidore felt like puking. He kicked his foot against the ceiling to moor himself in the bunk. "Yes?"

"Fuck no! I put him in the hold. And when we got out to sea, he been in there a day and a half and he wasn't screaming no more and the locker smelled like a toilet. And I said to myself, 'Chips, you can't use this locker no more for your whiskey bottles. It smells like a fucking toilet.' And I threw the whole thing overboard. What do you say to that?"

"I say, I'm glad I can't fit in your footlocker."

Happy hooted and laughed hard at that. "I say, you're right about that, Schooner Rig!"

Isidore could hear the Red Stag bourbon sloshing in the footlocker, and in a rhythm syncopated with the bottles in the locker another bottle sloshed in the lower bunk, along with personal noises of lips and wet exhalations.

Daylight did not bring calm. They adventured through mountains of water big enough to spin ten thousand tons; white trails of foam rinsed down the dark mountain waters like branches of lightning. When the wind came in, the waves got even bigger, and the bulkhead lamps popped and fell down and rained on the halls a ruin of mosaic glass. In the hold, crates went wild and blew up into splinters and nails.

It occurred to him that ships did sink, that misfortunes were littered over history like shipwrecks on the sand beds of the world, and he tried to talk to Laura in his mind.

"Don't drown," she seemed to say. "Don't get killed by a drunk."

"Where are you?" he said.

And there was no answer, even in his mind, a silence like a death. In the middle of the night, when it began to rain hard against the porthole, he wondered if he'd ever get home or if he might die there alone in this raw black cold wet desert place and he'd sink and his bones would be gnawed by cold, blind hagfish. Death seemed so lonely—he felt death out there in the sea and it seemed that Laura was the only thing attaching him to the earth. Without her he might sink to the bottom of the sea or fall off the earth and into the bottomless black hole of space.

But then the foghorn stopped blasting and he fell asleep, and in the morning the ocean was calm. At 6 A.M., they went down into the hold, where pillows and feathers and socks had spilled everywhere and the splinters and nails grabbed your clothes and your skin. And though they had cowhide gloves, they had to take them off and tuck them inside their belts to hold a nail or use a tape measure, and their blood began to spatter the bright broken wood. But he felt grateful, in a way, for the disaster, because of the industry and the exercise of matutinal reason it demanded of him after his night of dancing with death.

"You're a strong bastard, ain't ya?" Happy said with an air of approval as he watched Isidore toss away a broken plank. "Last time this happened was in the South China Sea. Coop was there. He'd tell you. You come into the China Sea and there's all these little Chink fishermen in their junk boats in the dark, like a bunch of fireflies all over, little boats lighting their way with lanterns, fishing for eels. They're too stupid to get out of the way, those junks! Or too slow. I must have run down a hundred of 'em in one night at the wheel, the stupid Japanese fuckers."

"Hey, give me a hand with this, Happy," Isidore said, lifting up one side of a broken crate and blowing at a floating feather. Happy helped him lift it.

"South China Sea is a beautiful place for pussy, Schooner Rig. Between me and Coop, we probably fucked every hooker in Hong Kong. I told you I got a tattoo on my prick in Hong Kong?" Happy said. "A little spot right there on the end. When it's hard, it says 'Josephine Cunningham.' You get it, Schooner Rig?"

Isidore hammered a nail into the side of the crate while Happy held the side in place for him, breathing out an acetone-ish air of cherry bourbon.

"No, what do you mean?" Isidore said.

"I mean—"

"I know, Happy, I get it."

They hammered together another couple of broken crates and Happy kept on talking and talking about his prick. But just when Isidore thought he couldn't take it anymore, Happy went climbing up the ladder with surprising strength and energy, up toward the blue light of the hatch with an anchor-chain link in his left hand—the hand missing a finger.

"See ya, Schooner Rig, my turn to drive."

That morning, Happy had emptied his last bottle of Red Stag cherry bourbon. "You're going to the wheelhouse," Isidore said. "You sure you should?"

"Coop and me used to take a bottle *into* the wheelhouse sometimes. We was hellraisers, me and Coop."

A gust of wind whooshed against Isidore's ear and banged loud on the hold floor next to his feet. The chain link that Happy had been carrying had dented the hold floor.

Happy looked down but didn't say anything.

"That link weighs thirty pounds!" Isidore said. "Jesus H. Christ!"

"So it does," Happy said. "You're learning more every day, I tell you."

Happy went on up the ladder, occasionally missing a rung and swinging off the ladder in a very unintentional yet balletic way.

At lunchtime, Happy didn't come down to eat. Isidore looked out a porthole.

"I don't think we're meant to be sailing into our own wake, are we," he said.

They said Happy, who had fallen asleep not at the proverbial wheel, but on it, would be put off the boat in Hawaii.

This led to a long period of uncharacteristic silence from Happy, who didn't laugh at Isidore's farts anymore, or even complain about them. The weather was fine and Happy slept much of the days.

But at Honolulu, Happy sat down to his food as though there were no trouble.

"This fish has been dead a long time," he said cryptically.

It was extra crowded in the mess hall. The crew of the SS *President Buchanan,* which was docked beside them, had come over to the *Garfield* to eat.

"Hey, Happy, isn't your friend Cooper on the *Buchanan?*" one of the sailors said.

Happy said nothing.

"Isn't that Cooper?" another man said, pointing to a long and lanky sailor with dirty brown hair sticking out from under a wool cap and big scarred hands clasped behind his head. There were moons of black grease under his fingernails.

"Yeah, that's him," another sailor said. "That's Cooper right there."

Cooper half-turned his head.

Happy didn't look up from his fish. All he said was "This fish been dead a long, long time."

Before he left the boat, Happy gave Isidore his sou'wester rain hat and his bottles of linseed oil.

"And you take these pants, too," Happy said. They were the army pants that Happy said he'd bought on the black market in Vietnam. They'd probably come straight off the legs of a dead GI. "Now you ain't Schooner Rig no more," Happy said.

"Thank you, Happy. That's real nice of you. It really is."

"You believe I killed that boy in Vietnam?"

"I believe whatever you say, Happy," Isidore said.

"Don't *believe* whatever I say. *Do* whatever I say. But believe this: you don't want to know what I done," Happy said, and he walked onto the gangway, perfectly steady, and whistling in the Honolulu sunshine.

That night Happy bought the drinks, and Isidore had no choice but to match him drink for drink. He got so drunk that when he came back up the gangway in the middle of the night alone, high over the black water where duplicates of the harbor lights burned and waved like fire upside down, he walked as slowly as he knew how, thinking, *I am too high up. This is the most dangerous thing I have ever done, this is the most dangerous walk I have ever made.* But he made it aboard again, and back to his bunk, which was not so noisy as it had been before Happy was put off the ship, but still smelled like engine oil.

Isidore returned to land, where the light of the table lamp and Laura's hairbrush and warm, dry, plaid bathrobe remained just as he'd left them. The death dreams fled. By comparison with the sea, medical school seemed civilized, the way a base camp at the foot of the Himalayas must seem civilized in comparison with the storm, snow, and avalanche above. And at the same time he felt a power gathering inside him to summit a mountain, and he smelled the nearness of the peaks in the sharp clarity of the air: he could do it. He was going to be good at this. He was going to do good.

6.

How Isidore Auberon Was Chastened and Bade Anon to Forswear His Penne by James Helpern, the Ghost Boy; of Librium Pills and a Cold Cup of Coffee

The candle that burned for his mother flickered on the sill, and raindrops traveled slowly down the dark pane facing Overlook Drive. On days like that Isidore read Keats from a wine-red book that still had the Harvard Coop sticker on the back cover, and he copied down a few phrases, which he would toss in a briefcase with poems he had written on prescription pad paper. *Sea-shouldering whales, vision of greatness, a new thinking into the heart.*

Isidore grabbed his rough red coat from the hook and said, "Did you know Keats's girlfriend was named Fanny Brawne?"

"What does a poem accomplish in this world?" James said. "If you're gonna waste time, wouldn't you rather waste it with me at the bar? Cripes, we have boards coming. If you're gonna read, read Stepp or the *New England Journal of Medicine* or something. You make me nervous."

"Okay, gunner."

"No, I'm just here to watch the Isidore Auberon story unfold, the hard-luck kid with the world-class arm, and I don't want to see you throw it all away on poetry, for criminy cripes."

"You can just say 'Christ,' James. He isn't listening."

"Not to a couple of Cleveland Heebs."

"That's what poems are for, by the way."

"For what?"

"To get you through life when no one is listening, you heathen. Get your coat on," Isidore said. "Sweet, sweet Fanny. Oh, Fanny Brawne, how do I love thee, let me count the ways. Fanny Brawne. I think I saw a case of that in proctology clinic."

"Speaking of proctology, how're the hemorrhoids? How's your ass?" Ghost Boy pointed to his own ass.

"Yeah, I'm presenting it at this month's M and M. 'My Ass: What Went Wrong.'"

And they went out together into the wet early-evening air of Cleveland in green, green summer.

Isidore and Laura were married at Glidden House on the campus of the university. Late that night, they returned to the Neuwalders' house in Shaker Heights, where they had first met out on the patio with the circling bees.

"You know why surgeons always stop elevator doors with their heads, don't you?" Isidore said. "Their hands are too important to their work."

Doc wiped a few tears away. He laughed so hard that he took his own pulse, then carried his plate to the kitchen, whistling, and joined his wife on the patio.

When he came back to the backgammon table, he smelled of smoke. "There's nothing like family," he said, and he put his arm around Isidore and Isidore put his arm around him and they felt each other warm and present through their shirts.

Doc dropped his matchbook back into the glass urn full of matchbooks and matchboxes. The urn was round and the matchbooks and matchboxes were of all colors so the urn looked like a globe mapping all the colors of the countries of Earth. It was very late and Isidore was still in his tuxedo with his bow tie loose around his neck. They could hear the girls talking quietly about their dresses on the patio, saying they would wear them again, and he wondered if they would. Bobby Kennedy was shot and dead, but Isidore was married. "I made it through," he said.

"You made it," Doc said. "We both made it."

He told Doc about the dog that barked all night and the boards coming. And Doc came over to Izzy's house and stuck two Librium pills inside some cold hamburger and tossed it over the fence.

James said medical school was like eating a hill of shit with a teaspoon. In fact, it was much worse than that. But it was also a crucible in which one was smelted and transformed and felt oneself being transformed, and for which four years of lifeblood was perhaps a reasonable price. Doc said that when the day came for the Hippocratic oath and the ceremony where Isidore would wear the green velvet trim of a doctor, Doc would be there to shake his hand and would be the one to give him his diploma. But that didn't happen.

Remains of breakfast: a cold cup of coffee, the slag of eaten toast on the china, an orange peel. Doc went to California and leaned his head on a steering wheel and coasted to a stop in the highway sun and he came back in a wooden box.

7.

How the Ghost of Dr. Austrian Appelled James and Isidore of Grievous Sins, and How Isidore Smote Off Its Head

IT WAS TRUE that in the old days, he felt that some people were rooting for him. He knew many of his teachers liked him. They liked that he'd been in a foster home and paid for his dinner by working a garbage truck and that he never complained (as far as they knew) and kept up with guys who had families and money and a tradition. He had a good attitude (or so they thought) and he figured he knew what to say, and he didn't ever give up. He was "tall and good-looking," according to Mrs. Polanska, but more than that he lived without a cushion. He lived hysterically on the knife edge of oblivion. Most people in the world are forgotten, there's no setting for them at the table, and that's the way it is and there's nothing they can do. But he was going to set his own place and pull up his own chair and refuse lost love its brutal victory and restore what should have been and realize what should be. He'd try it even if he sometimes didn't believe it was possible, and looked around at others and thought they were chosen for success and he and his people were small and selected for pain and destruction. He would love life even though it played dirty and kicked in the balls. And some people saw this and wanted him to make it, and that meant something.

But now Doc was dead and he was an intern and nobody gave a damn if he fell off the apple cart. In fact, they hoped he would.

James the Ghost Boy's eyes were red and the collar on his white coat stuck up on one side. The rubber loops of his stethoscope spilled out of his coat and drooped and bobbed over the edge of the chair. A penlight, dog-eared index cards, a laminated Snellen eye chart, and a green booklet of antibiotics bulged in his breast pocket.

"It's really true," James said. "You fleas don't know when to get off a dead dog."

"You called the consult," Isidore said.

"I called in a consult, not an air strike of hypodermic needles," James said. James and Isidore huddled together over lab values on the wavy pasted printouts in the back of the nurses' station. James groaned. "What was the potassium?" he said again.

Beyond the dark doorways lay patients in stocking feet, with faces that reflected your gaze from out of the darkness with wet, shining eyes. Sometimes the patients sat before windows of square twilight with their bowel-prep drinks hissing ginger air beside them on the table. Sometimes they shuffled from the bathroom in feces-stained gowns.

The team met for rounds in the Austrian Room, a conference room on the general surgery ward. Dr. Stepp produced his stack of blue index cards and prepared to hear lab values on his patients. High on the wall behind him was a portrait of the leaden-eyed surgeon, Dr. Austrian, in a cracked frame. If you looked at it directly it would turn you to stone.

"I'm giving him a ride home," Isidore said. "All right if he sits in?"

"Who," Dr. Stepp said without looking up.

"Dr. Helpern."

"And Dr. Helpern is?"

"He's the surgical intern," Isidore said, "that called us to consult on Mr. Healy."

Dr. Stepp said no more and still did not look up. Isidore looked at James and shrugged.

When Isidore said Mr. Healy's bilirubin was missing and would have to be ordered again, Dr. Stepp's head shot up and his eyes broke from their card-reading squint into an imperious stare. "Well, we need to know that bilirubin right now," he said, and turned to James. "Did you order it?"

"Yes."

"Well, where is it, then?"

"It was missing from the chart," James said.

"Well, we need it right now," Dr. Stepp said.

James said, "Yes, sir, I already drew another—"

"I don't care whether you drew another," Dr. Stepp said. "I care whether I have it in front of me. You drew another, you say—did you send it stat?"

"No, sir," James said. "Would you like me to draw another and send it stat?"

"I said," Dr. Stepp said loudly, "I need that value right now."

"Yes, sir," James said, and pushed back from the table.

"I'll go do it," Isidore said, and sighed loudly.

"What are you sighing at?" Stepp said. "I've heard the jokes you tell, Dr. Auberon. Is that how your mother raised you to behave in a public elevator?"

"Is that how *what?*" Isidore said.

"Did you know about that missing bilirubin?"

Isidore stared at Dr. Stepp. The silence grew uncomfortable. Then he said, "I was more worried about the missing chest X-ray."

"I didn't write for a chest X-ray."

"Oh," Isidore said.

"You ought to worry about yourself, young man," Stepp said. "You may have been Leonard Neuwalder's chosen one, but I didn't choose you. I've heard the jokes you tell. Are you one of those weird people?"

"No, I vote Democrat," Isidore said. Stepp seemed to want to say something about this but Isidore said, "Mr. Healy's got pleurisy on the right."

"So what?"

"The nurse agreed."

"So, what does that mean!"

"So I thought you might want to get a chest X-ray."

"No. If I had wanted a chest X-ray, I surely would have written that in the chart and our trusty surgical intern here would by now have procured it." Dr. Stepp glanced over at the GI fellow, who was on the phone. "You tell me Mr. Healy has right-sided pleurisy. If you're presenting to me, then do it right. Vitals? Does he have a fever? Did you examine him? Does he have a fluid level? Did you percuss?"

"I'm not certain about a level," Isidore said. "I heard rales. He doesn't have a fever. But he's on steroids, isn't he?"

"Yes," Dr. Stepp said in an evil way, "he's on steroids." And he laughed.

Isidore didn't care if he ordered the chest X-ray or not. Mr. Healy was a doomed shade of yellow anyway and there wasn't anything Isidore or anybody else could do about pancreatic cancer. And Burt had wrecked his car and broken a tooth and had come over unannounced asking for money.

As they were leaving the Austrian Room, Dr. Stepp said to James, "Go ahead and get a chest X-ray on Mr. Healy. This is a teaching hospital, after all."

"I already ordered it," the GI fellow said as he vanished into the stairwell.

"Good," Dr. Stepp said. "Dr. Auberon will evaluate it."

Tireless Dr. Stepp and the tireless GI fellow trooped onward from room to room while the tired interns hurried after them.

It was half past ten by the time they dragged themselves to Isidore's car in the dank parking structure. Water was dripping from the concrete ceiling onto the steel hood of the car. The GI consult service was supposed to be an easy month, but Dr. Stepp had made sure it would not be.

"Is that how my mother raised me. Is that how your mother raised you, you prick? To go around talking about people's mothers? Fuck you. What is wrong with that guy?"

"I strongly suspect micropenis," Ghost Boy said.

"Looks to me like plain old astrocytopenia."

Before going to sleep, Isidore pulled the prescription pad from the drawer.

Laura opened her eyes and began to cry.

"No, no," Isidore said, and petted her hair and her great big belly.

"I know you must be tired," Laura said. "I don't want to disturb you."

"Is it because I yelled this morning?"

"No," Laura said. "I just wish Daddy would have at least known about the baby. It wouldn't have mattered. But I just wish."

"I'm still here. It's you and me. It's been you and me. It would have been you and me, anyway. I'm not going anywhere."

Isidore jotted down a line—*faces in the cracks in Hell's hive, they reflect your passing inquisition, and damn* you—and a poem, which he called "The Austrian Room":

> *Dr. Austrian:*
> *Would you have said*
> *(If you weren't dead)*
> *"Do you like surgery?"*
>
> *Would you have spoken?*
> *Or, manly, dealt your silent token,*
> *Condescending vision*
> *In your eyes of molten lead.*

8.

How Isidore Spake to His Aunt at the Feast of Saint Rufus, and How He Behaved Him There; How He Went with His Lady into the Country without Regard for His Aunt's Rebuke

"Why are we doing this, again?" Isidore said through the bathroom door.

"Because the baby needs people to love it."

Even at full term, and huge, in fact looking like she was about to give birth to an elephant, she hid her body functions from him, but he couldn't hide his.

"That's something you should know about me by now," he said through the door.

"What?"

"My guts. I have a special brand of *kishkes* made unpopular by the Jews of eastern Poland."

"I see. And Hungarian Jews have better stomachs?"

"I don't think you understand what you've gotten yourself into, here. You marry an Auberon and you marry his ass.... Put it this way. There would never be such a book, because it would be extremely boring, but if there were an Auberon family history, it would be titled *Inherit the Wind*. You get my drift? This is something you should know."

And he proved his point with a long, low, tuba-like sound. "If you think it's horrible to hear that, you should try producing it."

"Gee, you're a hopeless romantic, Izzy," she said.

When he had completed the act and stepped out of the bathroom and into the kitchen, he said, "Actually, I am," and he twisted at a cowlick on top of his head. The Friday-morning light lit up the wet grapes on the table. They were soaking through the pages of the *Cleveland Press*.

"Let's get it over with," he said. He squashed a handful of grapes in his mouth and spat out a stem.

And they went back to the neighborhood of early-morning garbage trucks, his father, the green bicycle, blistering white snow, and dry, guttered glaciers that lay there in the roads unconquered and gray well into the spring. It had risen above freezing and was cool to warmish in the bright sun, but not warm enough to melt much. Any patches of exposed grass lay flat, as if the grass had memorized the weight of the snow so well that it could never stand again.

"I see why the Jews came here from northeastern Poland," he said.

"Why?" she said.

"They must have taken one look at all this Baltic slush and felt right at home." And before opening the car door, he said, "Like I was saying, Laura, you ask very little. And you'll get it."

"You may be surprised," she said.

His mother's brother, Mo, looked guilty as hell and fumbled around with a bottle of gin. "Can I get you some, Isidore?" he said, before any introductions had been made, and he didn't offer anything to Laura, not even a glass of water.

Isidore introduced Laura, who stood there with her huge belly waiting for a chance to be nice to someone, and it was Isidore who asked if she wanted anything. Aunt Mara did not get up.

"Why didn't you call?" Aunt Mara said. "He's been back in Cleveland for years and he doesn't call," she said to an old lady who was sitting on the sofa and neither gave herself a name nor was given one. It might have been Tante Faige, who was apparently not dead yet.

Laura said to Aunt Mara, "You have a lovely home, Mrs. Alman."

Mara said, "Isidore, you should ask your father if he plans on repaying Mo." She leaned nearer to the old lady sitting next to her and explained, "His father, Ezer, ruined Sophia's stomach, he gave her the cancer, and *we* paid her radiation treatments. This, after I went to Poland myself to get her and we paid her passage to America."

Isidore put the glass of gin against his face and heard the ice cubes start to melt and settle in the glass.

"Sit down, Laura," Isidore said, "here." He tossed a pillow aside.

Aunt Mara watched the pillow as if she were concerned for its well-being.

Nobody said anything for a very long time. The Cleveland Browns were on the radio and they all sat and listened to the game.

"You follow football?" Isidore said.

"Certainly," Mo said, with a fairly strong Yiddish-Polish accent.

"Who are these guys? I've never heard of any of them," Isidore said. "Doug Dieken? Who the hell is that?"

"He hasn't had much time for sports in the last few years," Laura said.

"I know this much," Isidore said to Laura. "The Browns win the division every year but they can't win in the play-offs anymore. Do you follow this lousy team, Mo? Do you, Laura?"

"No," Laura said. "My father was named for a third baseman for the Indians, though."

"Is that so?" Uncle Mo said. "Here, have some more, Isidore." He reached out with a gin bottle in one hand and a bottle of seltzer water in the other. "Do you want something to eat?"

"Just the drink, please," Isidore said, and Mo poured with one trembling hand and then with the other. "I didn't know Jews drank gin," Isidore said.

"You do, apparently," Mo said.

"At a family gathering," Isidore said, "I'd drink turpentine."

"So you started working?" Uncle Mo said. *Voiking.*

"Yes."

"Where does he work?" Aunt Mara said.

"At the hospital!" Uncle Mo said.

"What kind of work do you do at the hospital?" Aunt Mara said.

Isidore stared at Aunt Mara, then he said sarcastically, "I'm a parking attendant."

The next morning the phone rang at eight o'clock. Isidore turned over and the box spring creaked.

"Go away!" Isidore said from under a pillow.

It was Laura's boss.

"She's at the school," Laura said. "She always fills out these forms from the state in triplicate. Nobody does that."

"Well, you're not going. It's Sunday."

"I don't know." Laura sat up, sighed, and tugged her nightgown down over her belly. "It's not worth fighting with her. I'm very good at keeping people happy, because I just give them what they want. It doesn't bother me."

"Ah!" he said, and sat up. "I'm afraid we have an appointment in the country that can't wait." He threw the covers off the bed and pressed his ear to her belly. "Hello in there! Can you hear me? This is your daddy speaking. We're going to the country to-day." He went into the bathroom and opened the faucet in the stained yellow bathtub.

When they were out near Chagrin Falls, he rolled down the car window and leaned his head out. "Do you smell that?" he said. "It smells like rotting leaves! Old stone fences! Horses! Barns!"

9.

HOW THE LORDS OF CHAOS CAME TO
ISIDORE AND MADE WAR AGAINST HIM,
AND HOW ISIDORE GAT HIM A SON AND THEN
ANOTHER, AND HOW WHEN LAURA WAS GREAT
WITH CHILD AGAIN HE TOOK HIM HURTS UNTO
DEATH; AND HOW THE QUEEN MADE HER A
NUN ON THE GLENCAIRN HILL HOUSE WHERE
THE CROWS VOLLEYED ACROSS THE GRAY SKY
AND ATE THE SEED MEANT FOR THE LAWN

THE QUEEN BORE her a child and named him Leodegrance after her father.

She strained and sweated in a vale of hot tears that weird December day of seventy degrees to push the baby through the wet well of pussy willows. He was a week late and they had to cut him out finally so his head was perfect, with black hair shining like a sea mink. And Mrs. Neuwalder said he looked like Mao Tse-tung and the queen didn't like that because Mao Tse-tung was as ugly as a sink full of dirty dishes. Mrs. Neuwalder was mad, perhaps, because her daddy had once left her and now he'd done it again and all the babies with their mommies and daddies could go to hell.

And Isidore and Laura took him home and sang to him, and

twilight came down soft as humid August tears in eclipse of winter.

Isidore sang the boy a sad song in the tiny closet room, *"Oyfn Pripitchik,"* though he'd be damned if he wouldn't be the best father on the face of the earth atwirl in its silent morning terrorglory.

In the hearth burns a little flame. . . . What insanity, a Yiddish lullaby: to teach infants in their cribs to learn by rote the Hebrew alphabet of tears, to inoculate their babies against the plague of years to come, or to inoculate them against joy before they had a chance to suck their mamas' breasts. He was sure it was his mother who had sung it to him, but then it seemed, in some dim and primitive remembrance, that it might have been his father.

How's your mother? Went over the falls in a barrel. Yours?

A baby was as light as a bird. Its head smelled warm and good like a peach, like milk.

By the time Leo could walk, Isidore wondered if it had been a year or ten, or only an instant finely dissected since the child was born.

"Look at those eyelashes!" the women said. "No fair!" they said.

Leo's skin was as soft as the belly of a cat or as a lilac silk blouse.

Isidore's own father was an evil old Saturn and a cannibal, and he'd never get his red claws near that soft skin. What was wrong with that lunatic old Saturn? It was easy to love a son.

"What will you be?" he asked the child.

The child looked back at him studiously.

"I think you will be great. I know you will be great."

They sat on the rug.

There was a future there, but they didn't know what it was—a future more exquisite and subtle, in fact, than a mere galaxy of dead rocks and stars. They would just have to wait and find out.

"We'll see, Leo!"

"Light!" the boy said.

Isidore carried Leo on his back to the edge of the little woods by the pond, where wind had raked half the water into slow little waves. The other half of the water lay still and clear as a sheet of acetate, and ducks slept on the glass above muddy tin cans.

"'We have met the enemy and he is us,'" Isidore said, and released a smoke ring into the air. "Not you, Leo. Pogo meant humanity, but not you. You are free of sin."

"Don't smoke near a baby, you fool!" a woman said.

Isidore couldn't form another smoke ring, so he blew out a great cloud of pipe smoke. "Get lost, witch," he whispered. When the lady was gone, he said, "Can you breathe okay back there?"

But he could see in his peripheral vision that Leo was totally oblivious to the smoke and to the lady in the stupid hat. Leo grabbed two tiny fistfuls of his daddy's hair.

"Careful, there, cowboy!" Isidore said, reaching back with his pipe in his hand and then remembering the pipe.

Before the sun had set, you could see a star or planet over the pond and in it, and the moon, and the silhouettes of the trees. It was as if he, Isidore, or he, Leo, or both, had called stars, planets, moon, and trees into being by a magic wish. They had found a lump of gold there: the first sight of dark trees waving before the moon and stars, of stars written on the heavens like a poem.

Isidore did not fill out the forms of the blue baby book, but instead wrote on the last blank page and inside back cover, leaving himself just the two pages to fill as if he secretly knew they would not have long.

12/73 Behaved beautifully at Dr.'s for 2 yr check-up—listened to preparation, said "I'm scared" but let pediatrician examine

*him etc. Opened mouth on request for oral exam. 1 and 2/74
Says "It's too dangerous" to certain prohibited activities. Now
tells of need to make poop or pee pee and gets both in potty regularly. Accidents are rare. Says "Daddy's doctor, I'm big boy."
Says "Mommy's big, I'm just yittle, Daddy's biggest." Noticing hairs on my arms and legs—wary of it. Does not like
my developing beard—tries to avoid kissing me directly—says
"beard scratches." Creating imaginative stories from pictures and
objects. Handling separations and fears better—pulls self together after initial tears and says "I feel better." Reassures self
that we "come right back." Now can identify objects himself as
"just part of bed; just pretend; just a friend" to reassure self
against fears. Starting to draw recognizable objects (barely). Has
been drawing faces for months. Criticizes own drawings— "not
good owl; not good plane." Whispers and says "Ssh, be quiet"
with finger over lips. Tells time—it's "free clocks" all day.
Asks me each morning "Daddy go work?" If yes, he is vis-
ibly disappointed and withdraws. Responds with glee at my
returns—running to me saying "Daddy, Daddy" over and
over. When I tap on his back, he says "Don't knock me,
Dad." Very sensitive to others' feelings—if you look sad etc.
he says "You're mad" or "You're sad," "Don't cry, Dad; feel
better in your eyes." Says "I need a hug; lemme give a kiss."
Memory fantastic—occasionally reminisces about things that
went on months ago. Imitates well—makes sounds of many
animals—e.g. squeak-squeak (mouse), hoo (owl), hello (par-
rot = carrot), caw (crow), roar (lion, tiger—we told him he
was named Leo for lion, roared like he was a lion), growl
(bear—high-pitch growl for "yittle bear" which he thought of
by himself). Brought me imaginary "candy turtles" to feed me
yesterday. Often says Jenny and Harvey and Grammy are in
planes he sees in books—says they are going "zoom" from*

"runway" coming to see him. To my declaring my mistake in putting "jammies" on backwards, he said "not on purpose." Gets control of tears quickly now, rubbing tears away and saying "I feel better in my eyes" as he struggles to maintain control. In response to my continuing to sing after his demanding I stop, he said "I mean it!" in exact imitation of my words and tone to him on other occasions. Interprets table's being set for evening company as "Happy Birthday" someone. Takes any opportunity to sing Happy Birthday song ("to Leo") and claps afterward in quietly pleased glee. In response to being told it was the wind whistling in his bedroom windows (which frightened him), he said, "it's not wind, it's snake in the window." Described a mouse being chased by a cat in a book as "cat frightening dat mouse." Knows meaning of number two, full and empty, close and far, and identifies "engine" and "caboose" ("parts of train"). Calls eyebrows "eyebrowns." Opens his mouth and shows you how "Doctor looks in your FROPE (throat)." Able to thumb through pages of books in perusal for items or subjects he likes (like "lotsa cars"). After tripping on shoelace, said, "Oops, Daddy, better tie my shoe!" While thinking of things to draw with me he said, "I got a idea." Of a bump that continued to hurt, he said to Laura, "Dat's a problem." Poses for camera, smiling sl. artificially on command. Blows kisses, hugs and kisses friends spontaneously now. Says "bless you" and "gesundheit" to sneezes. On 2/10/74 handed me an old letter and said "sign your name." 2/16/74 learned to use drinking straw. Referred to self as "a little guy." Copies pediatrician in playing doctor—examines your mouth ("open mouth"), says "you're fine," offers a lollipop. Says "I'm de doctor"; "I'm big boy doctor, you're daddy doctor." Takes his toy toolbox and says "I'm going to work"—returns in a few seconds, running in with arms wide, hugging us and say-

ing "I missed you, good to see you. I wove you. I come back, see?" Pretends to exercise on living room floor, demanding our participation and saying "like Grammy." Puts a plastic cup over one eye, squints with the other and says "smile for the camera." His imitations show amazing attention to detail and nuance. 3/4/74—says "I'm so pretty and proud;" "I keep my pants dry and warm and comfy;" told me while sitting astride me on the floor, "I'm imagining I'm riding a horse." 4/74 Says "Mommy bought me a wonderful present." Frequently ends requests with "or sumptin"—e.g. "Daddy, give me a ride, or sumptin." In car says "Oh God, de traffic." Makes faces to scare me. Says "I fink we going outside" as a hint; or "Maybe we'll go for a walk or pway in puddles, or sumptin." Says words with great animation and inflection. Using complex sentences and questions, with many appropriate "ands" and "buts." Realized he couldn't see his eyebrows on 4/18/74 and thought he'd lost them—cried till we showed him he could feel them with his fingers; his joy was immense. In response to being told we'd have a baby someday by Laura said, "You will change the diapers, and I will go to work, but don't worry, I will come home for lunch." Said to a neighbor girl, "Larissa did you know I can go to school and I can read?" 4/29/74 —Leo asked Laura, "Mommy, is there a baby growing inside of you?" [Yes.] "In your tummy?" [Yes.] "I got one too" he said, pointing to his tummy. Says "see dat" finally as he explains things to you. Appropriately identifies TV characters as "wonewy (lonely)." Tells us when we or others (even on TV) are "upset"—wants to know "what's matter." Says of scary TV scenes, "It will frighten you away." 5/7/74—Told me this a.m. that "I dreamed a man was scaring me." Says "be gentle with me." Refers to "our mommy" (mine and his). Almost able to ride his new (used) tricycle.

Said "Mommy you're special." Learned to put his hands in his pockets; stands around like one of the Dead End Kids now. Sits between and hugs both of us together around the neck, showing great pleasure to have us close in a trio. Making real buildings with blocks—builds carefully and when very tall, squeals to us with glee and pride "Isn't it beau'ful?" Says of many things "It's so funny." Said on my accidentally bumping him over "dat rockled me over." 5/24/74 "I used to be a doctor; now I'm a cowboy!" In response to request for a kiss said, "I'm too busy now; I'm too tired." 6/74 Said, "I want to be a fire engine when I grow up, and help people." Rode tricycle well and alone for first time. Says "upside up" as opposite of upside down. Told me "Trees are made of wood." Says "hi, lady" to Laura and says "Hiya, Dad, how ya doin'?" to me. Calls either of us "young man." In tub said, "I found the ocean." 7/74 Put his hand on Laura's belly and said, "Don't worry, Mom, I won't hurt the baby growing in your breast." Knows whole alphabet and counts to 20. Calls me "sir" jokingly on occasion and "Daddo" (like Leo), and says, "Is he, Izzy?" Told Laura that "whoopsie daisies are flowers." Laura had hair in pigtails after swimming. Leo said, "Oh, Mommy, you look like a girl." Told us a few days later, "Mommy got her hair wet and then looked like a girl." Was using 2 hands as puppets, with one saying "I will help you up the hill, Daddy." When he saw I was puzzled he showed me "this is hand Daddy and this is hand Leo." Says "a monster makes me mad at John (next door 2 yr old)." 8/74 Now says L's correctly (instead of like W's) and relishes repeating L-words correctly. Says "Sorry you yelled at me, Dad"—a left-handed apology. Describes dreams now, usually regarding witches and "gophs" (ghosts). If our hair is wet or rearranged slightly differently he says "That's not you" and gets upset until correction is under way. Then says, "Now *it's you!" After months of resisting my kissing him due to beard or mustache (12/73—8/74) his first comment to me when I shaved my beard was, "Now you can kiss me."*

Doc had died before he could write a letter and so had not been able to help at NIH, but Isidore won the fellowship anyway, without any help. That summer of 1974, when they were living in Rockville, Maryland, in a duplex they rented for $145 a month, Isidore drove Leo into Washington, DC.

They went together to the Lincoln Memorial and stood before the giant statue of Abraham Lincoln.

"That's a big man," Leo said.

"Yes, it is."

"Is that you?" Leo said.

"That's Abraham Lincoln."

"Chase me, Daddy," Leo said. "I'm faster than you."

"Okay, but let's put your coat on."

"No, I don't think I need my coat," Leo said.

Leo probably didn't need a coat. But that was not the point. Isidore said, "Get your coat on, Leo."

"No, I don't have to."

"Leo, just put it on."

Leo started to spin around and sing.

Isidore said, "Get your coat on, Leo, or I'll kill you."

"Don't kill me, Daddy," Leo said. "Please, don't kill me."

The sun was blue.

The statue was bright.

When they swam together at the public pool, Isidore said to jump, and Leo ran and flung himself at Isidore without pause, without ever knowing that there was such a thing as gravity.

A world had opened like the world of the matchbooks in the glass urn.

They made still another world, and they thought she'd be Sarah if she was a she, or Max if he was a he, because Laura didn't like Martin. And doctors rubbed Laura's belly at the Bethesda Naval Hospital. And what was bad was done. What was good was yet to come. The house of Auberon rebuilt by a Jack Tar with garbage gloves and a stethoscope.

When they got back to the house, Isidore put on a record, *The Roar of the Greasepaint—The Smell of the Crowd*. And Leo danced to "A Wonderful Day Like Today" on the living room carpet that was painted light green with sun.

They should have known it, because the sun winked twice and became neeve. The lords of chaos had come. And not long after that, it was Halloween.

The jacks scared all their mummies and yawned with toothless smiles all strung with mushpearls. The odor was cold stars and swampy pumpkin as the evening went afire with fright flames. Plastic junkwalkers in fake teeth began to scowl the dark dog-walks. A skeleton mooned the children with his ischial tuberosities and a Franken lowered his flattop. On batblack night of All Hallows' Grieve the green Frankencorpses yowled for candy and fought to be at the darkness door like mutant dreams fighting to be in the sleeping breast of Mary Shelley, dreams of her mother that died in the doo dah tree. Double bubble boil your ruoyliobelbbubelbuod. Roy Leo: Bell Bubble Bood. Say it again but add more blood. Blood of infant babies, a Maxwell broken forth from the life maw of the seawater womb, when the dead with their crazy legs and their bad breath, and their squid black eyes like nevi looking blindly, shew themselves up from the grave, and a door where the candy yowlers fought to be in green plastic masks and fake teeth.

★   ★   ★

Before the lords of chaos hurt him in his brain so he couldn't speak, and he smashed the IV pole to the ground since he had no words, Isidore wrote a letter and sent it into the breach.

Ms. Edith Wainwright
Chief of Nursing
Department of Nursing
NIH

Dear Ms. Wainwright,

As a hematology-oncology fellow I had a brief experience with you in which I found you to be a strong advocate of the patient. Therefore, I am writing to you at present to apprise you of certain complaints generated by my own stay as a post-laparotomy patient in the NIH surgical ICU during the period of August 23–25, 1974.

In comparison with the nursing care delivered to me personally on floors 5E and 4W during a two-month hospitalization, the care in the ICU was an absolute nadir. I was repeatedly made to feel as though I were a nuisance, and the clear preference seemed to be for comatose or semiconscious patients who apparently presented less disruption to the order of the unit than I.

It was, in fact, reported to a nurse on 6E (a friend of mine) by an ICU nurse that I was a "terrible patient"; I was not aware that postoperative (or other) patients were required to conform to behavioral standards defined by the nursing department.

I was ignored when calling for a nurse on numerous occasions when I could see at least one nurse sitting in the nursing station. My earliest response to the ICU nurses' efforts to help me in and out of bed was fear that this would cause increased pain and I therefore resisted. As a result I was assisted with ambulation but no one had the patience to teach me the easiest way to enter and exit the bed. On 5E I was finally shown how to minimize pain in doing these tasks; I was no less fearful of second-party intervention at that point, either.

Furthermore, my bed curtain was often pulled halfway closed for no other ostensible reason than to obscure my view of the ICU clock. I was using the clock to judge the time for delivery of pain medication and was clearly annoying nurses by reminding them early of my need for it; however, the clock was also the single device by which I was able to orient myself in the most dehumanized and disorienting setting I have experienced. The clock was an essential companion in the face of the extreme dearth of human interchange provided by the ICU nurses. There were, in fact, only three nurses (whose names ever reached me) from your ICU that I would allow to care for anyone who meant anything to me, given any choice. The rest were fit for the care of the half- and near-dead only; i.e. those patients beyond placing any direct emotional demand on nursing.

My experience on the ICU will linger in my mind for years as a nightmare. I am, by the way, not the first person to observe these things regarding these highly trained "angels of mercy."

Thank you for your attention. Hopefully you will be able to bring some changes to bear in what I feel is a weak link in an otherwise strong nursing department.

Regards,
Isidore Auberon, M.D.

He had said exactly what he had to say. It seemed, however, that nobody was listening.

★   ★   ★

But he did get better, thank God. Better enough to stand up straight like a man on the edge of the thunder hole and breathe carefully, though it hurt, though he weighed a mere hundred and fifty pounds now, which he had not weighed since he was fifteen. He felt better enough to hold Maxwell with a great hope, an expectation even, that he would someday throw a baseball with him (and Mack, as his younger son would later be known, would one day exceed all others in his family at throwing and catching baseballs, he could even pick up a short-hop without thinking). Isidore held the new infant and sang him a song, Sambamba, nobody nothing nemo nun.

The Auberon house was leaning on its nails, but he thought he would get better. He couldn't open a jar anymore, but he called the new chief of medicine on the phone and agreed to chair the house staff advisory committee next year. And he lifted up a box filled with new dishes that Laura had bought and he said to Leo, "Next year when I'm better we'll go swimming again. I'll teach you to swim. I'll teach you to dive." It hurt the bottoms of his feet to walk on the cold floor and he hopped and staggered on skinny legs and had to put the box down in the wet sink, where it didn't belong.

"Whatsa matter?" Leo said. "I'll help you." And they both fell on the floor and broke all the new dishes that had flowers on them.

"I'm sorry I broke the flowers dishes," Leo said. "I'm sorry that you don't feel good in your arms."

And Isidore thought that Leo would let him rest, because it seemed that he half-understood, but Leo said, "Play with me, please, Daddy, please." The boy's eyes were live as the eyes of a person who's laughing, eyes struck by an inner fire burning hard at some reserve of love, eyes that burned love and need and wasted the things they sought. Isidore saw that Leo couldn't understand, and couldn't wait, not even for a minute.

Isidore left the dishes broken on the floor and played till the wind was gone from his lungs. He tried to lift Leo up onto his shoulders but he was afraid he'd drop Leo down the front steps and crack his head open.

"I'll crack your head open, Leo!" he shouted angrily, because the boy was climbing on his back and laughing a delirious loud laugh.

Leo said, "Play, play, play, please, Daddy, please." If there had been any comprehension of lymphoma and chemotherapy, then love burned it off like impurity until what was left was just love, pure, empyreal, uncomprehending, fragile as an ancient bird condemned to saintly extinction.

Isidore was too tired to move his mouth.

"Please, please, please, Daddy. I will help you, I will help you, Daddy."

"Just give me a second to rest."

Leo turned his back meaningfully, theatrically, and looked over his shoulder with eyes suddenly smoked up and gray with the grayness of a disappointing sky, of clouds and shadows.

"Okay, let's get out the truck," Isidore said, and he went up on his frail, skinny knees and then stood and fell onto the sofa, shaking, eaten up by love. "You can get it, it's there in the cabinet there."

His son was a carrion-eater.

Then he woke up in the night with a pain in his mind and Leo and the baby went to Aunt Jenny's house and Laura and Isidore went to the hospital. He would have said he felt the hole where the clot had torn loose from his heart, but he couldn't talk. It was a stroke and now he was burned through to a terrible underworld purity, like his son.

When you talked to Isidore he seemed to know what you had said, but he didn't answer, and it was as if he was too sad to answer, even to answer his own son; he would just look at you with the eyes of a cow going to slaughter, and he didn't get up anymore since there was no point. He lay in the bed and didn't even grope for the water cup anymore, even when Leo held it up to him. He was a little bit his old self, but more so not himself, as if he'd been replaced by a wax model. It was the same daddy who'd carried Leo on his shoulders and held him up in the sky at the pool and kissed his belly, but those motions and actions were gone out of him; he didn't hold up and he didn't kiss. Then one day Isidore groaned and wailed liked a baboon wailing in a tree while a lion eats her baby underneath it, except that Isidore was wailing not only for his babies but for his own lost future and his fatal powerlessness before the irrevocable harm of this place that's the universe, and all the doctors went into the room and when they came out he was still moaning, and Leo plugged his ears but could still hear him. Two days later the moaning ended.

Before Isidore died, a great many people and places, or their simulacra, siphoned through him against his will like verses of a sentimental song, jumbled out of order: the crusts of toast and Laura in the garden full of flowers. And ten thousand pounds of doorknobs asail for Hawaii. The sun was like a red gong over the South Pacific sea. He remembered the lightning rinsing down the water mountains and the raw, cold smell of sea wind. He remembered throwing the crowbar in the snow and his garbage truck route when the ragweed pollen was killing his eyes and he wanted more than anything to scratch but he couldn't touch his face because of his filthy gloves—he and that huge guy Jeffords, the lineman at Wisconsin, would eat on the sidewalk in front of somebody's house, and if somebody saw them, he and Jeffords would drop their brown bags over an empty trash can and pretend to be eating their lunch out of the garbage! And his friend Mrs. O'Keefe, a patient, looking up from her hospital bed with eyes pushed halfway out of her head by an old case of Graves' that had ravaged her thyroid and her orbits, and how she'd itched all over, and he'd had to tell about her high creatinine and that she'd need dialysis. She knew it was the end, that once on the kidney machine, there was no coming back off, and the bulging eyes then glowed in the dark face with tears of total defeat, and she got pneumonia soon thereafter and left the hospital straight for the funeral parlor in a bag zipped over her face. He remembered the morning he went off to Harvard—Dennis leaving him there in the house alone because the bells would soon be ringing at the high school, but Isidore was done with high school and he still had an hour before he needed to go to the bus station to ride up to Cambridge, and he told his brother, "You'll be okay, you know how to handle the old man now," and though neither admitted it, a certainty had grabbed them both in the guts and they knew that nothing would ever be the same. And there by himself in the quiet living room where Ezer had once slammed Burt's fingers in the sewing basket, he'd played a Tony Bennett record on the ancient Victrola, and the singer's voice had seemed to echo forth, faded and diminished, from some obsolete dance hall ages past. And nothing ever was the same after that. They were right.

It seemed to him that the memories dragging through him were not only his soul being ripped out of him; they also screened something even more vital and unremembered, they moved past him like a wind opaque with blowing sand and obscured a sacrifice even more terrible than the flight of his soul to oblivion. The moving memories obscured perhaps the loss not of his past but of his future, not of his mother but of his sons, whose faces, by some miracle of corticosteroids, he could not see, not even Leo's, who had become in just a couple of years the pith and center of his life. He wanted more than anything to say all that and something more to Leo, or at least to write a letter to his Leo and to Maxwell, too, but he couldn't speak or write a word. The brain injury was a wall that had bricked him up in Hell.

Then when he was almost dead, he had a morphine dream. He was climbing down a tree and he was very tired, but he had to get to the bottom, there was something very important at the bottom; he saw a pair of worms and the first worm said, "Stop and chat for a bit," and the other one said, "I need you, I'm having a birthday party," and he said, "I'm sorry, I have to go." And he said, "I'd like to stay but I have no time for that now." He couldn't figure why, but it was a horrible dream, a dream that stabbed into him like a knife between the ribs, and he wished for the total oblivion of death with all his might.

At last the name Lefty Paradise came to him out of a fog and a great distance, like an ambassador from a magic land. Lefty Paradise: a figure in some story he'd once read or made up. "I loves those combed-cotton sheets of yers (I feel like I'm in a hotel)," he'd once said to Laura. That was a while ago.

So Laura wrote the last little paragraph in Leo's baby book.

He will never be the same and neither will I. Says "I'm sad about Daddy. I'm mad about Daddy." Says "I yelled at you and you yelled at me. So-oo-oo shut up." Strokes my cheek. "Remember when Daddy used to do this to you?" At night crying that he was sad about Izzy. When I told him I was too and that he had me and I would always take care of him, said "and Uncle Harvey cause he's a men." I said, like Daddy was? He nodded. Swings his arms "like my daddy does." One night crying he said was afraid if I rocked too hard in the chair the house would break. I reassured him and he said "but who will fix it? My daddy could but he's not here." When I cry he often tries to comfort me. One night "soon it will be late and the people I love will come home." When asked who he meant said "I love my daddy but he's not here. But there are other persons that I love—like Uncle Harvey and Aunt Jenny—and soon they will come." Grammy showed him places on the globe. Next day he pointed to Turkey, asking "Who lives in that chicken?" Has developed his own curse words: "I scrumped you off, Bummo." Talks about being like Daddy who is "the biggest." Said "if my daddy was here I would play tackle with him." Said "When I'm bigger I'll dive in the water and my daddy will watch me."

Hic jacet Isidorus, Rex quondam, Rexque futurus.

In 1984, on the weekend of Leo's thirteenth birthday, James Helpern came by.

He squatted in front of a fern in his madras shorts and said, "Your mother never could take care of a plant." He had piston-hard calves that looked as though he'd pulled a rickshaw all his life and a black, somewhat satanic mustache. Leo's mother and Philip, his stepfather, had gone to buy a new set of glasses before the party. James plucked a yellow leaf off the jade plant or whatever sort of plant it was, dropped it in the pot, and sat down on the gray porch couch, which was slightly damp. He looked at Leo as if he were peering inside him and reading the label on the back of his skull.

"They used to call me Ghost Boy, you know," James said, lightly stroking his mustache and speaking as if from inside a deep reverie. "I was pretty fast when I was in school. Barry Cohen named me that. Your father knew him. He said, *the Ghost Boy, so fast he wasn't even there.* I ran the hundred and two hundred. Of course, in those days, we didn't have good shoes."

Leo had seen Barry Cohen's note in his father's yearbook, a dark-green book on the shelf next to the window where the icicles always hung down. And James the Ghost Boy he had met a few times before. He was a surgeon. Was it Ghost Boy who had given him the doctor's bag?

"You know your father was one of the great men," James said, plucking off another yellow leaf. "I always thought, he was *rough-hewn by life,* that's how I always put it to myself. These other guys, they had money, they had family. But he didn't. He had his character. He did it all purely by the force of his personality." He stared at Leo again as if he were looking into Leo's soul, and shook his head. "And he was as strong as a bear." Ghost Boy grinned like a devil and concluded, "You look more like your mother."

There be nine worthy and the best that ever were.

Before bed, Leo looked at the picture of his father and then went to the mirror with it. Leo was thirteen now, but he felt he looked twelve, with no muscles. In the picture his father looked thick and powerful in the green-gray twilight, with arms like a steamfitter's. Behind his father there was gray lake water, subtended by horizon and shore, and distant trees, August light fading as the picture itself was fading from too much sun. Leo thought he hadn't cared well enough for it and now it was damaged beyond repair. You couldn't see any bugs in the photo, but you could infer they were dangling there in the mystic twilight, dancing on skin still damp from a shower and tacky with new sweat, landing on your clean pressed shirt and then reconsidering and flying away and dithering still more and landing again in the exact same spot. There he was, his father, tobacco in his pocket, biting a pipe, relaxed, happy. What lake? Erie? Was it on South

Bass Island somewhere? Leo had never been there. You couldn't see much of the island in the picture, but it, too, was real, as his father had been, and the water was in fact real at the moment of the picture, even though Leo wasn't there, real and wet to the touch, a real lake of water like a great dark mirror, ticked with midge rings. In the other picture: his father's jaw, from below, slightly blurry—turning away, refusing to be paralyzed by the camera, turning away from Leo but back toward life and motion and time, an unshaven face blurry and dark as burnt bread. That picture was kept in a frame with chipped silver paint.

Leo put the badly faded picture of his father back on the shelf and took the birthday card with red balloons to the garbage can, a steel oval cylinder with a Mercator map of the world wrapped around it. *The world is my garbage can.* He let the card fall loudly to the bottom. Then he lined up the milk crates and boxes on the floor of his room in two rows. The row of blue plastic crates started at the base of his actual-size poster of Marilyn Monroe, with whom he'd recently become infatuated. She looked at him askance, standing up in high heels and a black maillot bathing suit. She held her down-turned hand under her chin like the *Thinker*, except only touching her chin lightly with the ends of her extended fingers and not supporting her head on them as the *Thinker* did. A centennial poster of Einstein had also recently gone up (1879–1979, it said on the bottom) in place of an old poster of Aquaman, the blond hero whom no one liked anyway because all he could do was swim, and not even swim all that fast, and breathe underwater, and talk to squids. Leo had only put him up there because of an idea he'd had while swimming in the Atlantic Ocean in a strong undertow, the kind of undertow that moves a hundred tons of seawater on a whim and then moves it all back to where it was before. The idea was that a hero doesn't overcome what can't be overcome, but sustains, survives, by endurance, by true grit and an instinct for the rhythms of the waves.

In the first crates went the *Star Wars* toys from his closet. The *Millennium Falcon,* the X-wing with trusty droid R2-D2 in the back (R2-D2 could be pushed down to open the spaceship's wings into the X formation), and all the miniature *Star Wars* people that didn't bend at elbow, waist, or knee: orphan hero Luke Skywalker, who came with a yellow light saber even though none of the light sabers in any of the *Star Wars* movies were yellow; old Obi-Wan Kenobi in an unrealistic chintzy plastic cape of a burnt sienna color; Darth Vader, whose light saber was an evil red; two Han Solos, one with a huge head, one with a normal head, now hard to find in the stores; a bunch of seldom-used Princess Leias in her various weird outfits.

The Legos, once dismantled, would have to go in the boxes. He broke apart the spaceships he had built, and the interconnected space stations where the Lego spacemen had made their home, bravely huddled in the heart of lonely crepuscular moonscapes and black empty space—they had but meager defenses in the bottomless abyss of the universe. When Leo was done, the shelves where the space installation had been were bare except for large balls and tangles of dust. The crates and boxes were loaded with a rubble of toys.

He opened up the mausoleum of his closet to inter the stethoscope, medical book, and pathology journal that James Helpern had given him. He hung his father's old stethoscope in the closet next to the black belt and the rough red shirt. He took down the blue box from Higbee's that had in it his father's T-shirt (HARVARD in block letters like a crimson badge at the breast, armpits stained yellow with aluminum—he would go there someday, to Harvard or Yale), and he took down the jewelry box that held the hospital ID card and the merchant marine license. On top of those things he laid the pathology journal. James said his father's pathology report was written up in it because the doctors had never seen that type of lymphoma before. Immunoblastic sarcoma. James said the doctors looked at the pathology and they didn't know what the hell it was his father had.

Leo opened the dusty medical book and saw where his father had written ISIDORE AUBERON, M.D. He stepped out of the closet and put the book on the shelf that had just been vacated by his Lego spacemen.

What must I do? Leo thought, giving a last look into the closet. What do you do? You make a black leather belt in the hospital playroom with a black lady with a pick in her hair, a stranger—fitting each soft leather piece into the next in a daisy chain; and you hang that belt in your closet like the shed skin of a black snake and let it hang there forever. Next to the dusty red shirt.

PART II

The Little Boys Lost

I.

GRAND CANYON

AT THREE, LEO was of an average weight and height, and of the usual tender flesh, but his mother thought that something inside him was different from other children she knew. He'd spoken a bit early, true enough, but it wasn't his aptitudes that struck her as unusual. She didn't care that much for aptitudes anyway. His heart was heavier, she thought. His face sometimes had a kind of medieval stillness and sobriety to it—like a face, say, looking out on the centuries from a unicorn tapestry that's itself unchanged and unchangeable. Any mention of his father would elicit the stillness, and so could many other unpredictable things. He seemed depressed. She sent him to a preschool that was run by psychoanalysts.

The child could not understand guilt, or grief, or defense mechanisms, or much of anything, really, besides life and death, and presence and absence, but he did understand and welcome one principle upheld for him by certain grown-ups: that he could call for help. The school seemed to be an island in a sea of helplessness and aloneness. He trusted the women there to answer him if he cried out. Elsewhere, among strangers, he could feel himself struggling and then actually drowning in a great, dangerous sea without anyone noticing or caring. He could feel a coldness about him like Atlantic water in December, all purple with the gelid blood of winter.

Very early, he developed radical, monastic convictions: he was a hero afloat in a storm sea strafed with winter winds. He was a poet at the mercy of the gods, looking in on the far revolving core of the universe. He had a destiny before him ruinous or triumphant, and everyone he knew belonged to this destiny, not least his younger brother, who he thought had been spared the tragic burden. It only remained to be seen whether Leo had within him ruin or glory.

As he passed into that period of life known to psychoanalysts as latency, his sense of destiny receded behind the normal affairs of childhood, but it would reassert itself at the most unexpected times and in the most unexpected ways.

By the summer of 1982, when all the bad things could no longer be clearly remembered, Mack followed his older brother, Leo, everywhere and in everything—and as far as Leo was concerned, that was as it should have been. If Leo took a pretzel from the ebony bowl at Grandma's (Philip's mother's) house on a Friday night and bit the sides off the pretzel, so that it looked like a little man, and then had the little man leap into his mouth to a death by mastication, then Mack did that too. If Leo and their cousin Todd slid down the polished floorboards in Grandma's front hall in their socks, then Mack did too. If Leo covered his door to their shared bathroom with Wacky Packages and *Star Wars* stickers, then so did his younger brother. If Leo trained himself to write in all caps like they did in comic books, then Mack trained himself to write in all caps so he could write like Leo.

And if at 5 A.M. Leo sat down in front of *The P.T.L. Club* to watch Jim and Tammy Faye Bakker crying about their sins, Mack watched it too. *The P.T.L. Club* was better than *The 700 Club* even though neither show made much sense. And even *The 700 Club* was better than no TV, especially on a day when there was Sabbath school, which they grudgingly attended every week at Park Synagogue near Taylor Road. At the Sabbath school they'd been told they were Jews, and they figured it was just as well, since the Bakkers made them feel that Christians were perhaps a bit weird.

It was understood that whatever the show, Leo would occupy the more favorable couch position—that is, the end farther from the TV—and Mack would sit at the other end, where you had to crane your neck to see *P.T.L.* at a fifteen-degree angle and were so close up to Jim and Tammy Faye Bakker that you could see the red, blue, and yellow pixels of their tears wiggling on the inside of the curved glass. Leo had once or twice tried sitting there himself, and from Mack's side, you could even reach out and brush the invisible, hairlike lines of static that stood up off the glass.

Did Leo call his dad Dad in the summer of 1982 or was he still calling him Philip? Such changes became mysteries. Dad or Philip, Philip or Dad—but not Daddy. That summer Philip flew them and their mother to Disneyland in California, where Philip took Leo on his first roller coaster: Space Mountain. Leo didn't get a bloody nose as he had that other time with Philip, in the bumper cars, when his legs were too short and he'd left off his seat belt to reach the pedals.

He didn't get mad at Philip when he got the bloody nose. Or when Philip dropped him into a pile of leaves and the hard frozen ground punched him in the lungs. When he crawled to his feet out of the warm, decaying, flattened underleaves, he tried not to let Philip see that he couldn't breathe, and that he'd gotten the seat of his pants wet. He didn't even pull the leaf out that was stuck inside the waist of his pants, so as not to embarrass his new father. Leo would not be mad, but he would also not let Philip throw him into any more leaves.

The past was not supposed to matter anymore, but it did.

From California, Philip took them into the desert of Arizona.

"Do you know how it is when your little brother's in the lower bunk and he won't stop talking?" Leo wrote in his diary while he lay on the top bunk in the sleeper car of the overnight train. And then: "We are having an adventure in the West. We are sleeping on the train. The bathroom is a shower with a sink and a toilet in it." His diary had a puffy blue cover with cowboys, lassoes, and sheriff badges on it. His brother had been given one with a puffy red cover with cowboys, lassoes, and sheriff badges. They both wrote about their feelings in there, because their mother had trained them to pay attention to those as opposed to doing what most other people seemed to do with theirs, which was to stuff them down like gunpowder into an old musket. "I am trying to think," Leo wrote, "but my little brother keeps interrupting me! Ugh! Little brothers!"

Yet he dared not write what he was thinking.

Leo had begun to think about things that were well beyond his younger brother's comprehension. Shameful, exciting things, such as "naked ladies." He wanted badly to see a grown woman's vagina, or at least an up-close breast. (He had seen a topless woman on a beach once, but she was far away, and people seemed to notice him staring and thrust their faces back at him in a mocking way.) A naked lady was a very scarce commodity, evidently. He had recently cut out a little picture of a naked lady from the Showtime pay cable guide, but it was a drawing, not a photograph, and only about an inch high and you could not see anything that looked remotely like a vagina. That was how desperate the times were. His friend Ted said that his dream job was to be a *Playboy* photographer. Leo had not thought of that possibility. He had seen *Playboy* in the magazine racks at Campus Drug, and he knew what was inside the pages without ever having seen. The idea that someone was employed to look at naked ladies all day gave him and Ted great hopes for the future. Once, Ted had pulled a *Playboy* magazine from the drugstore rack, and they had seen the face, necklace, and bare shoulders of the centerfold, but then they'd been apprehended by the fat and fully clothed lady behind the cash register before they could see anything else. Naked ladies were fiercely guarded treasures, that much was clear; the universe legislated against their seeing one. They had to carry on with the certainty that naked ladies existed, even though they might never see one. They had to carry on with belief and hope.

When Leo awoke from his reverie about naked ladies, he saw that where his felt-tip brown marker had paused, the brown ink had leached into the page in a big wet dark spot. The train began to sway and caused his pen to record its movements. After a minute or two, the movements of the train had drawn a little supernova.

Mack did not understand about the larger world out there rushing past in the darkness, the wilderness of sagebrush and naked ladies. He only wanted to think about *Star Wars*. But there was more to life than *Star Wars*.

Philip took them to the Anasazi cliff dwellings, to the place where you could stand on one foot in four different states all at once, Utah, Arizona, New Mexico, and Colorado, to a dude ranch outside of Tucson where Leo looked for snakes at night and saw every star, and to the Grand Canyon, where people were making a movie. Chevy Chase came down the front steps of the lodge while Leo was climbing up them. Chevy Chase was very, very tall, especially when he was standing at the top of the steps. Leo recognized him from *Seems Like Old Times* and *Foul Play,* where a dwarf rolled down the street in a garbage can, just about the funniest thing Leo had ever seen. (After seeing *Foul Play* Leo began his own mystery in a spiral notebook. It was called "Murder in the Bathtub," which he drew in creepy slanted bubble letters, and he planned for it to be four or even five hundred pages.) When Leo came back from the bathroom and out of the lodge and down the steps, he told his mom that he'd seen Chevy Chase, and then he saw Chevy Chase again, under a big umbrella, kissing and kissing a young woman with yellow hair and a yellow blouse, kissing to the point where Leo thought it must be boring, like when you chew gum for too long. Leo's mother was looking another way and she said, "Harold Ramis? I love him!" and the man called Harold Ramis, who was not as big a star as Chevy Chase and seemed pleased to be noticed, turned and pointed to himself and mouthed the words "Who, me?" and Leo's mom loved that. The movie people never seemed to do any acting. They just stood around and ate grapes. Leo and Mack sat on their suitcases. It was very sunny and very hot.

The joys of that trip seemed very natural. They were a family. Leo's mother was happy. Leo and Mack were having their adventure, new phases of which seemed to unfold by the hour. One forgot, even, that it had ever been different.

"Alaska," Leo said in the backseat of the rental car, and he threw his arms around Philip's neck and pushed his face past the front seat and up against his dad's rough face.

"I love you, boy," Philip said, quietly, almost confidentially, and pressed his hand against Leo's cheek. "And how is Fly back there?" he said, peering into the rearview mirror. "Hello, Fly!" Fly was what Philip called Mack when he wrestled or tickled him because, he said, Mack weighed as much as a fly.

"Hello," Mack said sedately. He was filling out a Mad Libs.

"You have an 'A,' Dad," Leo said.

"I have a what?"

"In Geography."

"Oh yes, an 'A,'" Philip said. "Hmm." He was not really looking out the windshield but digging between the car seats for a morsel of blueberry muffin and steering the car with his knee. He seemed to be at the same time sifting distractedly inside his mind for a geographic rarity, a bauble of suitable glitter for a boy, as he generally did when they played Geography. Finally, he said, "Andalucía." (Abidjan, Amman, Antananarivo, and Ankara, perhaps, dropped back carelessly to his heap of jewels.)

Philip's mind possessed a thousand highways, the currencies and civil wars of foreign lands, their crops and ideologies, and all their history buried below. He was not afraid of plane crashes and didn't notice when he cut himself, which he seemed to do with some regularity. He seemed in no danger of dying at all. Philip and Mack went hand in hand right up to the edge of the canyon, where you could fall down a thousand feet. They stood together on the edge of the chasm without fear with the man's sure grasp on the boy's shoulder while Leo lay down and hugged the dirt, more than twenty feet away from the edge. He gripped the weeds in his fists.

"You'll fall in!" he said, and laughed, though it wasn't funny.

Philip laughed.

Mack said nothing.

Leo's brother and dad looked out over a chasm of blue sky.

Leo took a picture with his Kodak Disc. When they came away from the edge, he hugged Philip tight around the middle.

"Yes, boy, I know," Philip said. "You're shivering!" He pulled off his sweater and gave it to Leo.

He was shivering but he refused the sweater. "Listen to this, Dad," he said, "I can imitate Gomer Pyle. 'Well, goll-y, Sergeant!'"

"Very talented, that boy," Philip said.

And the boys ran away laughing about the Irish Rovers song about the two brothers where the toy horse's head falls off.

Months later, the brothers looked at the picture.

"Weren't you afraid?" Leo said.

"No," Mack said, and pulled at his lower eyelid, which he always did when he lied.

When they got back to Cleveland, the boys went to a new camp called Red Barn. It took an hour by school bus every single day to get to the camp in the woods and an hour to get home.

Neither boy had friends there, and they were not in the same group because Leo was ten and Mack was only seven. Still, they saw each other on free periods and at lunch, and Leo said he would protect Mack from the cicadas, and in fact he usually did have to pluck the cicadas off his brother's red T-shirt or disentangle them from his brother's hair while Mack closed his eyes and held perfectly still as though he were covered with a hundred tarantulas like Indiana Jones in the Temple of Doom. Leo couldn't remember ever having been irritated with his brother then. He hungered to be with his brother every second of the day, especially at the end of the morning bus ride, a moment that without fail harrowed in his stomach.

That was when the bus drove up the gravel road to the camp and the dust flew in their eyes, and the gravel clinked like shrapnel on the sides of the bus and clicked on its windows now and then with a sound like a lady's fingernails. But the motor of the bus didn't stop. When the gravel road protested, the engine roared louder, inexorable when Leo's heart protested, and they got out and went as if to their deaths into the lonely, lonely woods that hissed and hushed, hissed and hushed on waves of high insect heat.

There were cicadas everywhere. (They came out every seventeen years, which was too often for Mack.) No matter where you were, they dropped onto your bloodred Red Barn T-shirt with an audible pat and onto your hair, not seeing you with their eyes like orange beads and their black helmet heads. Most days Mack hid from them in the lightless terrarium house, pretending, should anyone enter, to be interested in the fern leaves and the stone-still lizards in glass cases there who waited for nothing. (The lizards were wrapped around branches with a silent endurance and agony entirely of a piece with the agony of a human day camper.) And the huge kid named Onessian with Chiclet teeth would hold cicadas by their translucent wings and stick their beetle legs kicking in your face or he'd hold them close to each other and the bugs would blindly claw at each other's eyes and pull at the back brims of their beetle helmets and almost separate each other's heads from their bodies, but never quite.

There were lots of kids who were friends with each other but not with Leo and Leo got into a fight with the younger son of James Helpern, that doctor and friend to their family who had known his father. Near the terrarium, where a tree root grew in the path, Leo tripped and fell and Helpern laughed and so Leo plucked the other boy's glasses right off his nose. The camp director walked past and looked ashamed of them but didn't intervene, just went off to write "safety first, last, and always" on a blackboard somewhere probably and then do whatever it was he did with all the spare time afforded by not doing anything besides going around saying "safety first, last, and always."

They had one overnight that summer where they ate hobo stew (hamburger and corn in a wad of blackened tinfoil roasted right in the coals) and it was surprisingly delicious, and the kid with the gums that were taller than his teeth narrated the whole story of the Melonheads and Mack was afraid of the kid's gums. In the middle of the night, Mack woke up crying.

"What is it?" Leo said. "Is it your ear? You have an earache?"

Mack couldn't say anything, couldn't even nod, he just cried, but that was what it was. Mack was always getting earaches.

"Don't worry, Mack, I love you, Mack, and I'll take care of you. Don't worry."

Of course Mack had to get an earache right then, the one night of their whole entire lives they were alone in the dark Ohio woods without any grown-ups, with tall shadows around the fires and bats in the dark and people not like them whom fate had chosen for laughter and fulfilled expectations, nobody near that cared a crumb about them, not even a female anywhere who could be made to care. But Leo could take care of it. He had something inside him that was special and terrible, even if he couldn't remember what it was. He had a duty to the past. He had a destiny.

"I'll take care of you, Mack, don't worry," Leo said again. "It's just an earache." He wished his brother would say something, but Mack wouldn't say anything. He just cried in silence, pushing on his soft, small ear, folding it into itself as if to eliminate the pain by replacing it with another of his own invention.

"I'll go get someone," Leo said, and began to try to reach his flip-flops, which were sitting just inside the tent flap.

"Don't leave me here!" Mack cried. "Not all alone!"

"Okay, Mack," Leo said. "I won't leave you. You'll come with me. Get your flip-flops on so you don't hurt your feet."

Leo got his flip-flops on and Mack tried to get his on while he held on to his ear with one hand, but he couldn't do it with just one hand. Leo helped Mack get the flip-flops on. It felt funny to wear pajamas with flip-flops. Leo and Mack never wore flip-flops at all, but their mom had bought them and packed them because they were on the camp's mimeographed packing list. Leo's said LEO AUBERON in indelible marker and Mack's said MAXWELL AUBERON. Mack had red flannel pajamas with white trim and Leo had blue checkered ones with a breast pocket.

Leo took Mack by the hand and they crawled out the tent flap together in their pajamas, into the darkness and the rough, high grass. There were some lit flashlights swinging away out there in the darkness and along with them, disembodied voices.

"Wait, I forgot the flashlight," Leo said.

"Then I'm coming back in with you," Mack said, holding on to his ear.

"All right." Leo held open the tent flap and Mack crawled inside again. Leo crawled in after and picked up the red plastic flashlight, which seemed to be running out of batteries already. He shook the batteries around inside it, but that only made the light dimmer and browner than before. He could look straight into the bulb without it even hurting his eyes. They went back out into the dark, where the flashlight illuminated not a single blade of grass. The darkness was awash around them, and while Leo knew that everything was supposed to be same at night as during the day, only you couldn't see it, that was quite obviously false: what was there at night that was foreign to the day was nothingness, blankness. And it wasn't just that you couldn't see anything, but that something from the day was in fact missing, and that was the people who had been in that same space a few hours before—the people and the ornate city of activated parts and relations connecting them—the people who had then decamped from that space like a traveling circus that leaves you behind. Leo felt the air through his pee flap and smoothed it closed.

"Mom asked them to put us next to Josh Helpern," Leo said. Josh was older than Leo by a couple of years. He hoped Josh's little brother hadn't told him about the fight by the terrarium, and about how Leo had snatched the glasses off his face. Josh was twelve. "Josh!" Leo whispered. "Josh, are you in there? We need help!"

There was rustling inside the tent, and laughing, and someone said loudly, "Get off me, dude!" and then Josh stuck his head out. "Who is that? Leo?"

"Yeah. My brother needs help," Leo said again.

"What's wrong?"

Mack was still curling up his ear and pinching it hard.

"He has an earache."

Josh pulled his head inside his tent and a flashlight went on within. He said something in a low, inaudible voice and the shadows of the other boys in the tent began to move around. Josh stuck his head back out and said, "I'm coming out. Let me get my boots on."

They followed Josh's flashlight into the darkness until they arrived at a little cabin, where a few counselors were sitting out on a slanted porch. They didn't see the boys until they were already standing below the porch and when they did see, they shifted suddenly in their seats as though they'd been surprised in the middle of something secret, though Leo couldn't tell what.

"What's up, Josh!" one of the older boys on the porch said. "That was a nice goal you scored today."

"These guys need to go to the infirmary," Josh said.

One of the counselors went inside the cabin.

"You guys okay?" Josh said.

Leo suddenly felt all swollen inside with forbidden tears. *No, no, no*, he told the tears.

"Yep. Thanks."

Leo and Mack waited together in the infirmary for two hours. When their mom got there her hair was still matted down on one side from bed and she squinted as though her eyes were still adjusting to light. She said she would bring Mack home and though Leo wanted to go home too, he knew that his mother had expectations and he had expectations of himself, so he didn't ask.

When Leo went to sleep that night in the tent, alone, he dreamed of an emergency room where doctors were trying to save a man who'd been mortally injured in a car accident. The man's heart and lungs were on one table and his lower half on another with guts spilling out that looked like a pile of chocolate mousse. The man's upper body sat upright on a third table with its eyes frozen open and a baby in its arms.

The first time Leo went to a place they called a summer camp, it was 1976, he was four years old, and he had a quarter in his pocket that his great-grandmother had given to him. On the back there was a man playing a drum and a circle of stars. She said it was the bicentennial, which was as good as crap. They had been back in their old house in Cleveland, without his father in it anymore, for a year and a half.

There were daily marches at camp, and bees in the grass.

He didn't know the songs. He looked up into the trees, which waved their fulsome leaves at him with a swishing like the swishing of his mother's robe, and the trees had nothing in particular for him to do. The others didn't think it was a bad place.

His mother stayed somewhere near but he wasn't sure where; she hid behind the dark building full of pipes and linoleum, maybe.

His fruit punch opened inside his *Six Million Dollar Man* lunch box and soaked the Wonder Bread pink in his peanut butter and jelly sandwich.

There would never be any lunch for him. He sat on his knees and watered the grass with a hundred gallons of tears until he had no more blood. He became a vapor and rose up the tree trunk to commune with its leaves and lie in the clouds.

2.

RED RIGHT 88 / THE WAMPA

OFFENSE WAS THE time when you refused to go down. Defense was the time when you refused to let go.

If he could forget that anything had ever been different in their family, it seemed that Mack wouldn't even need to forget, since he'd been just a newborn baby when the bad things happened, and nothing had been subtracted from his life but only added to. But Leo's mom said that Mack looked at Leo as more than a brother because there had been no father there at all for Mack for the first three years of his life. And being more than a brother was both a good and a bad thing, she said, for both of them. Leo and Mack were still best friends, at least Leo thought so, but there was a little worry in the back of his mind that something had changed.

It was a perfect day for a football game, with a Cleveland

Browns sky of unbroken gray, leaves as bright red and orange as tulip petals and also as damp, and a novel air of cold and rot. In a football game on a day such as this, and there had been many, when Leo tackled or was tackled, he landed on acorns that had already been stamped into the soft earth, and slid on his shoulder pads through chilled mud and wet leaves. The muddier his Cleveland Browns jersey, the more he felt like #43 Mike Pruitt running the ball through the gray gridiron rain at Cleveland Municipal Stadium or #57 Clay Matthews stopping a run dead in the gray gridiron rain. None of Leo's friends could bring him down single-handed except Ted, who was almost a year older.

But Leo didn't play football at Mack's birthday party that fall of 1982. The last time he'd tackled his brother, Mack had strained his groin, and the time before that there had been blood. Leo and Ted went up to Leo's room instead and listened to his 45 of "Twelve Days of a Cleveland Browns Christmas" and tried to play with the yellow Lego castle. But Ted didn't know how to play with Legos like Mack did. Ted imagined at the wrong scale and couldn't make it into a story. Besides that, he kept looking out the window at the younger boys playing football in the yard. Ted had taught Leo how to throw a football, and why the 1980 Cleveland Browns were called the Kardiac Kids, and what yardage was. (Leo had called it "yardilage," like cartilage.) The year of the Kardiac Kids, the Browns' quarterback Brian Sipe won the MVP but the Oakland Raiders beat the Browns in the play-offs because of a disastrous play called Red Right 88. The Oakland Raiders went on to win the Super Bowl that should have been theirs. Boys and men alike understood what a serious thing it was: the eyes of all the nation had been watching Cleveland's team, and a football team was the best expression of what a people were capable of in one area of the country, and the people of Cleveland had tried and failed. Even places like Pittsburgh and

St. Louis that Philip said were smaller than Cleveland managed to produce winners, and while they used to produce winners in Cleveland, they didn't anymore, not for a long time. Their luck had run out in the sixties, and now men talked about Red Right 88 at Friday-night dinner.

Leo changed the speed on the record player to 33⅓ rpm so that the player ran too slow and it sounded like the singer had had a stroke: "A Rutigliannnno Super Bowwwwwwwwl team." He didn't like the name Kardiac Kids, as it made him think of heart attacks and strokes.

"Let's go out and play football," Ted said.

"We can't. We're too big. My brother will get hurt."

"Then we'll coach. Or be official QB. You be on one team and I'll be on the other."

They went out to the game in the backyard. Mack was in his #17 Brian Sipe jersey. Mack didn't like to be tackled, and managed to avoid it by either being the quarterback or catching the ball in the end zone. He could catch anything that came near him, so Leo said he ought to wear #82 Ozzie Newsome's jersey. Ted coached Mack's team, since Mack was not going to be bossed around by Leo when his friends were there. Leo didn't even bother to ask. He just went to the other side. Ted and Mack's team won the game by a score of 56–21.

Mack made three touchdown catches and four interceptions and every time, Mack would look at Leo with a barely concealed smile of total glee. Leo found it somewhat annoying that for the next two months almost, Mack would be allowed to think of himself as only two years younger instead of three.

> *(O, when degree is shak'd,*
> *Which is the ladder of all high designs,*
> *The enterprise is sick.)*

Everyone had pizza and watched a pirated Betamax tape of *The Empire Strikes Back.*

When the Wampa ice-creature clawed Luke Skywalker across the face, Mack said, "I used to be afraid of that part."

Leo didn't say: You're still afraid of it.

"Oh yeah, I used to be afraid of that too," another kid said seriously, "when I was, like, two years old. I was really afraid of it."

"The movie came out last year," Leo said. "So you didn't see it when you were two. But," he added generously, "I used to be a little afraid of the Wampa. And of the part where they show Darth Vader without his helmet on."

"Afraid of *Star Wars*?" another one of the little kids said. "I was never afraid of *Star Wars.*"

Then they debated until cake about whether or not Boba Fett would be a main character in the final episode of the *Star Wars* trilogy. Some said the last movie in the trilogy would be called *Revenge of the Jedi,* someone said *Return of the Jedi.*

"No, it's *Return of the Jedi Race,*" someone else said.

Leo said, "I don't know what it is, but it's definitely not *Return of the Jedi Race.*"

"I heard Boba Fett can fly," Ted said.

All the kids sat at the dining room table in their Browns jerseys, and Laura brought in the cake. Hough Bakeries had made a football on it in chocolate frosting, and eight football player candles stood around the giant ball like blockers with flames coming out of their heads. The ball read MACK across it in cursive orange and brown. Their mother was almost recovered from a virus that had paralyzed half of her face (and had required of Leo's disease watch list two new medical phrases—"Ramsay Hunt" and "Bell's palsy"). The half of her face toward Leo looked mean and serious, especially in the candlelight from below, which made her eye socket look deep and dark like the eye of a witch. The other half of her face seemed to be smiling. Philip sang in loud meandering bass notes that weaved just above and below the actual melody of "Happy Birthday" as though he were drunk, even though he wasn't. (This was the normal manner of singing with Philip's family, the Zajacs. At Zajac Friday-night dinners when Philip sang with his brothers it sounded a little like someone had dropped a set of bagpipes.)

Mack's face was nearer to the candles than their mother's and the many small lights caused his face to glow entirely. It was very nice to see Mack's face lit up by the candles. The birthday candles illuminated a face that looked almost surprised and grateful, a face of total humility—as if it had been more than likely that no one was even going to remember his birthday. Mack utterly valued every candle, you could just tell, every guest, every gift. A mere football game was something to remember just because it had happened at all.

"Well, how is your birthday party, you think?" Leo said.

"I thought the football game was pretty fun," Mack said.

"Who are the Browns playing tomorrow?" Philip said. Philip took them to Municipal Stadium sometimes, to a loge where there were free hot dogs and you were safe from drunk people spilling their beer on you. (The stands of that stadium were a place of stagnant clouds of burped-up peanut gas and cigar smoke, where drunks whistled at unnatural volumes and sometimes laughed at you in the sticky bathrooms as you stood on tiptoe, trying to pee with your child-sized penis over the edge of the clogged horse troughs they called urinals.) But Philip didn't know a thing about football. He usually sat in the back of the loge and read the newspaper. Many other times Leo and Mack just went with Uncle Harvey, and Philip didn't go. Philip did important things like build buildings, but he also liked silly things, like Inspector Clouseau in the Pink Panther movies. He just didn't like sports.

"Are we going to win?" Philip said.

"There's a strike, Dad," Leo said.

"Oh, yes, the strike," Philip said, laughing a bit, as he often did about sports—at the idea, maybe, that anyone could patronize him over something so trivial as football, or at himself for not knowing about the strike. Or maybe he was laughing because football could make a ten-year-old aware of a labor dispute. "Yes, there is a strike, after all, isn't there. . . ."

"He doesn't like sports," Leo explained.

Ted seemed to have a lot of respect for that, sort of like how you respect someone who has cancer or who has only one leg.

When everyone had gone and Leo had helped his mother clean up the wrapping paper from the presents, Leo and Mack played a game of dice baseball at the low cold slab of crannied stone that was their coffee-colored coffee table. Their uncle Ollie had taught them the game. One summer vacation in Amagansett, he'd taught them how to make a grid on notebook paper and score a baseball game on it and how the thirty-six number combinations possible with a roll of two dice could be assigned to mean thirty-six different possible outcomes of an at-bat on a baseball field. A one and a one, for instance, was a home run. A four and a three was a ground out to the second baseman. Leo had then created the DBL (Dice Baseball League), with made-up teams and players, like Douglas Kramer, a reliable extra-base hitter and left fielder for the New York Blazers. In the early days of the league, he'd ask his uncle to make up names: like John Kastelonits—despite high expectations, the dice had withheld their blessing—and like Rocco Fuschetto, an excellent shortstop, and Rope Roubles, the storied catcher for the Boston

Shamrocks. Leo was the commissioner of the league, and also an active player (he made himself a pitcher for the Long Island Streakers, whose team name was not, to him, funny), and Leo had named the annual best pitcher award, the equivalent of the Cy Young, the L.A. Award, after himself. It seemed strange, even to Leo, that a pitching award would be named after an active player, especially one with an ERA perennially over 5.00 (the mercurial dice hadn't deigned to bless him in that way). But Mack accepted such institutional biases in silence. The main thing Leo regretted was giving his father's name, I. R. Auberon, to the Blazers' catcher, who struggled every year just to reach the shameful Mendoza line.

That night was the first-ever play-off game between the New York Blazers, whom Leo managed, and the team that Mack both managed and played for, the Boston Shamrocks. The New York Blazers had by then won the World Series three times, so it seemed only fair to both boys that the Shamrocks might break through. But they agreed beforehand there would be no rerolls unless the dice fell on the floor; and Leo was careful not to react with excessive celebration when the Blazers' batting champion, Wally Pina, cleared the bases with a triple.

As it turned out, those were the Blazers' only runs anyway, and the Shamrocks rallied against the Blazers' star closer, Thomas Blue.

The Blazers lost in disgrace.

"That's awesome, Mack," Leo said magnanimously, even though it had been a painful, last-minute loss, and damaging to Thomas Blue's pristine career stats. "And you hit two home runs yourself. Wow."

Mack tried to cover his great pleasure at winning by actually putting a hand over his mouth.

"Don't give me that smiley face of yours," Leo said in what he thought was a friendly voice.

"I didn't have a smiley," Mack said calmly, still vaguely smiling. "You're just mad you lost."

"But I'm *not* mad," Leo said.

"Okay," Mack said.

"Why do you say it like that?" Leo said. "And seriously, give up the smiley. You've been doing that all day."

Mack rolled his eyes with irritation and also evident fear. "You always do this," he said.

"*You* always do this!" Leo said. "You're making it a fight, not me. 'Okay,' you say, like that. And you just love to win *so* much. I shouldn't have let you have that reroll. The die wasn't even on the floor."

He felt a magma of hot rage boiling up inside him, and things did not seem then the same as they were before. The good times in their lives seemed like a fragile armistice with fate that was soon to crumble. Things had been bad and they would get bad again. They would get worse. Hadn't he had it worse than his brother, who had never lost anything?

"You *always* get mad at me!" Mack said.

"*You* always make me mad!" Leo said. "I don't just get mad all by myself, out of the blue, like it's magic!"

"Oh, really?" Mack said. "That's not what Aunt Jenny says."

"Aunt Jenny?" Leo shouted. "You've been talking to Aunt Jenny about me?"

"I'm not talking to you anymore," Mack said, and he turned away.

"Well, you have to!"

"No, I don't."

"I'll make you listen!" Leo shouted, a shout with all his wind that made his voice hoarse. "I always look out for you!" Leo said, coming up very close to his brother, who cowered. "When do you ever do that for me?"

"Boys!" their mother said through the doorway. "Leo, move away from him."

She entered the room.

Leo turned and looked at his mother's mean, half-paralyzed face. He heard his mind say, *You used to be beautiful.*

"*What* are you so mad about?" his mother said.

There was never any explaining when it came to Mack. He couldn't explain it. Mack smiled again and covered his mouth with his hand, and Leo roared and pushed Mack off the ottoman. Mack seemed to fling himself off the ottoman with much melodrama, and then suddenly he was loudly crying.

"Leo!" his mother yelled. "Just get out of here!"

Even before Mack sat up and held out his small hand with a bright ribbon of blood across it, Leo felt doom and criminal banishment from his mother's affection begin to close over him like a cloud shadow.

"Look what you did, you *idiot!*" Mack yelled. "You broke my tooth! He broke my tooth!" Mack's face crumpled into an expression of pure terror. "My grown-up permanent tooth is broken! Look!"

Now Leo saw that in addition to blood, Mack had spat into his palm what looked like a triangular shard of bloody tooth.

"Oh no!" Leo said.

"It's not broken," their mother said.

"Yes, it is! Look!"

"That's not your tooth."

"Yes, it is!"

"Oh," their mother said, looking more closely. She sighed. "Leo, would you go get a towel and some ice cubes?"

"That won't work," Leo said, "a towel is too thick. You can't feel the ice through it—"

"Will you just get it?"

Leo ran to get the towel. Philip had gone to a shopping center convention in Las Vegas, so the hall upstairs was perfectly still and the linen closet cursed with Saturday-evening gloom. Leo grabbed a hand towel and ran back down the stairs and into the kitchen. He filled the towel with a small pile of ice.

"I'm sorry, Mack! I'm sorry," Leo cried. "I didn't mean to! I didn't mean to!"

But Mack's glacier-blue eyes beamed icicle rays at him from across the stone coffee table. Leo had destroyed the joy that the birthday candles had brought. It was his fault. And he could see Mack sitting there thinking, *You just had to ruin my birthday. You just can't let me have* anything.

They watched their old pirated Betamax tape of *Sleeping Beauty* without talking and Mack held the ice cubes in the hand towel against his upper lip.

The movie sang: *I know you, I walked with you once upon a dream. . . .*

"I think you must have banged into the table there," Leo said, pointing to the Lucite table by the couch.

Mack just stared at Leo with the ice against his face.

"I hate that table," Leo said, loudly enough for his mom to hear. It was hard and sharp and he didn't understand why anyone would intentionally make a piece of furniture that looked like the windows at the bank. He didn't like the coffee table, either. It was cold as Dr. Barr's stethoscope when he rested his bare feet on it in the morning and with all its gaps and crannies it was not good for drawing on. "I didn't push you that hard," he said in a pleading voice. "Mom says the dentist will fix it." He kept thinking of that surprised and grateful look on Mack's face when their mom brought out the birthday cake.

Mack just stared. He was smart, all right. And he didn't have a sympathetic bone in his body. It was as though they were still caught up in some kind of game, and Mack was going to kill him at it.

Leo stared back at Mack with the rage again boiling up. His brother didn't know anything about death or about his sorrows and didn't care to imagine. He was in fact an ice-man who didn't care. Or if he cared, his compassion was buried in a snowdrift.

Mack stared back with grand indignation, the way a defenseless villager might stare at a Viking who has just finished up burning and raping everything and everyone. He had his indignation, at least. And he wouldn't let that go.

"You don't care about me, you Wampa," Leo said, and smiled hopefully. It was supposed to be a joke. The Wampa was the ice-creature on the planet Hoth in *The Empire Strikes Back* that Mack was still somewhat afraid of, which fact Leo had not pointed out. He couldn't remember what had been said or how they'd gotten into the mess. He couldn't remember what had once been different in their lives, and preferred to think there wasn't anything much, preferred to think that he remembered all but the details from the time he was lifted from his mother's belly in the operating room. But it was hard to deny that a mysterious influence had today entered the solar system of their family and distorted the orbits of normal life. And the dark energy that had disturbed affairs in their dimension might as well have been that forgotten once upon a time—what else should it be? The past was maybe even bigger in size than the visible here and now—as if the past were the larger, lower part of the iceberg that the ship's lookout doesn't see. The lookout just sees a little climbable, hospitable ice-world in miniature with glittering shelves to use and facets to sit on, a white-blue island of charming scale like the asteroid that the Little Prince lived on, an island no bigger than a whale and rising just above the ship's gunwale, fit for a child's imagination. And down below is something of a more adult size with a more adult meaning.

Leo contemplated Mack in sorrow and Mack stared back at him with glacier eyes and the towel full of ice held still against his mouth.

3.

LABIAPHOBIA

SOME YEARS, LEO promised himself that this time, this spring, he would not get sad, and some years he forgot that anything bad happened in the spring and entered summer with a naïve optimism, but every year it was exactly the same: spring's end aggrieved like the end of time and his depression humiliated him publicly and mercilessly as though he were naked and kneeling in a stockade. By the time he was fifteen, he had hopes that a summer job would relieve him of this syndrome. He went to work as a lifeguard at a camp, and he wouldn't let himself cry then. Fifteen was too old.

Mack went to a day camp in Cleveland called Anisfield. Leo went away to Camp Wise in the Ohio woods. He thought he could do it. Because it was a coed camp, he thought he might even have sex—he wanted to have sex—but then the summer came and "orientation" and he just watched that girl bend over to tie her shoe with a genuine lump of pain in his throat. Backpack buckles clinked and clinked in a row of cheerless little bells. From ahead came a voice that sounded like one of his friends from home, but was not his friend—he heard it like a rescuer's call that he couldn't answer, like he was buried under rubble and his diaphragm could barely move so that he hadn't the air to make a sound while someone called his name above.

"Are you okay?" someone asked.

Got a feelin' inside that I can't explain.

His friend Ted had just been there beside him. Now he was not. "No problem," Ted had said, "I'll take you to pick up the film," and Ted, who was a year older and could drive, had driven him to Fairmount Circle while the *Who's Greatest Hits* tape played on the stereo. He could see Ted like he was standing right there. But he wasn't. On the ground were leaves and two crossed sticks. Mack was at home in Cleveland, and completely fine without him. There were no beetles that needed picking out of his hair and there was no lizard tank this summer. Leo would kill for Mack, but Mack didn't give him a thought anymore, not the whole year and not now. Next year, Mack would go to the junior high.

Leo trudged on with the Who lyrics going over and over in his head. It had to be less than an hour now till camp, where the others would eat without looking at him. He hadn't really spoken in four days—a few words maybe, but not a conversation. There was that boy who never laughed but had the broad still smile on his face when they joked with him, who chose sometimes to read by himself in his tent, who drank one beer, then stopped. Maybe he could be a friend. Leo tried to switch the music in his head onto another song but a different one by the Who just took the first one's place and kept going and going and going: *Captain Walker didn't come home, his unborn child will never know him. . . .*

At the campsite: tin pots on the ground and balanced on rocks, some with peeled potatoes in them under clear lake water like stones, some freckles of dirt or a pine needle spinning slowly on the meniscus. The bend-over girl with big breasts came close to him and mimicked his grave expression. She brushed a leaf from his hair. He said hi and looked away, blushing. Her opinion was on him like a fever on his skin. His blush was a chain reaction that crescendoed and exploded on his face.

"Stop the world—I want to get off," he said, and he wondered if he'd made it up, because if so, it should be a saying. It sounded clever enough to be a saying, but it didn't make him feel any better.

In fact it was the title of a musical that his mother and dead father used to play on the record player, but Leo didn't remember that until many years later after a great deal of psychoanalysis. Years later, he found the record. There was a clown on the album cover. There was another record behind it called *The Roar of the Greasepaint—The Smell of the Crowd* that he remembered slightly better. The same pair of Englishmen, Leslie Bricusse and Anthony Newley, had written both, and years later Leo remembered dancing to the song "A Wonderful Day Like Today," dancing when he was so short that he could see the individual piles of the green shag carpet and the hairs on his daddy's legs and the shine of his mommy's nylon knee-highs in the prismatic light of the living room glass.

> *On a wonderful day like today*
> *I defy any cloud to appear in the sky*
> *Dare any raindrop to plop in my eye*
> *On a wonderful day like today*

On a wonderful morning like this
When the sun is as big as a yellow balloon
Even the sparrows are singing in tune
On a wonderful morning like this

On a morning like this I could kiss everybody
I'm so full of love and goodwill
Let me say furthermore
I'd adore everybody to come and dine
The pleasure's mine and I will pay the bill

May I take this occasion to say
That the whole human race should go down on its knees
Show that we're grateful for mornings like these
For the world's in a wonderful way
On a wonderful day like today

But he didn't remember any of that yet, only the title of the one musical, and he thought maybe he'd invented it, and decided to write it down.

The skeleton of tent poles had entangled him. When he'd got the thing up at last, he crawled into his tent, dragging in with him a lot of dirt and pine needles. The tent had a bad sweaty air that made him feel he was inside the body of a dead fish. He opened his bag and his mother's handwriting on the packing list jumped out and struck him in total silence like a pit viper. He pulled out his yellow legal pad and wrote, "Stop the world—I want to get off." He wrote after it, "Ha ha ha," as if it were a joke, but really he meant it. The measure would be if he'd been with a girl by the time he was eighteen. If not, he'd kill himself. He took some comfort in the idea: he would not be tortured or alone forever. He could stop the world and get off.

Time went as slowly as if he'd taken a drug, as if a drug like marijuana had confused the labels on past and future and kept him spinning in the present like the pine needle on the surface of the pasta water. He felt the nanoseconds.

Evening. The tent walls hung close. He heard the voices by the fire. His clothes and the sleeping bag felt tacky and damp. Rocks gouged his side and his hips, and the wall of the tent pressed against his feet; by invisible increments he was undeniably sliding toward the tent flap. The beer-smelling Gore-Tex and insect repellent worried his nerves at all times. The repellent felt like gasoline on the skin. He thought of the lonely places that awaited him, the fire circle, the path between the showers and the barracks, the bright burning wastes of the sports fields where the grass dried in the baking heat. An exile that hurt so badly but could not be understood from without, even by himself, when he thought back on it from someplace or sometime else. Inside the barracks the smell of cedar, itchy army blankets and thin mattresses unrolled on sagging metal chains. Mesh on windows without shades or curtains. Blaring music that was not of his choosing, en masse toothbrushing in cement-floor bathrooms, standing in damp flip-flops that his mother had bought at the beginning of the summer and checked off a typed checklist. Fluttering coma of moths around a bare bulb. Supposed to be teaching kids to swim. Supposed to be administering candylines and bug juice. And the whole time feeling every pound of saltwater inside him and drowning in it.

He stood in the circle of tents in the dark of the middle of the night, alone. Someone snored. The darkness seemed to move. Rocks did curvets like black horses down into the gorge. He knelt on the lichen before the gorge. His father was Harvard and merchant marine and doctor and man. He felt for his father in the rocks and looked for him in the tree where the cold lantern hung.

In the morning the breasts approached again.

"Are you sick?" she asked. She made a ponytail of her dark brown hair. He looked into her loose sweatshirt at her tits.

Everything worried him like a bad condition of the air.

"I get depressed," he said. "I'm not always like this, but I'm like this now."

"Oh, you're all right," she said, and watched him for a little bit. "Wow, you really are depressed, huh?"

"I can't explain," he said. *Quoting the Who. Ha ha ha.* "I'm an anachronism."

"You're a deep kid, aren't you, honey," she said.

"It's like there's an evil hypnotist in control of me," he said.

"Huh! Have you been hypnotized?"

"No. I mean a hypnotist makes you feel things that don't make any sense." He had other theories but that was all he dared to say. He'd read parts of medical textbooks because he worried about his brain. He'd also read Viktor E. Frankl's book on existential logotherapy to try to cure his blushing. He tried to thrust his red face out brazenly as Viktor E. Frankl would have instructed. It helped a little.

The girl brandished a wooden spoon at him. "Rrrrrr, I'm a killer," she said. "Just kidding. Come on, help me make breakfast."

Before the talent show, he saw her change her clothes. She pulled her skirt down and stood before him in black tights. She caught him looking and looked down at herself. The crotch was swollen but not like a man's. Her belly was flat, a smooth clean sweep from up beneath her red chamois shirt all the way down between her legs. She pulled on her jeans and zipped them without turning away from him and her fingernails scratched on the denim as she buttoned the pants. Her breasts jutted before her like sister stemheads on a pair of boats.

They thought he was funny because he couldn't shit and he did stand-up about the rocks up his ass with a loop of toilet paper sashed over his shoulder like he was mayor of Turdsville. Which he had anointed himself.

But in the evening in the field behind the pool where dandelion tufts floated like fireflies drunk on nectar, she said, "You're beautiful. I'm sure you know that."

It remained a remote possibility that something could happen with a girl that summer: the thought returned. The sports counselor taught him how to drink beer in a parking lot. He coached him to "double-swallow." He was good like that, that kid, he understood the in-between steps. Taught Leo finally how to shoot a basketball, too: "Just wave good-bye." They played basketball with the hoop in the pool and Leo didn't need anybody to teach him to swim. He was a born porpoise because his father was the keeper of the Eddystone Light and he married a mermaid one fine night. The kid said, "If I could just get you on a basketball court on dry land, you bastard." The kid did tricks with his scrotum—could make his balls click, or seem to, and could empty his sack—stuffed his balls up their canals or something and made them really disappear and flapped his empty scrotum around like an empty coin purse. Said Leo should get started fucking girls, God bless him.

"You're beautiful," she'd said, "I'm sure you know that." Even pretty girls liked him sometimes. There was that girl Kathy Main at school who people said liked him.

The darkness lifted with the little crumbs of love he got with his jester act and he thought he might even lay his eyes on his very own "naked lady" that summer—it was a little like that dream he'd once had where some fuzzy little creatures had opened a window for him (a literal one with panes and sashes), opened it on the harmony of the universe, and he believed, he believed, all he wished for could be true.

On a wonderful morning like this
When the sun is as big as a yellow balloon

But he was just a jester, just the mayor of Turdsville, and she had a boyfriend to whom she gave a blow job in the first-aid closet at the pool and she showed up to a meeting with come in her hair, which was much talked about for the rest of the summer.

At least the darkness had gone. Just as easy as waving goodbye.

In the fall, Mack started at the junior high and he brought a girl home with him on the first day. She was kind of cute, with cheeks still round with baby fat and braces, and a freckle on her nose. Mack brought her upstairs to his room, and they closed the door and didn't open it for hours. Leo wondered what of a sexual nature could go on in that time capsule Mack called a bedroom, with the same football posters and dwarven bookshelves, and buckets of toys that had been there since the third grade. Leo wondered, too, why his own room was so virginal a place, with its austere grown-up desk and ink blotter and black-humored comic strips tacked to the wall. One of the clippings was a photo of Woody Allen with the caption, "I don't want to achieve immortality through my work; I want to achieve it through not dying," and another was a *Bloom County* strip with a guy worrying about getting run over by a bus or catching AIDS from a dirty soup spoon. He had a poster of Einstein next to the strips.

He wondered why he had a framed Philippe Halsman portrait of Einstein on his wall but had never had a girl on his bed.

He wondered and worried and wondered while he sat in his history class, and pretended not to look in the direction of Michelle Katz. She played field hockey, might have even been the captain of the team, and she made all the posters for the theater department and the art for the school newspaper—a girl with a mannish love of being the best, and yet soft and feminine in her body, and she sat at her desk with her head slightly lowered. She won all those things and said straight out: no way would she let anyone beat her at art or on a hockey field. And yet at the awards ceremony last year when she'd won the freshman-sophomore art prize, she'd come up onstage with red ears and head slightly lowered and took the certificate with a somewhat childlike expression of surprise and gratitude, as though however much she'd coveted and anticipated the prize, she was not thoroughly convinced she really deserved it. She was soft when she looked at him, and he wondered if that soft look was just for him or if she gave it to everyone. She was *popular*.

She looked up at him.

Fool! Could his smile have looked as tense and awkward as it had felt? No, not possibly so bad. Maybe she couldn't tell. Still, you had to consider it in contrast to her ex-boyfriend, Josh Helpern. Was he tense and bad by contrast with the Helpern kid, an older male whose self-assurance was presumably the template by which Michelle judged potential successors? Of course he looked bad by comparison with Josh! Look at her, gone cold now. Her initial gesture of friendliness was already being reconsidered and withdrawn. She could smell his fear. Like a dog. Though he was in fact incredibly brave and stout of heart, this he knew! He was a hero in a wind-shot sea! Sometimes he was. Maybe it had been fear, then, of a temporary nature. People don't like to be around that, the camp sports counselor had said, the one who taught him how to shoot a basketball and drink a beer. And they don't like to hear you're depressed. You're making me depressed, the sports counselor would say. Don't show that, the sports counselor said. Don't be yourself, then, the sports counselor said. Or were the drops of dried semen in his boxers perhaps subliminally detectable to human smell? Or the sweat in his boxers from having done it after his shower? (He'd been late to school because of it.) His mind was a stockade that ridiculed him with paranoia: *She thinks you're a freak! She knows you're a pervert!* But maybe he did better than he thought. Or maybe every girl, every person for that matter, could see his nervousness right there in plain sight, and something that might have gone well went instead, each time, badly, or did not happen at all. Like at the camp. Maybe endowments meant nothing next to self-confidence. Someday he'd go to Yale, where people would be sensitive and thoughtful, and wouldn't judge others superficially. Was he a narcissist? The horror of it. Someone had called him a narcissist once, a girl who liked him whom he didn't like back. You must like narcissists, then, he'd said. What exactly was narcissism? He had seen it in Viktor E. Frankl's book. God, that blushing. Was he blushing even now? Damn the corpuscles, full shame ahead. God, his blushing would ruin him. Then all those people like Josh Helpern would go around feeling sorry for him. Probably, they already did. *No, you don't feel sorry for me, I feel sorry for you, see!* But every year the record of all his accomplishments, which couldn't even show all he was capable of, that record was over and over wiped clean, every summer in fact, when people just took him in their eyes for a second and shrugged, said "prove it" and—

Mr. Herhal was looking at him with scarcely veiled desperation. No one would raise a hand to answer him about the Magna

Carta. "What does the book say about this?" Mr. Herhal said. "Leo? What does the book say?"

"It says that feudalism gave rise to constitutional democracy because the nobility were to a degree independent from the monarch and that they codified their rights in the Magna Carta," Leo said. "But I don't really see how that's so. Baboons are to a degree independent of their monarch. Ants are to a degree independent. Constitutional democracy and the social contract was an idea before it was a system of government, it was an Enlightenment idea, and that idea sprang from the secularism of the Renaissance, not medieval piety and divine right and all that."

He couldn't look at Michelle. He was afraid he might blush. He wondered if she still went out with Josh Helpern or if Josh had moved on. He heard Josh was on to someone else now. He heard the scratching of Michelle's pencil resume, and with his left forearm he covered his own drawings of Captain Change, which were just storyboards and not real drawings—but he could make real drawings, he really could! He would not speak to her. He'd tried to overmaster that nervous feeling with his speech about feudalism, but he'd been arrogant and now he looked like an ass. She thought him an ass. It was over between them. *Michelle, we've been through so much during the last twenty-five minutes. Is it really over?* What a pathetic fool he was, a nonentity, unfit for survival in the human race, a Cipher in the Snow. He wrote these things in the margins of his notebook, as if by writing them they could be precipitated from his mind, or out of reality even, onto paper, where they became mere shapes of symbolic graphite, and not true.

Why was he like this? In health class they had to make an album cover that expressed their personal selves and choose an animal that represented their personalities. He'd called his album *Undertoe.* He'd chosen a turtle.

143

The nervous feeling had come in sixth or seventh grade and had not gone away; he was on year three or four of it now. He'd been happy at first, he'd been president of his class in the seventh grade and slow-danced with a cute girl named Heather with a turned-up gentile nose and afterward smelled her perfume on his banana-yellow polo shirt—how he had breathed that perfume in an opiate trance and refused to wash the shirt until the Heather smell of her had faded away—and then things kept getting worse and he made more and more lists of his worries:

I am not brave
I am not good
I am not smart
I am not funny
I am selfish
I will die
I will fail
I will lose all my friends
I will get infected by a trichina worm
I will never get married
I will never have a beard
I am getting dumber
My penis is too small
My voice is too high
I will get that disease I saw on Nova *that made the hockey player*
   get breasts and stop scoring goals

And it had gotten quite bad. In Rome he'd almost lost his mind. (It was only a month ago that he'd almost lost his mind, just after camp ended, but it seemed like more now that he was sitting in school again.) In the impure darkness of the churches of Rome, metal crucifixes transected the air like scalpel blades, people whispered in occult passageways, and old rags and bones in glass cases that were supposed to be holy seemed instead to be cursed. Jews were not supposed to fear damnation, and anyway angels and devils belonged to the Great Chain of Being, and signified the Ptolemaic order in the universe (how he longed for the innocence and order of a math textbook then). But try as he might he couldn't stub out the smoldering conviction that a chaotic magic of devils and angels far more ancient than Ptolemy lurked in the darkness of the churches. He would not step on cracks, especially in the church floors, because that superstition seemed to him not at all childish but rather august and ancient. He knew the Devil would try to outsmart him, would sow his malevolent power exactly where it was least expected, within the clichés of floor cracks, broken mirrors, fallen picture frames, but outside his own traditions; the Devil would ambush him not in the boring bourgeois daylight of a synagogue with photographs of businessmen on its walls but in the dark Catholic air that smelled of the thurible, like burned brass, charcoal, styrax gum, candle wax, rose oil, flame, earth, stone, sweat, tears, historic skeletons buried with gold swords. He had to be smarter. He feared contamination by certain chemicals and diseases and cursed objects (such as an oxidized green nickel he found on the carpet in his hotel room in Rome) and he compulsively washed his hands to rid himself of chemicals, grease, and germs. But more than anything else, he conducted rituals to avoid dangerous thoughts: anytime he found a fallen eyelash on his shirt, for example, he kept his mind a blank while he swept the eyelash away because he couldn't remember whether wishes made on eyelashes were supposed to come true or were supposed not to—either way was dangerous because it could cause the death of loved ones (he could involuntarily wish for his mother to die and his wish might be granted, or wish for her to live and the opposite might come true)—and because he really couldn't help thinking of the Devil every time he farted (it had become automatic sometime after he saw *The Exorcist*) he always said to himself after farting *flo, flare, flavi,* which he felt protected him from the Devil like a Latin prayer to blow the evil away. Demonic magic was imminent in every church and crucifix and fart; symbols were dangerous portals that could not be opened or even looked through; the thoughts must be controlled in the presence of symbols to keep the door closed on Death and the Devil; but a door could fly open at any time; it was very, very dangerous; one had to be vigilant. He wrote pages and pages of theories on his compulsions, but they were not meant to understand, they were meant to keep the Devil away.

He remembered the foreign smell of the Tuscan air, like arugula leaves or a spice he didn't know the name of, and the caretaker's advice to bar the door "because of Gypsies"; like a dream, the little house required that you unbar the door and actually go outside to climb the stairs and so if Gypsies came, Leo and Mack would have to deal with them alone and could not get to their parents. In the daytime there were empty rows of cypress trees, which were beautiful, yes, but he felt himself like a tree of suffering all day and all night, like Cyparissus, who shot his pet stag, like a tree with a poison nail in its heart and copper up and down its water column. One day in the shower, while his eyes were closed, his tube of Neutrogena shampoo jumped up and hit him in the face, banged right on his right eyeball. There was no one else there; he was forced to conclude the Devil had flung it at him. *This must be what it is to lose your mind,* he thought. On the walls of the hotel room in Venice, red and green roses wreathed the green lines of the wallpaper and in the roses he saw skulls, because they were in Italy, where Satan lived, underneath the Vatican.

In the hotel room, Mack agreed to make up a silly story where they each did the dialogue for one of the characters. Leo would try anything not to think about the Devil, so he said he would be Ixion and Mack could be Tantalus, but then he realized he was thinking of Hell again, because Ixion and Tantalus were in Tartarus, which was Latin Hell, and Mack didn't want to be Tantalus anyway. So they decided to just be X and Y. They laughed for a little while until the "X"s began to look like crosses on the notebook page and Leo ran out of jokes.

Franco, the tour guide in Rome, had hairs on top of his nose and other places Leo didn't know hairs could grow, and Franco trotted out his rehearsed little list of facts, with which Philip politely agreed, saying, "That's right," and then elaborating, and in the act contradicting and replacing Franco's dates and facts with new ones that were presumably more accurate and certainly more interesting. Philip taught Leo about the ruins of the Forum from that mental encyclopedia of world history he'd amassed—and there was something relaxing in the idea of ancient Rome, before Christ and Satan and all the bad things began, and something relaxing about Philip, whom Leo had resented just a couple of years before, Philip who never minded change, who swam in the waters of change like a salmon while Leo's mom got constipated if they went as far as Florida. His heels had beaten the pavement of every European capital in wind, rain, or sun with boundless energy and he was indestructible; he ignored a knife cut on his finger or a burn on his leg and went straight on without fail, without fear, thinking of the ancient Romans and the Visigoths and Raphael and the Borgias and wanting everyone else to see and enjoy, and having five different restaurant reservations, and then making unnecessary excuses in Italian to cancel them (usually fake medical emergencies), and dabbing at his nose, which ran constantly because of his polyps, and changing the hotel room to get a better view. In Rome they had stayed in the same hotel as Kurt Waldheim, and all the Zajac aunts and uncles whispered that he was a Nazi.

When the touring was over at the end of the day, Leo wanted to die and his soul went into withdrawal, and he was more ashamed of this instability of self than anything, this copper inside him; he would do anything to scour it off his soul and family name. When they got back from Italy they sent him to a psychologist, who said it was to do with his dead father.

When the sun is as big as a yellow balloon

And, lo, the psychologist said, "You're ahead of the game intellectually but you're behind the game socially" and that wounded Leo like a razor cut to his knees. And he thought he would show that shrink: he would kiss a girl now or die.

The bell rang.

"What did you draw?" he said.

"Oh, nothing," Michelle said, and stuffed her notebook into her bag, but not before he saw: she'd drawn Josh Helpern's name and a design that looked like a heart. "You know a lot about feudalism," she said.

"I have a medieval mind," he said.

"What?"

"Nothing. It's a joke."

"There's a lot going on in that mind of yours, whatever it is," she said.

"What do you mean?" he said.

"I just mean," she said, "you do a lot of thinking."

"Yeah, probably too much," he said.

"I'll bet there're a lot of interesting things going around in that head of yours."

"I guess," he said.

"I was thinking you should do more talking," she said, "not less thinking."

He had to think about that.

That day that he blushed before Michelle and disparaged the Magna Carta in history class, a kid said something mean to him, something about his backpack, something he didn't hear completely, something like "Mr. Wears His Backpack on Both Shoulders" (when he in fact wore it religiously on one shoulder like everybody else even when it had fifty pounds of textbooks in it). The kid said it in health class (where they had last week watched *Cipher in the Snow*). He would let it go unchallenged. He would not stoop. He would let the kid be wrong. And yet that wrongness abraded the mind. It remained in the universe when it should not, radiating out into space forever like all those episodes of *The Beverly Hillbillies,* going on and on inexorably out into the cosmos and embarrassing all humanity before the superior races of the Andromeda galaxy.

It was a Friday.

That night his brother the ice-man went out (he never said where). His parents went out. His friends were going bowling. They had invited him, belatedly, but it seemed the plan had been conceived without him. So let them go. He picked up the picture of his dead father and then the one of his dead grandfather and namesake looking out from in front of sea rocks. Every other night of the week he studied until midnight at his desk or in the computer room. Under no circumstances would he work on a Friday or Saturday night.

"Mr. Wears His Backpack on Both Shoulders," the kid had said. Another time the same kid had said, "You know *his* report card: all As and a B in gym." And the kid and his friend had laughed and laughed. All As and a B in gym. Of course it was true. And he felt branded with a scarlet letter "B" on his breast, though he knew it was ridiculous, though he knew that his sensitivity itself was the very feminine, weak, socially vulnerable part of him that caused him to hang back and get those Bs in gym, the weak part that demanded extirpation. He ought to have said in a friendly, teasing, manly way: "Better than all Cs and an A in gym, muthafucka," like Josh Helpern might have. Or maybe Josh wouldn't have cursed, maybe he would have said, "Sucka." But he couldn't have said it in a friendly way like Josh, who seemed at ease at all times, he could only have said it with all the tormented murderous spite he truly felt, so he said nothing. And the other one had said, "Look at him, he probably got girls crawling all over him, probably got hisself a car," and he wasn't sure if that was stated sincerely or in ridicule or envy or what, and it had been worse than that, because then the first one had said, "He ain't never kissed a girl, neither. Just look at him. He wouldn't know what to do."

And the shameful truth was: he was sixteen (but just sixteen) and had never felt a girl's lips against his own.

Though it took over forty-five minutes sitting by the phone with a bounding pulse, he did finally dial the number. And when Kathy Main's mother answered, he didn't hesitate and asked for Kathy (though it felt like someone had cranked a valve on his larynx so that the air squeaked out comically). When Kathy got on the phone, he asked her without preamble if she wanted to go to a movie. They had not spoken at all in two years, since he had been editor of the *Shaker B* and she had lined up to join the staff.

"Your name?" he'd asked.

"Kathy," she'd said, as if they were meeting each other, and not just recording information on a list. She had bright blue eyes like his brother's.

"Your full name," he'd said.

She'd laughed and told him. He'd not laughed, but perhaps had smiled at her mistake. Maybe that was why she'd liked him, because he'd been behind a desk. There was the rumor out there that she liked him still.

It seemed to be true. She said yes. She said she was planning to go to a party, but she'd go to a movie instead if that was what he wanted.

He picked her up in a light-gray-on-dark-gray Plymouth Horizon whose bumper was tied on with twine. (He liked to point that out to people in a self-deprecating way, but really he believed it gave him a certain street cred.) She didn't wear a coat, just a pink sweater. He was wearing a too-warm ski jacket that puckered out in the front. They barely spoke. At a stop-light a man in another car rolled down his window and yelled at him angrily, but they couldn't hear him. It seemed to be about the bumper tied on with twine. Leo laughed nervously and she laughed and said, "Jeez." All that mattered, anyway, was whether he would kiss her.

There was no movie showing that he really wanted to see, and she expressed no opinion. (There was an appealing softness about her, an old-fashioned deference—she let him decide everything.) So they saw the movie *D.O.A.*, a remake. It was in black-and-white and had Dennis Quaid and Meg Ryan in it and the guy who'd played the villain in *Dreamscape,* a movie which had caused Leo to fear his own dreams for months. Leo sat paralyzed beside Kathy in the dark. Once or twice he looked over at her and she looked back at him. She was very pretty, but he couldn't enjoy her smooth bare arms (she had pulled off her pink sweater) or her long hair or her nice new breasts or glossy lips.

Her prettiness seemed to indict him with errors: he did not deserve to be there with a girl who looked like that, who was popular. But he was going to do it, do it come hell or high water. He wondered if he should do it there in the theater, but his arms lay straitjacketed at his sides. He couldn't be sure what she thought of him anymore. Maybe if he were back behind the desk.

There was a clock ticking affectedly throughout the movie and it seemed to be ticking down for him: *when time is up, you must act.* He paid no attention to the plot, which had something to do with the murder of a young novelist, and watched the entire movie with boredom and anxiety as if he were watching instead a long spilling of sand between the bulbs of an hourglass. Dennis Quaid's character said that the unpublished manuscript was the best book he'd ever read. Funny to call a manuscript a book. The credits rolled up the huge screen as the final particles of time rolled down the hourglass neck. Leo's heart again became a fluttery bird trapped inside his ribs.

They drove in silence up Cedar Road in the Plymouth Horizon. He didn't even turn on the radio. He listened to the sound of the heat blowing through the vent and the car engine groaning over the cold street. When they finally arrived at her parents' house, they sat for a minute parked in the drive under an elm tree. The birdwings inside him were flapping so wildly he thought she could see the blood fountaining up his neck. All he could think of was Dutch elm disease and whether it was an elm and whether it would die. Did he even say anything? Did he say "Good night" or "I had a nice time" or "Thank you"? Certainly he had not complimented her on how she looked. But he leaned forward to kiss her and she didn't stop him. Her lips were soft and wet and cool. His lips were compressed and firm like the tip of a pool cue. She began to get out of the car, backing away quickly as if from a spill that would ruin her clothes. "Wait," he said. "Let's try that again." She let him, but he was just as stiff the second time, and the light had by then gone out of her eyes. She ran away from the elm tree and went into the house and it was true that after that she would not look over at him anymore in biology class. The sight of him did not cause pleasure to her mind anymore.

He was so ashamed that he drove home with his head hanging below the steering wheel. He had to look up over the dash-board occasionally to make sure he didn't drive into a telephone pole. The words "Let's try that again" played over and over in his mind. This noise in his head really would kill him someday.

4.

The Island of Neverything
Ad Ban Cappen

As the candles were burning down on the dining room table, and with them the last hours of 1988, Leo watched the cars rolling through the darkness of Shaker Boulevard in front of the house and thought that nothing good would happen in the world in 1989. What good could arise in the free world when its leader was George Bush, the man without a plan? What good could arise on a cold, black New Year's Eve without a female heartbeat anywhere in sight or hearing? At the family party there would be his mother and father, his aunts, uncles, and younger male cousins, his grandmother and two great-aunts, the one who'd never married and the other who made blintzes and never talked. This year the blintzes aunt's husband had wasted from cancer and died, so Leo's great-uncle, who never talked even when he was alive, would be more silent than ever, and furthermore not there. Then Leo's friends would be getting drunk at Singer's house and watching the entire miniseries *V: The Final Battle,* about man-eating reptilian aliens. Jesus Christ.

His friend Singer was a lothario who had sex with all the girls in the theater department. Singer was Adam this year in the winter production of *The Apple Tree* and Leo knew for a fact that Singer and Eve had already tasted of the tree of knowledge together. It was nothing to Singer to spend an evening laughing at, or even seriously enjoying, *V: The Final Battle* with a bunch of fucking nerds.

Mack brought a huge steaming pile of brisket and mashed potatoes to the table. No matter how much Mack ate, he seemed to weigh forty-five pounds.

"Hey. What are you doing later on, man?" Leo said.

Mack paused with his fork in front of his mouth. "Do you mind if I eat something? I just sat down."

"Uh, sure."

Mack went on chewing, then shook his head slowly back and forth as he loaded up another bite.

"What, is it a matter of national security or something?" Leo said. "I just—"

"Going out with friends," Mack said.

"Yeah, where?"

"It's really none of your business."

"What? It's none of my business?" Another of Mack's mind-fucks. Leo felt vaguely like crying. "Wait. What are you talking about? Because I'm just talking about what you're doing later tonight, because my plans suck."

"I feel like you're trying to make it out like you're being normal," Mack said, practically holding his breath to keep the nerves and the anger out of his voice. "You're making it out like that, but you have an agenda."

"It's not an *agenda,* Mack, I'm just—whatever."

After dinner, Leo's mom asked him to get the candles from

the "bar," the weird closetlike room with a sink in it and wood shutters that unfolded into the den on brass hinges. WASPs had built it before Philip bought the house. Leo went inside the bar and opened the low cabinet and found a funny little candle in a jar. It had a blue-and-white label with two small Jewish stars on it next to the bar code and tiny Hebrew letters and it said in English MEMORIAL CANDLE and DISTRIBUTED BY GENERAL WAX CO. It was a *Yahrzeit* candle, a Jewish candle for the dead. He brought it out into the hall.

"Hey, Mom," Leo said. "How come we didn't light this, this year?"

Leo's mother stopped in the hall with an armful of wrapped presents. "I was going to light it, but I actually didn't want to make you think about it if you didn't want to."

"Oh."

"Did you want to light it? Because we can light it right now. Come on, we'll light it right now."

"No, that's okay."

"Are you sure? I just want to do whatever works for you, honey. Are you okay? I just decided, you know, I think about him whether I light a candle or not."

"Yeah, I'm okay."

"Do you need to talk?" The presents were slipping out of his mom's arms. She lifted one leg up to keep them from falling.

"Here, let me help you," Leo said. He took one of the presents, and the others fell on the floor. He and his mother bent down to pick them up.

"Whose is this one?" Leo said. "It feels like a book."

"That's for you."

"Oh, good, I'm excited to see what it is."

"You know, I've been thinking that this is a hard time of year for us," Laura said. Her eyes seemed suddenly to fill up with the sight of her son and nothing and no one else. The presents lay littered on the floor around her. "There's truth to the idea of an anniversary response."

Philip came into the hall holding a big tarnished silver menorah by its neck like a strangled goose and he leaned through the double doors into the den and gave a loud, perfunctory roundup call: "Okay, boys, it's-time-for-candles-and-presents! Turn-off-the-TV!" He turned and saw Leo and his mother there, and said somewhat absently in the same perfunctory singsong, "Come on! Let's go! Everybody in!" Then he said in the lower register of his regular speaking voice, "Laurie, do you know where the candles are?"

One might have concluded that he didn't perceive the electromagnetic intensity between mother and son. But Leo knew that he had perceived it, and also that he didn't like it. Otherwise, he would have asked for the candles in a happier way and called Laura "my dear." He didn't like it if Leo made his mother upset, an attitude Leo couldn't understand very well because he wasn't married and didn't know what a pain in the ass it is to have an upset wife.

They celebrated Chanukah on New Year's Eve. Between the ages of six and twelve, the holiday had not been about time or stalagmites of old purple wax at the base of the tarnished menorah. But it was about time now, as it had been in the beginning for Judah Maccabee.

The gift from his mom and dad was a copy of Locke's *Second Treatise of Government*.

"You must be the only sixteen-year-old in America who asked for John Locke for Chanukah!" Philip said. He patted Leo's back.

Maybe his dad wasn't mad at him.

Three more hours till midnight. He went to get water.

Uncle Ollie was on the phone in the kitchen.

"Dr. Greenblatt," he said. "I received a page." Uncle Ollie pretended to pant and rolled his eyes. He'd been sitting in the living room for a long time with the great-aunts. "Is it midnight yet, boy?" he whispered, and flickered one of his eyelids like a lizard. "Can we turn the clocks forward?" Then he picked up a pad of paper, turned to the stainless steel countertop, and identified himself again in the uninflected, bureaucratic manner of doctors answering pages, giving rude treatment to the cherished Greenblatt name.

Leo sat in the breakfast room, where the white clover patterns on the wallpaper swam in your eyes, and listened to his uncle. He wondered what the words meant—"creatinine," "albumin," "sodium." Albumen was in an egg. Sodium was in a salt shaker. Creatinine sounded like an epoch you'd see on a chart at the natural history museum. *Long before the Pleistocene was the Creatinine: when the cells got together in the primordial piss.*

His mom came in.

"Mack doesn't care about me," he said, though he knew it was a craven tactic to pull his mother into it.

"That's not true," she said.

"It is."

"Why are you saying that? He worships you."

Leo laughed seriously.

Laura went out and came back to the breakfast room with Mack, who was in his winter jacket, a ski jacket with the Peek'n Peak tag still attached to the zipper.

"He thinks you don't love him," she said to Mack.

Mack said nothing.

"Well? Do you love your brother?" she said.

His face said it all. Cold air was flowing into the kitchen through the garage.

When Mack had gone, Laura lit the *Yahrzeit* candle and said she could never remember the mourner's kaddish. She said that anytime they went into a synagogue.

Why should anyone remember it? The mourner's kaddish was a sick and twisted thing, written no doubt by some Dark Ages rabbi who knew that disaster and grief debilitated faith in the fairy tale of a personal God. And so you were asked in your moment of grief to think not of your own feelings or of your loved one's, but of the feelings of the medieval rabbis, who were very worried, the poor things. For their sakes you were asked to attest to what you knew to be false.

The Mercator map was rolled down like a window shade. Again total silence. Snowflakes hurried in every direction outside the window. The sky was gray.

Michelle sat at a desk with illegible graffiti on it in green Magic Marker. He sat at one that said LIFE SUCKS in pencil.

Josh Helpern was waiting for her outside the classroom, talking to some other girls.

"How are you?" Leo asked with incredible insouciance, his arm draped casually over the back of the chair.

"I'm okay, I guess."

"You guess? Everything all right?"

She said her parents were getting divorced. "I don't know why I told you that," she said. "Sorry."

"Divorce," he said. "Sorry. That sucks." Plagiarizing desk graffiti. Snow swirled past the window. The American flag snapped, the rope jerked, and something metal lightly clinked on something else metal and clink-clinked, and the cracked wooden flagpole rumbled in its holster.

"What are you doing for this project?" she said.

"I'm doing something on the cycle of mistrust between England and Spain as an example of an arms race. It's really no different from what's going on now with the Russians."

She said nothing.

"You seem like you're mighty impressed with my idea: the Cycle of Mistrust."

She watched him: he supposed she thought he was a rampaging nerd.

"I sound like a dork, huh?"

"Noooo," she said, and he couldn't tell if she was being sarcastic or not.

Well, they didn't get it, his peers. *You are walking on thin ice. Reality is not nice. Everything bad can happen and does, all the time.* He wrote it down.

> *You are walking on thin ice*
> *Reality is not nice*
> *Everything bad can happen*
>
> *Who yare alking won in thice*
> *Eality ris ot nice*
> *Neverything ad ban cappen*

But he had his books and his poetry to protect him. He was a rock. He was an island. And a rock felt no pain. And an island never cried. He could be alone forever, even with his Deprivations. He could persist in the wasteland by an exercise of indissoluble will, like Captain Change. And he didn't have to feel ashamed. It wasn't his fault he was cracked. He would fix the crack with a great career. He would go to Harvard or Yale because he was *that* good. He was a rock, he was an island that felt no pain and got all As and would be a writer-doctor like Anton Chekhov or a doctor-writer like Sigmund Freud (not Michael Crichton, Dr. Spock, or even Oliver Sacks).

5.

THE ABATTOIR

WHEN, FINALLY, LOVE visited itself on him, for a reason unknown and at a time unforeseen (in fact it had happened two or three times, before he had any hair on his groin or under his arms), when it did visit with that weird genius of Love, it did it in the jaded last days of his life at home, the summer he worked in a hospital.

While he was dreaming, at least, it seemed he had been to the hospital before. The Bethesda Naval Hospital, he assumed, went a thousand stories down into the earth in the fall of 1974. There were blind giants in that hospital. Someone had taped to their cheeks and brows metal plates, pricked with little holes like a colander. The light in the hallways was as apathetic as wood lice and discovered everything like a spy satellite in the sky—blankie-humps, tantrums, whining mommy-love, urge to poop, freckle, homicidal jealousy, sadistic wishes, etc. The light was very much unlike the lustrous wholesome sunshine of his tricycle handlebars when the sun was as big as a yellow balloon; this fanatical light dulled everything within its penumbra, turned platinum to tin, diamond rings to glass, people to fear. The light smelled cold, and like paper, empty, like the inorganic antiseptic matter out in space. The people with the metal plates in their faces were led around by the hand. They had seen things they were not supposed to see and copulated with machines made of rubber tubes and glass and transistor radios and now they were monsters with metal holes in their heads who wandered the Abattoir hallways. He who looked with curiosity upon their deformities was wounded in his own eyes.

It was called the Bethesda Naval Hospital because his brother crawled out of a belly button there. (The sightless giants did the rock star deed and then hid their babies in drawers full of surgical instruments.) The giants, the babies, the bad people, the good people: they all howled and wept in elevators. Mayhem, happening and happening without purpose in the empty corridors of the universe, happening without any people in it, like the infinite regress of the opposed bathroom mirrors when there is no one between them, empty and deep as the thoughts of God.

And there were many other miraculous weird happenings around the Abattoir. For instance, women ate men. Sometimes, the female began to eat the male even before copulation with rubber hose and glass radio balloon had been completed. Oh no? Well then, how do you think the mommy got so big and round with child while the daddy wasted away to bones and died? She ate his flesh and put it in her belly to make a baby out of it, as one makes a gingerbread cookie of dough. Then the daddy tried to get his body back by sawing her belly open with a bread knife and the doctors sewed her belly with hanging black strings. And then nobody liked each other anymore and their teeth were false and they wished they had never started to hurt each other and could go back to the old house and never hear the howls of pain in the birthing room and they could be happy again and not all alone with nobody to help anybody else.

His daddy died in the Abattoir, where he had been a doctor once. Then his mommy couldn't open any jars and cried into her *shiva* mayonnaise salads. His daddy used to open the jars, but then some mystery enshrouded him, and he moaned like an injured animal and died. Leo preferred to think he dived, but anyway, they buried him with his watch.

Leo couldn't open the jars.

Visitors came in the weeks after. Now his daddy was dead and his mommy had babies to take care of and was bewitched like a nursemaid to Satan. In a few more years, grief would permanently disfigure her face, though the police (doctors) said her face had been vandalized by a lunatic named Ramsay Hunt. The visitors knelt on the floor and played with Leo, but not very well—they rolled him the sticky red truck but they didn't understand him when he said, "You be the rug." They were meant to take the part of the rug and say, "Where is my lamp? Someone moved it and now there's a hole in me. I miss the lamp. Come back to the hole where you used to live and we'll have tea and cookies, lamp." And then he would be the lamp and come back. They didn't understand. They left while he was right in the middle of saying something to them about the hole and the lamp. Sometimes he was dropped off at someone else's house where the ice cubes smelled. They left his blankie behind. Then back home among the legs. New legs came. They cooed at the babies. "You be the couch," he said. "'Someone took away my afghan.' Say that." They knelt on the floor. They rolled the red truck. He smelled his blankie and it made him sad because it smelled like the bed and he wasn't in his bed anymore. There was a real question of who, of where, of if, of if, of if.... Someone needed to give him some pants. It was too cold on his legs.

Sometimes he cried. There were endless strangers, endless auditions. But he had to try or there would be no one to keep him company. The constant auditions were so much work that he became physically exhausted. When he woke from naps, he saw that he had missed out on too much, and he went back to his auditions and worked twice as hard as before.

Sometimes he dreamed that his daddy was still alive, living with another family. Or that he was somewhere lost in the Abattoir, if Leo were only brave enough to go back and find him there.

The Abattoir: sink into the wet and sorry holes of the earth and hide in old junk from the riot of the winds. But in order to survive, go back out into the winds. Audition. Go out and try also to understand the universe, which you are here to witness alone.

Dr. Helpern's secretary's office had a Georgia O'Keeffe ox skull in a brass frame and no windows. Dr. Helpern asked the old lady sitting at the computer to call up radiology for him. There's a plaque dedicated to your grandfather, Dr. Helpern said, on the fifth floor. *Heavy hitters,* Dr. Helpern said: Leo Neuwalder and Isidore Auberon were heavy hitters. Doesn't seem like the same place since he and I were residents here, he said. Medicine is really changing, he said, some would argue not for the better. Leo followed Dr. Helpern out of his office through the maze of spaces within spaces, where men copulated with rubber tubes and with machines behind tinted glass and inside a silver orifice. Attached to every windowless exam suite or lab were windowless offices where computers fanned themselves idly like butterflies, thinking on the horrors of life and death without feeling them.

"You look nervous," Dr. Helpern said, checking his watch.

"How was your graduation? We had our doubts about you, you know, Leo!" he said, and he laughed.

They passed a lady on a hospital bed laden with tanks and saline bags. She was screamingly, ragingly, crushingly old, silenced and flattened by time, and wreathed in tubes like vines on a gnarled old tree, and vessels coiled around her like old vines and many brown growths grew on her head and arms like toadstools on an ancient log. She didn't move. She was time-ravaged. She was fallen.

Dr. Helpern saw him looking. "And she's one of the winners," Dr. Helpern said.

There was no real light—windows that no one bothered to wash looked onto gravel roofs—no one bothered to look out of them. They went to the basement and followed the pipes on the ceiling. The basement halls were like the tunnels of the London War Rooms and lined with canvas carts, the carts mounded with clear plastic bags, the bags filled with crumpled blue polyurethane, the polyurethane soiled by blood and iodine.

People in scrubs and funny paper hats passed them or walked beside them. People in white coats passed. It felt the same as when he saw the Cleveland Browns practice in Berea and Brian Sipe and Ozzie Newsome came right up to sign autographs. They did what he could not do, did not have the skill, strength, or courage to do. The people in the white coats were talking about "the albumin," and he wondered again what that was. They said "hematocrit" and he wondered what that was. They said words like "supraventricular tachycardia." Leo felt a sordid fear grabbing him. *Your father did it but you can't do it,* it whispered. *A man stands his post and takes care of business, knows what to do. If you don't know what to do. . . .*

"Okay, Doc," Dr. Helpern said as they stepped out of the elevator. "Go do some surgery."

Josh Helpern and his friend Steve Zenilman would be doctors too. They had finished a year of college but Leo had just finished high school. The three of them scrubbed in on surgeries and then ate lunch in the hospital cafeteria, where Zenilman talked every day about different girls he'd fooled around with (everyone was back in town from college by now and the parties had started again). He said what was different about this or that girl's legs, or nipples, or vagina, or personality, and the girls of his stories were always willing and somewhat unwitting accomplices to his Roman appetites. They were always getting caught in their underwear or exposed in some anatomical quirk like hairy arms or cellulite hips or a bifid uvula. They smoked pot and did whip-its (nitrous oxide, Leo learned, inhaled from whipped cream cans). The girls of the stories were always betrayed by their bodies, whose menstrual periods gave them away by smell or even, unbeknownst to them, stained their jeans with blood, whose little movements and moans of excitation seemed preposterous and embarrassing when scrutinized in the clinical light of a hospital cafeteria. All this Zenilman studied and reported with the thoroughly good-natured enthusiasm of David Attenborough observing muskrats or sea lions. Poor chaste Leo preferred to doubt the sex stories of males, but Zenilman's stories, unlike those of other males, were not boastful, and furthermore Leo had witnessed for himself Zenilman's extraordinary social ease with girls and even with grown women. Josh, too, was at ease, with girls, with women, with Zenilman and his stories, even with Leo and his stiffness, which kept him from saying much of anything at the hospital lunches, gnawing on his cafeteria hot dog. Leo was sure that Michelle Katz had surrendered up her virginity to Josh, but dared not ask. In the afternoons, they restocked the shelves of the semisterile areas behind the operating rooms, where the wheel locks of the autoclaves were lined up in rows. The wheels made the autoclaves look like submarine hatches.

One night, at a swimming pool at the top of a hill (you got there by flagstones that led from the driveway past a wild raspberry bush), he saw her again, Michelle, though he hadn't expected to see her there. And she saw him splayed shirtless on a raft, and she later told him that her friend liked the look of him too and said someone needed to jump his bones. (He didn't like the expression "jump his bones," as it reminded him of death. . . .) He floated himself over to the edge of the pool next to her bare and tan legs and she crouched down, lowering the most interesting parts of her anatomy to the level of his eyes. He told her that he worked with Josh, and where was Josh? She said Josh didn't tell her where he went anymore. She had the sad-happy expression on her face that he remembered from the day in class when she said her parents were getting a divorce.

His friend had to tell him: I think you like her.

"You like her, oooooo!"

"What?" he said. "Shut up. No, I don't."

But why did he say that? He did like her. He asked her to dinner and took her to a restaurant called the Cheese Cellar, which his mom had recommended. He took the recommendation with his teeth clenched tight, hoping that his mother would say no more, and then tried to own the information as if it had not come from a maternal source. But then he had to ask her where it was.

After the Cheese Cellar, he took her to Bonsdorf's ice cream shop, and only after they had sat down at one of its refrigerated tabletops did he realize: this place, too, belonged to his mother's world, to his mother's time. She talked about "malteds" and "root beer floats" and other things from a hundred years ago. She talked sometimes about nice old Mr. Bonsdorf, but the Mr. Bonsdorf that ran the shop now was not the old Mr. Bonsdorf, but young Mr. Bonsdorf, the son, and he wasn't nice. He seemed to judge them unkindly from behind the counter, which he polished and polished with a stringy, holey towel. It was as if selling fudge and serving ice cream to the grubby kids who stole his candy canes were some purgatory to which he'd been assigned. People said he was mean because of his acne. The candy on the ancient table in the middle of the floor, meanwhile, looked like it had been unloaded from the back of his mother's very own time machine. It was like eating ice cream in a morgue—which he would have been happy to do, as long as Michelle came with him.

Michelle's mother, who had long ago put Michelle's cat to death, at least didn't bother them and they watched TV in the dark while the dog's tail swished against their legs. They watched and watched late into the night, breathing in the warm, dry odor of dog, the talcum on the dog, and the odor of the disused winter coats on the rack by the door. Leo thought and thought about the undiscovered country of the naked girl sitting next to him under those clothes, her female shape readily visible through the tight T-shirt and jeans, a shape that conformed more or less exactly to a preexisting ideal in his mind, but he sat there as if shot with curare. This happened perhaps five nights in a row, and each time when it got very very late—so late that they would both have to go to work in a few hours—each time when even the cable stations ran out of programming, he went to the door and, like a nineteenth-century gentleman, kissed her demurely on the mouth, then departed in his two-tone Plymouth Horizon love chariot. The gray vinyl on the dashboard had been cracked since Kathy Main had sat before it. (He'd hammered his fist on it.)

He pulled back the Foley catheter tray. The ventilator went kush, kush, kush. A series of beeps caused the anesthesiologist to touch the bank of lights and dials and the beeping stopped. The resident painted the skin with a sponge dripping yellow iodine, draped the blue polyurethane paper on top with the square hole in it, and taped Tegaderm onto the yellow skin and drew a dotted line on the Tegaderm with a purple Magic Marker. No one paid attention to that. Leo helped the scrub nurse open up his table. When the scrub nurse was all ready and the sterile light handles were all screwed on and the doctors all scrubbed and gowned, the resident came back to the purple dotted line across the yellow skin and traced the line with a scalpel so the skin parted and after a moment blood welled up along the line rather like tears welling a beat after hurt feelings (the other doctor mopped up the blood repeatedly with a lap pad) and the resident pulled the wound wider apart and when blubber appeared, he pulled apart the blubber, too (the other doctor zapped bleeders with the Bovie and said, "Cauterize from the top down so you can see what you're doing," because the blood ran from the top of the wound down), and each time the resident traced his scalpel down the seam it split wider than before. In every knife stroke you could see how sharp the scalpel was and how soft the body. A third doctor waited before the body on the table with white hands clasped low against his chest like a priest.

On the sixth or seventh night, she didn't let him give his demure kiss, but told him to go to his car and she'd meet him out there in a minute. Leo waited outside by his car in the street. He couldn't see any stars because a streetlight was shining right over him.

She came out fifteen minutes or so later, shivering and holding her elbows, and didn't speak to him.

"So?" he said.

"I have to go to sleep," she said, and yawned.

"Can I see you tomorrow?"

"I'm seeing some friends tomorrow."

"What about me? Aren't I your, uh, friend?"

"Yeah, Leo." Then she said bluntly, "I want you to know that I think of you as just a friend, okay?"

He did not allow himself to move. "Wait, do we really have to talk about this out here?"

"What is there to talk about?" she said.

But they went back to the den and the coatrack by the door and sat in front of the TV again. He said carefully, "And why do you think of me as only a friend?"

"Because we haven't even fooled around!"

So that's how it is? He was pissed, and he felt suddenly in his element. He put his arm around her. He kissed her with an open mouth, pushing hard against her so that his tongue was flat against her lips and he tasted her skin on his tongue and felt the fine hairs of her face on his lips. He rubbed her breasts on a wild guess, enjoying none of it, but feeling a little bit as he had on Space Mountain—*Hey, I can do roller coasters!*—and shortly thereafter he lovelessly plunged his hand into the front of her jeans. He felt nothing on his fingers before she stopped him, didn't even feel her underwear when he touched it, as if his hand were anesthetized.

Unconscious people just barely closed their eyes, as if they had just closed them for a moment, as if they were feeling something good somewhere distant in their bodies, like a foot massage. The lids on the old lady were almost translucent, too, like the lids of eyes on dead bird chicks that you saw in the grass in the spring, covered with flies; you could faintly see the blue bulbs inside.

The next night, he didn't wait at all. He kissed her with an open mouth and tasted her tongue with his mouth and thought of the cow tongues at the West Side Market. He wondered with each movement whether he had done as Josh Helpern had done or Steve Zenilman would do and he soon found that the old and churned saliva, hot on their faces, was somewhat stale and gross. Then, just as he grew bored with kissing, she dropped her hand down, grazing his chest as she did, and grabbed him with great sureness through his shorts. She kept her hand there all the way to the end, beyond the end in fact, and he apologized that he wouldn't be able to do it again just yet, because it seemed possible that other boys had been so virile as to do it twice in a row and perhaps that was what she expected of him.

Surgery was performed in the morning, Dr. Helpern said, because you weren't allowed to eat before it. That was called NPO after midnight. Nihil per orem. Maria undique et undique caelum. But one afternoon there was an emergency. A post-op patient was coming back to the OR, the surgeon said, and he was going to "reopen her."

"Why?" Leo said.

"To see what's going on," the surgeon said. He was the one who wore cowboy boots into the locker room and Hawaiian shirts and he had a long gray ponytail.

By the winter coats, long unused, in the little coatroom lit only by the streetlight at the end of the drive, they hugged so there was no space between them and they fit right together like two puzzle pieces meant for perfect apposition. He felt on his own chest the soft successive rise of hers against him, like the susurrant camber and retreat of waves on the sand. Her eyes were so alert and open and he was so close to them he could see splinters of topaz shining in her green irises. He supposed he must have been this close to another person's face before, perhaps when he was a child, perhaps when doing an Eskimo kiss, but he couldn't remember the last time he had looked so closely at another face, especially at that of a girl.

He'd entered a parallel universe, one where girls like Michelle gave away such gifts for free, a universe where the pleasure of perfect apposition was okay and free. It was just okay and there was nothing bad about it and no price. There was no evil waiting for him in the road, no red pupils and white irises in the backseat like two drops of rabbit blood on snow, no devil or broken glass, no maggots, no car accident, no fight even. There was nothing but the soft and divisible night air that withdrew before him no matter which way he turned. He could go anywhere. There was nothing to be afraid of and nothing on earth to stop him. He had blundered into the temple.

When they wheeled the patient in, she was yellow-gray and damp, eyes open but unseeing, hair matted like the hair on an Egyptian mummy. The mummy was breathing with great spasmodic gulps of air, her spine arching and mouth snapping open to the maximum excursion of her jaws as a great gust of air was consumed, then falling back to the gurney, her mouth nearly closed. A feeble little wheeze of escaped air would follow, billowing the ropes of white saliva that bridged her parted lips like spiderwebs. Then all was still. Her elbows were bent and her hands lifted slightly, fingers frozen in imprecation like the fingers of dead soldiers in history books. Then another breath would come that would rack her whole body, a spirit taking hold of her completely only to release her completely once again.

Now everyone was in a hurry. They scrubbed in a rush and when they entered and gowned themselves, she was naked with a row of five or six stitches down the front in fat plastic sheaths, puckering her abdomen like the seam of a football. The gray ponytail doctor didn't wait, but stepped up and snipped the sutures, then yanked them out with a needle holder. He tossed the instrument onto the scrub nurse's tray and began with his fingers to peel open the bloodless pink incision that had just begun to heal. It separated easily.

When the internal sutures were cut and yanked loose and the last layers prodded apart, a brown liquid rose up from the wound with a sewer stench. "Jesus," the surgeon said, and leaned backward. White intestines lay sunk in a bog of greenish-black water. He reached in and began quickly seizing up loops of bowel, hauling them up from the black water, searching the bowel as if looking for a leak in a hose, and dropping the searched loops back in. Everything that came out of the opaque foul water was gray and white. "She infarcted her entire fucking bowel," he said, then added loudly to the resident, "Just close her." His eyes met Leo's for a moment and he said, "Sorry, that's the way it is." Then he stepped back from the body and grabbed his gown by the front and ripped it off, popping the ties in the back and uncovering the palm trees on his Hawaiian shirt. He balled up the dirty gown and gloves and stuffed them in the waste bin, punched the plate that opened the OR barn doors, and left. The resident began to close the belly with a huge curved needle like a hook for a swordfish.

Leo went out into the hallway too. Dr. Helpern talked to the doctor with the ponytail there. Leo heard him say, "SMA occlusion."

The universe continued to make room for him in the most unexpected ways: Michelle's friend went to France with her parents and left Michelle the keys. They watered the plants in their wet clothes and kissed by the refrigerator, where a wedge of dull light slanted across the ladybug magnets and old grocery lists. He was not afraid of empty houses anymore.

They went upstairs.

"Did you see that angel with ivy all over it?"

"In the fountain."

"It was beautiful," he said. "I didn't know private homes had statuary like that." They had gone trespassing in the backyards of the country homes to the east, in the woods.

"'Statuary.' Who talks like that?"

"Don't make fun of me!"

"I'm appreciating you, silly."

"Sure you are. Sorry, the 'statue,' then. Wasn't it cool? I thought it was."

"I didn't really pay attention to it. I was trying to get you to take your clothes off and come in."

"I did. I stepped in the fountain."

"But in your clothes."

"Captain Change always swims in his clothes."

"I thought you were Aquaboy."

"He swims in his clothes too."

"Oh, he swims in his clothes, does he?"

She always seemed to want to laugh at him, and around her he was always saying things that were laughable. She didn't really like him, he thought. He had merely exhausted her of the energy to resist him all those nights at her house on the border of Warrensville.

He tugged once at the waist of her jeans and she lifted her hips and wriggled out of them. He walked his fingers over her disorienting body, starting with her panties. They didn't have a little silk bow at the top of them or lace like girls in *Playboy*. They were just plain white cotton. She complained that her underwear was a money issue.

When he'd once again mapped this foreign land by touch, and guided his fingers to their target by an inevitably crude stereotaxis of hard pokes and pinches (for he had not ever exactly seen her down there and her legs remained undiscussably closed), he commenced to try to please her, sustaining pressure on the hard and mobile rib of flesh so as not to lose his place in the darkness.

"Stop," she said. She grabbed his hand.

There was silence in the house, just the sound of the rain creeping down the shingles. He left the room, humiliated. At such moments he was weak and his will leaned downward with a love of dirt, like rain tempted down, down, down into a hole. Rainwater in gutters and drainpipes, seeking out the wormy bowels of the earth, or in rivers running down to the sea as if tempted by it, as if in a swoon.

She didn't come after him. He waited awhile longer so as not to forfeit absolutely all of his pride; then he went back into the bedroom.

"She's one of the winners." Meaning, the aged, because they had sur-vived, they had met and conquered every one of the eighty, ninety, a hundred years that went before. He saw a young man in the pre-op wait-ing area, maybe thirty or thirty-five. He looked well. His wife was there. She carried a huge shopping bag with all their bedding in it, a big soft white down comforter and a pillow with a lacy fringe, looked like it had come straight off their conjugal bed. He'll be acting funny after, the nurse said. He always acts funny, the wife said, pretending not to be scared. The man was in a wheelchair and every time they came to some auto-matic double doors, the man raised his hand up just as the transport guy touched the metal plate on the wall and the man said, "Use the Force, Luke," or "Open sesame," as if he'd caused the automatic doors to open by magic, and then he'd look around at the transport guy and at his wife and Leo, too, for approval of his joke. When they came to the last set of doors, his wife said, Can I stay with him through here? No, she couldn't, the transport guy said. And the man said he didn't see why he had to take off his wedding ring. And he said, I love you, and as the doors were closing, he said it again.

When he was fifteen, Leo had had surgery, when he broke his arm. They took away everything before it, your underwear, even your glasses, even a magazine, and then it was just you alone, and then they shaved him under the arm and he looked at his armpit and sud-denly remembered very clearly what it had been to be twelve years old. Then they covered you in paper and put in an IV and gave you something to make you sleepy and took away the last thing, which was you yourself.

I love you. The words had come of their own accord, tapping

on the inside of his skull, wanting to be heard, until he finally listened to them and said them aloud.

Dollar bills and coins from her work apron lay all over the bed. He wanted to tell her he'd pay for airplane tickets when college began in the fall, but she said she wouldn't talk about money today. She was brave like that. He held on to her tight with the coins cold on his naked back, and she said, "When will you know your phone number at school?" He would be going away soon. The cold swirling ironwork of the chair on his back—he remembered that. July. Behind his grandmother's empty house, shadows on the grass were cool undertoe, and many sunbursts hung high above them like day stars in the high canopy of the trees. He'd sat by himself while she swam and he watched her, and the chair tattooed cold arabesques onto the dermatomes of his wet warm back. He'd wanted to ask her, Are you a virgin? But he couldn't make himself say the words. Then they'd lain in the hammock and she didn't tell him, because he couldn't bring himself to ask. Go back to July and arabesques of ice.

"I can't be away from you," he said. So that was love. Not caring about anything or anybody else in the world. Falling. Falling.

6.

YALENSIS

What needs my Shakespeare for his honored bones
The labor of an age in piled stones?

—Milton

HE HAD KNOWN for some time it must be Harvard or Yale. Only deeds of that caliber were sufficient to redress the destruction of a life. But then he went to the Berlin dinner at Sammy's in the Flats with the lights on the factories out the window and up on the Detroit-Superior Viaduct and down on the Cuyahoga River, too, on a boat or two, shining through the dark windows at many depths of field like Christmas lights strung across the riverbanks. It was Bab Berlin's seventy-fifth birthday.

Leo's uncle Harvey was married to Laura's sister, Jenny. He was the eldest of the four Berlin brothers and the only one who'd stayed in Cleveland, a natural host, a pillar to his family; he was a champion toast-maker and inveterate crier.

"You've heard of the sins of the father being visited on the sons," he said into the microphone. "What the Bible doesn't tell

you is that the big asses of the fathers are visited on the sons."
Laughter came out of the tables with many different colors and
at many depths of field, like the lights over the river.

That was why they called the Berlin patriarch Bab: it was from
his army nickname, B.A.B., Big-Ass Berlin.

Despite their possibly big asses, however, and despite being
raised on the crooked brown river where the football and baseball teams always stumbled and fell like a deer on rolling stones,
and despite their descent from a race of shtetl dwarves—
despite even their congenital hearing loss, which began with
their mother's streak of white hair and trailed the next gener-
ations with incomplete penetrance—the Berlins were men of
strength. They'd fed on the flesh and milk of American cat-
tle, not Polish turnips, and were physically big and tall. They
were good swimmers and had followed Harvey to Yale—the
youngest played water polo. Harvey, like Leo's father, Isidore,
and his second father, Philip, had been of that first generation
of Jews to pioneer the Ivy League. Harvey had gone to Yale
without a precedent and established one for his brothers, just as
Isidore had done for his younger brother, Dennis, at Harvard,
just as Philip had done at Columbia. When Harvey's kids and
nephews and nieces were of age, they would presumably head
on up to Yale too.

Leo watched his uncle Harvey standing up at the microphone
before his father, Bab, and his younger brothers and his sons, and
Leo knew right then it would not be Harvard but Yale. To repair
a legacy that lay in ruins was no easier or harder, he reasoned,
than to start one from scratch. To restore his own fallen line, he'd
require in his person that same strength that Isidore and Harvey
proved they possessed when they founded a legacy from nothing. To use his legacy at Harvard would be to cheat and to lie to
himself and leave the question open of just how strong he was.

If he couldn't get into Yale without a legacy, then he figured he hadn't the strength of character to do much else required of him for restitution against his father's death. If he couldn't get into Yale, he might as well give up.

Father:

I will fulfill your promise.

I will avenge your death with my success. I will be the best that ever was, and you will look upon my deeds from Heaven. They are for you—you are not finished. You are not reduced to a few yellowed envelopes in a nurse's filing cabinet. Let me be your voice. I am you, I am you, I am you, I am you. I fight on for you here in the land of the living with all the strength that belongs to me. I am strong of body and mind. And all the adverse forces of the universe—ALL—will bow before me like sheaves of wheat in the dreams of Joseph.

I will be a "heavy hitter" like you were and you will hear the bugle call in the famous halls of the dead and you will be publicly, proudly vindicated, you will feel my love in all the hard work and battle I've done for you and you will love me with a father's proud love.

(What other purpose is there to life but to do great things, to create beauty, knowledge, and joy for all humankind forever, and with greatness to decimate mediocrity, and bend the stone will of the universe to the feeling sensate human will? Our will, Daddy.)

And you who are emblazoned on my heart will live on. My rivals have fortune and they don't know it: they live out their legacy of father and son, they have in their war chests their standard-issue ingot iron and javelin, and I am jealous as the bottom of the sea is jealous of the jewel lights on the waves. But bare hands can do more than mediocre iron when one acts with indissoluble will.

I represent our house alone now. But I can do it. I am touched by lightning.

I declare war on our rivals. To those who stand between me and that which you and I justly deserve: beware. Stand aside. I will reach into

your chests with my bare hands and rip out your hearts and eat them
and I swear to it by all I know and love.

I bring the barrow hailstorm; I wield the barrow lightning.

We will have our recompense and resurrect our legacy in a great des-
tiny, Daddy.

I take up your mantle now.

Even when you just visited Yale, you could see destinies and
legacies unfolding all around. There were societies, monuments,
secret tearooms, fabrics and shingles and stone that had long ago
exhausted their colors on the litany of passing years, and now
were muted, fine, august, and gray in self-remembrance; there
were windows that shone gold in autumn with the luster of centuries, polished oak tables in heroic, dim dining halls, and the
gloom and gloam of time upon every sunken stairstep and every
quiet courtyard. That was Yale: a great, grand triumphal legacy
of truth and beauty asail on the sea of the ages. He loved the idea
of Yale like he loved the Renaissance and the Enlightenment, but
even more in a way, since Yale was the door through which a
young living man like himself could pass in order to link hands
with the men of the Renaissance and the Enlightenment.

And he wanted more than anything to be a part of this
knighthood of enlightenment, to walk those halls and courtyards
beautiful as the church, with people inside as enlightened as
Voltaire. Surely, this monument to truth and beauty would see
and appreciate his love. For he was like them. True, he'd been
surprised by some pretty unintellectual types at Shaker Heights
High School who'd gotten into Yale in recent years, presumably
because of their extracurricular activities. And he had quit the
debate team, yes. And been offered the editor-in-chiefship of the
paper by the journalism teacher, Mrs. Bernstein, and had de-
clined in order to conserve his energies, the better to carp and

moan in the opinion pages. He'd not gone out for tennis or swimming (at which he naturally excelled) and while he'd been president of the class in seventh grade, in the eighth grade he'd chosen like Cal Coolidge not to run again, as the student council was a stupid popularity contest (which he was likely to lose now that the Woodbury kids had mixed in). He'd acted before his friends but never in a play, hadn't prepared for the annoying SAT for more than an afternoon, and hadn't shown his lifelike drawings to anyone. He'd long ago given up the boring, rote drills with that dangerous and disgusting trombone that was always a millimeter from knocking over a lamp or jabbing his dog in the spine, and the trombone teacher with his gray toupee slightly greenish as though he moisturized it with the drippings from a brass spit valve. But any sensible person would clearly see in those decisions his seriousness of purpose and his priorities in the great contest with death. Knowledge was all in that contest. Science was all. Art was all. Not student council! Not "Hot Cross Buns"!

He was tall and girls liked his face and he had tried, alone and with all his might, to understand the universe he was there to witness. He took no one's opinion for his own and without help figured everything out down to its rudimentary particles and underlying vectors, and though he didn't have great extracurricular activities, he had the most substantial proof of his talents and his devotion: his grades. He'd obtained the best possible grades on the actual work he'd done to educate himself, in direct competition with a wolf pack of the best new minds in northern Ohio. He had done the work and they had done the work. He feared them and they feared him. They had all tested themselves against the exact same problems, hard ones like Johannes Kepler had faced in his charts of the planets, and out of this melee came inevitable confidence, even to a conscientious boy so lacerated with doubts as Leo. He believed in the other young wolves and they believed in themselves; they believed in him and he believed in himself. He had emerged from the wolf pack a straight-A student (except for the Bs in gym, of course, fuck gym) in strictly Advanced Placement classes. Four semesters of AP math, two semesters of AP physics, four semesters of AP Latin, two of US history, two of modern European history, and four of English: A, A, A, A, A, A, A, A, A, A, A, A, A, A, A, A, A. His report cards were a bandolier full of As. Whatever else the rest of the wolf pack had done, there were very few who had done that, and he knew that because of his class rank! He had even set the curve on the final exam in one of the two semesters of AP calculus, even though he lived and breathed words, not numbers, and could barely calculate the tip at a restaurant. And his letters of recommendation would show how good he was, how tough, how brave, and how vicious the competition had been for those As. Or so he had to believe.

And so it was with a great sense of destiny and old apprehension, too, that Leo appeared before the Yale alumnus for his college interview.

It was when the Berlin Wall fell—before Michelle, before the spring, in November 1989, Shaker Heights, Ohio: by day, blazing white snow, cold; at night, snow melting off boots inside the door. His lungs were overfilled, his joints tight. The alumnus was a lawyer with white hair on the temples and a narrow face—a nice man, a man of rectitude with the sort of stout WASPish last name that could belong to a president: Eastman. His daughters went to Yale. Leo remembered the younger Eastman girl: dark hair and no makeup. An athlete. He didn't know about her grades.

Yalies were able to see what others failed to see, and they walked among others like calm and unassuming praetorians who could secure with their talents whatever they wanted. The crests on Mr. Eastman's blue Yale tie tantalized Leo like keyholes to the doors of a palace. Like the seal of the Order of St. Arbuthnot's Finger. Leo sipped from a glass of Coke by the warm hearth in the fine home, in the bright room of books in whitewashed bookcases, ice melting off his shoes by the door. Mr. Eastman said to Leo, "I expect you'll get in," and read one line aloud from Leo's college essay:

. . . Changes always carry for me some intimation of loss. . . .

Still cold in December. His early application was deferred, but a note arrived from Mr. Eastman that said, "I spoke to Ewell Bryant, the director of admissions for the Midwest area, and I feel sure you'll get in in April."

And all that winter and spring, Leo felt the key to the Order coming to him, Yale, coming from afar, like an angel drifting across the millennia to meet him and be his escort into the future.

Now, I am eighteen, a man. Now, you return to me, Daddy. I am tobacco in your pocket. I am your will, a circle you drew in the sand. I know you will come back to me.

When he left the Shaker Heights High School oval and pulled his Plymouth Horizon up the drive that day in spring, there were workmen on the roof, and his mom and his aunt didn't hear his car or even hear the door to the mudroom open or shut.

He climbed up the steep back steps as he usually did (because they were harder to climb than the ones in the front hall and proved the enduring strength of his knees) and dropped his backpack on his bed. He sat on the toilet for a while listening to the workmen talking in Polish just outside the bathroom window. He could hear them talking quite clearly and smelled the tar or whatever it was they were laying down on the roof, and he hoped they couldn't hear him or God forbid smell him farting and grunting and plopping. When he came down the front steps, he heard his mother and his aunt Jenny in the living room.

They talked on quietly as if they hadn't heard him. (Maybe they didn't hear him, or maybe the sounds of his feet on the staircase had been camouflaged by the sounds of the workmen on the roof or going for the tools in their truck.) His mom and his aunt Jenny were having one of those sororal conferences unique to them, talk of their families plaited with psychoanalysis and female empathy, a conference possible only between two daughters of a psychoanalyst who had themselves trained in the mental health field and had cinched themselves together in order to survive a series of premature deaths. Their words were quiet and logical and slightly wonky with analytic technical jargon, but also mixed with tears; they were like a pair of structural engineers crying over a bridge.

Leo froze when he heard the louder-than-normal sniffling. Shit: his grandmother must be dead.

"I'm not saying he won't care," Aunt Jenny was saying in her most calm and mollifying tone, "I'm just saying he'll be okay, because it's not really about this."

"I mean he *really* cares," his mother said.

Leo sat down on the stairs and his eyes dropped instinctively to the YALE letters at his breast.

"Nobody's to blame here, honey," his aunt Jenny said in that pacific voice that he didn't completely trust.

"Maybe it's a man thing," his mother said. "I didn't pay much attention to it, the applications and everything. I mean, who cares where you go to college?"

"This is his life."

"I know. I've never seen anyone plan like he does. From the

time Izzy died he knew what his future was supposed to be like. That was very relaxing to me, in a way. He didn't ask for any help with that part of life, he was just going somewhere all on his own, going after it relentlessly, like a heat-seeking missile. I couldn't have stopped him if I'd wanted to—not that I tried. It wasn't like he was planning to be a drug addict. He was planning to go to Yale and be a doctor. What mother stops a child from going to Yale and becoming a doctor? It's like with Leo he plans to impose his will on the world and on the future and make it turn out a certain way, and if it doesn't go exactly the way he planned, he considers it a referendum on him, and then he—I don't want to see him hurting is all. I just want him to be happy. I think he deserves to be as happy as anybody else. I look at other people's kids, and mostly they seem happy, they seem fine, and I think that's because they had two basically fine parents and Izzy wasn't fine, and I wasn't fine. I let him down. We let him down."

"Well, first of all, you did pretty well—I was there," Aunt Jenny said. "And second of all, I'm not sure other kids are as happy as you think. I get to hear in my work what they say when their social masks are off, and I can tell you, everybody has to struggle. Everybody has to struggle just with being a person."

"Well, that's true," his mother said.

"You know what I think: his thing with Harvard and Yale is an identification. It's an identification with Isidore instead of the opposite, and he'll have to figure it out. He thinks he wants to *be* Isidore, but what he really is, is just a son that wants his father back. He wants his father so he doesn't have to feel everything he feels about his father being dead. And he would have had to figure this out regardless of where he went to college."

Leo had heard enough. He almost left right then but then his mother began to say more about him and he couldn't stop himself from listening:

"That may be, but he hasn't figured it out yet," his mother said. "And he's like a keg of TNT. He's going to explode when he finds out. And in the end it always comes back to it being his fault. Like he should've done better, he should've known better, he should've been stronger. And then—"

Jesus, his mother was really worried about him. (She also knew him very well.)

"A conscience like that is what *makes* you into a powder keg," Aunt Jenny said. "It's what makes you driven to control everything, and to be the biggest and the best all the time. That's what you do when your conscience makes you feel infinitesimally small. He'll figure it out. It's up to him."

That was all he could take. It was easy for her to say, since she went to Yale! (God, was he totally fucking insane or what?) Leo went back up the stairs slowly and quietly and came back down stomping the steps as noisily as he could. He would show them he wasn't upset about not getting into Yale. He would act surprised, but not upset. He would have a sense of humor about it. There was still Harvard, after all, or if it came to that, Princeton. His high school career had not yet burst into outright flames, though there was a strong odor of scorch in the air now, he had to admit.

When he entered the living room his mom stood up and came toward him with red eyes and held out two thin envelopes. One was from Yale and the other was from Harvard. He saw the blue vein in the thin-looking naked wrist of the hand that held the envelopes, which were already open. Poor hand. Poor vein. The hand and the vein were the reason he'd wanted to get into Harvard and Yale in the first place, to make his mother happy and proud, like the mothers of people who went to Harvard and Yale, instead of defenseless and sad, to safeguard her from cancer and doom and mediocre human susceptibility, and buoy her with his lionhearted powers of flight and imagination.

"Jesus, I thought Grammy was dead," Leo said.

They didn't laugh. Aunt Jenny seemed to be looking at his sweatshirt with YALE at the breast. It occurred to him that he'd been wearing it compulsively in the last month, perhaps even every day, the same way that he used to like to wear the sea-green frayed surgical shirt that his uncle Ollie had given him when he was seven.

Harvard, too? He wanted to scream into somebody's face, anybody's face, *"I'll show you, you stupid fuckers!"* but instead he kept himself perfectly still.

It occurred to Leo that he shouldn't have written Philip's name down on his Harvard application. But it was too late now. Philip had adopted him and it had seemed wrong and ungrateful not to put him down in the space where it said: Father. But he should have just put his dead father down in that space to make it clear. He hadn't thought he needed the help of his father's legacy. He didn't *want* that help. How could they reject a kid who was first in his class (or would have been, had they weighted journalism the same as band)? *This would never have happened if his father had been alive.* All that outlining and memorizing and all those problem sets, all his "conceptualizations," as he called them, and all the furious exercise of his "integrative intelligence," his insatiable hunger for final answers and relentless pursuit of them, and all his savage battles for supremacy with Geetha Gurubhagavatula and John Posey De Polignac and Susan Fishman and the other AP wolf cubs on this most significant of all battlegrounds— knowledge of the real world—all of that would have paid off. He would be headed, if not to Yale, then at least to Harvard. Or he should have applied somewhere else he wanted to go besides Harvard, Yale, and Princeton. He should have ignored Philip and applied to Columbia and fulfilled his legacy there if he was going to use Philip's name on his applications.

"Well, there are children dying in Africa, for Christ's sake," Leo said, trying to sound nonchalant. But what he was really thinking was: *I don't care whether this is important in the grand scheme of things or whether I'm important in the grand scheme of things. The grand scheme of things doesn't give a shit about me or my mom and dad and my brother and I don't give a motherfucking shit about it. I don't care what I deserve. I don't give a fuck about Africa. I care about my father, my line, my greatness, and I will stamp my will on this mediocre earth whether anybody likes it or not, now get the fuck out of my way before I break your fucking skulls.* But he said again, "There are people dying right now, for no reason whatsoever, as we speak! People dying everywhere! What does a thing like this matter by comparison with that?"

He went to the junk drawer and got out a long pair of gold-plated scissors blotched with rust. Philip had once cut a ribbon with them in Tucson. Leo went upstairs then, and pulled off the sweatshirt that said YALE at the breast, pulled it off so fast that it pulled his Cleveland Indians T-shirt off with it, and he stabbed the sweatshirt and the T-shirt both with the gold scissors and stabbed them again. He shoved the rusty gold-plated scissors into the first stab wound and cut the YALE letters out of the sweatshirt. He tore the rectangle of cloth with the YALE letters in his teeth. Then he put the sweatshirt back on over his bare chest and the next day wore it to school, too, with the hole in it, right over his heart.

He said it was no big deal, even though his nipple was hanging out.

Mack didn't come to his graduation. He said he couldn't make it.

Leo said, "Why not?"

Mack said, "I'm busy, okay?"

"O-kay."

Mack seemed to think this was a moment for him to be brave

and stand up to some institutional evil in his life, though Leo didn't know what evil it was.

"You honestly should not be asking me that," Mack said. "Mom already asked me what I was doing. It's not your business what I'm doing and it's not her business, either. I don't want to be judged." All of a sudden Mack was breathing quick and shallow, and he swallowed once and then swallowed again. "You guys have this agenda, but I don't have to go along with it."

"Okay, Mack, okay."

"Don't act like it's abnormal for me not to go to your graduation. You always act like I'm abnormal and you have all the answers, and I'm sick of it."

"What would be abnormal about it? You went out with your friends instead of coming out for my birthday, so why would you come to this? I assume the Changs are having a cookout or something?"

"This is so typical of you. You and Mom are always imposing these expectations on me. You act like everybody normally goes to their brother's graduation. You don't know what's normal and you don't know what's abnormal about you and me."

"Okay, forget I asked, Mack," Leo said, and pulled at the hole in his Yale sweatshirt. "Do whatever you gotta do. Sorry I asked."

So he guessed Mack could just go and fuck himself. He supposed Mack had his own troubles, his own reckoning with the past and with the absences in his life. But Mack had not been interested in the least expression of brotherhood for years now and if Mack wished that he didn't have a brother, then Leo would fulfill that wish, he would in fact use Mack's skull like a basketball hoop and slam-dunk that fact right into it and Mack could just go fuck himself. *You think you're the only one who can handle an icicle? You think you don't need me? Well, let's see. You have no fucking idea what you're in for, Mack. You better wear your fucking mittens* around me from now on, 'cause if you're not there for me, then I'm not there for you, and it's going to be cold. Good luck in your grand future with all your devoted friends, I'm sure the Changs will take real good care of you through all your major life events, you dick.

And he tossed Mack away like a beloved old shirt that's finally shrunk too much or is torn beyond repair. He would expunge Mack even from his dreams if he could help it.

Summer came. Michelle came. Mack was gone.

At the very end of the summer, days before he'd be leaving to attend the University of Michigan, another letter from Yale arrived. That powder-blue "Y" with its just-so serifs like spandrels on a Gothic arch: he still loved it just a little. This letter was none too thick either, but its envelope was cut from paper of a heavier-than-usual weight. There was a crest on it too with a big red "X," which in Leo's case meant, he guessed, fuck you, go home. Above the big red "X," there was an image of an open book with Hebrew letters saying *Urim v'tumim*. As a child, he thought Yale was "Jewish"! But he didn't know what these letters meant as he looked at them now, and he felt quite sure they were not deployed in the way Jews had intended but rather had been stolen and repurposed like the art collections of the dead Jews of Vienna. The letter read:

Jack James
Dean of Admissions
Yale College

August 28, 1990

Dear Leonard Auberon:
  I write to inform you of the outcome of certain discussions be-

tween the Admissions Office of Yale College, the Office of the President of Yale University, and the Yale Alumni Association of Cleveland.

Over the summer, members of the Yale Alumni Association of Cleveland made it known first to my office and then to the President's office that they disagreed with our decision to reject your application to the College.

We receive applications from the finest students all over the world and take great pains to insure that our admissions process is fair, thorough, and accurate in its assessment of applicants' potential contributions to the Yale community. Your application was no exception. After careful consideration we concluded that you would not contribute to the Yale community in the manner of our best candidates and that a decision to accept would be contrary to our historic mission.

The Yale Alumni Association of Cleveland has no insight into the admissions process, let alone privileges in making admissions decisions, the sanctity of which, we believe, is critical to Yale's historic mission, which antedates the American Revolution. Under no circumstances is any Yale alumnus or any alumni association whatsoever empowered to make assurances regarding an applicant's candidacy with the Yale College admissions office.

That said, a member of the Yale Alumni Association of Cleveland has given us to understand that he made inappropriate contact with you, without the knowledge or consent of any personnel in the employ of the admissions office, in the form of a written communication, and that that communication could have been construed as an assurance. Therefore, in order to obviate any possibility of unfairness to you as a Yale applicant, the Office of the President has instructed me to offer you a place in the Yale class of 1994.

I extend this offer on behalf of my employer. In my tenure of over two decades at the Yale Office of Admissions, no student has *ever been admitted by the Office of the President. Consequently, I have tendered my resignation and will be assuming new duties as Master of the Branford residential college at Yale.*

Yours sincerely,
Jack James

It was the first Leo had heard of this.

He went to the bathroom to throw the letter away.

But when he stood in front of himself, and saw the blue polo shirt he had on, he thought of people dressing themselves in the morning: whatever my grievances with others, I agree to shop in the same stores as everybody else and put my socks and shirt on in the morning one foot, one arm at a time. He thought of his naïve and hopeful cooperation with everything he'd been asked to do in high school and how little fun he'd had, how much he hated his life, and he blew up:

"Are you fucking kidding, you sanctimonious *bootlicker*—"

"Leo?" his mother called out. Chair legs grunted on the kitchen floor. He met his mother in the dining room and waved the letter at her.

"This midget Jack James quit his fucking tacky, insignificant job to keep me out of Yale. *Me, Leo Auberon!*" He pounded his chest. "When I would give my life for Truth and Beauty! Have practically already given it! And they accepted whatsherface with the 1100 SAT—because she was a second-rate swimmer! She couldn't even *spell* 'hypocrite'!"

"What did you say?"

"I need to get out of here." Leo squeezed the letter in one fist and held it up as if watching Jack James's blood wring out of the letter and run down his forearm, then stormed past his mother into the kitchen. He mashed the letter between his palms and spiked it into the kitchen garbage can, which, he noticed for the first time in years, was an old diaper pail with the outlines of a teddy bear on it, stamped into the plastic.

"I look stupid?" he yelled down into the garbage can. "I look like a fool spiking a ball of Yale stationery? Because the ball is so lightweight and made a little pathetic puny rattle in the bottom of the trash? Yeah? Well, watch this!"

He went to the mudroom and took the Yale "Blue Book" off the lid of the bin full of boots and gloves, where the book had sat since last spring—it left behind a white rectangle in the dust. He opened the course guide to savor one last time all its delicious course titles printed in that Yale font of refined serifs, and pulled an aluminum baseball bat from the heap of sports equipment. The door to the yard stuck in the muggy August heat and when it opened it made a sound like a live branch ripped from a tree.

When he was standing in the grass, he tossed the Blue Book into the air and chopped at it with the aluminum bat. The book dropped noiselessly onto the grass. He tossed the course guide up again and leveled his swing and clipped the book but it just spun in place and then flopped on the grass again more or less intact. He tossed it up a third time and that time he nailed it right in the spine with his bat, and the pages of the Blue Book sprayed across the yard like flames from a flamethrower.

(This was probably what Jack James meant about not contributing in the right manner.)

"That's right!" Leo shouted. "I'm a nutcase!" He thought of Poppy Bush pounding his glove at second base or whatever position he played. "Hurray for dear old Eli, dear old Eli! Hear, hear!"

It took a while for his heart rate to return to normal. He peeled open the sticky door to the house and wiped his face off with a wet paper towel.

He sat down on the couch, feeling indecent and sweaty in the cold pure air of the house, and he called up his uncle Harvey, who had gone to Yale.

He told it like this: here's a wacky thing that happened today. Uncle Harvey listened and then there was a pause.

"Well, are you going to consider it?" Harvey said.

Leo laughed. "Of course not. I already threw the letter in the garbage."

"I think you should consider it."

He was not about to consider it.

He was not.

But that night buildings and strange landscapes occupied his mind. He saw Harkness Tower black with dusk, many-steepled with striving ornaments like the missiles on a ship flying heavenward, and he heard its lovely bells with their cold metal tones, each one different like colors assorted on an autumn day. He saw dark stained glass divided by muntins delicate as dark winter branches dividing a Connecticut dusk. He smelled the chimney smoke floating over the unlit courtyard. Michigan's clock tower had hardly any ornament. Its buildings were giant and modular, pharaoh tombs drenched in freezing sunshine. They were public works, Himalaya-sized post offices, train stations that dwarfed their own trees.

Grief: never what it is, an envelope that used to hold airplane tickets.

Half an hour before he had to get up. An unwelcome arc of light lit the wall and the bureau. They had no shades or curtains, as though they lived in a cavern, but the cavern was a century-old stone Tudor gatehouse with battlements on top and the naked window looked onto the blood-tinted stone of the Yale History of Art building. The room smelled of the cologne and shaving cream on the bureau under the window, fresh, like a bathroom after a shower. Reaching his hands out of windows whose sashes were barely opened: a dream. He was wrested from its dilatory time-flow.

Soon Corey, Leo's roommate, would leap up from the lower bunk with undepressive brio, then go to the cassette deck, which was the first place the sun alit every morning, and he'd slap a tape in and stride on to the bathroom, prongs of sleep-matted hair nodding like the leaves of a plant (Corey was the only male he'd ever known to use hairspray, but then Leo's friends were the sort who watched *V: The Final Battle* on New Year's Eve). Seven-thirty was coming down like a train. Leo's heart bumped hard against his ribs, he squirmed in the rugae of his upset sheets, and he thought of the miles of ugly highway and empty airspace between New Haven and home, between New Haven and Ann Arbor, where Michelle was now marching around campus on her work-study job, unhappily stapling posters on bulletin boards, or sleeping, posters under her bed. He kept a portrait she'd made of herself behind the bureau and when he was alone he held it sometimes in his lap and stared at it.

It was a Tuesday. There would be standard enthalpies of reaction in the chemistry class in Frankenstein's castle up on the hill, Descartes in the chapel with stained glass, and *Waiting for Godot* around the corner in Linsly-Chittenden with the mummified old professor with sagging male breasts. A rock, a tree, nothingness.

In the Vanderbilt courtyard a fusillade of cold rain drubbed the cobblestones. He had no umbrella.

The Yale grounds crew were hauling trash bags out of the Dumpsters under the archway; their blue Yale garbage truck beeped and beeped. Yale, Yale, Yale. The name was everywhere on campus, name-branding everything, the garbage trucks, the blue uniforms of the dining hall servers, the campus police. Nothing common and generic, everything *Yale*.

He passed through the arch onto Old Campus. The arch was supposed to be on the other side; someone had dug the foundation backward and they'd had to build Vanderbilt Hall with its back turned to the rest of the school. He turned around to look at Vanderbilt's steep fortress wall, from which prep school assholes launched water balloons at you as you crossed the Old Campus green to Battell Chapel on Yom Kippur, dressed up in your blue blazer and striped tie, one of two in your closet, both of which Philip had bought for him at the Peer Gordon men's store at Fairmount Circle.

But there he was, where he had dreamed of being, Yale-Valhalla, hall of the slain warriors, the place where he might have knelt beside his father's ghost and drunk the bright-green mead from the bowls at Mory's. He wasn't good enough, they said, but he went to Yale anyway, to the land of giants, so high above the rest of the mortal world that the blood turned blue and all the squirrels grew gray-blue coats, and even in summer the ghost squirrels skittered across dead leaves and up the bark of gray trees. Yale's leaf-strewn arches opened onto a monkish quiet and the halls of its colleges a monkish dim light. Future presidents and information barons walked the stones, sorting themselves according to suit and rank and playing practical jokes on outsiders. It was not meant for him in any way; the blue fifty-foot-long hundred-thousand-dollar Persian rug stretched in the foyer outside the Berkeley dining hall seemed to reject his footsteps. (It had probably been stolen directly from the Ottomans by Elihu Yale but like an admissions officer had by now come to lie at Yale's feet with servility, complacency, pride. *I would not let just any feet tread and mash my face, for I am a Yale rug, and only Yalies may tread and mash my face with their stank, gum-tarred shoes, because it is Yale stank, and Yale gum.*) The dining hall was still and dim behind the glass with a World War I plaque on the wall to honor the slain Yalies of Berkeley College, and below it, on an antique sideboard, there were sterling coffeepots polished to mirrors, and the master of the college, the professor of French history who was so annoyed with him when he said he wanted to transfer to Michigan, seated there beside the undergrads who had really gotten in, their elbows reflected in the dark lacquer of the tables, all dwarfed by soaring stone and chandeliers. There was never anyone in the foyer—only someone talking quietly on the phone in the dimly lit alcove with the pay phone. No one played the grand piano.

He thought of his father at Harvard, in Cambridge. He thought of it in winter. On a winter night with five inches of slush in the streets, his father would buy his books in the warm light of the bookstore, stacked to the ceiling with Henry James and Marcel Proust, unread novels as warm and long as hours in the L and B at Yale. The faces before the shelves would glow yellow over the table lamps, and those outside in the cold slush would envy them. They'd stop, even, and peer in through the snow sifting down the latticed windows from the cold lead sky.

His father's name was typewritten in places, in the mailroom, at the registrar, on letters from the dean with a Harvard crest stamped in the corner. In his mind, he saw his father's mail in the mailbox with the official letters: I-S-I-D-O-R-E A-U-B-E-R-O-N.

At Yale, all the names of the freshmen were typewritten in their mailbox windows, except Leo's, which was handwritten.

He had failed his father.

Leo sat in cold sunlight in the huge granite quadrangle outside the Beinecke Rare Book library. Its 250 slabs of Vermont marble were white on the outside, but within, where the stone filtered the light that fell on the written treasures of the world, the marble glowed with veins of perfect gold (other frequencies of the visible spectrum, regretfully, were turned away). "How is my second mix coming?" he wrote. Michelle had given him a mix of her favorite music and used a Miró reproduction as the album cover for the cassette. She'd probably cut the picture from a library book, but he didn't want to know. "It takes years to find the nerve to be apart from what you've done, to find the truth inside yourself, and not depend on anyone. . . ." That was her favorite song.

In the afternoons, on his black Panasonic CD player, he played Squeeze, which she'd introduced to him along with the Cure and the Smiths and other girl music, and he looked out the window of the common room at the blood-tinted stone of the History of Art building. Michelle was in the art school at Michigan. She said the shadows on her lithograph were meant to interact. The arc of the shadow of the bench enclosed the shadow of the girl.

Every night, he sat in the hall, away from his roommates with the phone hot on his ear and the pulling green phone cord tethering him to the base of the closed door.

"What's up, freak?" she said, happy, chewing. "I'm eating Reese's, sorry."

"Help," he said.

She swallowed, and she said, "No, no, no. Noooooo."

Then he would wander upstairs into the dim feminine lair of the Asian girls, green-and-blue paisley sheets draped over futons and hung up on the wall, posters of the Cure and Morrissey, Enya playing while they studied equilibrium constants. Or he'd go study and quickly fall asleep in the L and B, where identical green leather chairs lined every wall (having passed from cow to chair without ever leaving the herd), their solid bones nailed with tarnished copper. The students read and slept in the chairs with their feet up on the wooden shelves, toes of their socks against the spines of the books. He admired, feared, hated every soul in the room. Corey said he was a misanthrope. Well, he had always been. He had failed in pursuit of a great destiny.

Corey said there was an undergrad production of *Hamlet,* and a girl in their doorway in Vanderbilt was acting in it. Corey was always on his way someplace. He never sat still, and he always invited Leo to come along. They went to the play on the night that the ground war began in Kuwait. They'd seen the bombs glowing green over Baghdad on Corey's antenna TV. "Here I am all safe and sound in New Haven," Leo said, "while they're fighting a war."

"Uh, safe and sound? In *New Haven?*" Corey said. "Those girls in Durfee got a bullet hole in their ceiling."

"Hang on," Leo said, "I see someone."

"Leo!" the Hillel rabbi called out. It was strange to hear anyone call his name. The chances of it were low anywhere in the entire city of New Haven. "Hey, Leo!"

Leo stood as the rabbi came over to him. The rabbi grabbed him by both shoulders.

"What are you doing here?" Leo said.

"What am I doing here? What are *you* doing here? You should be in the cast!"

"Which part?" Leo said.

"What do you mean, which part? Hamlet!"

The rabbi had gone to Yale a long time ago with his uncle Harvey. Leo liked the rabbi. For a rabbi, he was very undoctrinaire. They went for walks sometimes and Leo had told him about the letter from Jack James, and the rabbi said Jack James was an old drunk. On one of their walks, when a homeless person asked for money, the rabbi had stopped and emptied his pockets of change, and then shrugged and said, "Sometimes I give and sometimes I don't."

"I'll get the key to that tearoom for you!" the rabbi said, and pointed at Leo as he turned and went back to his seat.

Leo sat down again.

"I don't know why he always calls me," Leo said, embarrassed.

"I think he thinks you're going to kill yourself," Corey said, and laughed. He often laughed at tragic things.

The play began. Hamlet wore a black turtleneck and sat on a black cube. The black cube sat on an empty, dusty black dance floor. When the ghost of King Hamlet entered, they lit the actor's face from below with a green filter, and a cool chalk-smelling mist slunk over the black floor from pails of dry ice. The actors spoke their lines flawlessly, and in scenes of high dudgeon they tore at their Renaissance costumes, their feet drummed the stage, their spittle seemed to catch fire as it sprayed across the stage lights. It was the best performance of Shakespeare Leo had ever seen.

The faintest inklings of rebellion in his heart. Shakespeare's son Hamnet died in his cocoon at eleven years. That is dying intestate, with one's will folded against the breast like flightless wings.

And the next day in Yale Station, the freshman mailroom in the basement of Wright Hall, Leo ran into the kid who played Laertes. The kid had had a nonspeaking part in the movie *Dead Poets Society.* Laertes had big bright blue eyes, and an inverted pyramid of blond hair just like a *Doonesbury* character.

"I saw you in *Hamlet,*" Leo said. "That sword fight was amazing. How did you do that? Was it improvised?"

Laertes gave a false and dramatic laugh, then cut his face dead, and said, "Yes, all improvised." Then he suddenly looked bored. "I'm fucking with you," he said. He stared at Leo, and Leo felt his mind very slow in tracking the changes of this quick-witted sarcasm.

The performance had been strong. The actor was mentally

strong. Was confidence the same as strength? People hated weakness because it made them feel guilty. Laertes looked hateful. *Why the fuck are you staring at me?* Perhaps they would fight.

"Big guy?" Laertes said, and pointed at Leo. "You're standing in front of my mailbox."

Just the week before, Corey had said, "Is nothing ever trivial to you?"

"I concede," Leo said, "that trivia is a theoretical possibility."

"But not a real phenomenon?" Corey had said.

"Life is a battle royale," Leo said. "Here, at least."

"Here? Where? Yale?"

"Earth."

Couldn't you just say "Thank you," Laertes? Is that too much to ask, Laertes? Laertes evidently liked himself quite a bit. And why not? He was in fact a good actor and a quick wit and he'd gotten into Yale and been in a movie and his prospects looked mighty good. He would probably be a person of some importance, if not substance, given his talents. He was already famous, wasn't he? But couldn't he—*shouldn't he*—have assumed he'd been standing before an equal? Or perhaps someone much greater than he—undoubtedly in substance—but perhaps in importance as well? Leo had paid Laertes a compliment and Laertes had condescended to him. He wished to say to this complacency and arrogance:

Laertes, with your fatuous view of the future—life is a battle royale. And I will win. Let's meet again before these same mailboxes in twenty years and draw our swords once more. If I am still alive.

But anything he said to Laertes seemed artificial, because at heart he knew that he only twisted and turned to tell himself he was good when he felt he wasn't, and the only sort of person who feels he's no good has a broken will and is therefore, in fact, no good. Yale had broken his will. Laertes was a winner and he was a loser.

Back at Vanderbilt, Leo went into his room and shut the door and beat on the door with his fists. He ripped Corey's plastic hooks off the door, spilling all the ties on the floor.

His roommate from Sri Lanka knocked on the door. "Leo? What's the matter?"

"The matter is that Yale is complete bullshit," Leo said. "The matter is that this place isn't a training ground, it's a finishing school, and it's not for the great talents of the future, it's for the *children* of the great talents of the *past!*" He said it, and he almost believed it. But it didn't do anything for that pernicious sense of failure that had dogged him since the previous spring.

"Are you going to go on again about Yale?"

College, and hence his entire life, was turning out to be a disaster. He had even shoved Michelle in a restaurant, and gone to see a psychiatrist, who was always late for their appointments and never talked about anything of relevance: only about conscience, when all that mattered was whether he was in fact any good or was worthless like the dean of admissions had said.

After Corey's birthday, Leo tried to begin again. And in truth, Leo and Corey had got along quite well. When Leo was sick, Corey brought him soup and Gatorade; on Corey's birthday, Leo wrote a note to apologize for the broken tie rack and gave Corey a red-and-brown striped tie (Corey was too truthful to say he liked it); and toward the end of the winter, when there was a huge snowstorm, Corey announced that they were going to get drunk and go to the Berkeley Screw Your Roommate Dance. Before the dance they read each other Trivial Pursuit questions and did a shot each time they got one wrong.

"How many eyes does an oyster have?" Corey said.

Leo was drunk by the end of the first card.

Wind lacerated the Old Campus snowdrifts, scoured and sculpted the snow in long rifts and canyons. Brilliant dark swords of ice hung from the gutters in darkness.

At the dance they drank watery beer. The girl was plain-looking, but funny, and he might have kissed her, but all he wanted was to go to Ann Arbor, to the South Quad dorm with its long institutional halls and stereo music and the sound of anonymous hair dryers and the smell of girls' shampoo. In South Quad, the football players pulled the fire alarms every single Friday and Saturday night, and every single Friday and Saturday night, the fire department would come and the RAs really made everyone evacuate their rooms and they all stood in the freezing vestibules and laughed about it and one time when he was staying there in Michelle's room, everyone started whistling the theme to *The Bridge on the River Kwai.*

At the end of the dance, Leo drank all the half-empty water glasses at the table, but he couldn't uncross his eyes.

When they returned to the snow field and the dark sea winds blasting against the church stone, he screamed. "Fuck you!" he screamed at the hanging swords of ice and the lampposts shining on the frigid beetle-back of the ice. A window slid open far across Old Campus and a voice faintly shouted back: "Fuck *you!*" In the common room, Leo kicked over the chair that sat before the ancient fireplace.

"Well, if that's how you hold your liquor," Corey said, "I see why you didn't want to drink," and he pulled off his tie. Leo couldn't help it; he was filled with admiration for his friend, the drunk Jewish genius of Nashville.

The cold air grew damp, the streets wet with melted ice. He hated everyone; he hated himself. Leo crossed Old Campus for the cocktail party, looking up at the deaf stone facades and ivy. Instead of victory, his father looked down at him and saw a failure who couldn't get into Yale and then, worse, humiliated himself with the most petty, ridiculous, broken-willed, and unmanly behavior. It seemed as though things had gone down a bad road, gone very far, and this was a last chance to make it work. The air was chilly and bright, and the grass was growing again. He knew a few people who would be there. Their names were Champion Harkness Killingworth, George Herbert Walker Bush, Fighting Bantam of the Army, Michael Gupta, Michael Chang, Michael Schwartz, Michael Ajayi, William Goodenough Pearse, Kenneth "Brownie" Brownridge-Brown, King Richard II, Winslow Nellius Pubert Potchcontrol Groton, and Dunster Neaves Cushing Lenonrind Bottlebook Scrambledeggs Milk Vaginahorn.

The room was packed with Yale boys in blue blazers drinking vodka and cranberry juice. Tall windows lit up the conspicuous dust whirling all around them while they stayed put in their blazers. The senior swimming star was there. Why would a straight male senior hang around a bunch of freshmen unless he was looking for girls? There were no girls here. Was he actually networking? He sang not just for a singing group, but for the *Whiffenpoofs*. (Under other circumstances he might have found it endearingly earnest that a school prized its singing groups more than its fraternities, and that the gemstone among them was something called in all seriousness the fucking Whiffenpoofs.) Champion Killingworth did not remember him. But another upperclassman whom he sort of knew, who had gone to his high school, invited him to play Ultimate Frisbee (Yalies loved Ultimate Frisbee). He said no thanks and left.

He went out onto Old Campus and around the Battell Chapel flowerbeds, where the daffodils were already poking through, then to College Street. He headed north, away.

Winter was ending and the days getting longer, but it smelled like fall and brown leaves were glued to the curb. The bright, heatless light caused him a shiver. He had walked past the giant cemetery four days a week on his way to Science Hill but he'd never been inside. He paced over the cracked sidewalk toward Prospect Street.

He stopped and pulled out his appointment book. To do:

—call Michelle
—mail withdrawal letter to registrar
—read V. Woolf
—pass before the indifferent gaze of those who will dis-
    miss you because of momentary reticence
—lament

He crossed the street and from there he could see the arch over the entrance to the Grove Street Cemetery. He passed his psychology professor, wearing sunglasses, probably going to measure whether people who are shown pictures of dogs remember dogs better than cats. Then that would be called the Dog Remembrance Effect. But it should be called the Waste of Grant Money Effect. What a fucking idiot.

Michelle had come for the last time. Leo's next trip to the New Haven airport would be to fly home to Cleveland. There were only two sliding doors at the airport and the one that led to the tarmac made a sound of tortured, dry ball bearings. Then you waited and you heard the turbines make a *yeeeen* sound in a high-pitched crescendo from the runway. Then the plane taking off, and the thunderclaps galloping up into the air and away. Then she was gone.

At the end of the summer, before college began, when everyone was disappearing, when time was flowing over a cliff like a waterfall, Michelle and Leo had sat in front of her mother's house on the small and overgrown lawn. Michelle couldn't find the easel she had used in high school.

"I can't believe it's over already," Leo had said. "Almost time to leave for good."

"I feel like it was summer for a year," Michelle said. "God, I missed a weekend shift just to come get the stupid easel." Michelle said her mother saved all her old school stuff, especially paintings and drawings. Michelle's sketches from fourth grade were still up on the refrigerator: precise, realistic renderings, in No. 2 Faber-Castell school-supply pencil it looked like, of a stuffed finch from the spooky taxidermy rooms in the Museum of Natural History. But her mother had chucked the easel, just like she'd put Michelle's cat to sleep. She was crazy, Michelle said. Michelle's room was apparently all redone too, the bed moved out, the wallpaper stripped. Leo had only seen the room once or twice because Michelle said it was too messy to let him inside.

"What happens when we die, do you think?" he'd asked her.

"Nothing. We disappear."

"That's it?"

"Yep."

"But you don't want to talk about this," he'd said.

"Nope," she'd said. "Be happy, Leo."

Then he had cried.

"Do you have the time? Do you have the time?" An old woman with crooked teeth and unwashed hair, humped over on a New Haven mailbox, wheezing, exhausted. Leo stared at his cheap Swatch and felt he couldn't read it, some anxiety attack he always got when people asked him the time.

"Five thirty-five," he said finally. *Out of my brain on the five-fifteen....*

He began to pull the letter to the Yale registrar out of his backpack, but the exhausted woman stayed slumped over the mailbox there, wheezing away. He put the letter in the backpack again.

It was the end of something. The new ideas of spring in the air seemed to refer backward, not forward, to springtimes gone and long ago. A beginning was an ending. Ends of summers. In the dining room with the pine table the size of a yacht in the house by the ocean at Amagansett that Philip had bought, there was a ship's clock that ran fast, an heirloom inherited from his dead grandfather and namesake Leo Neuwalder. Dinging ceaselessly and advancing too fast, like life, charming and jingling with mini-knells, announcing, "Time is running out." Marking time with dings just audible in every room of the house.

The last summer was gone. How he had feared the end of their vacation in Amagansett! Fog all the way down the beach, gray day, coolish, glasses misting and unmisting, terns flapping, skimming low over the waves, fishing. "I think you could catch a fish now if you tried," Leo said. He remembered saying it and thinking, *This moment will soon be long gone,* and now it was. Few umbrellas. Gray houses embanked behind a hundred yards of dune grass, and windows in the houses that were mirrors full of ocean sky.

He and his cousins walked down the long pebble-strewn drive across the street to get to the beach—cars had cleared the pebbles from under the paths of the tires so two strips of gray-black pavement showed through. A papyrus-brown hive of wasps hung in the tree along the road. The weather was always hot when you walked there. It never rained on that road. Because you were going to the beach and would not have gone if it had been raining. They passed through a verdant tunnel behind a hedge. Prickers grew up in the path after Philip's cousin, another Zajac, another builder, who owned the house beside the path, separated from his wife. The tunnel opened out from under a tree limb to the path through the dunes. There was a secluded pool there that no one ever seemed to use. There was a cast-iron statue of an eagle on a pedestal rising somewhere out of the green-black brush. The sedge tickled the ankles as you walked down. Then you dropped folded chairs in the sand.

Face on the sand, on the plain of miniature bright dunes, where derelict skate cases and crab claws lay half-embedded, crab exoskeletons dead but with a lilac bloom and shiny like the skin of an eggplant. He'd invented his own aphorisms one day on the beach, like this:

"Hot Cross Buns" is an obscene song and should not be left out of any porno.

—*Jack James*

His brother and half of his cousins and Aunt Anne and Uncle Ollie left three days early.

The door to the porch hall hung open, and the lights in the rooms off the porch were out. It was quiet in the house. Leo won at Boggle, Uncle Harvey was mad, Leo was nervous to have made his uncle mad. The unused darkness from the living room turned the dining room half-dark. The CD player played Peter, Paul, and Mary. *If you miss the train I'm on, you will know that I am gone. . . .* The music was like looking at the picture of his young dead father at Harvard in the red jute shirt or one of Aunt Jenny at Yale—the picture in the navy peacoat on York Street in New Haven. The music was like a hot day on the campus of Yale outside the building with the classroom of cracked plaster and latticed glass all cracked, the building by the private tearoom that the rabbi was going to get him into. At Thanksgiving Leo had told Uncle Harvey that he'd made friends with the rabbi and that had pleased his uncle, but when he said that the rabbi hated Yale when he was a student there, the light in Uncle Harvey's big hale face dimmed a little.

He could remember very distinctly when half the group left before he did at the end of the summer. He had trudged alone to his bedroom then. Mack's bed was empty, still unmade. He felt deserted, sorrowful, hopeless. Afraid of insanity, like some evil hallucination would divorce itself from the world of dreams and burst forth into the room, because the world wasn't making much sense, the world where we die.

On the last night, the smaller group, a huddle of survivors, sat together on the deck. In the vaporous darkness above, a few stars proved they existed, then disappeared. Philip carried out glasses of wine on a tray and pea pods with black sesame seeds. Leo tried to be festive and lit a cigar, which was slightly embarrassing to do with his elders. The air was too cold to sit out. The wood under his bare feet was damp, and Leo felt rotten, afraid of being laughed at, and he said someone should find out what "bad chemicals" were in the pool. Didn't anyone care what the "bad chemicals" were? Uncle Harvey said, "I'll tell you what, Leo. I'll give you the number, and you call and find out about it."

Too much in his thoughts—he'd step in some real New Haven dogshit if he wasn't careful. Someone cried out and Leo looked up. Ahead on the sidewalk a boy on a skateboard almost ran into a man pushing a baby stroller.

Accidents killed people. At the ski resort, the year he'd broken his arm, the woman who wiped out on the slope knocked herself unconscious, skiing; then she fell and instantly stopped moving, lay crumpled on the snow. Took some time for it to sink in that she was really hurt. Her husband crouched beside her, tentatively dabbing blood from her nose. Leo was on the lift, floating high above among sparse snowflakes, moving ever so slowly as in a dream. The gears of the slowly passing towers tugged the high cables with the smallest of squeaks as they turned, a muted chirping in the snow-hushed air like the sound of Swiss clocks. The tall white steel arose from pure-white snowdrifts.

Some people shouted: "Don't move her!" A child in a puffy green snowsuit lifted mittens to his face. In the lodge later that day, thawing skiers with matted hair and rosy cold-scalded cheeks advanced over the wet wood toward their hot chocolate in an atmosphere of vaguely sweaty woodsmoke, taking giant clomping steps in stiff ski boots. The kids who'd been behind Leo on the lift turned up, the kind of coarse children he'd encountered everywhere, and he heard one of them say, "Bam, she totally wiped out. Ha ha ha, and the little kid was cryin', 'I want my mommy, wah, wah, wah!' Ha ha ha!" Never found out what happened to her.

Watch for dogshit. Look out. Listen. A Rasta man on the street corner shook the change in his Styrofoam cup. Photocopied flyers for the endless Yale clubs papered over the building behind him and sidewalk beneath him. The flyers were taped to the sidewalks, to the doors on the buildings, to kiosks around the campus. Their stapled corners twitched by the tarnished brass doorknob on the locked, windy door. "Some change, man," he said to Leo. "How 'bout you give me some change. I don't got nothin' and you got somethin'. Oh, I see, at Yale what you got don't matter, huh, schoolboy, 'cause you ain't a material guy, you a liberal Michael Dukakis motherfucker, huh. Hey, you, how 'bout you give me some change." Falsely accused: he was not one of them, a Yalie.

Chilly. Leo stopped by a low brick wall and yanked at his tie until it slithered through his button-down collar. He took from his bag the old eviscerated Yale sweatshirt—the sweatshirt with the frayed hole at the breast—and pulled it down over his head.

He could still hear the bum shouting behind him, down the street. "You don't got to worry 'bout no kinda AIDS an' shit like that, I got to worry 'bout AIDS. 'Bout pneumonia! 'Bout my people. Come on now, big up Yale!"

Leo could see a short way into the cemetery. Nobody in sight there. On the arch, letters. THE DEAD SHALL BE RAISED.

The sand on the street crunched under his shoes like the bones of birds—a bit of ocean beach orphaned on the cold New Haven cobblestone. The beach and the long grasses shining on the dune. A full moon over trees, with the faint lunar seas embossed on the moon like a president's face on a coin, and the moon a silver seal on the sky. Dark sky, dark sea by night, stars rolling deep on the face of the sea like dust motes in eddies of sun. By day some days the sea refuses to be lit. Deep, impenetrable blue or even gray. Leo had found the ocean in a tub. He walked down the beach alone. *Do I even leave footprints at all?* Uncle Harvey's thick body stooped, dripping saltwater from his stubbly chin as he searched the cooler for a plum. Uncle Harvey sank down into a folding chair from which he watched the boys in the waves and bit into the fruit, teeth popping the wine-red water-beaded skin. Leo's uncle had gone to Yale, given Leo a first Yale sweatshirt in elementary school days, the treasured one with the bulldog on the front. When he got home he would cut the sweatshirt to ribbons with the rusted gold scissors. What had he done with it? It was in the bottom of a drawer now. Long ago, he'd made an effigy out of it, a man. Stuffed it with old towels and tucked it into some stuffed jeans. Folded some rags into an old undershirt for the head. It started with the Harvard sweatshirt. The housekeeper gave him an old wig stand to play with and he'd tucked it through the neck hole. A joke, right? *That's a joke to play with a wig stand is all.*

Uncle Harvey was a lawyer. He taught Leo to bodysurf and

showed him which was a good wave to take. He assessed the waves with something like jurisprudence, all the great intelligence that was in his mind. "That's chop," he would say, rejecting a wave, elbows lifted above the windy water, thumbs hooked upward, advancing with pivoting shoulders through the chest-high surf. *It's a five o'clock world when the whistle blows, no one's got a piece of my time.* He was the first one that Leo and Mack had looked to to be their dad.

There were two uncles from the old days, before Philip came. Uncle Harvey and Uncle Ollie. Uncle Ollie and Leo fished together in the Atlantic. Together they caught twenty blues and Leo caught one mackerel, what he had been hoping for, one special speckle-backed fish among all the snappers. "My boy, you got yourself a fine-looking fish," his uncle said, looking out over the fading light on the salt marsh and reeling in line. Ollie wore an old-style Red Sox cap that was too small and sat on top of his head because he liked to steal his sons' hats. He wiped the fish scales on his jeans and rooted in the brown grocery bag he'd brought, neatly rolled so he could grip it in one hand and the tackle box and rods in the other. He took a big lusty bite of the pastrami sandwich Aunt Anne had packed. Aunt Anne was a Shakespeare scholar who packed lunches. The air smelled like sea salt. The sunburned waves sloshed into the dock piles where the gulls stood with beaks facing into the wind. A spider crab clutched one of the piles just below the rising and falling surface of the cold water like it was waiting for something.

On the fishing boat, Leo leaned against him and heard his uncle's mind, beautiful madrigals woven of funny things and of Uncle Ollie's sapient love of the system of living things in the world. With sure hands Uncle Ollie slit the belly of a snapper by inserting the tip of his knife into the fish's anus and sawing up ventrally to the jaw, gathering scales on the blade as he sawed.

They had discovered in the stomach of a bluefish a snapper in whose stomach was a baby eel chomped into three parts. That made Uncle Ollie laugh and say *Gulp, gulp, gulp.* If they were using live minnows for bait, sometimes he ate one himself. He was a doctor, too. He had mudpuppies in his lab because he was interested in their kidneys.

Leo almost remembered the attic of the old house, where, in front of the gray dresser, he had pretended to serve his aunt and uncle's toes coffee, milk, Coke, water, orange juice. The painting of the mother bird and the baby birds—it could be hung horizontally or vertically because the baby birds poked out of the nest in a direction perpendicular to their mother's body, the three birds in the thicket in the middle of a great big tree, where direction doesn't matter anymore and there's no down or up, just branches and a place to sit every which way.

Iron railings on the row house steps, like the railing behind Winston Churchill in the picture where he raised his fingers in the "V" for victory. Just they two upon the steps, the sun on their shoulders—Isidore's wide as an armchair, Leo's narrower than his tricycle handles. Playing on the floor inside, where the cool refrigerator presided over the shadows. Playing with "lotsa cars."

Uncles. He could see them, but he couldn't see Him, not even his own memories of Him. The memories were known as a black hole in space is known, by gravitational field. He spoke to Leo through envoys only now. Leo felt his big body, saw his dashing mien, through their bodies, their faces.

A mosquito hawk dances on the wall.

A body lying still under six feet of dirt, the length of a man, a barrier through which no air could move. Long ago, Leo had tried to think of a way that air or food could get down there to his father. *Don't worry, Daddy. The others have forgotten, but I will bring you my macaroni and cheese. I didn't eat all of it. I will save it where no one will find it, behind the bed, where the mosquito hawk danced. . . .*

His father and grandfather, great heroes. Those two men had sailed the cold oceans; truly they had braved the seas, the ruthless crashing cliffs of brine and spray falling from a standstill, high as a clocktower. Verily, they had winched steel and manned decks, trimmed the glim of the human hearth in the sea to keep it afloat and afire, they had sailed into the mouth of the titan waves that ate bow decks and fly bridges, that gulped freighters and battle-ships like toys. His father, the merchant marines. His grandfather, the navy. Two Jews among the rough sailors. Two doctors.

That was what they said, *Your father was one of the great men,* his father's friends, walking around Leo as though he were a statue. They missed Izzy, they said. It was hard for them, they said. How hard was it to figure out what a son needs to know — that his father loved him is all, that his father would have loved him. *That's all I ever wanted to hear, you bastards. I wonder how much he'd have loved you, how grateful he'd be for what you've said on his behalf to his son. Would he say, thanks for speaking to my son for me, because as you know I'm dead, and you said just what I'd have said to my son if I could: Leo, I was one of the great men. No, I'd not have said with my last breath: Leo, I love you. I'd have said, Leo, remember, I was one of the great men. Actually, you didn't know Him well enough is the problem, or didn't love Him well enough to think of his wishes. All I have done for the last sixteen years is think of how he must have felt. I loved Him. I lost Him. Not you.*

But then maybe they thought it was obvious that a father would have loved his son and would have said so. Maybe they thought it didn't need saying.

He didn't know if his father had said "I love you" in the end. He had that stroke. Maybe he had said nothing at all.

Where is my father, Doctor? He is destroyed by heat. It will come,

214

the time will be now. All will be lost. He would stare down the blast pipe of the end of life. He would be destroyed. *Me, this body.* He would lie belowground in darkness, the roof of a coffin just inches from his blind eyes. Time would finally run out. Strange. Like the rings of Saturn.

Look the fly, Daddy.

It's a mosquito hawk, Leo.

It's a mosquito fly. Shoo, fly! I blow it, Daddy!

Tolstoy lost his mother at two years old. Fallen like Ozymandias. Perpetual winter of his invisible planet. Alone. *How did I get here, to New Haven, so far away from home? I'll ride my bike back to Cleveland. It will take two hours if someone comes to meet me halfway.* Dear dead days beyond recall.

Watch me blow the butterfly. It's on the wall, Daddy. It's so funny. It's so scary.

Leo peered into the darkness—the toasted bread jaw with the pipe; it could have been from photographs. He peered onto the deep, the continent of darkness. He couldn't see, but only hear. He heard the clattering and scything, the snap and click of the surgeon's gloves as he ties a suture, prods an organ with perfunctory fingers, separates the wet spools of intestine to peer in at the diseased *machina.* Pupils fixed and dilated. His own father, still warm with eyes of wet glass that did not react to light. Dissected, drained of blood, and buried.

Dead eyes were strange. They were just objects. If you thought of them as objects, living eyes were strange too, so that you had to use another language for them. *Yeux:* two spheres darting and flicking in eerie unison like the heads of two synchronized birds perched on the cheekbones, round and radially symmetric like flying saucers. Like aliens, filled with jelly, nutrition pumped into their skin by snaking vessels.

Watch me, Daddy!

Where are you going, gollywhopper, flipadoodle?

Hello, daddy longlegs.

Jump, Leo. I'll catch you!

I can dive like my daddy does!

At his feet, once, there was a brittle crab skeleton, bleached white, cured with sea salt, picked clean by the fishes. Leo searched the beach with Uncle Ollie for crab skeletons. Uncle Ollie knew about skeletons and sea life. Leo was starting a dead crab collection. He had just picked up the skeleton when another boy took it and crushed it. The boy wore a white braided band on his right wrist. *Where are you now? I would meet your hard opposition with my own, much harder than you could ever muster in all your life. My indissoluble will. I am unbreakable.*

He saw the sand which his chemistry professor said forms glass. The burette nozzle dripping in his dream—urine? That made him a man, a boy, of glass. A girl in the lab had dropped her burette and broken it. He was broken glass.

The decrepit car there on Prospect Street, like the rusted dead cars and cracked windshields abandoned in the weeds along the Metro-North line. *Decrepit,* from the Latin *crepere,* to creak, rattle; akin to the Sanskrit *krpate,* I wail, cry (his red bar mitzvah dictionary signed by David B. Guralnik said); and to the Old Norse *hrafn,* raven; and to the Cymric *cre, dychre,* cry, clamor. And *broken,* meaning split or cracked into pieces; not in working order; disrupted; or reneged upon, as a promise. Also, subdued and tamed. Subdued and tamed. See: The Theory of Breakage. *How death tames.*

Jump and I'll catch you! One, two, threeeeeeeeeeeeeeee!

Do it again, Daddy!

One, two, threeeeeeeeeeeeeeee!

I can dive like Daddy!

Ah! Leo came out of his thoughts as the clouds moved on and

the sun blazed out above the cemetery arch. It flooded his eyes in red and blacked out the arch and ate its words. He imagined the panel from the comedy group that had rejected him, listening in on his thoughts. He bowed his head and blushed, then raised his face again to the blinding sun.

you will see his eyes, gray eyes the color of a wave below the curl, below the storm winds that smite the waveheads and shatter the spindrift on the white air, Captain Change and his indissoluble will

Leo leaned against the arch. Two pigeons bobbed their heads as they wandered the sidewalk. One was fat, with a healthy green shine on the feathers around its neck. The other was skinny, and had been splashed with tar, its useless feathers black and glued to themselves. It was missing an eye.

"Looking *good,* brother!" he said.

Where was his "hour of splendour in the grass"? He could forget about illness and death—if he could spend the days of his youth in bed with Michelle, without fighting, just peace between them, her naked body. The screen of the sliding door would admit the odor of the sky and ocean. The room of a beach house would smell like fresh linen and there would be sand in the carpet. In Amagansett she would press her naked left buttock into his rough-haired groin, in private. A girl: wears lipstick, perfume, has long hair, armpits with scarcely a shadow, wears a dress, is prudent and wise about her ring finger, about her eggs and her vagina, which she maintains with regular service calls like some men do their brake pads.

He remembered the pictures of Michelle in the yearbook. Solitary, pensive, sober, dappled, under the tree. And the field hockey pictures. She once said she liked to run past other players like they were standing still. That was the person who thought that when we died we became nothing even though he argued that from a Berkeleyan standpoint this was impossible. The person whose mind housed many unlike things: a waitress shift schedule, Stafford Loan deadlines, long shadows of unhappiness and how they would look on a lithograph, "pretty pictures." She'd lived on the same street as his friend David Kim, whom he'd teased for being Korean—imagine that, teasing a kid about his eyes. Not funny. That was Ohio for you. David lived farther up Fernway, maybe. He wasn't even sure anymore. Once, in the middle of the night he saw two black guys in matching red T-shirts jogging down that street with javelins. It was true.

Leo passed under the arch, and wandered on amid the graves. On his father's tombstone was a line from *Macbeth*:

> *Your cause of sorrow*
> *Must not be measured by his worth, for then*
> *It hath no end.*

Then he is dead? Ay, and brought off the field. Had he his hurts before? Ay, on the front. He's worth more sorrow and that I'll spend for him.

The chill deepened over the quiet graves as the sun went down. No trees resisted the dominion of the falling star and it raked the naked cemetery with orange fire and thrust into it long spears of darkness. The shadow of the angel with the broken wing crept far out onto the grass, and orange light ignited the western facets of the headstones and obelisks. Leo's skin felt cool. The embarrassed angry blood in his face had drained.

He could see a girl, back toward him, sitting on a bench on the other side of the cemetery's pointed black iron bars. She was hunched over some papers on her lap. She could have been Michelle. The same brown hair, falling over the shoulders in the same way, tucked behind one ear in the same way. It was her! his heart said, leaping up. He had seen her head move in just the same way, looking from one piece of paper to the other on her lap. He could envision Michelle's face with the body of that girl. He experimented: It was really her, merely yards away! It was her! They would go to a restaurant and she would tell him about Miró.

The girl looked up for a moment as if she had heard her name; she had a piggish nose, looked nothing like Michelle. But when she looked back down he could practically see again—turned away from him, looking down—Michelle's face. Her army-green coat that was too thin for winter (she always shivered in it), the coat with the leather collar. Her jeans. Her breasts. Her hips. It was her!

Ah, fuck, it was nobody.

I came here looking for you, Daddy, but you aren't here. I guess I wasn't good enough after all. I'm only my pitiful small self, my irrational self, raving with wounds. Self-pitying fool!

Yes, but can't anyone take pity on a boy who is unknown to himself, and wild with grief?

The rabbi pities you. Yes, you're a case for the clergy now. But they don't quite get it, do they. Always bow it around to the useless mystery of God. Then you're alone all over again.

But someone took pity on Lear. The fool, was it? Ape Tits says— yeah, I call my professor Ape Tits, shoot me—Ape Tits says the fool never exits. Or was that the kid with red hair. Kid with red hair never exits, just sits in Linsly-Chittenden. The kid with red hair must have said it. Remember? Ape Tits says nothing. He's a "New Critic."

You just leave me here? To wander the tombstones? No word of help or regret? No blessing? No compliment? Because I am too raving mad? Fucked in the head, Corey says. You don't know him. You don't know about John Lennon or the Berlin Wall or the Gulf War or Star Wars or anything after 1974. You never even got to see Europe. But you knew about cemeteries. And Keats. And the moon like a seal on the sky.

Leo stood in the cold wind. The tip of the cloud-capped sun had impaled itself on a mausoleum.

A mosquito hawk dances on the wall.

Look, Daddy. I blow the butterfly.

Leo, Leo, Leo. It's okay, Leo. Daddy's here. That just scared you. The mosquito hawk scared you. Daddy got rid of it. I shooed it away, Leo. Okay, put your head right there on Daddy. You're okay.

It will frighten you away!

you little gollywhopper

you prince of the dashing mien, you Apollo and sailor of the seven seas, doctor-man, Harvard-man, pipe-man, beard-man, go-to-sleep-on-your-chest-man, daddy longlegs. You Young Siward

we're are best friends, we're are a family

They buried whole families together in the Grove Street Cemetery. Eli Whitney and Noah Webster's bones were lying somewhere here. But they wouldn't bury Leo in New Haven, that was for certain. If they did, his putrefying corpse would get up and flee.

Leo jogged along the path back to the front gate of the cemetery. The wind blasted against him as he ran, biting through the hole in the breast of his sweatshirt. There was another mailbox outside the cemetery, this one without a homeless lady on it. He pulled out the letter of withdrawal addressed to the Yale registrar and flung it down the throat of the mailbox, slapped its blue mouth shut with a clank.

He wandered east, toward the Town Green. There were more dead there under the grass. But before crossing Elm Street, and for no reason he knew, he stopped. He had never noticed the building there: Branch Four of the New Haven Free Public Library.

It looked like an old fire station. He climbed the steps and passed through the double doors, whose gray paint was badly peeled. The library's one room was pitiful compared to the magnificent Yale libraries. Dusty fluorescent tubes, exposed by missing ceiling tiles, cast a tepid light down onto stained yellow window shades and dying plants, wall-to-wall brown carpeting, blue plastic chairs, and round tables with faux bois veneers and steel legs. A sign on the checkout desk said the library was only open until 6:30 P.M. You couldn't even study there if you were in school. The place was useless. He sat at the round brown table.

"Closing soon," the librarian said. She was a high school girl.

Leo understood the place very well. He'd been in a public library before. It was a hushed place full of books available to anyone who wanted them. There were quiet, organized people there called librarians, who guided you toward the explanations, exaltation, escape, or help you sought in books. But this library couldn't save him, with its shabby little collections, its early closing time, its oblivious teenage librarian doing her homework, making fat redundant loops of blue ballpoint ink on some wide-ruled notebook paper. So this was the decayed land outside Yale, where he now made his way; this was home now, not a home but a wasteland. Leo looked around the children's section, which comprised half the room. The library was for the children in the New Haven public schools and Leo felt sorry for them. He pressed his ear to the table.

"Leo." He heard a whispered voice: "Leo."

It was his father.

"Yes?" Leo said.

But there was no one really there. The Greeks were vanished into whispers in the graveyard—a memory of a man reaching down for a plum, his big body providing shelter from the wind.

Good-bye, Daddy.

He raised his head up off the table and scanned the shelves as if some book might redeem the place or the moment. He shored himself up: he would swim for his life in the changing fortune and convoluted currents of the ocean, which glittered and destroyed. He pulled out a notebook and wrote on the lined paper in blue ink, AQUABOY.

And when he had shored himself up, Branch Four of the New Haven Free Public Library offered up its redemption, on the colorful covers of the children's books. He read their titles to himself. Stars. Bees. Summer. They were arrayed at brave angles, like doors half-open to the worlds their titles named. It was closing time, and the adolescent librarian ushered him out. He stepped outside into the street.

PART III

Highway 1 and Highway 2

I.

Lizard Tail

WELL, AS SO often seemed to happen after about the middle of June, it was now: late June. Say June 22, 1999. And that meant he was on an airplane halfway up the precipice face of giant clouds. He was there to launch his brother on a new life. Also, to see what had healed, if anything, and what more, if anything, could be healed without any near-fatal conversations. To quarry some magic from the banks of the Elwha River or up on the Rocky Mountain slopes, though neither he nor his brother believed in any magic. And finally to return to their point of origin, which was Cleveland, Ohio, where Leo had another wedding to go to, and stand up in. A couple of Jewish brothers from Cleveland on their way back home, to Lake Erie, to that old industrial port where the Indians played, the

city that helped to win World War II and then never won anything again. In 1969, on the first wedding anniversary of Leo
and Mack's parents, Isidore and Laura, the Cuyahoga River
caught fire and everybody in the whole world laughed like
somebody's mother had stepped in a pie. Right on June 22,
that very day. (Probably all Jews were by then somewhat sensitive about fire.) And apart from the Superman story, that's all
you need to know about being a Jew from Cleveland. Mistake
by the Lake, my ass. Burn on, you big ruined river soaked
in tar, burning with the blood of old war machines. From
Cleveland the brothers would carry on, together or apart, to
Philadelphia, New York, and the future.

The flight attendant came by with the cart and everybody ate
with chilly silverware and arms drawn in like praying mantises
in the dull blue nitrogen glow of the sky. Out the window,
symphonic five-hundred-story clouds rolled like glaciers on the
upper atmosphere. The sun gilded their arpeggios and from the
west, *lontano, morendo, misterioso, mesto ma non troppo,* bossed with
heavenly light their shadow-forked clefs.

Leo and Mack had not spoken for such a very long time, except for exchanges like this:

Leo: "Save some brisket for the rest of us, man."

Mack: [silent for eight years]

It was impossible to tell how far away they were, those slow
and giant nomad clouds. Nothing up this high to scale them.
Very far, probably. A far cloud god presided out there on the mist
plateau like a sphinx.

Come, his brother had said.

There were palm trees in West LA along La Cienega, there was
stucco on the houses and Spanish tile on the roofs and rarely a
second floor. Mack gave Leo the bed and slept at Will and Zhi-

lan's house. At about 6 A.M., there was an earthquake, which knocked over a guitar.

Things were in boxes and, aside from the bed, all the furniture was gone. There was nothing in the refrigerator but a very, very old lemon. Leo got himself water and sat on the kitchen floor in his bare feet. There was a stack of paper on the floor. The papers said at the top

Remembering the Year with Mr. Auberon

and each of Mack's students had filled one out and the first one Mack had filled out himself. It said

My favorite memory was ___ TERRENCE LEPLIE'S TINY TURKEY
I improved most at ___ TEACHING
My favorite story was ___ THE LEGEND OF SLEEPY HOLLOW
The funniest thing that happened was
___ CHARLES HAD HIS PIMP SHIRT OPEN
The best science project was ___ MEAL WORMS
The best art project was ___ SNOWFLAKES
The best math lesson was ___ TIMES TABLES
The best afternoon activity was ___ SILLY PUTTY
Next year I hope ___ I AM HAPPIER
I will miss LIVING THIS KIND OF LIFE AND ALL THE PEOPLE

A student named Eddy Fariss wrote specifics for everything, except for "best science project" he wrote "all of them." Some kids wrote "I will miss him," as if, for a personage so important as their teacher, the pronoun "him" needed no antecedent, as is sometimes the case with God; "Him"—who else? Another kid wrote that the best math lesson was "okay." A student named Exeline Ward had filled out her page like this:

My favorite memory was _____ NOTHING

I improved most at _____ NOTHING

My favorite story was _____ NOTHING

The funniest thing that happened was

_____ NOTHING

The best science project was _____ VOLCANO

The best art project was _____ NOTHING

The best math lesson was _____ NOTHING

The best afternoon activity was _____ NOTHING

Next year I hope _____ NOTHING

I will miss _____ NOTHING

Henry Vincent didn't fill out anything. He just drew a picture of himself smiling, holding hands with Mr. Auberon next to a stop sign, which, if you knew anything about Henry Vincent and all his trouble and all his good intentions, was fairly tragic.

They drove to Mailboxes Etc. to mail Mack's wire hangers. He said he was mailing half and the other half he'd bring with him in the car. Leo said he was crazy to mail wire hangers *or* to bring them in the car, which started everything off all wrong. But it didn't really matter much.

"See all the traffic?" Mack said. "And the smog? Those are the only ways LA lives up to its name."

"Yeah?"

"Okay," Mack said, "here's the famous intersection of Hollywood and Vine. That's right. It's a gas station and a 7-Eleven and... wait, there's nothing else. It's basically just Warrensville."

"Warrensville. Ha." Warrensville was a borderline neighborhood in Cleveland and it was pronounced with just two syllables and a long "o" as in "worn out"—"Wornsville."

"What's funny?" Mack said.

"You."

"Why? LA is the worst city in the world."

"You mean Compton."

"No," Mack said. "Compton is fucked up, but at least it's real. LA is the fakest place in the world. I'm not joking."

"I know," Leo said. "But you said the same thing about Brown. A lot of people like LA. It's a whole entire city. A lot of people like Brown."

"Oh, you mean lesbians? Yes, Brown is good if you're majoring in penis-machete, yes, that's true."

"Ah, yes, penis-machete. I forgot about that major. Hard to get a job with it these days." Leo sang the words "vagina dentata" to the tune of "Hakuna Matata," which was an old joke of Mack's. The words were from an English class in which Mack had been assigned a story about "Amazonclitwoman."

They both cracked up until they drove past a restaurant and Mack got angry again and said, "Oh, and that dump is supposed to be some famous place."

Before they went back home to get ready for dinner, Leo said he wanted to see the ocean, so Mack took him to the Santa Monica beach and they got out. It was six o'clock but it looked like the middle of the afternoon and the air itself seemed to be shining with sweat and everyone was shirtless and some black dogs were running with crazy tongues hanging out.

"By the way," Mack said, "that's not sand. It's dirt."

That night the other Compton teachers from Teach for America threw Mack a going-away dinner at a hibachi place. They gave Mack a Philadelphia Zagat and a city map.

Leo sat next to a Compton high school math teacher and his wife, who taught English.

"He calls himself Max now, right?" Leo said. "Yeah, Max here gave me the Pessimist's Tour of LA."

"LA's not so bad," the English teacher said, and asked her husband, "don't you think?"

"It's a good place to do community service," he said. "Better than Ghana."

The teacher husband and wife were from Wisconsin and no older than twenty-five. The wife was better-looking than him, as though they had paired off in some small town that didn't have any good-looking men in it. She had big healthful blue eyes, so healthful they didn't look quite made of flesh and blood—they had no red vessels or tears in them, but seemed wholly mineral, white as new snow with irises gemstone blue—and she was blond and peach-pale with big heifer breasts, and looked as though she had never had a cold. She ate every bite of her teriyaki chicken before Leo was half done with his miso soup.

Leo already felt a craving for Wisconsin breast milk when the wife said she didn't like her haircut.

"Something about layers," the husband said. "Looks fine to me."

The somewhat dowdy, cheap haircut and the husband's comments on it were so domestic, husbandly, and proprietary, Leo thought he ought to sweep her away and go have seven children with her on a dairy farm somewhere north and cold where the haircuts were really bad and everyone had faultless skin.

Mack wanted to remember LA, and his friends remembered things for him. They remembered the smog, seeing no stars, seeing no hill. "Remember the time there was so much smog, you couldn't see the smog?"

They really seemed to like Mack. But as soon as they'd begun to laugh and remember together, Mack began to bite his lip and grew younger before Leo's eyes. When people teased or made idle jokes, he got stuck on them as if they implied some criticism or hurt feelings, something he'd done wrong to lose his friends' affection, and he worried aloud that he'd given some offense and he hurried to explain things that needed no explanation and apologized for things that needed no apology, rather like a salesman who is down to his last customer. And he said crazy things that everyone except him knew to be false—like "*I* certainly expect to be friends with you guys for the rest of my life, assuming you guys do, are you in?"—and he was so earnest in this that Leo began to feel blushy and hot and ticklish in his esophagus.

Leo noticed Robby looking at him from across the hibachi grill. Robby was the oldest one, whom they called Gramps (he was twenty-nine).

"So you're out here being the good big brother," Robby said, "helping the little brother move."

"Yep," Leo said.

"Max keeps you quite a secret," Robby said. "I pried out of him that you were in medical school. And you dropped out?"

"Nope. Went all the way through."

"Oh," Robby said. "So you're a doctor."

Mack bit his lip and nodded as if he'd been caught in a lie, but he wasn't sorry about this one, Leo guessed, he was only sorry that the lie wasn't the truth, and that Leo was there to hear it.

There was something odd about Robby and his questions. The brothers and their unsolved mysteries had piqued something in him. And now it was Leo who felt the need to bring something to light, to explain that which needn't be explained, that which he couldn't quite explain, anyway, even when he tried.

"Our father was a doctor," Leo said. It was 9:30 P.M. now and the jet lag was falling. He felt he could go right to sleep and his left eyelid drooped down over half his eye.

Robby turned to Mack and said, "Your father is a doctor? I thought he was some kind of businessman."

Then Leo said the man was dead. This brought more unwanted questions, about ages and time and place, and Leo gave the answers.

"So you guys are from the same father, then," Robby said.

"Same one," Leo said.

"When you said three years old, I thought you must be from the same mother but different fathers," he said to Leo. And he turned to Mack and said, "How come you never told me?"

And Mack looked guiltier than before and wouldn't meet Leo's eye.

"We've had some heart-to-hearts," Robby said, "but he never mentioned this."

"It didn't seem relevant," Mack said.

After dinner they went back to Robby's place in West Hollywood— maybe Robby was gay—and Leo tried to stay awake and not be crushed by the depression of Robby's questions and his matchstick blinds, the same ones Leo had had in his own room in Baltimore, bamboo matchstick blinds hung on nails, which bespoke rootlessness and budget and playing house. They drank warm beer and when they had to go, it seemed that Mack said good-bye to everybody at least twice.

And then Mack and Leo drove home and Leo said, "Just think of the open road out there, Mack. All the cities and places and people out there in the dark. It's like, have you seen those *Viking* pictures of Mars? Mars is a place, you know? With shadows and rocks and hills and a horizon, an entire planet full of places and they're all out there, existing, right now. The massive simultaneity of it, you know? And here, this huge country is like that, but it's full of people and not just red rocks and sand. It's full of girls, Mack. It's all just waiting for us to explore it." Leo was young and single and girls had always seemed to like his face and he'd at long last taken to heart the importance of drink, as well as trained his liver to handle large quantities of it. There was no reason why on the road he shouldn't fall in love again or have sex again or talk literature with some girl under a bridge, watching the marina lights wink on and off.

"You make it sound good," Mack said, apparently a little unconvinced, like he knew that Leo was convincing himself.

Mack took him back to the empty, bare apartment and left him there alone.

The day before they departed they went to brunch with Mack's college roommate, Nathan, who had starred in the Disney flop *Newsies* and was a stand-up comic on the Sunset Strip.

They sat outdoors. All the men wore yellow-tinted sunglasses and all the women were beautiful in a way that ached in the teeth. Nathan said the waitresses had to audition for their jobs. They were even more beautiful than the girls sitting at the tables with their mimosas, and were bare-legged except for boots that came up above their knees. They seemed to be wearing bikini bottoms. Leo felt the foreign attitude of the place, the people, burning on his skin like the sun, like the smog. He was wearing a shrunken gray T-shirt and he needed a haircut. When he'd looked in the mirror that morning, his hair was bulging out on the sides so his head had the shape of a lightbulb.

"Yeah, this place has a very LA vibe," Nathan said.

While they were eating their feta and tomato omelets, a blue SUV rolled up in the street and two men climbed out of it. The bigger man lifted a large and professional-looking movie camera out of the back of the SUV and then the two men slowly approached the tables with the rear doors to the SUV left wide open. The tall cameraman had a long ponytail and carried the big camera over his shoulder. The other man looked like a Jewish lawyer or professor who'd gone off his lithium. This manic, smallish man was well into his fifties but he was wearing a sort of trendy-looking green bowling shirt. He came right up to the tables and said, "Hiya!"

Then he tried to do a headstand and failed and the girls at the next table applauded. The stoical cameraman pointed the camera down at him with care and concentration and evident indifference to his antics. When the man got up he said to Leo and Mack and Nathan, "You're too good to applaud?" He had a look of misery and a look of euphoria coexistent on his face, sort of like someone who's just completed a marathon or had several teeth extracted. With rapid little steps on the grass the cameraman circled around in back of him. "What's the matter with you, you look scared," the man said. "The girls over here aren't scared. Why don't you talk to them? Or you're here together? Are you guys *feygeles?*"

"Yeah, that's right, we're *feygeles,*" Nathan said. "And what are you?"

"Me, I'm famous, that's what. See the camera? Who are you? You're just a bunch of schmucks eating your breakfast. I'm managed by Hob Lewis, you know who he is?" He sang what he said with so many levels of irony it seemed he didn't himself know quite what he was up to.

"Never heard of him," Nathan said.

"I'm a comedian," the man said, and smiled confidently at the girls, who encouraged him with cheers and woo-hoos.

"Oh yeah?" Nathan said. "And where do you perform?"

"All over. Contact my manager."

"Oh, all over. Meaning open-mike night at the Highland?"

"I'm on TV! I'm on the radio! I've been on Howard Stern! Forget comedy, I'm a bodybuilder!" And he struggled out of his sad trendy shirt and pretended to flex his muscles with a perverse

234

trust in self-mockery as his ticket, evidently, to a small taste of fame, fortune, or love. Clearly, he had gone too far down this road to turn back. The girls laughed. "What are you? What are you?" he hooted, and waved his arms. "Forget the *feygeles*. These guys are very serious over here." He went on to another group of tables with his impervious smile.

"Jesus, look at you guys," Nathan said to the brothers.

Nobody said anything else until the waitress came by and Leo suddenly barked, "What do you have to do to get a fucking glass of water in this place?"

Nathan stared into Leo's face. "I actually have to go pick up my girlfriend," Nathan said. He dropped some bills on the table and took off.

In the afternoon, Leo and Mack went to the service station to retrieve Mack's car, the green Saturn in which your ass rode approximately one and a half inches from the road.

"I guess you'll want to see Hollywood now, huh?" Mack said. "It's obligatory."

"Okay."

Tourists crowded in front of Mann's Chinese Theatre and pointed to the concrete slabs imprinted with celebrities' handprints, shoeprints, signatures. Many of the tourists had come from across the Pacific Ocean, it seemed, and one Asian man shouted, "Gally Coopah! Gally Coopah!"

"America is of extreme interest to other people," Mack said.

The stars on the Walk of Fame were frequently people unknown to Leo with Jewish-sounding names. The whole area was horribly depressing and unglamorous as anyone might guess, with the names of absent rich and famous people stamped into the grubby materials of everybody else's lives—long vacant avenues and cracked concrete. Each palm tree promenade framed a screen of gray blank sky, as empty as a soundstage, and sometimes, depending on which way you looked, they framed that Hollywood sign, distant and faded and looking like a letter or two was about to fall off the hill. *The Muppet Movie* was wrong and Mack was right; LA was just a bunch of ghosts of things that were supposed to be famous but looked like a gas station. And Leo was just beginning to see that glamour itself was not glamour, but a mirage that withdrew wherever you wandered.

They went back to Mack's apartment because they were out of other ideas and sat in the hot, depressing, packed-up apartment, and listened to the ceiling buzz with the upstairs neighbors' surround-sound and to the heels of little children drumming up and down the floor above.

Mack felt better about the brunch incident by then, but Leo was upset all the way until they got to dinner at Will and Zhilan's with their baby who crawled with his left leg hooked underneath him, and their twin Stanford degrees and lightning-quick new PC, and Honey Nut Clusters cereal that the baby ate off the shining hardwood floor. Will's family was from Mexico and he was a DA, but he said people in restaurants often mistook him for a busboy and that it pissed him off, and you could see that it did, in fact. They grilled out and the light behind the house was beautiful, the sunset was beautiful. They played hearts until late.

"Hey, man," Leo said to Mack, "I'll sleep on the floor tonight, I don't care."

"I don't know," Mack said. "Okay. I guess so. Yeah. That's right. Or I could take the floor."

And they walked home together under a sky of reflected city light. Not only was it never cold in LA, it was, apparently, never even night. The sidewalks were brighter than the moon.

The next morning they set off up Highway 1 to San Francisco with thirty tangled-up wire hangers in their trunk.

2.

THE PORTLAND ROSE GARDEN

SOMEWHERE NORTH OF the Santa Monica Bay, the last waves of the LA radio stations died out and "St. Elmo's Fire" came on and Leo sang along with it, loudly, with the windows open and their asses one and a half inches over the flying pavement of Highway 1.

"'You know in some ways, you're a lot like me, you're just a pris-on-er, and you're tryin' to break free! I can see a new horizon, underneath a blazin' sky. I'll be where the eagle's flyin,' St. Elmo's fire!' Don't laugh at me, man."

"It's 'higher and higher' there," Mack said.

"Oh yeah," Leo said. "'Gonna be your man in motion, da da da-da da da. Feel like a man again, I hope I get hi-igh!'"

"Lord, he was born a scramblin' man," Mack said. "That's not even the right words. But at least they're in the wrong order."

"See, Mack? Life is beautiful," Leo said. "I'm gonna find a beautiful biology professor out there in the mountains with wild-flowers in her hair like in *Refiner's Fire* and make her my wife, Mack."

The road looped around another misty hill and they could see mist lying over the Pacific Ocean below, a tier of white unbroken clouds, and with the Saturn pitched upward as it was, it really looked as if they had launched into the sky.

"Fuck LA, man," Mack said. "I am so glad to be out of there."

"Good-bye to LA and all the beautiful people," Leo said. "And Nathan."

Then they found "Here Comes My Baby" by Cat Stevens and they sang it, too, and drank its syrup while they stared covetous up the steep green misty hills and breathed cool wet air that smelled of salt and sea and they imagined it could be theirs.

They planned not to stop and they didn't stop, except for food and gas and taking leaks and one long excruciating dump that was of such a legendary, heroic character that in later years they would both try to claim it as their own. By the time they got to Big Sur, Leo felt ill from all the twists and turns and they were so sick of driving they could hardly enjoy the views.

That night in San Francisco, in their friend's apartment with the flight of fifty stairsteps, they lay on air mattresses in the dark and Leo said, "I love that song, 'St. Elmo's Fire,' cheesy though it is."

"I don't think it's cheesy," Mack said.

"But I never like the first verse."

"Why?"

"Everything else in it seems right, but not the first verse. It's not true. Not for me."

"Why?"

"It's about shedding your naïveté, isn't it? Thinking you're hot shit when you're young and realizing things later about how the world is."

"You were never naïve?" Mack said.

"Not for very long."

"You mean everything with Daddy?"

"Yeah," Leo said. They had learned to be careful of each other by now.

"I mean, I've had some comeuppances. But that's not the main thing in life. Not in my life, anyway. It's about a certain darkness in the beginning that's just radiated all the way through. It's about a weight to carry."

"But I feel that way too," Mack said. "And I think that's what the song is really about, anyway. I don't think the first verse means what you said."

"No?"

There was a long silence, during which they listened to the sound of a motorcycle going down the hill.

"I told you those hangers were gonna be a pain in the ass," Leo said, and rolled over. And they listened to the sounds of the unfamiliar house, the roar of engines toiling loudly on the steep city streets and the sudden quiet when they coasted down, some buzzing somewhere of a refrigerator or a lamp, the sound of the cat dropping down from the arm of the chair.

They hiked to the top of Mount Tam with Leo's med school buddy John, who'd been a state soccer champion, and John's friends, a husband and wife, serious runners who loped uphill as though it were downhill and made the brothers both feel, in the words of the Enemy Brunch Dwarf, like *feygeles*. The husband and wife were in town for a wedding: Gavin was tall with a lean, knobby strength about him inherited, probably, from the Canadian voyageurs somewhere up in his bloodline;

he was like Marshall Pearl, Mack said, but more self-effacing; Bailey was short and blond and pretty and though her last name was Soudard, she was not Canadian and had never been. Her family had come over from France many lifetimes ago, and she had a French beauty about her, which is to say a dignified beauty cultivated like a crop by hundreds of years of genetic snobbery and excommunication of ugly people. And mixed with her easy, stainless French beauty was an American ruggedness and openness. They had met, of course, while in college at Brown.

"I thought you said everyone was ugly at Brown," Leo said. He was so tired he couldn't even brush flies from his eyelids like an African child dying of kwashiorkor. He leaned over and spat into a bush.

"Yeah," Mack panted. "I guess there are exceptions to everything. Shit, I feel like I just blew my liver through a flugelhorn. Do you have a stitch? I have a stitch."

"What's with these people?" Leo said. "I actually run in the park a couple days a week."

Gavin and Bailey had vanished up the trail ahead and John only hung back to be sociable.

"Look at that view," John said. "Look out there."

"Yeah, beautiful," Leo said. He imagined that this was how people felt when they had a chest tube between their ribs, a fairly barbaric-looking procedure.

Mack did not answer. He was gray.

"All right, pick it up, Auberons, I'm trying to get a workout here," John said.

They hiked some more and John said, "Make sure to look at the view, guys. Are you appreciating this?"

"Unh. Beautiful," Leo said.

Mack just made a noise that sounded like "Hee."

They hiked some more and a third time John said, "Would you look at that? That's just amazing, don't you think?"

"I can't look at the fucking view would you stop asking me to look at the view I'm just trying," Leo shouted, "to."

"You're trying to what."

He had to spit a few more times violently into the brush before he could say, "Oxygenate."

But eventually Leo and Mack did make it to the top, and when they had sat on a rock for a while and caught their breath, they could see quite far in the cloudless daylight over Napa and Sonoma, over the pastel buildings of San Francisco on the hill, and the bay full of sailboats.

"Well, it is beautiful, yeah," Leo said.

"I don't know why I was so keyed up for you to see it. Like I'm mayor of San Francisco," John said.

"So Emmy had to model," Leo said. "It's hell being married to a Harvard JD slash weekend model, huh?"

"Yeah, bait and switch, man. I thought I was marrying a dumb blonde. Ah, well. She'd never come up here anyway. Have to bring her in a wheelbarrow." John dropped and began to do push-ups.

Leo did not like to lose. He sat down on the grass next to Bailey, who had sweated through to her bra and was stretching out her calves with her legs flung wide apart and her fingers pulling on the light blue sole of her running shoe. Though he knew it betrayed an anxiety common to bachelors of a certain type, he asked Bailey how she and Gavin had met.

"We were hallway neighbors freshman year," she said. "I guess you could say we were soul mates." Leo couldn't tell if this was just woman talk or not.

★   ★   ★

Back at the apartment with the long flight of stairs, Leo asked Mack, "Don't you hate those two just a little?"

"I was thinking they're pretty nice," Mack said.

"They can afford to be nice because they live like God in France," Leo said. "But they are nice, yeah." He almost stopped there, but then he added, "And that makes me hate them even more. Plus, they look down on me."

"I don't think they look down on *me*."

"Oh, come on, yes, you do."

"You don't know what I *think*," Mack said.

Leo picked up his book and tried to read it. He had to admit that there was another way to look at things, Mack's way, that perhaps he'd been collared once again by that perniciously depressive mind-set from childhood. Perhaps life was not in fact a battle royale, and in fact everybody was in it together, struggling along, everybody scared shitless by death, and no one was judging him, not even Bailey and Gavin. Why should they judge him? *Because,* another voice said, *you don't look at things Mack's way. For that very reason. Because you're bitter and jealous and insecure, the very opposite of what people find attractive.* He gave up on the book and closed his eyes. How was he to escape this trap of self-hate if acknowledging the trap just led to more self-hate? This was why he felt himself to be a dog scratching at a flea collar, a wolf chewing his own leg off to get out of a bear trap. He couldn't win. He could see how his friend's wedding would go at the end of the summer: miserably. He would get miserably drunk and eat his salad with his bare hands again.

In the evening they went to eat at the House of Nanking, where the waiter brought menus and then collected them again without taking their order and brought them plate upon plate of delicious fish, rice, green beans, mushrooms, soup. John said, "They don't do this for everybody. They know us here." Bailey told Leo how she and Gavin had so loved it at Brown, how they met on the first day of orientation, waiting in line to get their student IDs, and found they lived on the same hall, how both had run cross-country in high school and loved the outdoors and had the same sense of humor and liked the same music and they had never looked back. Soul mates.

"Well, that's good luck," Leo said, and he coveted that dream life and despite his desperation to buck all self-hate, he felt that he and his brother were deeply inferior and that Gavin and Bailey felt them to be inferior but were too polite to say it. Bailey asked Leo about himself and he tried to explain about being a doctor and quitting or anyway taking a leave, and he told her how he had written something about the death of his father, and he very much expected her to say something irritating about student loans and debt or about how everybody was writing about their dead father. Maybe mortality touched everyone and maybe those who didn't know death in their childhoods or other insults to their naïveté had plenty of empathy and imagination. Maybe he was obscene to complain with all the death everywhere in the world. Or maybe, to gods living in France, death was just a fable.

She asked him some more questions about his father, and some of them were medical questions, because she was in medical school, and he answered those in medical terms. Then she started to ask about him and Mack and about his mother, and here Mack put down his wineglass and leaned his face closer. (Mack didn't drink beer because he couldn't burp.)

Leo had had plenty of beer and with Bailey asking such questions, listening so compassionately, and watching him with eyes puritanically blue, he thought he might kiss her even if Gavin attacked him with the giant wooden oar a man like him presumably kept in the trunk of his car.

Then Bailey said, "Where are you guys headed?"

He explained about the road trip and the wedding in Cleveland, where he was to be a groomsman.

"Because I think I know someone very much like you, Leo."

"Yeah?"

"Yeah, your soul mate!" Bailey said it was her favorite person in the world and best friend. She was a resident in pediatrics in Chicago and she also wrote and she said she didn't think she could have a relationship with someone who hadn't experienced loss.

"Huh," Leo said, and he kept up a poker face, even though it pleased him that Bailey didn't think him lesser, if she would set him up with her best friend.

Mack spilled his wine into a pile of chicken pieces. "Ah, shit."

"We met at Brown," Bailey said. "She was engaged but her fiancé died."

"Huh," Leo said. "Is it crass to ask what she looks like?"

"Oh, she's beautiful," Bailey said. "Very soft-looking. Her name's Berry. Not like Manilow. With an 'E.' Like in 'raspberry.'" Bailey's love for her best friend, Berry, made him love Bailey all the more, and he let himself imagine himself with Berry, his soul mate, on a yacht somewhere in the Greek islands, floating in a nirvana of starlight and prosecco, ocean wind and wave, a consonant chord of keening love to bind two souls and bodies together forever. (This was why all his friends were married and he was not; he was married to his own preposterous dreams.)

Mack, meanwhile, was trying to mop up the spilled wine with one soaked little napkin. To rescue him, Leo explained about the Enemy Brunch Dwarf and giving people three names, a kind of haiku, such as the brilliant haiku name Mack had given to Charles Barkley: Trrbll Donut Idiot. And the one for Terry Bradshaw: Bald Depression Touchdown.

The others wanted Mack to give them haiku names and Mack was more than willing, but Leo warned against this. Instead, they settled on pursuit of a nickname for Leo, who had never really had one, and Mack suggested the Assface. And it was agreed that Mack and his brother, the Assface, would borrow Gavin and Bailey's tent to take to Olympic National Park, under strict instructions from Gavin not to bring any food into the tent, because any bear within a hundred miles and ten years would discover such a breach of protocol and eat whoever was inside the tent then, probably Gavin and Bailey.

And the next day, when Leo and Mack went to Alcatraz with Mack's friends, Mack gave every word to his friends and not a one to Leo, but not on purpose, it seemed, as if a prison sentence of sorts had been passed on the older brother by the younger without the younger even knowing it. And Leo felt alone with the huge immaculate gulls high over the bay, screeching and swooping to defend their nests on the decaying buildings, which were ruined with wildflowers. It was bright and windy as a mountain and gardenlike in its ruins and flowers. And inside, the cells seemed to remember the bad men who lived bad lives there, and the air was heavy and cloying with their absence.

And in the morning, on the way up to Oregon, Leo said he was excited for Chicago, when he would meet Berry.

And Mack said, "It seems like you want me to be happy for you about it."

And Leo said, "Well, maybe I do. What's wrong with that?" And the temperature inside the Saturn seemed to drop by several degrees and the air inside the Saturn became unbreathable as it had been between them for years, the same kind of deadly cold cavern air for which the trip had been intended as anodyne. Leo wanted to say he was mad about Alcatraz, but he knew much better than to open the door to another ice age.

They listened to the Beatles, and Mack said that people were unfair to Paul, and that Paul was the genius.

"Who's unfair to Paul?" Leo said.

"Everyone," Mack said. "It's always all about John."

"Well, John was a genius too," Leo said. "And he's dead. People always revere the dead. He was also the leader, wasn't he? He started the band. He was the oldest. He spoke for them. He set the tone."

"See, that's what I mean," Mack said, and he was mad. "You know who wrote 'Sergeant Pepper'?"

"I think they're both awesome. They're both the poets of lost love. They both lost their mothers. Then they lost each other."

Mack looked straight ahead furiously. "No, they didn't. John left Paul. You know why Paul wrote 'Hey Jude'? He wrote it for Julian Lennon because he was more of a father to Julian than John was."

"I know," Leo said. "I saw a thing where Julian Lennon said his father told him he came out of a whiskey bottle on a Saturday night."

"Told that to his own son," Mack said. "John raised Sean but not Julian, and everybody knows what it did to Julian. What a great man. What a great father. He ruined his own son."

"Aha. Well, his own father wasn't really around for him, I think," Leo said, and wondered if his brother was really so blind that he couldn't see what they were really talking about. "Lennon's father was a sailor. You know, the yellow submarine. And then his mother, Julia, died in a car crash—left *him*. Isn't that the story?"

Mack had begun to rein himself in but still looked like he had a worm in his boot.

"You're totally nuts on this subject," Leo said. "You always have been. Same with Mafia movies."

"Why am I nuts? The entire world is nuts for liking Mafia movies. I'm the only one who's sane."

"It's just never about what it's about with you. You think it's about Mafia movies or John Lennon. Come on."

"Well, what's it all about, then? Since you know everything." Mack couldn't look Leo in the eye, and the fear was a measure of the rage, and the rage would turn the trip into something like the *Eiswelt* at the top of the Alps.

"Okay, Mack. Let's go back. I didn't mean to get you upset or to be a jerk about it. You're my bro."

Mack was quiet. He still had the worm in there.

"There's a lot of history between us, Mack. And a lot of attitude to that history that's quite complicated."

"What? You mean what happened to us?"

And Leo felt he was standing on the edge of a cliff, and if he said the right thing, things would go a certain way, and if he said the wrong thing, they would go another way. But the question made him feel something, a very awful, very deep, powerful feeling, like a malady of the pancreas, and he was still steaming about Alcatraz and he said, "Us? *What* happened to us?"

"How we lost Daddy."

"I have sympathy for you, Mack," Leo said cautiously. "But you didn't lose him, because you didn't ever know him to begin with." It was a thing that should not have been said, at least not in that way, but his pancreas made him say it. It seemed to him that it utterly had to be said, because his pitiless brother could for once in his life have some imagination and feel some kind of compassion for him about this. And he did not say, *If you had a clue what life is about, how much death and trouble there is in this world, you'd know we ought to stick close together, but you don't have a clue.*

He didn't say it in part because of the look on Mack's face. The worm was gone. The boots were gone. It was nuclear

247

fission, something that didn't need to come to pass, but once it had, it could not be turned off.

And Mack said, "Well, the thing with Mom's face..." and he trailed off. And Mack wilted like a plant.

And they didn't care about beauty anymore and they took Interstate 5 because it headed straight for the middle of Oregon. And they didn't talk until lunch at McDonald's in Redding off Interstate 5, where they played chess with their grandfather's pieces. Mack won in twenty-three moves, and while they put the wooden pieces with their mostly scratched-off gold filigree back into the cigar box, Leo told Mack what idiot mistakes he himself had made and Mack on the other hand reviewed what nifty pins and discovered attacks he'd made and how they had each one been fully intentional and planned. They folded the banged-up Milton Bradley checkerboard and went on.

The ice came with them like comet dust up to Sunriver, outside of Bend, Oregon, where they met up with their cousin Todd and Todd's girlfriend of ten years, Jen. The first thing they did was to play basketball and Leo knew that when Mack was depressed he played his best basketball. He wanted Mack to play his best basketball because he thought it might serve as antifreeze, and because he felt he'd said the wrong thing, and because it feels so good to beat the living shit out of other males at anything at all anytime at all, and because he loved Mack so much he would lie down in front of a train for Mack. That was something he couldn't make Mack understand, and maybe Mack didn't care. Maybe Mack didn't need such love because he didn't know what it was to have it taken away. But Leo would do it even in the middle of one of Mack's Arctic winters. He would walk straight into that ice-wind for his brother, or into a flood or a fire. It was just him and Mack against the whole world.

Mack had not permitted Leo to score a single basket in a game of one-on-one for more than five years. He could jump so high, he would just block every shot Leo put up, and he would shoot right over him and he never missed. And while Mack sometimes froze when he played pickup, he never froze up when he was depressed.

Mack brought the ball up and one of the strangers on the other side called out, "Let him shoot! Let him shoot! He can't do nothing!"

And Mack spotted up and nailed a three-pointer and then backpedaled and he had that old Mack-like sorrow on his face, the quiet, still, unbroken sorrow of an old pond without any birds. He looked like a kid at a fair where they were giving away puppies and everybody got one but him and somehow he had known that would happen.

On the next play, Leo set a pick for Mack and cut to the hole and Mack passed it to him and Leo fumbled it and the other team got it and ran it up the court, but Todd slapped the ball away and then threw a baseball pass all the way back to Mack and Mack jumped up and slam-dunked with two hands. He had a very nonviolent, somewhat slow way of dunking, a very elegant way of playing basketball altogether, very soft hands, and he could see over everybody because he jumped so high and knew how to float, and he could see through everybody because he had X-ray vision when he was depressed. Even the dunk didn't make him smile. He just kept watching the ball with the same expression of exhausted excellence and concentration that Galahad presumably had when he knocked his father off his horse.

After the game, Leo put his arm around Mack, but Mack only looked at the gleaming sweat of the arm with evident disgust.

Leo wanted to say, "I would take a bullet for you, Mack, but you would watch me drown." And it was possible he had said such things before, because he couldn't count on Mack, but whether or not he could count on Mack, he knew better by now than to say all those things about bullets and drowning and counting on.

When they had showered, Mack got out his guitar and Leo knew it would be hours of command performance and betrayal with Todd's friend, who could play the blues. *Mack, you would let me drown.*

Long ago, when they'd visited his soon-to-be grandparents' house at the top of a hill on North Park, where some of the wealthiest families in Shaker Heights lived, Leo's mother fell. A servant had opened the door to the Zajacs' house, a massive door with decorative hasps like you'd see on a very old book, and a brass handle that was fashioned to look like an enormous key in an enormous lock. They had gone into the front hall and saw there a tree arising miraculously out of a little indoor pool filled with stones. And his mom had reached out with one foot as if to touch the water, and had seemed all of a sudden to be dragged down into it. She had fallen into the pool and soaked her dress. "I thought it was glass," his mother had said, as if that explained, and Leo had watched the mobile sculpture hanging by the tree, the silver glyphs slowly turning on invisible strings, and hoped that the Zajacs would still accept them into the family even though they were klutzes. The spring after Laura changed from Laura Auberon to Laura Zajac, when Leo was six and Mack was three, Mack had fallen into the swimming pool at the same house and his mother had had to jump in fully dressed to save him from drowning!

The Zajacs didn't fall into pools. Their name, which meant "rabbit" in Polish, had a strong cachet among Cleveland Jews, and even throughout the gentile whole of the city. The Zajacs were builders. They owned Cleveland's main landmark, the Ter-minal Tower. Their family business, a real estate company, was traded on the New York Stock Exchange. Philip flew on business every single week and so did his brothers.

Todd Zajac was Leo's age. When they were eight, Todd's fa-ther had given him a Swiss Army knife, and Todd had brought it on the Zajac family canoe trip and had used it to whittle a stick. Leo had asked if he could try whittling.

"No," Todd had said. "You'll cut yourself."

"But you're using it," Leo said, "and you're my age."

"I know how to use it," Todd had said.

"I won't cut myself," Leo said.

Todd gave over the knife. Leo admired the blade and the other tools inside it. There were a screwdriver, a scissors, and even a magnifying glass. He used the knife to try to strip some bark off the stick.

"See? I told you," Leo said to his cousin.

Then when he tried to close the knife, he closed it on his thumb and he bled and bled.

Leo had always known that Todd was cool but at the charity event on the Sunriver green, Leo finally understood what "cool" meant. It was not a social construct like the bullshit vendors in his literary theory class said. It referred to a real character trait, a real phenomenon. It meant the emotions were cool; Todd did not get mad or nervous. And that was socially pleasing, as it caused everyone to forget about frailty and death.

Families picnicked on the green and cheered on the firemen in suspenders and bunker pants, who dueled with spraying fire hoses to push a red ball along a wire. Everyone, everywhere, was thoroughly white and all the land seemed to have been put just where it was on purpose, by a bulldozer, and then covered with a pelt of transplanted grass. Cries of joy. Leo ran grimly after the Frisbee, berating himself for dropping the Frisbee on so many one-handed catch attempts, and thought seriously of suicide. Todd never dropped the Frisbee. Death was nowhere to be seen. No death and no black people. Todd's friend was so blond you couldn't see his eyebrows. He flicked the Frisbee back to Todd behind his back while coasting away on a skateboard, deadpan, hidden behind sunglasses. Leo wanted to dig a hole and bury himself under the green pelt of the grass. He didn't know why he felt suicidal again. He hadn't felt it since his surgery rotation. The sun baked him red.

Then they went back to Todd and Jen's friend Melody's house—or rather it was Melody's parents' house where they were all to stay that night. Todd and Jen said they wanted to set him up with Melody. (After four years of medical school in Baltimore, four years of flaying onanism, Leo had made his needs loud and clear.)

Over the huge TV set in Melody's parents' living room, there was a landscape painting in a black-and-gilt frame, the sort you see dragged onto *Antiques Roadshow* from someone's attic and want to avert your eyes but you can't—like a car accident, except much more boring. Cast-iron statuettes of a golfer and a grizzly bear stood on either side of the mantel. There was a statuette of Santa Claus, too, wearing real clothes, actual red-and-white fabric. Everywhere there were pictures of golfers and bears.

"So is Santa nude underneath?" Leo whispered to Mack.

"What do you mean?"

"I mean is he nude or does he have iron clothes under his fabric clothes?"

"Why?"

"Never mind," Leo said. "I just thought it was weird either way."

When they had dropped off their bags and washed up a bit,

they went to dinner in Sunriver: Leo and Mack, Todd and Jen, Melody, and a couple of other friends of Todd and Jen. It took forever to find a place to seat them all that could also accommodate all their dietary restrictions.

Melody was a full-time animal rights activist and, like Todd and Jen, a vegetarian but not a vegan. One of the other girls was a vegan. When they finally did find a suitable place, the busboys had to drag two tables together to fit them all, and Leo blushed. The others had all known each other for years; he and Mack had pushed the head count to unmanageable numbers. But he was light-headed from sun and from dehydration and too little food. He had detected on the menu a turkey club with steak fries and had his mind on a Coke as well, and was literally swallowing back gobs of automatic drool when the vegan girl tossed the menu down and said: "I can't eat anything here."

Leo watched Todd to see how a cool person would handle this sort of insurrection by a vegan. Leo himself had zero ideas. He wanted to slit the girl's throat with a laminated menu and carnivorously drink her blood. Leo swallowed his drool and watched Todd. Todd merely waited; in chess that was called *Zugzwang*— when you waited for your opponent to break the status quo and let victory happen by his action, not yours.

"Why can't you eat here?" Leo said impetuously. (He was always too impetuous for chess.)

"There's nothing for me to eat here besides salad."

"Okay," Melody said calmly, sweetly, "we can find another place."

Todd said he thought he knew of a sandwich place to try that wasn't far away, though it was takeout only.

"Let's do that," Melody said.

Leo wondered, what do Vegans eat besides salad out there on their distant star, Vega?

★   ★   ★

It seemed odd that Melody was single, since she was sexy with dark hair and a clear gentile face and had such a nice-smelling bathroom. And people who were friends with Todd and Jen had a certain cachet in Leo's mind, they had a certain social facility, and Leo believed that such people didn't have his problems, and must all be paired off and happy. But then Melody had this very intense relationship with her droopy-face springer spaniel, Deedee, who slobbered and sporadically barked without cause—as if responding to internal stimuli, as they used to say in the ER of psychotic or delirious patients. Despite being a female, Deedee would try to mount any visitor she deemed a threat to her owner and though Melody was continually embarrassed by her dog and called her spoiled, it was also clear that she evaluated men according to how they got along with her dog. The dog mounted Leo immediately and continued to mount him at any opportunity.

Melody was very motherly in a certain way. The next day she set the table formally for lunch and served cookies (no butter or eggs or milk or other animal products, they tasted like shit) and fussed over them and asked if there was anything she could get for them. She started unloading the silverware from the dishwasher and then stopped. "Is this too noisy?" she said. "Is he asleep?" "He," like Mack's students would have said.

"Is he asleep?" Leo repeated. It was 2 P.M. No, Mack was no longer asleep and in fact was sitting right over there playing the guitar.

It was hard to believe she wasn't a Republican with a nose like that and so many pictures of bears and golfers and such nice etiquette, but she took Echinacea every day and had, according to Todd and Jen, hot-tubbed naked with them and ten other friends, and had, according to her, gone to many strip clubs, both male and female, and she had voted for Ross Perot.

"Oh, fudge!" Melody said. She had dropped a plate.

Leo went to help her clean it up and while he was squatting with the dustpan, he kept imagining her without her pants on, but he couldn't think of anything to say that might bring that about, and said nothing. *Zugzwang* worked for Todd, but it would obviously get Leo nowhere.

She asked him what he was doing in New York. He explained about the monkeys and the lab and how they had wanted him to do surgery on monkey brains.

"Oh no!" she said. "They should go to jail for that."

"Yeah. It seemed like a possible waste of monkeys," he said.

She looked at him as though a beetle had just climbed out of his mouth. He realized too late that he was surrounded by fervid antivivisectionists. Melody's girlfriend the vegan came into the room with a look on her face that brought to mind a vinegar-dressed salad and said, "*What* did they do?"

"I didn't take the job! I didn't take the job!" Leo said. And Deedee came and mounted him.

Love that knows no bounds can never be requited. This even Deedee the droopy-eyed springer spaniel seemed to know, with all her mounting and barking.

While Todd's friend with the Boris Becker eyebrows played the blues, Mack again studied the finger positions and tried to catch up. He made a racket and ruined the music, though Todd's friend didn't seem to mind.

Leo went back into the living room.

"Hey," Leo said, "you guys going to see fireworks?"

"Oh, is the Fourth of July a big deal on the East Coast?" Melody said.

"Uh..." Leo said.

He watched the Boston Pops play John Philip Sousa on TV and watched fireworks shoot off into the green darkness over Boston Harbor. The big TV under the landscape painting seemed puny and cheap in its total failure to reproduce any of the sights and sounds of fireworks. He remembered a Fourth of July he'd spent on the Mall in Washington, DC, and the Lincoln Monument. He'd always liked that place.

Leo didn't know why he was so depressed and further sinking, but he certainly was.

At night they played Taboo and drank beer in the stink of the dog's farts. They laughed, and the mood lightened. But he also asked himself: *Am I a fool? Will I be alone forever?*

And he went to bed and hid from the guitars under a pillow, but even after the guitar music had stopped he couldn't sleep. He got up. Mack was not in his bed.

Leo went out for a glass of water, and there was Mack in the kitchen leaning forward in a slightly awkward way with his hands on Melody's arms and they were licking their tongues together.

They went back to Portland with Todd and Jen. On their kitchen refrigerator was a picture of a cat and a pig and the words: "One you pet, one you eat. WHY?"

"Because," Leo said, "cats don't taste like bacon." Nobody laughed.

Todd and Jen had seaweed shampoo in their bathroom and a compost barrel behind the backyard patio. There were many stacks of CDs, bands and albums that Leo had never heard of. There were Nike sport-hiking shoes and many cats with honey fur and swaying, fat, low bellies. The Russian Blue was too scared to emerge from under the bed for more than a few minutes at a time. A serious backpack hung from the door, as if a hike were imminent at any time.

They went to the Rose Garden and Leo made a point of having ham at lunch. There were hundreds of breeds of roses, pink and orange roses so bright and stark against the dark-green grass it was not like a natural sight but rather like the shining spectra before a migraine. Mount Hood loomed over the rose-lined terraces, and Mount Saint Helens with its top blown off, snowy peaks at silent unreal distances like that of the moon—visible but too far to ever get there and following you wherever you go.

And right there in the Rose Garden in front of everyone, Leo said, "You don't care. I would die for you, and you don't care. I could be drowning and you wouldn't even notice unless somebody pointed it out to you. And then you would let me drown."

"Yeah, that's right. I would let you drown. What's wrong with you?"

"I was drowning two years ago and you didn't even know. How could you know? You'd drop everything and fly to China for one of your friends but I could be on fire and you wouldn't even notice, much less do anything about it, unless I said, 'Hey, I'm on fire, could you help extinguish me, perhaps by using a bucket of water?' and even then you'd just say you couldn't make it and wouldn't tell me why and the reason would be you were going to your friend's nephew's birthday party, something really important like that."

And Mack said, "*I* don't care about *you?* You say you care, but all you care about is yourself, *asshole!*"

"*I'm* an asshole? You didn't come to my graduations. You didn't come to my birthday. You're never there at all. When I broke my arm and called for you, you just left me lying there. When our canoe flooded, you remember that? You just swam ashore and left me in the river by myself to hold the canoe against the current alone and rescue all the gear by myself! And that tells it all! You're a *motherfucker!*"

And Leo couldn't stop it and he did what he had never done, he hit Mack in the face with a closed fist right there in the garden, right there among the roses bright as a migraine headache.

Leo jumped on top of his brother and punched him a second time while he lay on the ground. "What's wrong with you?" Leo shouted. "Why don't you fight back?"

But all Mack did was crawl back onto his feet and touch his fingertips to his bleeding nose and, as he had always done, let Leo's guilt do all the punching for him. And then Leo realized that Mack had stripped the watch off his wrist, the Raymond Weil inscribed to him for his twenty-first birthday by his aunt and uncle. He found most of it lying in the grass and held the broken watch out to Mack in his unsteady palm as if he were showing Mack his broken heart.

"They're brothers, they're brothers," Todd said. A policeman had come into the garden.

In the morning the Russian Blue came out from under the sofa and killed a spider and ate it. Separately, but within hearing of each other, Leo and Mack apologized to Todd and Jen about the scene in the garden because they both were really very grateful for being hosted and for the sleeping bags and backpacks and they felt taken care of. But they didn't apologize to each other. They said good-bye and drove to Olympia, Washington. They took Route 101 North along the misty Hood Canal with the Olympic Mountains on their left, on up past Dabob Bay, and followed the highway around to the west. In Sequim they bought stuff to take with them into the hills: smoked turkey, Muenster cheese, sourdough bread, some apples and bananas and baked nacho tortilla chips, and Leo also bought a Timex digital watch. They drove on between the mountains and the Strait of Juan de Fuca and the road ducked around to the south into a sad country of tree stumps. Leo swore to himself he would never apologize to Mack again. Every tree stump in the clear-cut forest was a one-sided apology Leo had made sometime somewhere for losing his temper.

"I'm sorry I hit you," Leo said, "I truly am."

"It's okay," Mack said, with eyes irreproachably calm but also blue and sad like that unvisited pond mirroring the sky.

And Leo wanted to hit him again and to hit the men who cut the trees down and to hit the stumps for being dead and to hit himself for using dead trees to write on and eating pigs he didn't have the courage to kill himself and for hitting his brother like a savage and he wished they would just terraform Mars already so everyone could just start over.

They drove south along the Elwha River and by the time they got to Lake Mills it was past four and wind was blowing false waves across the lake. They were going to drive another five or six miles up the Elwha River Road to the trailhead and then hike another two miles to a campground that Todd had shown them on the map.

"The road's washed out," the ranger said, and looked at the green Saturn where they sat with their asses one and a half inches from the road. "You could try it, but you won't get far in that thing." If they wanted to hike all the way, it would be seven and a half miles.

The sky blew dark and gray. If they made the hike in three hours, they'd only have an hour or so of light to pitch the tent, collect firewood, build the fire, and eat dinner, and that was as-suming it didn't rain.

"Shee-ut," Leo said. They had been listening to Jon Krakauer read *Into Thin Air* on tape, so they were well aware of the mortal peril that faced them. "We face mortal peril," Leo said.

"Fuck it, let's do it," Mack said.

"Skin-ut," Leo said. He didn't know how to use movie quotes the way Mack did. Mack didn't skin it.

They each loaded up the borrowed backpacks and Leo slung his frayed old MEI school backpack on his front as well and they set off up the road into the unspoiled world of the Olympic wilderness.

Once or twice they passed another couple of hikers. Sometimes they saw distant mountains that stood tall and blind with their peaks in the clouds. Sometimes they saw hills dark with lonely pines, which stood erect and waited for rain in that mute and homeless way of trees far up in secret hills. They sweated plenty into their T-shirts, and knew they would sleep in their sweat.

"My head is encased in three inches of ice," Leo said in his best Jon Krakauer.

"My brain screams for oxygen," Mack said.

"We're doing it, Mack. We're looking at the Western Cwm ice valley from the top of the world with our own eyes, Mack. It's just too bad I'll have to leave my left leg here in Tibet."

They hiked some more and Leo worried over the silence.

"What if I was X and you were Y?" he said in a harried, worried way. They called each other X and Y sometimes, some old reference that was by now partly forgotten. He thought it was something that happened on a family trip to Italy. They were playing at something and Leo had said he'd be Ixion and Mack should be Tantalus. Leo thought of that because it seemed that he hung himself on a wheel of fire and Mack held himself out of reach of love. But Mack didn't want to be Tantalus and they'd changed it to X and Y, something neutral and without meaning but that had somehow become funny to them in a now-forgotten way.

Mack didn't laugh about X and Y, and Leo thought he'd pressed too hard for an old shared memory. But then Mack said, "I'd say, 'You don't have any legs, X.'"

"I don't?" Leo said, surprised.

"You never did."

"Are you implying I'm an egg?"

"If the chromosome fits."

"If the chromosome fits you must acquit," Leo said. "Got the man out of jail with a rhyme."

"Don't put him in jail, *mmmf* this Pringle is stale!"

"Johnnie Cochran, standing before the judge, surprises himself by stuffing a bunch of Pringles into his own mouth! *Mmmf!*"

"We almost there?"

"No."

"You ambulate well for an egg."

"How did we get in Tibet?"

"We walked."

In the pitched ferns and moss on the forest floor they saw a grouse with two chicks. They saw many wildflowers, but didn't have time to get out the Audubon field guide to identify them. And when they got to the Boulder Creek campground up in the mountains, near the hot springs that the Elwha Indians said were the frustrated tears of two dragons who had fought to stalemate, there was nobody there. Nobody but a big buck elk wandering unafraid in the unhuman, lonely place, and it was so unafraid that it watched them come and they had time to count the points of its horns.

"I get twenty-nine," Leo said, and he didn't even notice the significance of that number. "Check me on that, Mack," Leo said, because he was bad at counting. He was better at calculus than he was at arithmetic, but Mack could do any kind of math without even understanding it, like an idiot savant.

"I get . . . twenty-two."

"Did you get those short ones there on the sides?"

"No, twenty-five. No, you're right, twenty-nine."

The elk turned away and then turned back so Leo could count again, and again he got twenty-nine. Then the elk turned and slowly walked off into the trees.

They pitched Gavin and Bailey's tent by the water music of the Elwha on a high ridge overlooking the river. The Indians said there used to be so many giant salmon you could walk across the river on their backs, but they didn't see any. As Mack preferred, Leo said where to pitch the tent and how to do it and where to make the fire and which wood was dead and which alive and no good for burning. The opposite hill was dark and distant and green with denuded tree trunks white like crazy needle teeth in the dusk.

Leo broke up a fallen tree limb by wedging it between two tree trunks and was pleased that it worked, as this would provide for a good long fire. They smoked cigars and watched stars appear and disappear as invisible clouds drifted by. Before bed, they hung their food up in a tree. If a bear came, Leo knew, it would be up to him to scare it away. He'd heard black bears outside his tent before and hyena even, when he was in Botswana, but he'd never had to run one off. Hyena could crack a man's skull with their jaws, he was told, and they'd proved it by biting through an inch and a half of Plexiglas. He could run off a hyena or a bear. He dared the mountain to challenge him when he was in charge of his brother.

"You remember when I left for college and I gave you that *Playboy*?" Leo said.

"Of course."

"1987. Luann Lee. Ah, Luann Lee. I had a lot of good times with Luann Lee. So did you like it? Were you glad or what?"

"Yeah! What do you think? I don't like to look at a *Playboy*?"

"I don't know. I couldn't tell if you were even interested in it. You didn't say anything at the time, so I thought, *Maybe he just thinks this is gross or something.*"

"No, man, I kept it for years."

"Did you have a girlfriend in LA?" Leo said, embarrassed that he didn't know, and trying not to be annoyed that Mack hadn't told him and that Mack wouldn't ask about his life in Baltimore or New York and didn't care.

"Yeah."

"Did I meet her?"

"No."

"Well, who was she? I assume you're not still with her, since—"

"Her name was Cindy."

"Yeah?"

"She was really funny but she had a temper. She once got mad at me because I beat her at tic-tac-toe. We played a bunch of times and I kept winning and every time I won I laughed, and she got mad. I was like, 'You're playing tic-tac-toe, I think you can figure out how not to lose. You're getting pretty angry.'"

"Was she in Teach for America?"

"Yeah, a kindergarten teacher. In Compton."

"Sorry if this is a weird thing to ask," Leo said, "but . . . did you have sex with her?"

Mack laughed with some embarrassment. "Yeah."

"I just wondered. So, was it good?"

"I guess so. We played hooky from school one day and just had sex all day. I remember we listened to the Dire Straits song 'So Far Away' over and over. That was nice. I don't know if you remember, but a long time ago I asked you about what to do with a girl."

"You did? No, I don't remember."

"We were on a Zajac vacation. You don't remember this?"

"No."

"I was in college. We were in a hotel room somewhere, each of us in our own bed, and we were talking about our frustrations with girls one night in the dark. I was thinking, *Who the fuck can I ask about this?* And I knew you'd had a girlfriend for a long time, and I figured you must know *something*."

"Ha!"

"Yeah, I figured you might like it if I asked you for your advice. You told me where the clit was and I asked you how do you do it and you said, 'You want to just touch very gently.' And I tried out your trick and it worked!"

"That's funny, I don't remember telling you that. But in my experience, it's true. And you know how I learned it? It's hilarious. I couldn't figure it out on my own, and every guy I asked was a complete idiot, and I asked Michelle and she didn't even know. I finally figured it out from reading the play *Cloud 9* by Caryl Churchill. She's a very edifying playwright!"

"Yeah, Cindy said I had magic fingers."

"But it didn't work out, huh."

"No, she was mad at me all the time. One time the Beastie Boys came on the radio. It was the song 'Girls.' Her brother really liked that song, and she was disgusted with it because it objectified women. Coming from Brown, I wasn't going to put up with that shit. So I said, 'You have a stick up your ass about this. Men like women. It's not a big deal. Plus, it's a song.' She got furious. I said, 'You're mad at your brother and me that we would like this song. Come on. And I don't even really like this song.' I told her if we were going to keep dating she had to tone down the anger, because I couldn't deal with it. And her response to that was to get even madder."

Leo slumped back against the log. But he was too tired to apologize again. He was too tired to point out the parallel between the girl's temper and his own, and he had no doubt that Mack would not see it anyway, even if he said it to him straight out. He was most of all too tired to tell Mack that Mack was mad as fucking hell too and had been bludgeoning him with rage for years but had turned that rage down to a temperature of zero degrees. He was sorry, he was sorry! He just wanted Mack to thank him for the *Playboy* and for teaching him how to deal with a clit, or to remember the times Leo had taken care of him. But sometimes Mack couldn't remember love, and sometimes neither could he. He looked out into the darkness beyond the fire and saw exactly nothing.

"You remember Red Barn, Mack?" Leo said.

"Yeah."

"What do you remember?"

"I remember it was pure hell."

"Remember the overnight? Your earache?"

"Yeah. Mostly I remember the cicadas. And the Melonheads."

The cicadas hadn't bothered Leo. He could show dominance to a cicada, a dog, a hyena, a bear, or a man. But not to those forces that made him weep in summer or fistfight among the painfully bright roses.

3.

THE CAIRNS OF THE KOOTENAI

LEO AND MACK took a picture of themselves in the dark sitting on the end of a log and smoking the cheap convenience-store cigars they'd bought in Sequim.

"It doesn't make you have to burp," Leo said, holding out a monogrammed flask, which had been a groomsman gift. "Hey, buddy, don't make me drink alone."

Mack relented and took the flask, drank, wiped his lips. "That's too strong for me. This cigar is already burning my throat. Isn't it burning yours?"

"Bah!" Leo dropped the heel of his boot into the coals and watched the red cinders fly up and barrage the darkness on long whirling braids of light.

"Careful!" Mack said.

Leo dropped his boot again and released some more fireflies, which puffed, paused, and then flew like Wile E. Coyote stepping off a cliff, pausing on the air, then falling. Leo had drunk enough to forget the fight in the Rose Garden.

"Why did Mom send us to that place?" Leo said. "What kind of mother sends their kids to a barn? A mother pig, that's who." He had to be drunk to bring up their mother.

"She did it for you, didn't she?" Mack said, with what Leo believed to be false innocence. "Because you hated sports camp."

"What do you mean?"

"I would've rather been playing baseball."

"I thought you told me once you were afraid of the ball back then."

"No. Not really."

Leo said, "She sent us to Red Barn because the Helpern kids went there." James Helpern's boys would all be surgeons, like their dad.

"Yeah, but Mom was worried about you. I remember."

His mom did worry about him, that much was true. How much he loved his mother! He could admit that to himself fully, proudly, when he was drunk, regardless of how his brother judged him for it. The most beautiful woman on earth, she'd been, before she paralyzed half of her face. At her wedding to Philip, she'd worn a silver silk blouse, the kind of thing Susan Clark wore in *The North Avenue Irregulars* in 1979, and she was soft and strong just like all those chaste, fair females of the North Avenue Presbyterian Church in the movie: Rookie, June Bride, Kiddie Car, and Phantom Fox (even Cloris Leachman had a pleasing shape in 1979, though he'd adored Susan Clark more in her shirtwaist dresses and Karen Valentine at the organ and Barbara Harris joking about her Saint Bernard; he'd adored them in a rather distant way back then, as one adores something very valuable that must not be handled, a mint-condition baseball card or the title to some estate cached in safe deposit). His mother was beautiful like those beautiful ladies in the movies and at heart as tough as those Midwestern matrons you read about who lift a truck off their children in the moment of need, and that was what his mom had done, in a way. He wished it were 1979, before his mom's face was paralyzed, before AIDS, and he could have sex with Miss April of that year, Missy Cleveland, who was nineteen and had real breasts with soft pink nipples and a huge blond civet-buttered bush.

"What, you think she wasn't worried about you?" Leo said.

"Not as much as you," Mack said, looking in the firelight noble and faintly aggrieved like an Indian.

Leo did not even let out the great big sigh rising up in his chest.

Not long after the sun came up in Olympic National Park, Leo went out of the tent and sat on a rock thinking. He remembered the smell of coffee and wind particular to canoe trips with Philip; Philip had been Dad for as long as he could clearly remember. And he thought for a long time about the elk and where it was right then and where it had slept and whether it had slept at all, and what it thought when it woke up (like, *I guess I won't brush my teeth again since I have no hands*). He listened to the running of the Elwha and wondered if he was enjoying the sound, which nearly moved him to tears (he couldn't let it, though, and so the tears remained a fullness in the rear passages of his nose and throat). Or was the sound of the Elwha the sound of the last good things on earth bleeding out to their tragic end as the human race fragged itself on its own unstable age of change? Or was it only the sound of his own minutes on earth trickling from the vein?

"You all right? You mad?"

"No, I'm not mad," Leo said.

They packed up and loaded up and left. Leo didn't care about bears anymore. He didn't care if he was eaten or not. He hoped he would be eaten and that Mack would run away and live.

They went to see the springs, yellow algae-bubbling pools that breathed a sulfurous steam among rocks. It didn't look like a good place to swim. They hiked back down and stopped for lunch beside a gray chill sky. They saw fallen trees, alpine forget-me-not, and sage buttercup.

Leo carried in hand his *National Audubon Society Field Guide to North American Wildflowers: Western Region*, heavy as a brick with its glossy photo paper, and he didn't say anything the whole way down. He waited for Mack to say something but Mack didn't say anything either.

When they reached the bottom the green Saturn awaited them one and a half inches from the mud.

They drove on.

They drove to Bainbridge Island and took a ferry to Seattle. There in that northwestern capital, on a Wednesday, they ate their lunch with the businessmen on the grassy embankment at Pike Place Market, watching tankers and ferries slowly cross Puget Sound. An old man with no shirt on and rings through his nipples and tattoos up and down his back ate a nectarine with his left hand and only his left hand, prodded his thumb through its rind and squeezed its juice into his mouth. Leo admired this act of gusto and thought the old man very wise. He said, "Mack, I need help."

"What is it."

"Something's going on with me."

"Why."

"You know, this happens to me sometimes. I'm sorry it's happening now, but it really is." Leo spat on the ground. Swallowing anything, even saliva, was like swallowing a nail.

"It's okay."

"Help."

"What should I do?" Mack said.

"I don't know. If I knew I wouldn't need help."

At the University of Washington a group of touring high school kids passed them twice. Both times Leo smiled at two pretty young girls and they smiled at him. They went to see a movie, *Summer of Sam,* and ate dinner in Belltown, where it was raining and completely dead and empty. The prawns scraped Leo's throat and the Merlot burned the scrapes.

He stayed awake in the Red Roof Inn thinking about time, thinking about how each passing second is different and smaller than the one before, because every new second adjoined to the seconds of memory has a smaller and smaller share of the total time lived, and week by week, year by year, the pace of time accelerates so that living is in fact diving headfirst into a screaming black hole. And he thought of last good-byes, how for every person he knew there would be one, a last one forever and ever, though neither he nor they might recognize the moment for what it was till after it had come and gone. And he thought of how the earth is filled with liquid—metal, but liquid metal (he wanted to write a story about a man who dug to the center of the earth and became the richest person in history with all his wealth in nickels that he piled on the moon)—he thought of how all people, splitting their seconds one by one like atoms, were living on a fragile floating rind, like ants on an easily punctured nectarine. Then all the products of human life and human beings themselves could be wiped out at one blow without a worry for all the hard and careful work people had done or for the billions of years it had taken for Earth and its people to get to that point, without a care for how people would feel.

In the morning they drove west on Highway 2 across Washington State, across the dirt quarry of the Columbia River Basin, dry and brown with vast Martian mesas of denuded earth and a few unnatural lakes here and there in the dark unnatural earth. As they passed through the irrigation district, Leo's heart sank deeper and deeper, city by city: Ephrata, Electric City, Coulee City, Davenport. They stopped at the Grand Coulee Dam, the largest concrete structure in the world, stuff of the Roman Empire, the New Deal project that bridled the Columbia River to make tanks and bombs and irrigate the desert east of the Cascades. FDR's wooden wheelchair rested there like a shed carapace, like the dam itself, a remainder of the Great Depression and the New Deal and the war. A Blackfoot Indian sat before a stack of pamphlets at the Grand Coulee museum, not saying anything. Leo went to the bathroom and took off his Cleveland Indians jersey with Chief Wahoo on it so he was wearing only his shrunken pit-stained white undershirt.

And finally, in Spokane they ate at Frank's Diner, which was in a real railroad car, and Leo thought of lying on the tracks, except that there were no tracks; it was just a railroad car turned into a little restaurant on a patch of weeds. The free newspaper in the vestibule rack said the Nazis were marching tomorrow morning in Coeur d'Alene.

"Let's go see what these fuckers think they're all about," Leo said, and in fact, at least for a moment, he felt he would slay the doom, death, and desperation in his mind once and for all and never again have the urge to lie down on railroad tracks.

The first things they saw were weird flags—Confederate flags, upside-down American flags, Nazi flags—and when Mack saw them he said, "Let's get out of here. This place is not good for us."

"Yeah, maybe you're right," Leo said. "Especially not me."

"Especially not either of us."

The avenue was lined with innocent mom-and-pop country-cute stores like you see in Chagrin Falls east of Cleveland, and there were decorations still up from the Fourth of July, lots of those half circles of county-fair red-white-and-blue bunting that call to mind grandmother aprons and butter churns. Leo looked at them and saw families hoping for customers and the Fourth of July colors on the embarrassed storefronts were like the color of their shame.

The people in the parade were shouting, "White power!" and a lot more people were shouting back, "White trash!" The king of the parade seemed to be an old man lying on a lawn chair on the back of a pickup truck. They were right up close; the old man had brown spots on his head and a tie with a swastika tie clip and a bullhorn. A big white dog lay next to him with its head between its paws on the flatbed and its eyes closed.

The old man said into the bullhorn, "I don't think there are too many niggers out there because my dog Himmler here's sound asleep. My dog doesn't hardly ever get to smell nigger, it drives him crazy. I'm glad I'm not a nigger. Himmler would chew my leg off. If you want to live under the thumb of the Jew dictatorship, that's fine with me, if you want your children's blood mixed with nigger blood, then go right ahead. But go do it down in the islands where nigger people belong, or in holes in the Ural Mountains where the Jew belongs, not in the USA. This is a land of whites and Christians. Now, some people think we're violent. That's what the Jew wants you to believe and what he tells you in the Jew-controlled mainstream media. In fact, we're not violent at all. We're just the same as anyone. We're not violent unless you threaten our children. That's when violence becomes the only moral choice. When the laws of God come into conflict with the laws of man, then it's your duty as a Christian not to follow the laws of man, laws written by a government of mongrels. But don't listen to what Jew newspapers and belly-aching niggers say. We're not violent. We just want to be left in peace. People ask me if I condone the actions of that fellow in Chicago who shot the niggers and Chinamen on the Fourth of July. I say, no I do not, as he then turned the gun on himself, and suicide is a sin against the Lord Jesus Christ."

There was a helicopter in the sky. There were a hundred policemen in riot gear, there to protect the straggly, pathetic little Nazi parade from the citizens of Coeur d'Alene, who were doing most of the yelling and were jabbing their signs at the sky. The green hills themselves seemed embarrassed by the basic irrelevance of it all and the green traffic lights, too, spearing the boring cloudless blue sky, unable to do anything about any affair of human beings but stand there and suffer in the harsh mid-morning sun over the eastern end of Sherman Avenue.

The Nazis seemed to take a peculiar pleasure in refusing to be deterred, like a child saying "You can't make me," and they threw a black baby doll onto the street and began to take turns gleefully stomping on it. A lady with a real baby in her arms, a white baby, of course, kicked the black baby doll as if it were an effigy and when a man in the crowd called something to her, she went right up to him and struck him directly in the face.

Leo was pushed forward up close to the lady with the Nazi baby and he said, "Let me ask you something! Let me ask you something! If you're so superior to the Jews—"

"I am! I'm white! I'm Christian!"

"If you're so superior to the Jews, then why are they running the world and you're out here in Idaho with your leader in the back of an old pickup truck?"

"You just admitted it! You admit you're trying to run the world, you kike parasite!" she said, and she reached out and swatted Leo in the face and her fingernails flashed hot across his temple. "This is a Christian country! Love it or leave it!"

"You Nazi bitch."

He couldn't see Mack anywhere.

He heard Mack calling his name but he still couldn't see him, and for a moment he wished Mack hadn't used his name because he thought the Nazis would come get him. Then he felt a big arm around him. Mack was much bigger than he used to be, a big lug now, six foot three, an inch taller than Leo.

The old man was raising his voice louder through the wobbly bullhorn and he had his arm up in a *Sieg Heil* salute.

"How could somebody that frail consider himself superior?" Mack said. "To anyone. The guy looks like Larry King."

"Isn't the car that way?" Leo said.

"It's up here," Mack said. "Let's get the fuck out of Idaho."

"I'll get bacteremia from the bugs that live under that Melon-head bitch's fingernails," Leo said in the bathroom of Dunkin' Donuts. He'd worried so much they had to stop and buy hydrogen peroxide, which fizzed along his scratches in the bathroom mirror.

They drove north through the purple hills of the Idaho pan-handle, back up to Highway 2 and then east into Montana, where they went to the forest and followed the cairns of the Kootenai. Even though it was too cold, they ate peanut butter and jelly sandwiches and potato chips and played chess by the windy waves of Lake Koocanusa.

Leo said chess made him sad. Once you move a pawn forward it can never go back, he said. That was sad. And a king, he said, once caged by a rook or a queen, can never go back again. A pawn can go back, Mack said, it can get promoted. To any piece except one, Leo said: king. And did you ever think how the king is never taken from the board at checkmate? Leo said. Like it's too painful to see him die.

"All right, let's play," Mack said. "You need some distraction."

"I'm sorry I've been so down," Leo said, and tears spilled out then where they weren't supposed to, right out into the Lake Koocanusa sun and wind. "And I want you to know, Mack, that I think I get it. The thing with Mom or other people worrying about me. I understand that's complicated for you. I want you to know I feel for you, too, and how cruel life was to you, too, and I feel terrible I hit you, Mack, I was weak. It's just sometimes I need you so much. Because I need Daddy, I still do, I guess, and it rankles in my heart. But I love you, brother." And the tears just ran like the Kootenai and he let them run and didn't even wipe them off his face, even when some hikers came hiking healthfully by and said healthfully hi without appearing to notice that his heart was broken.

Mack clapped his hand on Leo's shoulder and said, "That means a lot to me that you say that, Leo. I love you, too. And even though we experienced different things, I'm beginning to feel more and more like we've been in it together."

Now Leo did wipe up his tears with his sleeve. Leo said that if you look at an endgame position without knowing all the moves that came before, that position implies a certain history of conflicts on the chess board, of decisions and mistakes, but you don't know exactly what happened, how it got that way, and a person is like an endgame position with certain pieces on the board, certain strengths and weaknesses and a certain direction and tendency and style of behavior because of what came before, but nobody really knows all the moves that came before, not even the person himself.

Then he wanted to tell Mack about *Zugzwang,* what the Germans called it when your opponent had no good option but had to move somewhere and you just waited, and Leo wanted to say that was a good philosophy of life in many ways. But Mack wanted to play on, and they did, and Mack kicked Leo's ass again without any *Zugzwang* ever coming into the game at all.

They drove into a minefield of bugs in the air between Montana lakes, bugs snapping like flying pebbles against the windshield and blowing up on the glass in explosions of white and yellow hemolymph. They listened to Julian Lennon's song, "Too Late for Goodbyes," and they stopped for the night at the Sandman Motel in a town called Libby. Leo had had a friend named Libby once, hadn't he? A good friend, a friend from the preschool years of his life who remained in his mind like a good genie. They took the only available room, a smokers' double, and there Leo had a dream.

Just before waking up in the morning, he dreamed that the Blackfoot Indian at the Grand Coulee information desk was working as an elevator inspector, and agreed to take Leo down to the sub-subbasement of an apartment building on the Upper West Side of New York where he was considering renting (except in the dream the Upper West Side looked like Carnegie Avenue in Cleveland). The Indian said he spoke to the dead. He said he'd spoken to Leo's father and that his father was an elk now. And Leo said, Can I speak to him? And the Indian said that wouldn't be a good idea, but he didn't say why. Then he didn't take him to the sub-subbasement, but instead just opened the doors to the elevator and they were still in the lobby. The elevator hadn't gone anywhere, and Leo waited to go down to the sub-subbasement, and that made the Indian very irritated, as though Leo was not understanding something he was supposed to understand, and the clear implication was that Leo was that overprivileged, overeducated type that might have a graduate degree but doesn't know how to dance or to say hello and good-bye or to look a person in the eye when you drink and say *Salud!* And he thought to himself in the dream that this was just so typical of dreams, so ridiculous, and he woke himself up by laughing even though it wasn't funny, it was infuriating. Mack woke up too.

"That was like sleeping in an ashtray," Mack said, and grabbed at his lower back and winced.

When they went to check out, Leo saw that outside the office of the Sandman Motel there was a large cigar store Indian with cracks running down his forehead into his nose from many days of rain and sun. Leo looked him in the eye and said, *"Salud!"*

They went farther east and got food and drink in Kalispell and then took the Going-to-the-Sun Road (as the Blackfeet Indians called it) into Glacier National Park. They stopped and ate their Kalispell peaches, white bread, and Gouda at a picnic table at a drive-up campground. A laminated card stapled to the table warned against feeding bears, but they didn't see any bears. Instead they saw Mennonites who rolled up in a giant white van and climbed out of it in their last-century cape dresses and pleated caps and gray jackets like they were climbing out of a very low-budget time machine. They didn't speak or laugh or smile, but two of the boys, with tragically monkish haircuts, ran straight to the brook, which was about one inch deep, and dropped in their fishing lines. Silent men pulled a cooler and a Coleman stove out of the back of the van, and women set up cans of some kind of Spammy-looking meat, bread, mustard, mayonnaise. The girls in their head coverings with the long white ties on them looked over at Mack and Leo with fear and Leo felt rough and terrible in their eyes. They made Leo sad.

"Will you stop with the sad," Mack said. "They're not sad, they're just Mennonites."

Leo and Mack hiked up into the mountains on a path dug into steep rocks and wildflowers, with long grass and purple flower petals growing out into the air above and below them, hanging out over the chasm, a huge volume of nothing and nobody before snowy Heavens Peak nine thousand feet up. Here and there rivulets of melted snow crossed the path from up above. Mack and Leo climbed up over purple-and-green mountain shale. Heavens Peak did indeed look close and faraway at the same time because in the clear air and bright sun you could see every detail of its faces.

As they hiked up toward the place called the chalet, the immensity of the mountains and the empty volume of sky below gave Mack an attack of agoraphobia. Leo continued on alone, hoping to reach the chalet, onward in blazing light, and had to stop to catch his breath and he stood and let his eyes absorb the storm of mute and glittering energy ringing through the sky of the Northern Rockies. The shale was often wet with trickling streams but he was parched and almost out of water. A descending hiker said he had more than an hour to get to the chalet, too long to leave Mack sitting there. The chalet was lost.

Back in the car, they listened to the soundtrack of Oliver Stone's *Born on the Fourth of July* and "American Pie" came on just as they were crossing the Continental Divide. At the Logan's Pass visitors' center Leo saw his red red face in the mirror and rinsed the salty dried sweat from his forehead and temples in glacier water. Skiers glided down the mountain above. Snow. Mack took a picture of Leo on a wall with his arms outstretched and the broad daylight of the mountains reprinted in his sunglasses so that it would look like Leo was flying. And in an instant, on the other side of the mountains, it was later in the day because the mountain wall behind them reached up nearly to the sun.

They sang as much as they could remember of "America

the Beautiful." They looked with their own eyes at "purple mountains' majesties" and "amber waves of grain," the blowing undulating grass of the buffalo plains of eastern Montana.

"It's like *The Muppet Movie* but in reverse," Leo said.

"And real," Mack said.

"Goddamn, this is a great country!" Leo said. "What those Founding Fathers dreamed up, it was a Newtonian, Lockean ideal, they went for it, they went all-in, and just look at it. Not only did it come to pass, it's more than they ever could have imagined. All this and we're free, too, to go wherever we want and do and be whatever we want. There's no place like it on earth. It's a dream."

"It's like a dream," Mack said, which was a quote from the movie *The World According to Garp,* the scene where Garp crashes his car and gets his penis bitten off.

"Should I stop talking about America?" Leo said.

"No, no, you're inspiring me."

They tried to sing "This Land Is Your Land" but they couldn't remember the words. "Something something that ribbon of highway and up above me a something skyway...uh...uh... this land was made for you and me!"

When they stopped, Leo wrote it all down in a journal of Venetian leather that Mack called the Grail Diary. He remembered the line in Woody Guthrie's song about the sign that said No Trespassin' and on the other side, it didn't say nothin' and he felt the need to explicate for Mack: "I love that because you can only see the back of a No Trespassing sign by disobeying it."

Mack said, "I didn't think of that."

And Leo sang, "Now, that side was made for you and me."

Altogether they sighted three dead deer in Montana, one scavenged upon until it was only a fly-ridden head. A bird took off from the grassy median while Mack was driving, a forward-looking bird ascending, aiming at the cerulean prospect of the late-afternoon horizon and feeling the sky, the future, the grass, with his unknowable bird's sense of things, only to be stricken—*thunk!* a sound like a glass cylinder vanishing in a pneumatic tube—at eighty miles per hour by their hurtling green Saturn. They drove on for several more hours and at the Comfort Inn outside of Sioux Falls, South Dakota, they found the bird stuck between the grille of the car and the hood. Mack was so repulsed he could hardly hold up the hood of the car for Leo to clean it off (the beater Saturn had no hood stand).

"Jesus, Maxwell," Leo said. "I'm the one who's cleaning it up." He'd said "Maxwell" to make it a joke but couldn't eradicate all the malice from his voice, the malice of old wounds, the malice of Nazis and Zionists and Muslims and all the grudge-masters of the earth.

"Okay, sorry," Mack said. But then he clutched at his face and said, "Uch! Oh my God! That is so disgusting, I can't even stand here!"

Leo tried to keep silent but said, "You're being a complete girl about this."

Leo saw Mack's soul begin to close on that remark like a Venus flytrap, and saw Mack fall righteously silent, and that made Leo even madder at this moment of heavy mortuary duty, shouldered, as ever, by himself and himself alone.

"Why don't you jam your hood open with one of your wire hangers? That would redeem their presence, grabbing on to my duffel bag like a gremlin that lives in the trunk every time I get my bag out."

"Will you shut up about the hangers already! Asshole!" Mack said.

A thunderclap of fear struck them both and they stood shaking like men on earthquake ground, waiting for an aftershock.

"Sorry," Leo said. "It's the bird."

"It's okay."

Leo recited: Mack is your truest friend, Mack is your truest friend and he invited you to do this once-in-a-lifetime thing with him! He invited you, fool!

Leo rolled the bird into a newspaper, sang the *Sh'ma,* and dumped the dead bird in a trash can outside Arby's. The next day there were still spots of black blood under the hood and a few yellow-and-brown feathers.

The carnage they left behind: nameless flying bugs, one butterfly, another big winged insect (Mack said a moth) caught under the wiper blade, then released by activating the wipers, almost a Montana deer and with it two human brothers from Cleveland in a crap-green Saturn tin can, and last one yellow-bellied leap-without-looking bird—*thunk!* into the pneumatic tube of death. A meat truck slowly receded next to their car on the highway. It had a goofy cartoon of a bull on the side, proclaiming its prey with no compassion at all, like Americans killing Indians and claiming their ground and naming baseball teams after them and putting caricatures of them on the baseball jerseys. *What an abattoir life is,* Leo thought, *everything fragile and constantly getting slaughtered under the carriage wheels of life and destroyed in its prehistoric jaws.*

To eat, Leo thought, *to drive, is to kill. To live is to kill.* And they went on down the road eastward in their terrible glory; alive; killers; lords of the earth. All the way through the Badlands, where Leo got a migraine with a double aura, which had never happened before, all the way to the great metropolis of the plains where his soul mate dwelled, Chicago.

4.

THE HOG BUTCHER

APPROACHING CHICAGO FROM the west on a summer's afternoon, the shadows point toward the city. As its towers rise in the distance, so you loom up on pillar legs on the burning pavement of the Kennedy. And since the long shadows are the forgotten trails of the traveling sun, you feel that you're going someplace you've already been. You see plane after plane screaming into O'Hare through a cloudless lavender sky and you see the sun flashing on every plate of airborne steel and every countersunk screw. And you do see freight trains and you see Polish churches. And you have traveled over the whole of the Great Plains and the city is the first vertical thing you've seen for fifteen hundred miles and is therefore lord and sovereign over those fifteen hundred miles and the Sears Tower is the sovereign skyscraper of the world.

You feel love for the lone giant of the Plains, standing on

hardy pillar legs before Lake Michigan in cloudless summer and casting stalwart shadows like the legs of your mother and your father used to. You feel an old and reverent love when you come to Chicago and a trust that the rugged, perseverant human race will figure it all out and propagate on and on into the far future, past the dying of the sun, on generation ships bound for new planets where people will still eat kielbasas and drink Budweiser on their roof decks and the Cubs will still lose.

He'd heard Michelle was living there now, but he hadn't talked to her in years. Had it been love back then? Or just the foolishness of youth and the first time? It had not been, in the end, the love of the pre-op man and the woman with the white lace-fringed pillow off their marriage bed. *Wonder what happened to them. Something. Wonder what happened to Michelle.*

As he approached the Regenstein Library at the University of Chicago, where Berry was doing her residency, he instructed himself firmly, firmly not to have overly high expectations, not to bring to the library his fantasy Berry, next to which poor real Berry would be destined to fail.

And yet she was named Berry. That was at once so evocative of fruit, ovaries, female sex organs, beauty, flowers, dessert, summer—at once all that and so unique. And her parents must have been unique to name her that, and her father was a doctor, but literate, he loved D. H. Lawrence, Bailey had said, and her mother was someone of importance, he recalled, so she was bred of good people, strong people, magnanimous and benevolent people. And Berry had suggested they meet in a library; perhaps she'd spent a good deal of her childhood in the library of some wonderful old summer home, reading her father's books, and had been bookish but had discovered sex in D. H. Lawrence and rubbed one out now and then to scenes from *Women in*

Love (which Leo had never read but presumed to be full of sex). And he had Bailey's account of her friend in his mind. The girl was clearly smart, given where she'd gone to college and where she was doing her pediatrics residency, and she was good in her soul, a doctor. She cared for children. It had to be. And the ivy grew lush on the neo-Gothic stone of the campus, and people walked their bicycles in front of quiet archways with oak doors, thinking, presumably, as he did about genes, energy, force, time, stained glass, Pericles, induction, deduction, Francis Bacon, anatomy, the Renaissance, *Hamlet,* Virginia Woolf, Rome, medicine, and John Stuart Mill. There were quiet low little houses behind whose arrow-slit windows sat deans and masters, leather armchairs and secret Persian rugs, young men and women preparing to rule the world, and silver flagons with a century of names inscribed upon them, just as it had been at Yale—though the buildings here were slightly more spare, with a wind-ripped Midwestern honesty about them.

Despite all self-instruction, he had a feeling of destiny.

The floor plan of the Regenstein building had the shape of the continental United States, with an entrance somewhere around Louisiana. The building looked like the modernist dorms at Yale, Morse and Stiles, buildings of morbid, water-stained concrete.

He didn't see her at first there in the student union, because she was not the dreamed-of Berry, but a different one, the real one, sitting at a table with her coffee in a paper cup.

She was indeed soft and very sweet-looking, thin, with eyes that were slightly red, the right more than the left, red from fatigue and from her contact lenses, which he judged she had worn for his benefit. And around her eyes there was a weariness that seemed to run very deep, a weariness of the spirit, as if she had been crying for a long time or had had all her blood taken out and put back in, and she had a kind of mauled, haunted gaze that looked out as if through a long periscope from the bottom of a deep well of overmastered pain. Her eyes were smitten by pain, he thought. Leo thought you could see clearly on her face that she had loved fiercely and lost; he thought of the poem where Catullus called his love a crushed meadow flower "ungently beneath the plowshare stricken" and you could see too that she was postcall. He'd said he could come see her another time but she said it was okay, she'd said you're only in town for a day, right? Maybe it wasn't the depths of grief there on her face, but just that drowned, waterboarded look of hospital house staff.

"Am I late?" he said. "I broke my watch." He had left the replacement Timex in his room since the band already smelled like feet.

"Not too much," she said, and stood up. They awkwardly shook hands. She said she liked to get coffee there at the Reg, to be on a campus, around books.

"I love this campus," he said. "The library is a bit modern for my tastes, though."

"I think they call the style Brutalism," she said.

"Brutalism," he said. "That's fitting."

"I just heard something about it on NPR."

"You're sure you're not too tired?"

"No, no," she said. "I have my coffee. What happened to your face?"

"Oh, this?" Leo said, touching the scabs where the Nazi woman had scratched him. "I ran afoul of some Chicago Bulls fans."

"Seriously?"

"No. You're not from Chicago, are you? Can I speak freely? This town doesn't know shit about sports suffering, man."

"What about the Cubs?"

"I know, I know, what about the Cubs."

He said Bailey had thought of their meeting because of his dead father. And the mention of death seemed to make her brain contract like a sea anemone contracting at the touch and the inwardness of her eyes plunged fathoms deeper than before. And he suddenly saw the irony: that they were the very two people on the face of the earth least suited for each other—a woman mourning a dead man and in search of a man to rouse her from mourning; and a man in eternal mourning, looking for any woman but one who was mourning a dead man. No, he would not ever compete with that, never, knew better by now than to try to compete with a dead man. A dead man would bludgeon him. Dead men don't play fair. They drown you in your own love for them until you can't compete with them or anyone else and you just knobble around on your knees for the whole of your life with your hands tied behind your back. No fucking way. He would crack and blow up like plutonium with her past dead love peering out of picture frames at him for the rest of his life.

5.

Dead Man's Curve

Jerry Siegel was from Cleveland. You know who he was? He and another Jewish nerd from Cleveland named Joe Shuster made up a story together in 1933, when they were teenagers, a story that soon afterward became very well known. The idea for the story came from a real incident: Siegel's father was robbed at gunpoint at his place of business, had a heart attack, collapsed, and died there on the floor of his secondhand clothing store. Afterward, Siegel dreamed up a story with a very profound wish in it, a wish for a small alteration in the universe such that people's fathers would be saved from robbers by a hero, someone who knew what it was to lose. The story was about Kal-El, a baby born on planet Krypton. Kal-El's father, Jor-El, was certain that the entire planet of Krypton was going to blow up and kill everyone on it. Jor-El decided to send his infant son in a spaceship to planet Earth. And after that, guess what: Krypton blew up. And do you know who besides the baby Kal-El survived the explosion of planet Krypton, which Jor-El predicted would kill everybody? Nobody did! Jor-El was right! The destruction of the planet incinerated Kal-El's entire family! And all the inhabitants of Krypton! Just as Siegel's aunts and uncles and all the other Jews of Europe would soon be burned up in Nazi ovens! (But nobody, presumably, used the body parts of Kryptonians to make soap!) End of paragraph!

So... Kal-El's spaceship landed on a farm, where he was taken in by the Kent family and raised with the identity Clark Kent. As Kal-El/Clark Kent grew up, he discovered something that set him apart from others: he had superpowers. Eg, he was faster than a speeding bullet and able to leap tall buildings in a single bound. Ultimately, he became an invincible flying vigilante with X-ray vision and a cape and he used his powers to fight for Truth, Justice, and the American Way. (Except he wasn't completely invincible because if you confronted him with kryptonite, being a remnant of the home planet that had crumbled and killed his parents, he crumbled too and lost his powers.) Shuster, who was a talented artist, illustrated the story for his friend, depicting "Superman" in his now-familiar attire. In 1938 they sold thirteen pages to the corporate forerunner of DC Comics for $130. These thirteen pages became the first-ever "superhero comic," *Action Comics #1.* And guess what: it was a hit! But DC Comics, stirred to sudden contemplation by the success of *Action Comics #1,* a single copy of which is now worth millions, concluded that Superman was, in legal terms, "mine hands off." Under the law DC was not obligated to pay Siegel and Shuster anything, and guess what: instead of anything, they paid them nothing. What they did do aside from paying them nothing was, in colloquial terms, "jack shit." And

Siegel became a mail clerk and Shuster went blind and died of congestive heart failure. The End.

Burn on, big river, burn on.

They drove east on the Indiana East-West Toll Road, through Gary and South Bend, to the Ohio Turnpike, where they saw KISS KISS COKE WHORE painted on a bridge. It had been there for years.

Leo said, "Didn't we just leave this party?" which was his favorite *Star Wars* quote. It was perfect for the occasion of re-turning and it was his favorite quote because it was one of two movie quotes he could remember. The other was Danny Glover in *Lethal Weapon* saying with slurred speech, "Put—it—in—your—mouth."

But Mack could cite *Forrest Gump, Ferris Buehler's Day Off, A Few Good Men, Weird Science, Rocky,* and *Star Wars* like the Talmud, and if anyone was listening they would have thought the two brothers were insane because they sounded like this:

Leo: "So, beetolay." (Greedo to Han Solo.)

Mack: "Uh, what country do you think this ee-is?" (Garage attendant to Ferris Buehler.)

And then Leo said in the voice of Paulie from *Rocky V,* "Tommy, you're a piece a garbage, you know that?" which cracked him up by itself but was mainly a setup for Mack to say in a severely brain-damaged Rocky Balboa voice, "You knock him down. Now you got knock *me* down!"

And Mack did say that. And he also said, "Yo, Mondrian!"

And Leo said in a high, tearful Australian accent like Meryl Streep in *A Cry in the Dark,* "A dingo ate my baby." That was the other movie quote he knew.

And Mack said in the same high, tearful Australian accent, "A dingo ate my pussy."

And Leo laughed about that all the way to Toledo, when he thought of how he had extorted the letter opener. He had been at his grammy's house when he was seven or eight and they looked at old pictures and he cried about some pictures of his dead father. And then in the little study with the bullfighter painting he had seen a golden dagger with a red hilt and when you pulled it from its gold-tipped leather scabbard you saw that the dagger base was filigreed with runic symbols in red and blue. (It was a letter opener from Toledo, Spain.) And he had coveted the gold dagger from Toledo, Spain. And he couldn't help it and asked his grandpa (not the dead one, obviously, but his grammy's second husband) if he could have the letter opener. His grammy felt sorry for him and guilty perhaps, because of the pictures, and with her eyes had told his grandpa to give up the letter opener and he could tell from his grandpa's eyes that he didn't want to, but he did, and the letter opener still leaned precariously in a mug full of pens in Leo's bedroom in Cleveland and Leo felt guilty every time he looked at it. He had even tried to give it back.

And at last they got off the turnpike, which Leo had driven a hundred times on his way to and from the University of Michigan, and they passed Cleveland Hopkins International Airport and drove on. They took the banked, curving underpass that Leo always thought of as Dead Man's Curve, even though the real Dead Man's Curve was on I-90. Leo thought of getting lost looking for the exit to the zoo with a girl in his car who wouldn't kiss, not even a peck on the mouth, and a very beautiful girl who worked in a bookstore and had practically no tits and had surprised him with a yes. He thought of the highway trips to see the Cavs, all the time he'd wasted rooting for those Cleveland sports teams who hadn't won anything since 1964 when the Terminal Tower ceased to be the tallest building in the world outside of

New York. Now that Albert Belle was gone to the White Sox he saw the utter futility of caring anymore, even when the Indians were in first place and Manny Ramirez was hitting like Jimmie Foxx. Manny would leave them too, no doubt about it.

The brothers were too tired to joke anymore by the time they took exit 25B around to soul-whipping Warrensville Center Road and the Heinen's that once stood for fried chicken, but now just stood, recalcitrantly ugly and refusing still to have any windows. And they passed the checkered flag of Conrad's Total Car Care, which was forever a symbol of saying good-bye (since it was on the departure side of the road) and they crossed great cracked seas of saturnine gray pavement in their saturnine green Saturn and rolled farther north into the elegiac Lake Erie twilight.

"This street looks like a Samuel Beckett play with skid marks," Leo said.

Then came the nerve assault of that treeless corner with Valvoline Instant Oil Change on the left and on the right the desert of concrete and dirt, the hell-mounds and the tiny dull and distant windows of the Thistledown Racetrack, and there were almost no trees until Warrensville Heights Middle School, where it started to get green and the happy Midwestern feeling of home wavered into being. Places along the way cast dagger shadows, though, even in Shaker Heights—like the Thornton public pool with that spongy gray caulking in the seams of the concrete that squished under your naked toes, and some nice memory of a babysitter there, or a girl, the wind blowing the tall grass behind the fence, and the doom smell of chlorine. Joe Sgro's Barbershop, where his father, Philip, went (Leo used to go to the other Joe, at Fratantonio's), and then the old trees, the curving streets and Van Sweringen mansions of Shaker Heights, like the Cotswolds, especially around those lakes where the ducks flew low in the morning mist and the willow tree branches bowed to their reflections. Except that the houses of Shaker Heights had central air, and were not meant for little seventeenth-century English hobbits but for big twentieth-century Americans with big dreams. Even the small houses of Shaker Heights had garages that didn't face the street, by city ordinance, and they sat on streets that looked so benign and tranquil it was hard to think of anybody dying there.

When they entered the kitchen with all the *New Yorker* death cartoons on the refrigerator door, their mother hugged Mack first and then hugged Leo, and Leo watched his brother watching him. Mack had that half-averted gaze and that waiting look of his that combined judgment and condescending sympathy—like he was watching someone litter or inject drugs or get into a public argument and he was too polite to comment on the ugly behavior and anyway considered himself powerless to intervene. *What the hell did I do, after all?* Leo thought, and he tried to shake off an inexplicable feeling of guilt and an urge, which came after the guilt and not before, to turn on the stove and put his brother's head to the flame.

Mack went out onto the porch.

"How are you?" his mother said.

"I'm fine," Leo said. "You don't need to worry about me."

"And you don't need to worry about me," she said.

"I know."

"You do know that, right?"

"I know, I know."

Leo went out onto the porch where his father, Philip, was on the phone.

"All right, Morris," Philip said, "the kids are here." He repeatedly called his brother Morris, even though his brother's name was Peter.

Philip had two other brothers in addition to Morris, named Don and William. William he called Bowser, and Don he also called Morris. Their father, an immigrant from Bialystok, Poland, who had founded a lumber company, was dead now, but his four sons were like him, hairy and indestructible forces of nature, captains of industry. They built cities, they had senators in their Rolodexes, they gave to charity such sums as affixed the Zajac name to many a wall, they bought Israel bonds, and rented entire houses in St. Maarten. They were not Bialystokers, they were genuine Americans, impervious to fire as Bialystokers had not been. From the beginning, they had treated Leo and Mack as if they were born into the family and not puppies rescued from a shelter.

Bowser, the youngest, had a huge mustache like Teddy Roosevelt, and as a wrestler in college, he'd accidentally crushed a man's ribs. Now he had a problem in his spine for which he took medicine, but it didn't keep him from the wilds of Maine, where Leo had seen him shove a canoe across a river. He was the only brother to survive forty years with a full head of hair. He told Maine stories in a believable Maine accent, and Leo had seen him like Paul Bunyan pull a dead tree out of the earth with his bare hands. On the same canoe trip, he'd cut his foot badly on the edge of the dry box, then rummaged in the box for a tube of epoxy he used to seal holes in tents — then glued his foot closed and resumed chopping a red onion. He was the chef de cuisine of those trips, the in-house outfitter and map reader. He made blueberry crepes at your request on a dented old green Coleman stove and he found Leo's movie opinions very annoying.

Philip was the next oldest, Philip who had sacrificed his own potential progeny for the sake of another man's, who had taught Leo to love Broadway and the beaches of Long Island. Philip had done a thesis in medieval history at Columbia and he was a man who knew exactly who Poggio Bracciolini was. He showed up dutifully, especially where his own mother was concerned. Though he complained of an indentured servitude, he'd made himself very, very good at the real estate business. And though he complained of his hair loss, he was very, very bald. He consumed every newspaper and periodical and took no man's opinion for his own. Sometimes he disappeared on sudden errands, sometimes he disappeared without going anywhere, as though he were hiding behind a life-size poster of himself. He had no mustache and in fact shaved scrupulously without ever missing a hair, though there would, sometimes, be a dollop of shaving cream on his ear at breakfast. He shaved even on canoe trips—crouched in the morning at the river's edge with a small mirror. He crouched there at the river's edge also late at night, to wash all the pots and the forks in cold water, as he had appointed himself the Martyr of the Dirty Dishes. Leo went down there in the dark to wash dishes with him at the river's edge, where it hurt his knees, as he had appointed himself Martyr of All Father-Martyrs.

"All right, Morris," Philip said. "Say hello to your lovely wife."

The Morris on the phone call, who was two years older than Philip, was also bald and had a huge mustache like an English inspector and did not build buildings but had gone to Harvard, spoke Danish and German, was a theoretical chemist, and had helped lay the groundwork for the field of molecular electronics. He called Philip Bise, pronounced like *bees,* after a restaurant in the south of France, and he and Philip could laugh and laugh for many minutes with only one or two private jokes passing between them now and then to stoke the fires. For example, he would say, "Mexican hairless, Bise," with his eyes full of tears and they would laugh on and on. And Philip would say, "Firewater, Morris," and he'd practically choke. And Morris would say, "Can you imagine, Bise? Firewater!" Morris despised D. H. Lawrence and *The Sound of Music,* ejaculated bits of high literature such as "Up from the spray of thy ocean-perishing—straight up, leaps thy apotheosis!" and the final line of *Finnegans Wake,* and he embraced you with a frontal bear hug to shock the wind from your lungs. He was unafraid to cry when he looked up at the stars and remembered the uncle who had taught him their names. *A way a lone a last a loved a long the*

"Okay, Morris," Philip said, as if it were a new idea to get off the phone, as if he hadn't already signaled the end. Mack and Leo stood waiting on the rug.

The eldest of the four was the other Morris. He had once played football in school and walked with a limp. He had trained as a lawyer but didn't practice law. He ran the business, which had changed from lumber to real estate. He used to pet Leo's head with a distracted love, and praise his long eyelashes and white teeth. When Leo rode a Honda ATV down a hill of pachysandra and got trapped underneath the machine with the hot motor burning his leg, his uncle had pulled it off him, and when Leo punched his fist through the window in the kitchen door and the broken glass cut his thumb to the bone, his uncle had squeezed his small thumb in a handkerchief while driving him to the doctor and didn't stop squeezing the thumb the whole way. The elder Morris's eyes were slightly Asiatic, like there had been a Mongol chieftain somewhere way up in the family line. He'd survived heart surgery, a car accident that flung him through the windshield, and a wife who deserted him, returned to him, and widowed him in one year. He married again and even sired another child, kept on living like a rugged plant that can't be killed by cuts, poison, frost, or drought. He liked nice clothes and good cigars and claimed he had never been drunk. He paddled a canoe like a painter painting the river, dip-ping the paddle almost soundlessly into a slow-draining soundless river that was a watercolor of green trees and dead tree limbs, an occasional dark bird slowly climbing the waves of green pines or a dumb brown moose shackled to the mud, brightness of yellow rucksacks and red raingear before the gray of rain and river rocks and smoke rising up into the rain from a corncob pipe.

Philip hung up the phone, greeted his boys with love and manners, and then went straight out the door to buy something without telling anyone where he was going.

Upstairs, in his room, Leo took down from the shelf his dead father's dusty doctor bag. He examined the old blood pressure cuff with ISIDORE AUBERON, M.D. on it in black marker and the dusty sextant whose origins he could not remember or never knew. Then he put the cuff and the sextant back on the shelf and took down the little green jewelry box with the rusted latch. There were some pictures of his father inside it, including an unsmiling hospital ID badge, and a handkerchief monogrammed RIA on the corner with yellow stains on it. In many reinforcing strokes of black ball-point ink, a child had written on the fake green leather lid of the box: ISIDORE R. AUBERON STUFF!! KEEP OUT!!

He might have said, had it been time:

Father.

All my life, you lie in your hole and drink my love. You drink my blood and your hole repays me nothing but the guilty black humors of the grave. And still my every cell dare not breathe, my very ribosomes dare not read the Book of Life without I honor you.

I tell you now, for this grave and silent treatment, I hate you. Not Yale, not my brother or yours, but you. And that's not all. I will be better than you. And my other father and uncles, too. It's not too late. This is only the beginning for me. You'll see. It's a noble thing to hope for, a noble thing to try for! NOT a bad thing! NOT an unloving thing. I go to it.

And I welcome you to come out of your hole in the ground and try to prove me wrong. If ever again I offer you my life, then my life is a brass knuckle fist and I offer it to your still and silent mouth.

But the time had not yet come. He collapsed on the edge of the bed like a suit of armor without a man in it and said only, "Daddy."

He put the doctor bag and the jewelry box back on the dusty shelf and went back downstairs. He went onto the porch, onto the still and empty kilim rug, where time stopped. There was no one there.

6.

Wedding at the Metropolitan Ballroom

In among the crazy palm leaves on the roof deck of the night-club called the Velvet Dog, underneath the Terminal Tower, which pointed up into the night and seemed to hang the moon up above them like a Chinese lantern, the friends of the bride danced while the friends of the groom stood around and drank. He drank but he wasn't listening. The boys were all married and talking about the off-season moves of the Cleveland Browns, an activity that ought to be catalogued in the annals of futility some-where between sorting books in a burning library, beating dead horses, and rearranging deck chairs on the *Titanic*.

"The Cleveland Browns are like a Samuel Beckett play with shoulder pads," Leo said. "Godot never comes. Moses never gets to see the Promised Land."

Leo looked out at the girls and thought, *Fuck destiny.* The re-hearsal dinner had come and gone, but he still had tonight, and the wedding itself, and the reception to make something fun happen. *When destiny sits over you jerking your reins then you're nothing but a mistreated horse.*

He went out onto the dance floor among the crazy palm leaves.

"Cheers," he said, and raised his glass of whiskey.

"Cheers," one of the girls said, but Dusty, the attractive one with the nice ass and big tits, wouldn't even look at him.

"Where did you come from?" he yelled over the thumping music.

But Dusty turned her back to him and continued dancing.

"This is our girls' weekend," one of the bridesmaids said. "It's like a reunion."

"I learned how to dance in Africa," he said to Dusty's back. "Once to the right and then farther to the right, once to the left and then farther to the left. How am I doing?"

Dusty looked over her shoulder at him. "Pretty bad," she said.

"What happened to your face?" the other girl said.

"I got into a fight with a Nazi," he said. "I like that name, Dusty."

"Thanks," Dusty said.

"Like Susan Clark in *The Apple Dumpling Gang*."

"Like who?"

"How did you get that name?" he said.

She turned around. "My dad was a fan of Dusty Springfield."

"Dusty Springfield? Didn't she do a version of 'Who Can I Turn To'? You know, 'Who can I turn to . . . if you turn away?'"

"Huh?"

"Well, your dad sounds like an interesting man."

"Not in a good way." (Her father, a balancing act of wounds upon wounds and cuts upon cuts who kept himself upright at great cost to his spine and his daughters, who smiled with brave shocks of pain in his teeth like a trained bear on roller skates, and in silence seemed almost to groan with the wind that sawed the abyss of his heart—her father would ask things of him one day.)

The song ended. Leo asked what she did in wherever it was she was from.

"I work for the Devil."

"Oh, for the Devil," he said.

"Marketing. I have to fly to Cincinnati all the time."

"Where else would the devil live?"

"Toledo, maybe." She lived in Chicago, she said. "I went to high school in *Toledo,*" she said, pronouncing it like Toledo, Spain.

"I've only ever just driven past the exit to *Toledo* on Four-Eighty."

Another song started but she didn't start to dance again. She asked about him then in a somewhat skeptical and hostile way and he said he was a doctor but he guessed he would be a writer now, and she asked him what he wrote and he said fiction, and she said, what about? He couldn't think of any answer except the true ones, so he said he'd written a story about the ghost of a woman who lived and died alone and decided to go out and try to meet other ghosts (no time like the afterlife), and another about a boy with a dead father.

"Oh yeah?" she said skeptically. "Did somebody die on you?"

"Yes, actually," he said. And he told her about his father.

"I don't remember my mother," she said. "The same thing happened to her."

"We ought to go buy a bottle of 1974 Burgundy," he said, since his father and her mother had died within a month of each other in 1974. "We ought to go out together and take the bottle and throw it off a bridge."

★　　★　　★

After the ceremony the following night, at the Metropolitan Ballroom, she wouldn't talk to him again. He said he liked her necklace, which had three tiers of silver and turquoise in it. (Months later, after he looked out at the Duomo through his tears, after the wine and pistachio-encrusted venison at Palazzo Ravizza and the cigar she bought for him, whose smoke annoyed the other Americans having drinks in the parquet sitting room, and after the photograph she took of him, laughing through the smoke—he said he would write a book that would be like hot artillery fired straight into the heart and she said she knew he would—after he was nearly slain by cigar and alcohol and then arose the colossus of Tuscany thinking himself able to speak Italian while the rainstorm battered the shutters, then he learned that the necklace had belonged to her mother.)

He stood over the girls' table in the Metropolitan Ballroom and offered his hand, and said anybody want to dance? Anybody? But he was looking at Dusty. Because fuck destiny.

"You're not gonna get me to dance," she said.

"The fuck I ain't," he said.

He didn't care if she laughed, or if he looked like a fool. She would only touch his damp shoulders with her fingertips and she did laugh at him, but he danced on.

"So you like to pick fights?" she said, looking up at the scratches on his head.

"No, I lied, actually I was bird-watching," he said. "People don't realize it's very dangerous."

"Yeah, a cardinal could peck your eye out," she said. "Or a nest could fall on you and really mess up your hair."

"Exactly. What's that move you're doing there?" he said, and tried to imitate it.

"I'm dancing," she said. "You look a little like a piñata I saw some kids smashing in Tijuana."

"I don't think so," he said. "You're the piñata, *ese.* I'm the stick."

"Oh, is that so?"

"Yeah, that's so."

The fast dancing stopped. Their friends the bride and groom cut the cake and violins played something old. He grabbed Dusty's hand and lifted it, tilted his head back gaily and laughed theatrically as though they were both wearing gold brocade and white gloves at some centuries-past ball. She said she always wished she could go to the ball in *Anna Karenina.* Then she looked over at a waiter like she suddenly needed a drink.

And then organ music started from the keyboard, and the singer said: "'Dearly beloved.'"

"Oh, shit, I love this song," Leo said. "You like this?"

"I like 'Little Red Corvette' myself."

"'We are gathered here today,'" the singer said, "'to get through this thing called life.'"

And then the drums started and this friend of the groom's, one of the last male gynecologists left in the world and a guy who hated himself and bought his women by the crate, came up to Dusty and grabbed her arm and Leo said, "Not now, dummy," and he incorporated into his ungainly dance a gentle stiff-arm and actually pushed off on the gynecologist's face, becoming the first and probably last man in the history of the universe to stiff-arm a gynecologist to the beat of "Let's Go Crazy." The gynecologist spun away and, surprisingly, stayed there.

And the singer said, "'In this life, you're on your own.'" And an electric bass note jolted the Metropolitan Ballroom twice.

And if the elevator tries to bring you down, go crazy

In his drunkenness, and inside the creative field and rhythm of the music (it was a very fine rendition), Leo heard the words with a completely sincere affection, like the words of an army captain under a hail of rockets, and he felt himself a warrior in his once and only skin against the heartless stone and calamity, against all the heartless ignorance of all the dunces of the world, and he felt that his sister-in-arms was right there in front of him and their wounded souls were joined by fifty-four thousand degrees of coursing barrow lightning; he didn't doubt it for even the mean life of a subatom; his soul moved at two hundred thousand miles an hour toward its secret desire; he wasn't joking at all; he would take all comers, kill and kick ass, and he would fuck this girl right then, that night. Watch out, motherfuckers! If you don't hear me coming, you're gonna feel it when I get there.

At the end of the song he chest-bumped with the groom, who was his old friend Singer. He would have liked the Kinks afterward to snap spinal cords with the whiplash sarcasm of "Father Christmas" or something like that, but it was just as well, as the Kinks might have caused him to kick over an amplifier or knock over someone's grandmother in an excess of enthusiasm (which would have been embarrassing).

When the reception ended, he followed her back to the Marriott. It was said that people were getting together at the Marriott in some room whose number he drunkenly repeated to himself. He didn't know what time it was because his watch was broken (and even he knew better than to wear an Actinomyces-reeking digital Timex to a wedding). But nobody had made it upstairs anyway, it seemed, they were just sprawled out on the chairs in the lobby letting the world spin and saying their good-byes, and Leo asked to see Dusty's hotel room. She sighed and agreed to show it to him, against her better judg-

ment evidently, against the principles of the girls' weekend.
They went up in the elevator without saying anything. Once
they were inside her room with the lights off he could see she
was afraid to trust him, and he kissed her anyway and swept his
hand over her dress, through which he could feel very plainly
her warm naked body. He could see that that was as far as it
would go.

She gave him her card. The company had been named for the
John Coltrane album, she said. The card said GIANT STEP. It had a
leaf on it. He was afraid to trust its symbolism.

"I'll come to Chicago," he said.

"No you won't," she said.

"The fuck I won't."

And as usual everything was all confused and painful, worried
and guilty and mad inside him; his own homunculus, which
jerked in his brain like a marionette, and all the simulacra of the
world that were imprinted inside him all fretted the inner crown
of his skull with ruts of hot pain. When he came out of the
hotel doors, his old friend Singer the groom said, Where were
you, Slick? And Leo must have looked pleased (he could see that
in their eyes all around him), sly and pleased like the cat who
ate the canary, and he said, I took a tour of the Marriott. And
Leo smoked a cigar with his friend the groom outside the hotel,
both in their tuxedos with their ties loose, both of them leaning
against the bricks on that warm August evening like two young
gods.

It was very late when Leo came back to the den and sat down
with Mack in front of *Sixteen Candles*.

"They could never get away with Long Duk Dong today,"
Leo said. "You never quote from this one. Or do you? *Sexy girlfriend!*"

"I actually have never seen it," Mack said.

"*You* have never seen *Sixteen Candles*?" Leo said. "Impossible."

"I don't know. I— It just happened."

"How was Dylan's?"

"It was good to see them," Mack said. "How was the wedding?"

"Good, actually."

"Really? Good.... Okay, man, I gotta go to bed."

"I'll come up in a minute," Leo said. "Do you want the bigger sink?"

"No, that's okay. You want to go see *The Matrix* with me tomorrow afternoon? I heard it's good."

"Sure. I haven't seen a matinee in years. What about Tom?"

"He's out of town," Mack said.

It was easy for Leo to see, as if for the first time, that there was no slight in this sort of invitation. Maybe it was the opposite of a slight, even. Also, it seemed that there was no need to question Mack's movie opinions, or to apologize for his own. He looked up at the picture of Isidore on the shelf. The dead man sat in front of that awesome portrait of Moshe Dayan in bars of blood and shadow. His father had his long doctor coat on, trailing around him and down the chair like the robe of a king.

"He looks like you, Mack."

"Yeah. No. He—" Mack said, and then laughed.

"That was an aposiopesis," Leo said.

"Remind me what that is," Mack said.

"From *The Aeneid*."

"I know it's from *The Aeneid*. But what is it?"

"It's when a god or somebody starts talking and stops in the middle before he gets all his words out, I think."

"Oh yeah. That's what it is. What it was," Mack said, looking at the picture.

Leo hugged Mack, and slapped him on the back to defend their masculinity, but then he put his head down on his brother's shoulder and they embraced for a moment and held still. They were Ixion and Tantalus and they'd climb out of Hell.

They parted and Leo said: "And Neptune arose from the waves and said, 'Where did I put my—'"

Mack said: "I sing of the arms and the end."

Leo laughed a raggedy, raspy laugh—his voice was almost gone—and it was probably a laugh that was slightly too desperate for mirth. He saw that despite the jokes, Mack had his depressed basketball assassin face on.

"All right, I go to—" Mack said, and pointed up.

"It's gonna get better," Leo said. "It's—" And Leo pointed up.

"I hope so," Mack said, and sighed.

Then Leo started the aposiopesis again: "And Neptune arose from the waves and said, 'Where did I put my—'"

And Mack finished it for him: "'—giant robotic dildo.'"

"'I know that thing must be around here somewhere,'" Leo said, patting his pockets.

"Sorry, I just assumed that was what you were going to say."

They howled and cried. "Goddamn, Mack, you are a funny man."

Leo asked Mack to come into the living room, where there was an old record player. He turned on the lamp with the bronze paint and face of a lion on the base. The lamp lit up the corner of the room well enough to see but its thick shade kept most of the room in darkness.

Leo went through the records on the shelf and found it with ease, as his parents had not touched their LPs in years: *The Roar of the Greasepaint—The Smell of the Crowd* by Leslie Bricusse and Anthony Newley, with a pair of hoboes on the album cover just as he remembered.

He knelt on the carpet in front of the record player. "Let's see if this thing still works."

When he dropped the needle, they heard the old familiar too-loud sound of the vinyl smacking the needle, then the rhythmic *click-clack* as the needle settled into its groove and trailed around and around through the dust. Mack smiled stiffly so as not to give offense at the eccentric experiment.

Anthony Newley sang:

> *On a wonderful day like today*
> *I defy any cloud to appear in the sky. . . .*

"Sorry," Leo said. "Raindrops in my eyes."

Mack clapped him on the shoulder. Their reflections in the imperfect plate glass looked unfocused and strange. Leo listened to the music and Mack stood by him, hearing it, maybe listening to it or maybe just waiting for the right moment to leave.

"It is," Leo said.

"It is what?" Mack said.

"A wonderful day."

ACKNOWLEDGMENTS

Above and beyond the thanks I owe to many others for their faith, material, resources, time, wisdom, edits, ideas, packaging, and assistance with promotion, I owe my brother, Danny Ratner, in particular for his contributions to this book. Heartfelt thanks to Larry Kirshbaum, who sold this book; to Reagan Arthur, who saw value in it and gave me the exact edits I needed to make it a full-fledged novel; to Barry Gordon and Julian Seifter for their detailed recollections; to Barbara Perris for a sharp-eyed copyedit that among other things corrected the tenses of my Middle English; to Allison J. Warner for her magnificent cover illustration; to Ben Allen for piloting the book through the production phase; to Tony Marra for his many insightful suggestions; to Evelyn Somers, who felt such enthusiasm for the short story out of which the novel grew; to Kristin Ratner, who saw the phoenix in the ashes of this story; and to many others, including Millicent Bennett, Marlena Bittner, Sarah Funke Butler, Ethan Canin, Susanna Einstein, Will Hammond, Leslie Hodgkins, Jonathan Kandell, Deborah Kaufmann, Blake Kimzey, Josh Lambert, Speer Morgan, Sarah Murphy, Edith Ochs, Tish O'Dowd, Miriam Parker, Michael Pietsch, Gabriel Ratner, James Ratner, Susan Ratner, Virgil Ratner, George Rohr, Sami Rohr, and John Burnham Schwartz.

About the Author

Austin Ratner's first novel, *The Jump Artist,* was the 2011 winner of the Sami Rohr Prize for Jewish Literature. Before turning his focus to writing, he received his MD from the Johns Hopkins School of Medicine, and he is coauthor of the textbook *Concepts in Medical Physiology.* He grew up in Cleveland, Ohio, and now lives in Brooklyn, New York, with his wife and two sons.